Penny Jordan, one of Harlequin's most popular authors, unfortunately passed away on December 31, 2011. She leaves an outstanding legacy, having sold over 100 million books around the world. Penny wrote a total of 187 novels for Harlequin, including the phenomenally successful *A Perfect Family, To Love, Honor and Betray, The Perfect Sinner* and *Power Play,* which hit the *New York Times* bestseller list. Loved for her distinctive voice, she was successful in part because she continually broke boundaries and evolved her writing to keep up with readers' changing tastes. *Publishers Weekly* said about Jordan, "Women everywhere will find pieces of themselves in Jordan's characters." It is perhaps this gift for sympathetic characterization that helps to explain her enduring appeal.

PENNY JORDAN
Collection

PRIDE &
CONSEQUENCE

ISBN-13: 978-0-373-24987-9

PRIDE & CONSEQUENCE

Copyright © 2013 by Harlequin Books S.A.

The publisher acknowledges the copyright holder of the individual works as follows:

VIRGIN FOR THE BILLIONAIRE'S TAKING
Copyright © 2008 by Penny Jordan

THE TYCOON'S VIRGIN
Copyright © 2002 by Penny Jordan

Recycling programs for this product may not exist in your area.

Printed in U.S.A.

CONTENTS

VIRGIN FOR THE BILLIONAIRE'S TAKING

CHAPTER ONE

'EXCUSE ME.'

Keira had been so focused on watching the bustle of guests in the ancient palace courtyard, where two of her closest friends had just married, that she hadn't realised that she was blocking the pathway to the garden. She had intended to make her way to one of the pavilions put up for the wedding celebrations, but had become distracted by the magical, intoxicating atmosphere of it all.

The male voice was authoritative and deep—velvet-rough, Keira decided, as though the nap of the fabric had been brushed to reveal the strength that lay beneath the silky surface. Just hearing it made her feel as though that same fabric had brushed against her own skin, and the sensual effect on her sent small electric shocks of awareness darting through her. His accent was recognisably English public school, and university honed: the accent of a man who took both position and wealth for granted as his right of birth. The accent of privilege, power and pride.

Would her accent give away as much about her? Would he sense the Northern accent she had learned to conceal beneath the tones she knew worked best for her in her business as an interior designer?

She turned towards him, her lips framing an apology for the fact that she had been so intent on watching what was going on that she had inadvertently blocked his way along the narrow path that led from the courtyard to the gardens. Her eyes widened as she realised she was looking at the most sexually compelling and dangerous man she had ever seen.

As though her whole body and all her senses had been hard-wired for this moment, every nerve-ending she possessed was reacting to him with a silent but violent intensity. It was like being physically attacked by her own body—like being mugged and having the protection of her normal caution stolen from her. She was frozen and wide-eyed, as aware of the dangerous nature of his impact on her as if she had been standing in front of an oncoming train.

The power of his sexuality slammed into her, leaving her unable to defend herself from it.

Jay didn't know why he was wasting his time standing here letting the woman stare at him in the way that she was, blatant in her awareness of him.

Admittedly she was beautiful. But she wasn't the only European guest attending the wedding, though with her looks and figure she would have stood out no matter where she was. Tall and elegant, she had a refined air about her whilst the lush curves of her body and the soft fullness of her mouth said clearly that hers was the kind of sensual nature he most enjoyed in a woman.

In bed she would display a sensuality that came straight from the most erotic pages of the *Kama Sutra,* enticing any man who became her lover into pleasuring her until she cried out against the intensity of that pleasure. He could see her now, her dark hair spread out against the pillows, her eyes luminous with arousal, the lips of her sex curving softly and moistly, waiting to open to his touch like the petals of a lily open to the heat of the sun, exposing the pulsing heart of their being, giving that most intimate part of themselves up to the sun's heat, spreading their petals in open appeal for its possession, the scent of their longing filling the air.

The sudden intensity of the sharp surge of desire hardening his body caught him off guard, causing him to shift his weight from one foot to the other.

At thirty-four he was more than old enough to be able to control his physical reactions to a desirable woman, and yet somehow this woman had him reacting to her so fast that he had been caught by the wayward direction of his own thoughts—and his desire for her.

She hadn't made any attempt to don the costume that the female Indian guests were wearing so confidently and elegantly, as some European women did when attending Indian celebrations. But none of those things would normally have been enough to counteract his belief that she was covertly suggesting to him that she was available, and thus by the law of probability was also available to any other man who might have chanced to cross her path. He waited for the desire she had aroused within him to be chilled by the distasteful idea he had deliberately conjured up, and frowned with the recognition that it had not done so.

He was even more stunned when he heard himself asking her, 'Bride or groom?'

'I'm sorry…'

'I was asking which side of the wedding party you belong to,' he told her.

His choice of the word 'belong' stung her pride and her mind with the familiar pain of knowing that there was no one in this world to whom she 'belonged', but it was somehow overwritten by the intoxicating fact that his question suggested that he wanted to prolong his contact with her.

He was undeniably handsome. Tension bit into her, as

though some instinct deep inside her had pressed a warning button, but to her shock her senses were refusing to
listen to it. How old was she? Certainly too old to stare
in open awe at a man, no matter how good-looking he
was. And yet, like a child hooked on the adrenalin kick
of sugar, despite knowing that it wasn't good for her, she
just couldn't stop looking at him.

He was wearing a light tan linen suit of the kind favoured by wealthy Italians, and everything about him
breathed cosmopolitan upper-class privilege, education
and wealth. His skin had the right kind of warm olive tint
to it to carry off the suit, just as his body had the height
and the muscles. Were his shoulders really that broad? It
looked like it from the way he moved.

And yet, despite everything about him that proclaimed
old money and social position, Keira could sense within
him another darker side, a marauding, dangerous ruth-
lessness that clung to him so powerfully she could almost
smell it.

She fought not to be drawn into the aura of magnetism
that surrounded him. If anything was intoxicating her then
surely it must be this most wonderful of wedding venues.

Originally a summer palace and hunting lodge owned
by an ancient maharaja, it had been converted into a lux-
ury five-star hotel. Formerly an island palace, it was now
connected to the shore by a handsome avenue, but the
impression created as one approached was that the palace
and gardens floated on the serene waters of the lake that
surrounded it.

If it wasn't the venue then perhaps it was the sensual
scent of the lilies resting on the still water of the pools that
was having such a dangerous effect on her senses? Whatever the cause, it was in her own interests to remember
that she was supposed to be a rational adult.

Keira took a deep, calming breath and told him firmly, 'Both. I'm a friend of the bride and the groom.'

A swirl of activity refocused her attention on the wedding party. Late afternoon was giving way to early evening darkness, and preparations were almost finished for the evening reception. The small flickering flames of hundreds of glass-covered tea lights were scattered artfully around the large courtyard and floating in the pools and fountains, and the lights reflected in the lake beyond it giving it a magical aura of romance.

Richly embroidered pavilions in jewel colours were being erected as though by magic, their gold threadwork catching the light, and the branches of the trees in the gardens beyond the courtyard dripped strings of tiny fairy lights, illuminating the paths that led to individual guest suites in what was now one of India's most exclusive hotel and spa resorts.

Soon the newly married couple and their families would be changing for the evening, and she needed to go and do the same, she reminded herself, and yet she made no move to step aside, thereby ending their conversation and allowing him to walk away from her.

Perhaps it was something to do with the late-afternoon sun that was transforming the sky above them from deep turquoise to warm pink, or the languorous heat turning the air soft with a sensuality that was almost like a physical touch against her skin that was causing her heart to thud with heavy-laden beats. Or perhaps it was the effect the man standing so close to her was having on her.

Something inside her weakened and ached. It was India that was doing this to her. It had to be. She was beginning to panic now, caught off guard and out in the open with nowhere to run by the shockingness of her own vulnerability to instincts over which she had previously believed she had total control.

She needed desperately to think about something else. The wedding she was here to attend, for instance.

Shalini had used the magnificent venue for her wedding as the inspiration for her choice of traditional clothes. Tom had thrown himself into it, and had looked amazing in his red and gold turban, his gold silk *sherwani* suit and scarf embroidered to match Shalini's gold and red embroidered lehenga.

Keira would have wanted to attend Shalini and Tom's wedding wherever it had been held; they, along with Shalini's cousin Vikram, were her closest friends. And when Shalini had told her that she and Tom had decided to follow up their British civil marriage with a traditional Hindu ceremony here in Ralapur, nothing could have kept Keira away.

She had been longing to visit this ancient city state. It had captured her imagination immediately when she had first read about it. But Keira hadn't just come here for Shalini's wedding and to see the city. She had business here as well. She most certainly hadn't come looking for romance, she decided, before elaborating on her presence at the wedding.

'I was at university with Tom and Shalini,' she explained, before asking curiously, 'And you?'

It was typical of her type of woman that her voice should be low and husky, even if the slight vulnerable catch in it was a new twist on the world's oldest story. He had no intention of telling her anything personal about himself, or the fact that his elder brother was the new Maharaja.

'I have a connection with the bride's family,' he told her. It was after all the truth, since he owned the hotel. And a great deal more. He looked out across the lake. His mother had loved this place. It had become her retreat when she'd needed to escape from the presence of his father the Maharaja and his avaricious courtesan, who had turned his head so much that he'd no longer cared about the feelings of his wife and his two sons.

Jay's mouth, full-lipped and sharply cut in a way that subtly underlined its sensuality, hardened at his thoughts. He had been eighteen, and just back from the English public school where both he and his brother had been educated. That winter the woman who had stolen away his father's affections with her openly sexual touches and her wet greedy mouth, painted with scarlet lipstick to match her nails, had first come to Ralapur. A 'modern' woman, she had called herself. A woman who had refused to live shackled by outdated moral rules, a woman who had looked at Jay's father, seen his position and his wealth, and had wanted him for herself. A greedy, amoral harlot of a woman who sold herself to men in return for their gifts. The opposite of his mother, who'd been gentle and obedient to her husband, and yet fierce in her protective love of her sons.

Jay and his elder brother, Rao, had shown their outrage by refusing to acknowledge the existence of the woman who had usurped their mother in her husband's heart.

'You must not blame your father,' she had told Jay. 'It is as though a spell has been cast on him, so that he is blind to everything and everyone but her.'

His father had been blind indeed not to see the woman for what she was, but he had refused to hear a word against her, and Rao and Jay had had to stand to one side and watch as their father humiliated their mother and himself with his obsession for her. The court had been filled with the courtiers' whispered gossip about her. She had boasted openly of her previous lovers, and had even threatened to leave their father if he did not give her the jewels and money she demanded.

Jay had burned with anger against his father, unable to understand how a man who had always prided himself on his moral stance, a man who was so proud of his family's reputation, quick to condemn others for their moral lapses, should behave in such a way.

In the end Jay had quarrelled so badly with his father that he had had no option other than to leave home.

Both his mother and Rao had begged him not to go, but Jay had his own pride and so he had left, announcing that he no longer wished to be known as the second son of the Maharaja, and that from now on he would make his own way in the world. A foolish claim, perhaps, for a boy of only just eighteen

His father had laughed at him, and so had she—the slut who had ultimately been responsible for the death of his mother. Officially the cause of her death had been pneumonia, but Jay knew better. His gentle, beautiful mother had died of the wounds inflicted on her heart and her pride by a tramp who hadn't been fit to breathe the same air. He loathed the kind of woman his father's lover had been— greedy, sexually available to any man who had the price of her in his pocket.

He had been reluctant to return to Ralapur at first, when Rao had succeeded their father, but Rao had persisted, and out of love for his brother Jay had finally given in. Even now he wasn't sure if he had done the right thing.

The boy who had walked away from a life that held the status of being his father's second son into an uncertain future where he would have nothing but his own abilities had returned to the place of his birth a very wealthy man, who commanded respect not only in his own country but throughout Europe and North America as well. A billion-

aire property developer with such a sure eye for a successful venture that he was besieged by people wanting to go
into business with him.

Now he was old enough to understand the sexual heat
that had driven his father to forsake the high-born wife
he had wed as a matter of state protocol and tradition for
the courtesan who had courted and mastered his physical
desire. Jay could to some extent exonerate his father, but
he could never and would never forgive the harlot who
had shamed their mother and stained the honour of their
family name.

Keira watched his expression change and saw cold hau-
teur replacing the earlier heavy-lidded sexual interest that
had darkened his eyes. What was he thinking? What was
responsible for that look of arrogance and pride? Did he
know how daunting it was? Did he care?

'You're here alone?' Jay cursed himself under his breath
for having stepped into a trap he had known was there.
But secretly he had wanted to—just as secretly he wanted
her, this woman with her high cheekbones and her soft full
lips, her golden eyes and her pale, almost translucent skin.

Why on earth should he want her? Women like her were
ten a penny. She wasn't wearing any rings, which might
not mean anything other than the fact that no one had ever
given her a ring expensive enough for her to want to wear
it. His last mistress had only accepted the end of their affair after a swift visit to Graff, the famous diamond house
in London, where she had quickly pointed out to him the
pink diamond she had obviously already picked out ahead
of their visit there.

If he hadn't already been tired of her the fact that she
had chosen such a gaudy stone would have killed his desire
for her. Like all his lovers, she had been married. Married

women were far easier and less expensive to leave when the affair was over, since they had husbands to answer to.

Jay had no desire to marry, though his status as the second son of the late Maharaja meant that it would be expected that he would make a dynastic marriage to someone deemed high-born enough to become his wife, their marriage negotiated by courtiers and lawyers. Jay had a deep-rooted aversion to allowing other people to arrange his life for him, aside from the fact that he had absolutely no interest in bedding a naïve, carefully protected 'suitable' girl, whose virginity would be traded as part of the deal in the negotiations for their marriage.

Such a marriage would be for life. The truth was that he was vehemently opposed to making a long-term commitment of any kind to any woman. No way was he going to be forced to part with any of the vast fortune he had built up through his own blood, sweat and tears to some conniving gold-digger who thought he would be stupid enough to commit to her in the heat of lust, and would expect a handsome 'separation' settlement from him once that lust had cooled and he wanted to get rid of her.

Keira hesitated, well aware of her own vulnerability. But it wasn't in her nature to lie, and even if it had been she suspected that Great-Aunt Ethel, the cold and embittered relative who had brought her up after her mother had died, would have beaten it out of her.

'Yes.' Somehow she managed to stop herself from saying those telltale words, *And you?* But she knew that they were there, spoken or not, and it made her realise how far she had already travelled along a road that she knew to be forbidden to her. If the great-aunt who had brought her up—reluctantly—after her mother's death were here now, she would make it very plain what she thought of her behaviour in talking to a strange man, giving him heaven alone knew what impression of herself, risking bringing shame and disgrace on her family, just like…

Keira's heart was thumping with all the driven intensity of the thud of war drums, menacing as they came ever closer, pouring the sound of threat and fear into the pounding hearts of their enemy. She wasn't going to be trapped by her own panic, though.

Perhaps she *had* looked at him for a split second too long, but that did not mean anything—not in this day and age, when a woman could look as boldly at a man as she chose. *A* man, maybe. But never *this* man. This man would see such a look as a challenge, an infringement upon his male right to be the hunter, and he would react powerfully to it, taking… Taking what? Taking her?

The unwanted direction of her own thoughts was so shocking that she immediately recoiled, fighting to push them away as she struggled to force herself to look at him without giving herself away.

Heavens, but he was good-looking—more than good-looking. He wore his blatantly male sexuality with the same careless ease with which he wore his hand-stitched suit. But she, of course, was immune to the message being subliminally relayed to her by the suit and his sexuality. Wasn't she?

Keira shivered. It was never a good idea to challenge fate. She knew that. This was a man who positively oozed a raw sexuality that had the air around him thrumming with male hubris and testosterone—a man who, without her being able to do a single thing about it, had got under her carefully constructed guard and forced her body to acknowledge his effect on it.

He wanted her, Jay admitted reluctantly. He wanted her very badly.

Her full-length cream skirt, worn with a round-necked

sleeved top, and the fine long cream silk scarf she was
wearing certainly stood out amongst the jewel colours
most of the other female guests were wearing, giving her
an angelic air despite the darkness of her hair. She looked
ethereal, and fragile, but there had been nothing ethereal
about the look he had caught her giving him a few seconds
ago: the look of a woman whose sensuality was aroused
and clamouring for satisfaction.

The courtyard was almost empty now, the other guests
having made their way to their rooms to change for the
evening reception, and they were alone together. A small
frisson of something that wasn't entirely a warning shivered over her skin.

This was getting ridiculous—and dangerous. She
should have stepped out of his path the second he had
asked her to do so, instead of… Instead of what? Standing
here, watching him, greedily absorbing every detail of his
vibrant maleness as though she was savouring some forbidden treat? What was she going to do with those stolen
images? Take them to her bed and replay them inside her
head whilst she…?

She had to get away from him, and from the effect he
was having on her. Keira turned to leave, and then froze
as he stretched out his arm to rest his hand on the illuminated trunk of a tree on the other side of the footpath,
blocking her exit. His fingers were long and tapered, his
nails clean and well shaped. She drew in a ragged breath
of sun-warmed air, inhaling with it the scent of the evening—and of him. She might as well have inhaled a dangerous hallucinatory drug, she acknowledged as her gaze
lifted compulsively to his face. His eyes weren't brown, but
the cool slate-grey of northern seas. Her gaze was drifting
downwards to his mouth, and Keira knew that no power
on earth could have stopped her looking at it. His top lip

was well cut and firm, whilst his bottom lip was sensually full and curved.

As unstoppable as a tsunami, a surge of sensation broke deep inside her. She took a step forward, and then one back, making a small sound that contained both her longing and her denial of it. But both the backward step and the denial came too late to cancel what had come before them.

She was in his arms, his fingers biting deep into the soft flesh of her own upper arms, and his mouth was hard and possessive on hers in a kiss of such intimacy that it tore down the trappings of civilisation.

Neither his kiss nor her own response to it could have been more intimate if he had stripped her naked—and she had wanted it, had completely offered herself to him, Keira recognised with a violent sense of shock. She could hardly stand up, hardly breathe, hardly think for the rush of physical hunger consuming her. It swept through her, obliterating everything that stood in its way, a violent storm of need that had her frantically sliding her hands beneath his jacket and then over his chest, trembling with her need to touch him.

His mouth was still on her own, both plundering and feeding the tight, hot ache of desire deep inside her. Panic pierced the hot sweetness of her own dangerous pleasure. She could not, she *must* not allow herself to feel like this. Horrified by her own behaviour, she forced her heavy-lidded eyes to open and focus on him. A shudder of denial gripped her body as she pulled herself out of his arms, and told him jerkily, 'I'm sorry. I don't do this kind of thing. I shouldn't have allowed that to happen.'

Now she *had* surprised him, Jay acknowledged. He had been about to accuse her of trying to lead him on and then withdrawing to get him more interested in her, and her almost stammered apology had startled him.

'But you wanted it too,' he challenged her softly.

Keira wanted desperately to lie, but ultimately couldn't.

'Yes,' she admitted. The pain of her own weakness and self-betrayal was too much for her to bear. It had to be the Indian air that was causing her to behave in such a reckless way, making her break every promise she had ever made to herself. It could not be the man watching her! *Must* not be him.

Panic clawed at her insides. No doubt he felt he had every right to be angry, every right to demand an explanation. But there wasn't one she could give him, so instead she turned on her heel, half running, half stumbling through the starry scented darkness.

Jay made no attempt to stop her. Initially he had been more concerned about his own unwanted physical response to her than in taking things further. It had only been when she had pulled back that he had felt that dangerous male surge of sexual anger at her denial. But then she had gone and totally disarmed him with her admission, her apology showing him a quirky vulnerability that right now was having an extraordinary effect on him. She intrigued him, excited him, piqued his interest in a way that challenged him mentally as well as sexually.

He had simply been walking through the palace gardens when he had first seen her. He had planned to spend the evening going over some important documents and making some phone calls, but now he was thinking about putting all of that on hold.

A woman who could admit that she was in the wrong in any way, and most especially in her sexual behaviour, was a very rare creature indeed in his experience. She was here alone, she had admitted that she wanted him, and he certainly wanted her. Jay's mouth curled in a totally male half-smile of anticipation.

* * *

Keira didn't stop to look over her shoulder to see if *he* was still watching her. Once she was inside her room with her door locked she leaned back against it, unable to move whilst cold shock and nausea filled her. She started to shiver. What on earth had she done? And, more importantly why had she done it?

How had she let that happen, after all these years—years during which she had worked so assiduously to make sure that it did not? Why, when she had so easily resisted the sexual appeal of so many other men, had she behaved like that with this one? What was so special about him that had so easily broken through the wall she had built around her own sexuality, setting it free to make its demands heard?

Panic was clawing at her like a wild animal desperate to escape captivity. She couldn't allow her sexuality its voice. She couldn't allow it to exist, full-stop. She knew that. Her great-aunt had warned her often enough what was likely to happen to her—the degradation she would suffer, the shame she would bring on herself and her great-aunt. Even though Ethel had been dead for nearly a decade, Keira could still hear her voice as she told her what would happen to her if she followed in her mother's footsteps.

Keira had been twelve years old when her mother had died and her great-aunt had taken her in—or rather had been forced to take her in or face her neighbours finding out that she had abandoned her. She hadn't wanted her. She had made that plain.

'Your mother was a slut who brought disgrace on this family. Let me warn you that I'm going to make sure that you don't turn out the same, even if I have to beat it out of you,' she had told Keira when the social worker who had taken her to her great-aunt's house had left, adding, 'I'll have no cheap little tart living under *my* roof and bringing shame on *me*.'

Because she was her mother's daughter, all it would take was one step in the wrong direction, her great-aunt had told her, to lead her into a life of sin.

And so Keira had learned to keep a guard on her heart and her body. When boys at school had called her 'frigid' and 'iron knickers' she had thrilled with pride rather than been upset. Slowly and carefully she had created for herself a non-sexual world in which she felt safe—a world in which she could never become her mother's daughter.

That world had been hers for so long she had assumed it would always be that way, and yet shockingly now, out of the blue, she had discovered what it felt like to want a man—and with such depth that it had left her reeling. And still wanting him. *No!* But the real answer was yes.

She went hot and then cold. She started to tremble and to shiver. Her whole body ached and pulsed with unfamiliar sensations and needs. She felt as though her mind was on fire with her own feverish imaginings, and her body too. It was like being in the grip of some kind of fever. Perhaps she was. Perhaps that was why she had reacted as she had. Was there a fever that could cause a person to desire someone like this? Of course she knew that there wasn't. So what exactly had happened to her? Why was her body still aching with the aftershock of what it had wanted and been denied? Where had it come from, that deep physical need so diametrically opposed to everything she had taught herself to be? Was this how it had started for her mother?

She shivered again, even more violently, feeling sick with fear and despair.

CHAPTER TWO

SHE COULDN'T STAY in her room, no matter how much she felt like doing so, Keira acknowledged tiredly. Someone would be sent to find her if she didn't appear at the evening reception.

She showered and changed quickly into her evening outfit, a full-length embroidered silver gown, simply cut and softly shaped without in any way clinging to her body.

Why had he done it? Why had he kissed her in the first place? What message had she inadvertently given him? What had he sensed in her?

Keira knew that question would torture her for a long time to come.

Reluctantly she left her room and headed out into the night-scented darkness, walking slowly along the pathway back through the gardens to the courtyard.

Dhol players had been hired to provide music to welcome the guests into the courtyard, magically transformed for the evening into a small city of jewel-coloured pavilions inside which buffet meals were set out.

Later there would be a disco and dancing. Would *he* be there? Stop it, she warned herself. If an attempt to subdue both her panic and her insidious fascination for a man she had already decided she had to forget she had even met, Keira tried to focus on something else.

When the wedding celebrations were over she would be meeting up with the two men responsible for financing a proposed new development of exclusive apartments in the new city that would house Ralapur's developing silicon valley. One of these men she knew well, and had worked with before, designing and furnishing the interiors of his apartments both in Mumbai and the UK, but the other she did not. It would be a huge step forward career-wise if she were to be appointed as the designer for this new complex, and one that would be very important to her—not just for the income, although with all the problems she had experienced with her business over the last few months she did need that too.

Keira frowned. The initial cause of those problems had been her refusal to sleep with a client who, out of spite, had then refused to pay Keira's bill, claiming that the work she had done for him had not been satisfactory.

With her good name at stake, as well as a sizeable amount of money, Keira had been advised to take him to court, but the costs involved had put her off. Unlike Bill Hartwell, she was not in a position to afford a potentially expensive legal battle. And of course there was no way she could prove that Bill Hartwell's malice sprang from the fact that she had refused his advances.

In her line of business it didn't do to attack the reputation of a client—a fact that had been reinforced to her when Sayeed had warned her that his partner was very strict about those who worked for him adhering to his own code, and had to Sayeed's certain knowledge terminated contracts with those who broke the rules he imposed.

'He's very shrewd, very arrogant, and very demanding. He has the highest standards for business conduct of anyone I know—a man whose word literally is his bond—and of course he is extremely wealthy. We're talking billionaire status, and all of it earned by his own endeavours—he's not inclined to trust anyone until they have proved themselves worthy of that trust.'

Sayeed had made him sound so formidable that Keira suspected she would have turned down the opportunity he offered if it hadn't been for the dire state of her current financial situation.

It was perhaps foolish of him to decide to position himself here in the shadows on the pathway where they had met earlier, Jay acknowledged, but he knew of old that women tended to relish such touches. And he certainly wanted her to relish his touch as much as he intended to relish touching her, he admitted, grimacing wryly at his own mental *double entendre*.

Where was she? The festivities would be starting soon, and he had planned to cajole her away before they did to somewhere rather more private. The courtyard was already filling with wedding guests, their voices and laughter almost drowning out the sound of the musicians. The smell of food spiced the evening air, and children ran giddily in and out of the groups of adults, giggling with excitement.

Keira had almost reached the point on the path where she had heard him saying that fateful 'excuse me' when she was hailed by Vikram, Shalini's cousin and the fourth member of their close-knit group of friends.

'Keira—there you are. I was just coming to look for you.'

She was swept off her feet and into a fierce hug.

'Vikram, put me down,' she protested.

'Not until you kiss me,' he told her, straight-faced.

Keira shook her head at him. Vikram was passionately in love with an eighteen-year-old cousin, and equally pas-

sionately determined not to allow both sets of hugely delighted parents to put pressure on her to marry him until
she had a chance to complete her education. When Keira
had first met him she had been eighteen to his twenty-
one, a new student at university against his seniority as a
third-year. Vikram had laid siege to her and done his best
to coax her into his bed. She, of course, had refused, and
instead of becoming lovers they had become friends. He
still liked to tease her about her 'primness', as he called it.

'You'd better put me down before someone sees us and
tells Mona,' Keira warned him teasingly.

'Mona loves you every bit as much as I do, and you
know it.' Vikram laughed as he set her down on her feet.

Imprisoned in the shadows, and unable to move away
without them seeing him, Jay saw the intimacy between
them. Hearing Keira's warning words, immediately he
stiffened. She had lied to him about being there alone—
just as she had lied to him with her false air of vulnerability and her equally false hesitant apology. It was obvious
to him exactly what her relationship was with the man
who was holding her.

'I'd better go,' Vikram told Keira. 'I've been deputised
to go and find Aunt Meena. Remember to save me a dance.
Oh,' he added, reaching into his pocket for his wallet and
then opening it and removing a thick bundle of notes, 'I
almost forgot—here's the money I owe you.'

He had asked her earlier in the year if she could help
him to redecorate the new apartment he had bought, and
of course she had said yes, giving her time and advice free,
and getting him discounts on furniture bought through her
own suppliers. It had still left him with a substantial bill,
which Keira had covered.

Thanking him, she tucked the money away in her
handbag.

Vikram, Shalini and Tom were her best friends, but not even they knew everything about her. There were some things she hadn't been able to bear telling them for fear of seeing them turn away from her in disgust and losing their friendship.

She watched Vikram lope away from her down the path, and then turned to continue on her way to the courtyard, her eyes widening in shock and the colour coming and going in her face as she saw the familiar figure standing on the path in front of her, his arms folded across his chest.

'Oh, it's you,' she said inanely.

There was something different about him—and not just because he had changed his clothes and was now wearing a dark suit and a white shirt with discreet gold links in the cuffs that looked every bit as expensive as the heavy gold watch strapped to his wrist. He looked—he looked frighteningly angry, she recognized. And something more— something that warned her he was dangerous which, incomprehensibly, her body found exciting.

'You'll have to forgive if me I was rather dense earlier. When you said no, I didn't realise it was because you're here to do business and we hadn't negotiated terms. You should have been more direct with me.'

Keira was stunned—and horrified.

'By the looks of it you left your last customer a very happy man.'

'You don't understand—'

'Of course I understand. You're a woman who hires out her body for male pleasure.'

'No!'

'Yes.'

When had he taken hold of her? She had no awareness of having moved, but she must have done, because now they were standing in the shadows off the path, and he had manacled her wrists in a grip that hurt. It hurt all the more so because she was struggling against it, and all her frantic attempts to break free of his hold were doing was bringing her up against his body, so that she could feel its heat and smell its alien maleness.

'Let go of me,' she demanded

'Did you enjoy playing your little game? Well, for your information I wasn't in the least deceived. It was obvious just what you are.'

'No—'

'Yes.'

They were only a few yards from the courtyard, but for all the attention either of them were paying to the proximity of the wedding guests they might as well have been isolated from the whole of the rest of the human race. The air surrounding them positively crackled with anger and sexual tension, to the extent that Keira wouldn't have been surprised if sparks hadn't suddenly started visibly illuminating the darkness.

Jay dragged her closer to him. He couldn't remember a time when he had ever felt this kind of male pride-induced anger. It consumed him, sweeping away his normal restraint. Seeing her being held in another man's arms and enjoying being held there had unleashed it, and now it was demanding appeasement. He lowered his head towards hers, seeking revenge for her insult to his pride.

The rush of sensation pounding through her veins wasn't just a mixture of anger and fear Keira knew that. But she still froze into rigid rejection when his mouth covered hers. Angrily he nipped at her lower lip, shocking the rigidity out of her body and replacing it with a primeval angry heat of her own that came out of nowhere, compelling her to respond to him with equal ferocity.

How could such blatant savagery be so erotic? How

could she feel as though something inside her was breaking apart and consuming her? How could she be standing on her tiptoes to take as much of his punishing kiss as she could get?

He freed one of her wrists to slide his hand into her hair, his fingers splayed against her scalp to hold her head still as he punished her mouth with kisses of such sensual savagery that they were almost a form of torture. A torture she never wanted to end.

The raw sound of their increasingly laboured breath broke the calm silence of the gardens with a raw sexuality that demanded greater intimacy—and privacy.

Jay drew Keira deeper into the shadows, his mouth still on hers as his anger burned into desire. His hand was on her breast, shaping its full softness. He felt her shudder when he rubbed the pad of his thumb across her fabric-covered nipple, tight and hard, already outlined by the moonlight for his visual pleasure. He could feel his erection straining against his clothes. He took her hand and placed it against it.

Keira closed her eyes. This could not be happening. But it was. And, worse, she wanted desperately for it to go on happening—so desperately that she would rather have done anything than stop.

Not even the full spread of her fingers was enough to encompass the length of him, hard and pulsing with a driving demand that her own flesh ached to answer. His tongue probed between her lips, his fingers plucking rhythmically at her nipple, swollen and tight in its eagerness to entice him and be pleasured by him. If they hadn't been out here in the garden he could have removed her dress and pleasured it properly, with his mouth as well as his hands.

As though he had read her thoughts she felt him reach

for the zip on her dress and slide it down. Instead of objecting, she shuddered with excited pleasure.

Jay felt her body's reaction to his touch, and a thin, cruel smile curled his mouth as he released hers from its possession. Not a true professional, then. If she was she would not have allowed her own desires to be so easily read. She was more of a greedy, highly-sexed woman, who had learned that men were willing to pay for her pleasure and their own sexual satisfaction.

Overhead in the courtyard fireworks started to explode, the noise shattering the highly charged sexual spell Keira was under and bringing her back to reality. As the first bright pink stars fell down to earth Keira pushed Jay away with a vehement, *'No!'*

What on earth was she doing?

Clumsy, but effective, Jay acknowledged. Get a man so wound up that he was prepared to do anything to get satisfaction and then demand a sweetener. It would be a new experience for him to pay a woman for sex—normally they ended up begging him for it, not the other way around.

Keira watched dazedly as Jay reached into his jacket pocket and removed his wallet. But it wasn't until he opened it to withdraw some crisp notes, demanding coldly, 'How much?' that she realised what he was doing.

Nausea clawed at her stomach, humiliation burning her like acid.

'No,' she repeated, stepping back from him so that he couldn't see how badly she was trembling, how dirty and ashamed she felt.

She was turning him down? How dared she—a woman he had already seen take money from one man tonight? Jay could barely contain his fury.

'I wasn't offering to pay for more,' he told her in a voice as soft as death. 'Having tested what's on offer, I find you aren't worth buying. I was simply offering to pay for what I'd already had. Here…'

As he stretched out his hand to push the money down the front of her dress Keira pushed his hand away and stepped back from him, telling him fiercely, 'I'm not for sale.'

'Liar.'

He had gone before she could say anything else, leaving her to struggle to re-zip her dress and then hurry to the nearest cloakroom to repair the damage to her face and hair before going to join the other wedding guests in the courtyard.

It was an effort for her to behave normally. She was still in shock—a double shock now, after the accusation he had flung at her. She felt more frightened and alone than she could ever remember feeling. Even as a young girl, when she had first realised exactly what her mother was.

'Your mam's a prostitute. She goes with men for money.'

She could still hear the sharp Northern tones of the boy who had cornered her in the school playground and chanted the words to her. She had been eight, and well aware that her home life was different from the lives of the other children at school—children whose mothers waited for them outside the school gates and pulled them away when they saw her, children who didn't go home to a mother who slept all day and 'worked' all night to pay for her drug habit.

Sometimes it seemed to Keira that she had always known shame in one form or another, and that it had been her single true companion for all of her life, shadowing her and colouring her life—her future as well as her past.

CHAPTER THREE

JAY WAS A man who prided himself on his self-control. It was that control that ensured he would never repeat his father's folly in allowing his desire for an unworthy and avaricious woman to rule and humiliate him. Jay could allow himself to satisfy his physical desire, but he must always be the one to control it rather than the other way around. No woman had ever been allowed to intrude into his thoughts when he did not want her to, and yet now here he was, wasting his valuable mental energy thinking about a woman he despised. The mere fact that she was there in his thoughts, occupying space that rightly belonged to far more important matters, angered him far more than the unsatisfied ache of the desire she had left him with.

Why was he bothering to think about her? She'd probably thought she was being extremely clever, that by offering and then withdrawing she would get far more from him than if she had simply gone to bed with him there and then, but Jay did not allow anyone to manipulate him to their own advantage—especially not the kind of woman who tried to play games with him. He had desired her, she had recognised that fact and responded to it, and then she had tried to make capital out of it. So far as he was concerned that meant game over.

Jay wasn't the kind of man who let his physical desires

rule him, and it wasn't as though he wasn't used to women coming on to him. Coming on to him, yes. But then walking away from him having done so? He wasn't used to that, was he? It stung his pride—all the more so because of the type of woman she so obviously was. She was a fool if she thought he had been taken in by her puerile attempt to make him want her more by pretending that she didn't want him. And she was a fool because she had already previously admitted to him that she *did* want him. But she had still walked away from him. That knowledge rubbed against his pride as painfully as the sand of the nearby desert could rub against unprotected flesh.

Jay and his brother Rao had ridden their horses there as boys. He had a sudden longing for the freedom of the desert now, for its ability to strip a man down to his strengths and lay bare his weaknesses so that he was forced to overcome them to survive. The desert was a hard taskmaster but a fair one. It taught a boy how to become a man and a man how to become a leader and a ruler. He had missed it in the years of his self-imposed exile, and one of the first things he had done on his return, following Rao's letter to him warning him of their father's imminent death, had been to have a horse saddled up so that the could ride free in the desert.

Rao would be a good and a wise ruler. Jay loved and admired his elder brother, and was grateful to him for the compassion he had shown in making sure that Jay had the opportunity to make his peace with their elderly father before his death.

The courtesan who had caused the original breach between them had long gone, having run off with her young lover and a trunk filled with not only the jewels her besotted lover had given her, but also some she had 'borrowed' from the royal vault and had never returned…

* * *

'I've set up an appointment for you with Jay. Unfortunately I can't stay with you, as I've got another meeting to go to, but he's cool about the idea of having you on board as our interior designer.'

While she was grateful to Sayeed for accompanying her to the meeting, Keira was also regretting the fact that she wasn't on her own and so able to study her surroundings more closely, she acknowledged as they walked together through the old city.

Somehow she hadn't expected the billionaire entrepreneur who was the driving force behind some of the most modern office structures currently going up around India to have his office in an ancient palace within the heart of Ralapur's old town.

'Jay doesn't make a big deal of it—as I've already said, he's fanatical about his privacy, and who he admits to his inner circle—but the truth is that his father was the old Maharaja, and until his brother marries Jay is his heir and next in line to the throne. The old Maharaja had been in poor health for a number of years before his death. He was very anti the modern world. Rao and Jay want to bring the benefits of modern life to the city and their people, but at the same time they are both dedicated to maintaining all those traditional things that makes Ralapur the very special place that it is. That is why all the new development will be outside the city.'

Sayeed was right in saying that Ralapur was a very special place, and Keira could well understand why the new Maharaja and his brother were determined not to see it spoiled. Her own artistic senses feasted on the array of ancient buildings. She couldn't make up her mind which form of architecture actually dominated the town. There was undoubtedly a strong Arab influence, but then according to legend one of Ralapur's first rulers had been a warrior Arab prince. The Persian influence of the Mughal emperors could also be seen, as well as the tranquil calm of Hindu temples. She would have loved to stop to explore and enjoy the city at a more leisurely pace.

They had walked through the town from a large new car park outside the walls, where everyone was required to leave their vehicles because of the city's narrow, winding and frequently stepped streets. Now they had emerged from the cool shadows of one of those streets into a large square in front of the blindingly white alabaster-fronted royal palace. Two flights of white steps led up to it, divided by a half-landing on which stood two guards in gold and cream Mughal robes and turbans, their presence more for effect than anything else, Keira suspected.

Facing each other across the square, adjacent to the main palace, were two equally impressive but slightly smaller palaces, and it was towards one of these that Sayeed directed her.

'Jay has taken over the palace that was originally built for a sixteenth-century Maharaja, whilst the one opposite it was built at the same time for his widowed mother, who had been a famous stateswoman in her own right,' he said.

Sayeed spoke briefly to the imposing-looking 'guard' at the entrance before urging Keira up the flight of marble stairs and into a high square hallway that lay beyond them. She was feeling increasingly nervous by the minute. It had been bad enough when she had believed that her prospective client was an exacting and demanding billionaire, but now that she knew he was also a 'royal' her apprehension had increased.

He might be royal, but she was a highly qualified interior designer, who had trained with one of the most respected international firms, and whose own work was very highly thought of. She had very high standards and took pride in the excellence of her work, she reminded herself stoutly. She was a professional interior designer, yes. But she was also the daughter of a woman who had sold her body to men for money to feed her drug habit. Where did that place her on the scale of what was and what was not acceptable? Did she really need to ask herself that question? Of course she didn't. The burn of the shame she had known growing up because of her mother was still as raw now as it had been then.

It hadn't just been her great-aunt who had rammed home to her the message that her mother's lifestyle made Keira unacceptable and unwanted in more respectable people's social circles.

After her mother had died and her great-aunt had taken her in, Keira had had to change schools. In the early days at her new school another girl had befriended her, and within a few weeks they'd been on their way to becoming best friends. Keira, who had never had any real friends before, never mind a best friend, had been delirious with joy.

Until the day Anna had told her uncomfortably, 'My mother says that we can't be friends any more.'

By the end of the week the story of her mother had gone round the playground like measles, infecting everyone and most especially Keira herself. She'd been ostracised and excluded, forced to hang her head in shame and to endure the taunts of some of the other children.

Keira had known then that she must never allow people to know about her mother, because once they did they would not want to know her. She had made a vow to herself that she would not just walk away from her past at the first opportunity. She would build a wall between it and her that would separate her from it for ever.

Her chance to do just that had come when her great-aunt had died of a heart attack, leaving Keira at eighteen completely alone in the world, and with what had seemed to her at the time an enormous inheritance of £500,000.

She had bought herself elocution lessons so that she could hide her Northern accent, and with it her own shame, and the money had also helped her to train as an interior designer. It had bought her a tiny flat too, in what had then been an inexpensive part of London but which was now a very up-and-coming area.

As a child Keira had loved her mother. As she'd got older she had continued to love her, but her love had been mixed with anger. Now, as an adult, she still loved her— but that love was combined with pity and sadness, and a fierce determination not to repeat her mother's errors of judgement and weaknesses.

Keira never lied about her past. She simply didn't tell people everything about it, saying only that she had been orphaned young and brought up by an elderly great-aunt who had died just before she started university. It was, after all, the truth. Only she knew about the darker, more unpalatable and unacceptable parts of her past. A past that would certainly render her unacceptable to someone of such high status as a royal prince.

They were being guided to the main reception room— a huge, richly decorated room with columns and walls of gilded carvings designed to overwhelm and impress.

Don't think about the past, Keira urged herself. Look at the décor instead.

An Arabic-style fretted screen ran round an upper storey walkway, allowing those behind it to look down into the hallway without themselves being seen. It seemed to Keira that the very air of the room felt heavy with the weight of past secrecy and intrigue, of whispered promises and threats, and of royal favour and power courted and brokered behind closed doors.

This was a different world from the one she knew. She could feel its traditions and demands pressing down on her. Here within these walls a person would be judged by who their ancestors had been—not what they themselves were. Here within these walls she would most definitely have been judged as her mother's daughter, condemned and branded to follow in her footsteps by that judgement. Keira repressed a small shudder of apprehension as she followed Sayeed deeper into the room.

The scent of sandalwood filled the still air. High above them on the ceiling, mirrored mosaics caught the light from the narrow windows and redirected it so that it struck the gaze of those entering the room, momentarily blinding them and of course giving whoever might be standing behind the screens watching them, or indeed waiting for them in the room itself, a psychological advantage.

Sayeed gave their names to the man who appeared silent-footed and traditionally dressed, and then bowed to them and indicated that they were to follow him down a narrow passage behind the fretted screens. It led to a pair of double doors, which in turn opened into an elegant courtyard. He led them across and then in through another door and up a flight of stairs until they came to a pair of doors on which he knocked before opening.

A man speaking into a mobile phone was standing in front of a narrow grilled open window through which Keira could see and hear the street.

No, not *a* man, Keira recognised with a sickening downward plunge of her heart as he turned round towards them, but *the* man—the man for whom she had broken the most important rule in her life; the man she had kissed and touched and told without words but with a feverish intensity that had been quite plain that she desired him; the man from whom she had then run in her shame and her fear. The man who had shown her his contempt and his evaluation of her by offering her money in exchange for the kisses they shared.

If she could have done so Keira would have turned and run from him, from all the dark despair of her most private fears—fears which he had given fresh life both through her own desire for him and his treatment of her. But she couldn't. Sayeed was standing behind her.

The slate-grey gaze flicked over her and rested expressionlessly on her face. He had recognised her even if he wasn't showing it.

Sayeed stepped forward to shake the other man's hand, saying to him jovially, 'Jay. I've brought you Keira, just as I promised. She's desperate for you to give her this contract so that she can show you what she can do. I don't think you'll be disappointed by what she can offer.'

Keira squirmed inwardly over Sayeed's unfortunate choice of words and all that might be read into them by a cynical, sexually experienced man who had every reason to believe he already knew what she had to offer.

'I can't stay,' Sayeed was continuing. 'I've got a meeting I have to attend, so I'm going to have to leave you to discuss things without me. However, as I've already told you, I've seen Keira's work, and she has my personal recommendation and endorsement.'

He had gone before she could stop him and tell him that she had changed her mind. That she wouldn't want this contract if it was the last one on earth.

Jay watched her. Unless she was a far better actress than he believed, she hadn't faked her shocked surprise at seeing him and realising who he was. So, a woman who hired herself out for sex? Or a professional woman who liked to let her hair down and play a game of sex tease with what she thought was the local talent? Or maybe a bit of both, depending on her mood? If so, perhaps she was more used to being paid off in expensive gifts rather than hard cash—although she hadn't looked unhappy to receive the bundle of notes he had seen her being given last night. She was dressed today for a business appointment—European-style, with a careful nod in the direction of Indian culture. He could see the faint beading of sweat on her upper lip—caused, he suspected, not so much by the heat as by her discomfort at seeing him again.

'You come highly recommended. Sayeed can't praise your skills enough.'

The taunt that lay beneath his words was barely veiled and intended to be recognised.

Keira could feel the slow painful burn of a feeling that was a mixture of shame and anger. That her own behaviour was the weapon she had handed him to use against her was the cause of her shame, and that he had not hesitated to use it the cause of her anger.

Well, she wasn't going to respond to his goading.

Jay frowned when she remained silent.

It irked him that he hadn't guessed who she might be, and it irritated him even more that she had brought with her into his office not just the scent of the perfume she was wearing but also the memory of his desire for her. And not only the memory, he realised as his body reacted to her against his will.

She wore her sexuality like she wore her scent, bringing it with her into his presence and forcing recognition of it on his senses whilst maintaining an air of detachment from it and from him.

He turned from her and strode the length of the room,

trying to force down the ache that somehow managed to surface past his angry contempt.

He was pacing his office floor in such a way that she could almost hear the pad of a hunting cat's sharp-clawed paws, along with the dangerous swish of its tail—as though her mere presence fed his hunger to destroy her, Keira thought sickly.

'Has Sayeed bedded you? Is that why he is so keen to secure this contract for you? Did he promise it to you in exchange for your sexual favours?'

'No. I don't go to bed with anyone to secure business. I don't need to,' Keira told him proudly. 'My work speaks for itself.'

'Yes, indeed. I saw that for *myself* last night.'

The blood surged and then retreated through her veins, causing her heart to thud erratically. There was no mistaking the meaning behind his words.

'You must think what you wish. Plainly that is what you intend to do.'

'It isn't my wishes that govern the logic of my thinking process, rather it is the visual evidence of my own eyes. I saw the man you were with handing you money—and rather a substantial amount of money at that.'

Keira had to defend her professional reputation. She wasn't going to get the contract, so she had nothing to lose in defending herself, had she? She took a deep breath and spoke swiftly.

'And because of that you leapt to the conclusion that I am…that I…that my body is for sale? That isn't logic. It is supposition tainted with prejudice.'

She was daring to argue with him? Daring to defend the indefensible and accuse him of being prejudiced? Jay could feel his fury pressing against the cords of his self-control, threatening to break free.

'He gave you money. I saw that with my own eyes.'

'He is an old friend. He was paying me for the refurbishment of his flat. If you don't believe me you can ask him—and you can ask Shalini as well.'

'Shalini?'

'The bride. She and Vikram are cousins. The two of them and Tom, Shalini's new husband, and I were all at university together.'

Keira had no idea why she was telling him all this. What difference could it make now? She had lost the contract, and despite the fact that she desperately needed the money a part of her was relieved. There were some things that mattered more than money, and her own peace of mind was definitely one of them.

Jay frowned. Something told him that she was telling the truth. Not that he had any intention of demeaning himself by questioning others about her.

And besides, there were other issues at stake here. She had an impressive client list, the majority of whom were women. That had been one of the most important deciding factors in his original decision to take her on. India's growing middle class wanted new and more westernised homes, and it was predominantly the women who were making the decisions about which developer they bought from. The interior of any new property was a vitally important selling point, and Jay knew that he could not afford to make any mistakes in his choice of interior designer.

On paper, this woman ticked all the right boxes. She had connections with an elite of London based Indian families—no doubt through the friendships she had made at university. She had worked for them in London, and he was well aware of the praise she had been given for the way she blended the best of traditional Indian and modern Western styles to create uniquely stylish interiors that had delighted their owners. She had also worked in Mumbai; she was at home in both cultures and apparently well liked by the Indian matriarchs whose approval was so vitally important to her business and indirectly to his.

His long silence was unnerving her, Keira admitted inwardly. It flustered her into repeating, 'My work speaks for itself.'

'But perhaps your body language speaks more clearly? To my sex at least.'

His voice was as cool as steel and just as deadly. Keira could feel it piercing her pride, taking a shimmering bead of its life force as though it were a trophy. Now that he had savoured his pleasure in wounding her no doubt he would close in for the kill and tell her that he wasn't going to give her the contract.

She lifted her chin and told him proudly, 'I don't see the point in prolonging this conversation, since it's obvious that you don't have any intention of commissioning me to work for you as an interior designer.'

He certainly didn't *want* to do so, now that he knew who she was, Jay acknowledged. But there was the delicate matter of losing face—both for Sayeed and in a roundabout way for Jay himself.

Sayeed might be a very junior partner in their current venture, but he would be within his rights to question why Jay had rejected Keira, after allowing the negotiations to get this far. Sayeed would be personally insulted, and whilst Jay was too rich and too powerful to worry about that, his own moral scruples were such that bringing his own personal feelings into the business arena was something he just would not do without explaining. That would cause *him* to lose face.

The situation was non-negotiable—both practically and morally. He had no alternative but to go ahead and formalise the offer of a contract, as Sayeed would be expecting him to do.

'Not personally, no,' he agreed silkily. 'So if last night's little game of tease was meant to whet my appetite I'm afraid it failed. However, when it comes to the contract for the interior design work at my new development, I am prepared to accept Sayeed's recommendation that you are the right designer for the job. Of course if he is wrong…'

Keira was struggling to take in the triple whammy effect of his speech—first the direct attack on her personally, then the surprise offer of the contract, and finally the killer blow, warning her that Sayeed would be the one who would end up losing out if she failed to live up to his recommendation. She was trapped, and they both knew it. Whilst she might have been willing to risk turning her back on the commission and fees for the sake of her own pride, she was not prepared to risk injuring Sayeed's business reputation by doing so. And she suspected that the man in front of her watching her, so cynically, knew that.

'Very well,' she told him, drawing herself up to her full height of five feet nine—which, whilst tall, was well below his far more impressive six foot plus, leaving her in the ignominious position of having to tilt her head back to look up at him. 'But I want it understood that the relationship between us will be purely and only that of developer and interior designer. Absolutely nothing more.'

She was *daring* to warn him off?

Jay couldn't believe her gall. Well, two could play at that game.

'Are you sure that is all you want?' he mocked her.

Keira could feel her face burn.

'Yes,' she confirmed, tight-lipped.

'Liar,' Jay taunted. 'But it's all right, because I assure you that I have no intention of our relationship being anything other than strictly business. The truth is that if you want me you're going to have to come crawling on your knees and beg me. And even then...' His gaze flicked over her disparagingly. 'Well, let's just say I'm not a fan of used goods.'

If she could have walked out, Keira knew that she would have done so. But she couldn't. Not now. He had trapped her with his implied threat about his business relationship with Sayeed.

The door to the room suddenly opened inwards to admit Sayeed himself, who told them both cheerfully, 'My appointment was cancelled, so I came back. How's it going?'

It was Jay who answered, telling him smoothly, 'Since Miss Myers comes with your recommendation, Sayeed, I am prepared to offer her a contract. Whether or not she chooses to accept it is, of course, up to her.'

Keira gave him a burning look. He knew perfectly well that her choices were non-existent. He had arranged matters so that they would be.

'Of course she'll accept it.' Sayeed was beaming enthusiastically.

'So that's agreed, then. Keira is coming on board as our designer,' Jay said briskly. 'I'll get my PA to sort out the contracts, and the three of us can have dinner tonight to celebrate and discuss everything in more detail. You're staying at the Palace Lodge Hotel, Keira? I'll have a car sent to pick you up at eight o'clock.'

It was a fiasco. No—worse than that; it was a total nightmare, Keira decided grimly later in the day as she walked through the city, trying not to let despair over her situation prevent her from enjoying exploring the city's unique cultural history.

Keira couldn't remember how old she had been when

she had first realised just what her mother was. But she could remember that she had been nine when her mother had told Keira that her father was a married man.

'Loved him, I did—and he said he loved me. Mind you, they all say that when they want to get into your knickers. Not that he were me first—not by a long chalk. Had lads running after me from when I was fourteen, I did. That's been my problem, see, Keira. I always liked a good time too much. It's in me nature, you see, and it will be in yours too—see if it isn't. We just can't help ourselves, see. Come from a long line of women made that way, you and me have. Some lad will come along, and before you know where you are you'll be opening your legs for him.'

Keira still shuddered when she remembered those words. They had filled her with a fear that her great-aunt's unkindness had reinforced. Keira had decided long before she went to university that she would never allow herself to fall in love or commit to a man because of the risk of discovering she shared her mother's weakness in controlling her sexual appetite, along with her inability to choose the right man.

Her horror of sharing her mother's fate was burned into her heart.

After university Keira had moved to London and found a job working for an upmarket interior design company at a very junior level.

Through Shalini and Vikram she'd been familiar with the ethnically diverse Brick Lane area of the city, and she had quickly fallen in love with the creative intensity it had to offer, putting what she'd learned from it into her own work and adapting it to her own personal style.

Soon word had begun to get around that she had a sympathetic understanding of Indian taste, and rich Indians had started to ask specifically if she could be part of the team working on their interiors.

With the encouragement of her boss, Keira had eventually struck out on her own, finding for herself a niche market that was fresh and vibrant and matched her own feelings about design and style.

She'd met Sayeed through Vikram, and had let him sweet-talk her into doing some room schemes for the rundown properties he was doing up as buy-to-lets. Sayeed had done well, and an uncle in India had taken him into his own property development business—which was how Sayeed had become involved with Jay.

Jay. The thought of him—or rather of His Highness Prince Jayesh of Ralapur—was enough to have her tensing her body against her own inner panic. How could she have let such a thing happen to her?

It should have been impossible for him to have aroused her as he had done. Not once before had Keira ever felt tempted to ignore the rules she had made for herself.

Yes, she had kissed boys at university—she hadn't wanted to be thought odd or weird after all—but once they had started wanting more than a bit of mild petting she had had no difficulty whatsoever in telling them no.

True, a certain scene in a film or a passage in a book might have the power to make her ache a little—she was human, after all—but she had never allowed herself to experience that ache with a real flesh-and-blood man.

Until last night.

For him. With him.

Keira paced the floor of her hotel room in agitation. She couldn't stay and work for him. Why not? Because she was afraid that she might end up wanting to go to bed with him? Because she was afraid that she might, as he had taunted her, end up begging him to take her?

No! Where was her pride? Surely she was strong enough not to let that happen? Where was her courage and her self-esteem? Let him say what he liked. She would show him that she meant what she had said. She would remain detached and uninterested in him as a man. Would she? Could she? She was a twenty-seven-year-old virgin who in reality was scared to death she might be in danger of breaking a vow she had made almost a decade ago, and he was a man who looked as though he went through women faster than a monsoon flood went through a rice field.

She mustn't think like that, Keira warned herself. She must remember the old adage that the thought was father to the deed, and not will her own self-destruction on herself.

The hard, cold reality was that she could not afford to lose this contract any more than she could afford to be sexually vulnerable to him. If she blew this, she would never get another opportunity to match it. Chances like this came once in a lifetime—if you were lucky. Her success here would elevate her to a much higher professional status. All she had to do was to keep the promise she had made herself not to allow herself to be physically vulnerable.

At exactly two minutes to eight, Keira walked into the hotel reception area and told the girl on the desk that she was expecting a car to be sent for her.

At five past eight Sayeed came hurrying through the hotel entrance, grinning broadly when he saw her.

'Jay apologises, but he can't make it after all,' he told her as he sank down into the plush vibrant pink cushions of the gilded wood chair opposite her own.

He put the A4 manila envelope he had been carrying down on the marble table in front of them before signalling for a waiter, and then, without asking Keira what she wanted, he ordered champagne for both of them, his dark eyes sparkling with excitement.

'He gave me the contract for you to sign. I'm leaving for Mumbai and then London in the morning, but I'll make sure I get it back to him before I leave. Oh, and he said he'll be in touch with you tomorrow about arranging to bring you up to speed with what's happening and what he's looking for you to provide. It's a great deal, Keira. A good payment in advance that will give you some working capital. One thing I will say for Jay is that he expects the best and he's prepared to pay for it.'

The waiter brought their champagne.

Sayeed picked up his glass and raised it to her in a toast. 'To success.'

Half an hour later the contract was signed and witnessed, Sayeed had promised to fax her a copy once Jay had signed as well—and Keira's head was swimming slightly from the combined effects of champagne and her own awareness that there was now no going back.

CHAPTER FOUR

KEIRA HAD JUST finished answering the last of her emails when she heard a knock on her hotel room door. Automatically she went to answer it, her body stiffening when she opened the door to find Jay standing there.

When Sayeed had told her that Jay would contact her she had assumed that he would telephone her, not arrive unannounced outside her room at such an early hour of the morning. Immediately she felt on edge and at a disadvantage.

'I thought we'd make an early start so that we can drive out to the site before it gets too hot. Then we can come back and go through what I expect from you and the timing,' Jay told her, stepping into her room so that she had to fall back.

It was a large room, with typical hotel anonymity, but somehow having him inside it with her made Keira acutely conscious of its intimacy and privacy.

'If you'd rung me I could have met you in Reception,' Keira told him sharply.

'If you'd had your mobile on you'd have known that I did ring you—several times,' he countered.

Keira could feel her face going red as she picked up her mobile and realised that he was right. She'd completely

overlooked the fact that she'd switched if off when she
was with Sayeed in the hotel foyer last night.

'You'll need to wear sensible shoes and a hat,' he told
her, causing Keira to grit her teeth.

'Thank you, but I have visited building sites before.'

It wasn't entirely true, but she wasn't going to have him
thinking she was totally incapable.

She paused, and then said steadily, 'I can be ready to
meet you in the hotel foyer very quickly. It won't take me
long to get changed.'

Jay's mouth thinned. Was she daring to hint that she
believed he had come to her room because he had some
personal interest in her? After all that he had said to her
yesterday? Was this yet another of her teasing games, designed to excite male interest? If so she was going to learn
that he was not easily excited, and when it came to playing games he always played to win...

'Any man who believes a woman when she tells him
that is a fool,' he answered. 'You've got five minutes.' And
then, before Keira could object, he had settled himself in a
chair and, having reached for the TV remote, was checking the stock market reports.

It took Keira precisely four minutes to get changed—
behind her locked bathroom door—into a pair of sand-
coloured and very businesslike cargo pants, a plain
short-sleeved white tee shirt, and a pair of comfortable
desert-style trainers.

Emerging from the bathroom, she gathered up a hat, her
sunglasses, and a long-sleeved cotton shirt to wear over
her tee shirt. She put them into the wicker basket which
already held her notepad and some pencils, all without
daring to look in the direction of the man seated in front
of the TV with his back to her.

She wasn't used to having a man in what was essentially her bedroom. His presence there was making her feel both acutely gauche and even more conscious of him, in a way that somehow caused her thoughts to slip sideways to a place that had her recklessly wondering if he would be watching television whilst he waited for her, if they were lovers who had just spent the night together.

Now her imagination was conjuring up images that made her hands shake, and she felt very glad indeed that he wasn't looking at her. He would sleep naked—but would he hold his lover in his arms after the act of possessing her, keeping her close as he slept? Would she wake to the intimate drift of his hands on her skin and his kiss on her lips? He would be a passionate lover, but would he also possess a tender side?

She would never know, because she would never know any man's passion or tenderness. The starkness of the feeling of loss that descended on her shocked her. She looked at the back of Jay's head, willing the unwanted feeling to disappear.

As she reached for her laptop and put it into the basket, Jay switched off the TV and stood up for all the world as though he had been able to see everything she had done and felt, even though he had had his back to her. It was an unnerving thought.

Five minutes later he was driving them out of the hotel grounds in a sturdy four-by-four, his eyes shaded from the sharp sunlight by a pair of Ray-Bans that made him look even more intimidating than ever.

They turned off the new road that ran from the equally new airport past the old city to the hotel complex onto a rough track, sending up clouds of dust as they went along that made Keira glad of the four-by-four's air-conditioning and comfortable seats.

'How far advanced is the building work?' Keira asked Jay.

'We're pretty close to completion and ahead of schedule at the moment, but that doesn't mean we can afford to relax. We're planning to launch the development well before the monsoon arrives, with TV and other media coverage in Mumbai, and a big event in the hotel, followed up by free look-and-see flights out for prospective buyers. That's why I've stipulated in your contract that I want you based out here, where I can keep a day-to-day overview of your progress and your exclusive services until your contract with us is complete.'

Keira tensed in shock.

'You want me based out here? I can't do that. My office is in London and—'

She gasped as the front wheels of the four-by-four hit a rut, throwing her painfully against her seat belt.

'I'm afraid that you are going to have to be. The contract makes our terms clear. Didn't you read it?'

'I must have missed that bit,' Keira fibbed. She could see from the look he gave her that he didn't believe her. It simply hadn't occurred to her that he would want to oversee her work. If it had…if she had thought for one minute that she would be working closely with him on a day-to-day basis…she would have… She would have what? Refused the contract? She couldn't afford to financially. But could she afford the emotional cost of the effect he might have on her?

'I'm going to have to go back to London if only to source things,' she told him.

He was looking really angry now.

'It is my express wish that all materials used in the interior design of this development are sourced as locally as possible. That is a key requirement of the contract and a key feature of the project. We have been extremely fortunate in securing both the land and the planning agreement for this project from my brother, the Maharaja, and his granting of that permission was conditional upon us meeting certain set targets with regard to benefits from the project for local people. It is his desire and mine that as a second stage in the redevelopment of Ralapur, the old city itself will become the favoured destination of wealthy cosmopolitan travellers. In order for it to have that appeal it is essential that its unique living history is preserved. Surely Sayeed told you all of this, and informed you that we are working very closely with the Maharaja and his advisers to ensure that his conditions are met? Conditions which, as it happens, I totally support.'

Well, of course he would, seeing as the Maharaja was his brother. He himself was every bit the royal prince, all arrogance and aristocratic pride. No doubt he was used to having his way whenever he wanted it and however he wanted it, with women as well as in business. Well, he wasn't going to have his way with her!

'I can't remember, Your Royal Highness,' Keira lied again, not wanting to get Sayeed into trouble. Normally she would have been filled with admiration for the stance being taken by both the Maharaja and Jay, but on this occasion she was all too conscious of how difficult it would make putting as much distance as possible between Jay and herself.

The look he was giving her was openly contemptuous, as well as grimly angry.

'It is not necessary for you to address me in such a manner. Since I have chosen not to play a role that requires me to use my title, I see no reason why I should be addressed by it.'

Now he had surprised her—but why should that bother her? She wasn't afraid of him, was she? She wasn't afraid that somehow she *would* end up begging him to make love to her? No, of course she wasn't. The very idea was ludicrous, unthinkable. Because if she did then... Her heart had started to pound and a now familiar and very dangerous ache had started to spread slowly but unstoppably through her.

He was driving them up to the top of a steep incline, onto a small plateau, the wheels of the four-by-four were still throwing up clouds of dust, and Keira didn't know what she would have done to stop that ache from spreading if she hadn't suddenly caught her first glimpse of the development site and realised just what it was that Jay was creating.

'You're building a copy of the old city!' she exclaimed in astonishment, as she looked through the dust towards the rose-red sandstone city walls and the open gateway into them, beyond which she could see a mass of buildings and workmen. 'Sayeed said you were building apartments.'

'We are. These are apartments,' he told her, gesturing towards the buildings inside the city wall. 'And once we've finished work on this we'll be building the office blocks that will house the new IT industry on the other side of the new city. The office blocks are going to be mirror-fronted, so that they'll reflect the natural landscape rather than intrude on it, and we're using an up-to-date version of traditional building and design methods where the residential area is concerned. The idea of an ancient city excites everyone's imagination, including mine, so we've decided to see if we can recreate it from the outside whilst making what's inside more suitable for modern-day living, as well as environmentally sound. For instance, the new city will be a car-free area, and each group of homes will share an inner courtyard complete with swimming pool and private family spaces. Flat roofs will be converted into gardens. We want the new community to be serviced as far as possible from within the existing population, rather than bringing in a workforce from outside.'

It was a hugely ambitious project, and Keira could hardly take in the scale of it.

'Ethically it makes good sense,' Keira agreed, 'but you have to consider that the local population may not have the necessary skills. Even if they do, they may not be able to service the demands of a large number of new households.'

'Which is why I am already in discussion with my brother and some of the local family elders with a view to setting up training schemes to be run by skilled local craftsmen to teach the skills that will be needed. By the time the office blocks are ready for occupation, it is my intention that all the necessary infrastructure and practical aspects of comfortable everyday living for the people who will work in them will be in place and working efficiently.'

Jay stopped the car on a dusty expanse of hard flat earth.

'The first phase of the housing development is almost finished. I'll take you over so that you can have a look at them. We'll have to walk from here.'

Two hours later Keira acknowledged that what she'd been shown was any designer's dream—or nightmare, depending on that designer's self-confidence and the support he or she would get from those in charge of financing the project.

The architecture of the residential area followed that of the old city very closely. The homes were grouped in clusters, each with its own personal, enclosed courtyard garden for privacy, and each grouping also shared a larger courtyard with formal gardens. The houses were mainly two-storey, with large balconies on the first floor and access to a sheltered flat roof space. They were either two- or four-bedroom, and each bedroom had its own bathroom. The master bedroom had a good-sized dressing room.

On the ground floor the smaller two-bedroom properties were open plan, with long galley kitchens that could be shut off from the main living area by a folding wall, while the larger properties had separate family-sized kitchens.

Each property had a small office space, and good access onto its courtyard, which was designed to serve as an extra outdoor living space. The concept was both practical and modern, whilst the look of the buildings was traditional, with the houses grouped around what would be an open 'market square'. There was also what looked like a traditional bazaar, but in fact, Jay explained to Keira, it would be a set of buildings housing modern coffee shops and restaurants, as well as shops selling food and other necessary staples.

The houses were to have traditional hard floors, either in marble or mosaic tiles or, for a more modern feel, slate. The look Jay wanted for the interiors, as he had made plain to Keira, was one of simple elegance, in keeping with the whole concept, with a mixture of traditional and modern styles and furnishings to suit the tastes of the eventual purchasers of the properties.

'I want a style for these properties which is unique, conveying a certain status and meeting the aspirations of the people who will live here. It must be individual with regard to each property, and yet at the same time create an overall harmony.'

That would mean using strong key colours that would both harmonise and contrast to produce individuality, whilst keeping to an underlying theme—perhaps with plain off-white walls throughout the interiors, but with very different fabrics and furnishings textures and styles, in a palette of colours. Sharp limes and cool blues, hot

pinks and reds, bright yellows and rich golds. Indian colours, but used in ways that transcended the traditional
whilst still respecting it.

'I shall need to know if you want each house within a
group to share the same style, with each group styled differently, or if you want a mix of styles within each grouping, repeated over several groups,' Keira told Jay.

'You'll be able to see the overall plan more clearly when
you see the scale model,' Jay answered her. 'Ultimately
we intend to give people both the opportunity to work and
live here, or to use it as a leisure facility. We plan to create
a lake within walking distance of the development for leisure purposes, which together with the existing lake and
hotel—as well, of course, as the attraction of the ancient
city—will make this somewhere people want to come and
visit, as well as live in. The hotel will be extended to include a facility for corporate entertaining, and we hope
with irrigation to be able to source much of the food that
will be needed for the new town and the visitors locally.'

Keira was stunned by the breadth of his vision. 'It's
a very ambitious project,' was all she could find to say.

'I'm a very ambitious man,' he told her.

And a very sexy man. An unnervingly charismatic
and sensually disturbing man. Surely it wasn't possible
for the space inside the vehicle to have become smaller,
so that she was forced to be more aware of his physical
presence as a man? It was the fault of the bright sunlight
that she had to turn her head to avoid its glare, and was
thus obliged to look at the way his hands held the steering wheel—as knowledgeably and masterfully as he had
held her last night.

How had her thoughts managed to slip sideways into
that forbidden place she knew they must not go? Keira
wondered angrily. It was almost as though her own body

was working against her in some way, trying to undermine her.

So what if he was sexy and charismatic and…and sensually disturbing? He was also cruel and unkind and arrogant, incapable of judging her fairly, and she would be a complete fool to let herself be caught in any kind of sexual attraction to him. But wasn't the truth that she was already acutely aware of him as a man?

Keira could feel her heart thumping. She must not give in to this unfamiliar and unwanted vulnerability.

'There's a fabric designer whose fabrics might work well here,' she told Jay, putting aside her personal concerns to focus on her work. 'He might be prepared to design and produce some fabrics specifically to order for us. What I'm thinking of is using the hot colours India is famous for, but in a more modern way—stripes and checks, perhaps, in thick hessian and slubbed linen, coarse cottons rather than sheer silks. Fabrics that have a modern appeal to them but still an Indian feel. We could have light fittings in coloured mosaic glass, but in modern shapes.'

Her own imagination was taking fire now, leaping ahead of her, illuminating the way just as the mosaic glass lanterns she was visualising would illuminate the cool shadows of enclosed courtyard gardens and rooms.

The fabrics she was envisaging would work just as well with modern pared-down minimalist furniture in plastic and chrome as they would with more ornate traditional things.

She was as fiercely passionate about her work as he was, Jay recognised reluctantly. He didn't want to acknowledge that they shared a certain mind-set, he didn't want to find that he admired her professionalism, and he certainly didn't want to have to admit even to himself that he had actually enjoyed talking to her about his vision for the future of this development because he had sensed that, unlike so many other women he had known, she was genuinely interested in what he was doing.

Instead he focused on the sensuality of the way she talked about her work. It was like watching an image come to life, her passion illuminating her expression. The same way she herself would come to life in his arms in the heat of passion, offering him her body and her pleasure, inciting him to take it and to take her, exciting and denying him until he was driven to possess her in every way imaginable.

His body tightened with a desire he had to punish her for causing.

'You paint a very sensual picture. Deliberately so, I suspect.' His voice was harsh and accusatory.

'I was simply describing a light fitting. If you choose to see something sensual in that then that is up to you.' Keira defended herself even whilst her heart thudded into her ribs.

'You did not consider it sensual yourself? There are those who believe that the underlying message of the *Kama Sutra* is that everything we are is designed for sexual and sensual pleasure.'

The shock caused by his words sent a sharp thrill zigzagging down her spine, as though he had actually touched her there himself. She could feel the warmth of his breath heating her skin, just as his words were heating her already fevered imagination.

The *Kama Sutra*! It was unfair, surely, that he should refer to a such a book after what he had said to her about her having to beg him for sex? Was he deliberately trying to test her?

'I wouldn't know,' she told him sharply. 'It isn't a book I've ever felt any inclination to read.' There—that should make it plain to him that she was sticking firmly to business.

'Because you don't feel you have anything to learn from it?'

'Books instructing women to debase themselves for a man's pleasure will never be something I'd want to learn from,' Keira hit back.

'The *Kama Sutra* contains no suggestion of debasement of anyone. Rather it is about the honing of mutual pleasure, the giving and taking of that pleasure, the sensual and sexual education of both male and female so that they can experience the greatest degree of mutual pleasure with and for one another. I am surprised that you did not know that.'

If she could have walked away from him she would have done so, Keira knew. Anything to get away from the taunting softness of that male voice, painting images inside her head that made her ache as though her whole body was on fire. Images which had no right to be there and which she did not *want* to be there.

'It's time for us to head back.'

His abrupt change of subject was a relief, but Keira still felt it wise to keep her distance from him as they headed back towards the four-by-four over the rutted and rock-strewn ground. He was walking very fast, his longer legs carrying him over the rough ground far more swiftly than her own, and in her haste not to look unprofessional and helpless she started to walk faster, ignoring the danger in the loose rocks and deep gulleys carved into the dusty road by the wheels of heavy excavation plant.

They had almost reached the four-by-four when it happened. A loose stone beneath her foot rolled away into one of the gulleys, causing her to lose her balance.

Jay heard Keira's exclamation of alarm and turned back,

moving swiftly towards her, reaching her just in time to catch her as she stumbled.

His chest was on a level with her eyes and Keira could see its fierce rise and fall. It mesmerised her as much as the hot male scent of his body, sending out a message that locked on to her own female hormones, dizzying and almost drugging them with awareness of his masculinity. She could feel the heat of the sun on her back, but it was as nothing compared to the heat burning through her from the grip of Jay's hands on her arms.

All he was doing was steadying her. She knew that. But to her body his hold was dangerously reminiscent of the way he had held her when he had kissed her, and she had to fight down its instinctive urge to close the gap between them. If he kissed her now he would taste of salt and heat and male hormones...

It must be the shock of her unwanted sexual response to him that was responsible for the feeling that somehow time had slowed down, and with it the beat of her own heart, as though both of them were caught up in some kind of mystical spell, Keira thought dizzily. She could see where the shadow was just beginning to darken the line of Jay's jaw, and she had an overwhelming longing to reach out and touch it with her fingertips, and then to trace the curve of his mouth. The sensuality of the contrast between them would, she knew, be burned into her touch in a way that would make her ache to feel that contrast against her own flesh. It would be so easy to do, so very easy.

He knew what she was doing, Jay assured himself. She was trying to use his own maleness against him, knowing what effect her proximity would have on him. He had never known a woman so skilled at using his own sexuality against him. Where other women were foolish enough to blatantly thrust themselves on him, for him to either take or repulse as his mood dictated, she was far more subtle and skilled. Dangerously so, he recognised grimly, since her subtle waiting game had already resulted in arousing him. He shouldn't have referred to the *Kama Sutra,* Jay acknowledged. Doing so had conjured up images inside his head that had weakened his defences: images of sensuality and love-play in which her pale naked body was his to arouse and enjoy.

If he kissed her now...

Panicked by what she was thinking—and feeling—Keira told herself that it was relief she felt when Jay removed his hands from her arms and she was free to step back from him. What was wrong with her? Didn't she recognise her own danger and how foolish it was for her to keep having these wholly inappropriate and unwanted thoughts? It was as though some stranger had taken possession of her, and she was no longer in control of her own thoughts and feelings.

'Thanks,' she told him huskily, striving to appear normal, but avoiding looking directly at him.

She had done it again, Jay thought grimly. She had aroused him and then walked away. No woman did that to him and got away with it—especially not this one.

CHAPTER FIVE

'ONCE YOU'VE SEEN the scale model of the project, I'd like to see some concrete plans and sketches for the interiors for the first phase of the apartments as soon as possible,' Jay told Keira crisply as he drove them back down the dusty untarmacked road.

He had removed his sunglasses now that they were no longer driving into the sun, but the light was still too bright for Keira to want to remove her own.

'I'm leaving for Mumbai tomorrow evening, which will give you just over twenty-four hours to come up with an overview for me before I leave.'

The speed at which he expected her to work was shocking.

'I can't possibly produce detailed interior plans in twenty-four hours,' Keira protested, her face burning slightly as she sensed from the sideways look he slashed towards her that he was taking her words as an admission of failure rather than as an honest professional assessment of what could be accomplished in such a limited time span. Well, she wasn't going to recall or deny them. Her chin lifted, and the look she returned to him said without words that she wasn't going to recant—or apologise.

Keira could almost feel his mind probing her silence and assessing it. Her chin tilted a bit higher, but she wasn't going to risk looking directly into those platinum-grey eyes. Just thinking about the power of their uncompromisingly analytical surveillance made her feel far too weak. Platinum. One of the most desired and valuable metals in today's world. Somehow the colour of his eyes was symbolic of the man himself.

'Overviews, I said—not detailed plans,' Jay informed her coolly. 'Themes, colours, some take on style, so that I can mull them over whilst I'm travelling.'

'I haven't got my samples with me, or a proper office, or…'

'You'll be staying in the guest wing of the palace whilst you're working on this project. I've already arranged for the hotel to shift your stuff over to it, so it should be waiting for you when we get back. The accommodation provided for you includes an office.'

As easily as the first Mughal warriors had taken possession of the land, he had cut the ground from beneath her feet.

Oblivious to the bombshell he had just dropped on her, Jay continued briskly, 'You'll find it much more convenient, being in the city, and I'll supply you with a driver so that you can go out to the site if you need to whilst I'm in Mumbai. As for your samples—I thought I'd already made it clear that I expect you to use locally sourced materials. I'll take you down to the bazaar once I've shown you the scale model of the site, and introduce you to some of the suppliers I've already sourced.'

'Are you sure that you *want* a designer?' The thought of having to share a living space with him had upset her so much that Keira was in a headlong flight that redirected her fear into sarcasm. 'It seems to me that what you really want is someone who says yes to everything you say.'

'Isn't that what all women secretly want?' Jay taunted

her softly. 'A man who can tame her creativity to fit his
own desires and tells her so? You modern women may
deny it, but none of us can go against nature. Isn't it true
that secretly you prefer a man to know himself and his
desires so that he can use them to become a truly creative
and imaginative lover, who can take you to a place where
every fantasy you've ever had can be fulfilled? Be honest and admit that it's true. A woman of your age living
in these modern times must know that truth—unless, of
course, you are still waiting for a man with whom you can
experience that degree of pleasure.'

How was it possible for her to feel so hot and so cold at
the same time, with her stomach churning with shocked
fear and her head dizzy with even more shocked excitement?

'Nothing to say? Perhaps, then, the lovers you've experienced in the past weren't as satisfying as they might
have been?'

What was going on? How had the conversation managed to go from a businesslike discussion of Jay's requirements to this? However it had happened, it certainly wasn't
kindly intentioned, Keira suspected.

She took a deep breath and told him calmly, 'I don't
think that this kind of conversation is appropriate, given
our business relationship.'

She was doing it again. Jay could feel the heat of mingled anger and arousal beating up inside his body, threatening his self-control. He had no idea what it was about
this woman that pushed against the boundaries of that control and threatened it so dramatically and with such speed,
but he couldn't deny any more that there was something
about her that did. It acted on him like a goad—irritating,
driving, inciting, making him burn with a need to make
her want him as much as he did her, to make her admit

that want and cry it out to him. Only then could his pride be salved. Only her pleas for his possession and her cries of pleasure could satisfy it. And him?

'Not given our business relationship,' he agreed. 'But what about *this* relationship?'

As he finished speaking he took his hand off the steering wheel, reached out slowly, and very deliberately rubbed his thumb across Keira's nipple.

The shock of his touch was like an electric charge shooting through her. Her body, already sensitised to him from their earlier intimacy, reacted with the immediacy of a monsoon downpour, drenching her with aching need.

One look at her blatantly aroused expression had Jay stopping the four-by-four abruptly in the middle of the dusty empty road. It was almost midday, and there was no escape for anyone foolish enough to be caught in the sun's heat as it scorched the scrubby patches of dried-out grass. In the distance Keira could see trees that would provide shade and protection from the heat. But, like the grass, she was exposed by her own foolishness, and there was no protection for her unless she herself created it. She could feel the heat pressing in on the four-by-four as though trying to possess and overwhelm its artificial air-conditioned coolness. Safety and security were such fragile things when they were opposed by the forces of nature. But they still had to be fought and an effort made to control them.

Her breasts ached heavily, her nipples hard with longing for what they couldn't have.

'That isn't a relationship,' she told Jay flatly. 'It's… it's…'

'Desire…need…hunger…'

Keira could feel her control being stolen from her.

'It's nothing,' she corrected him.

'Nothing? Are you sure?'

'You've hired me as an interior designer. That is the only relationship I want there to be between us.'

Keira held her breath, waiting for him to call her a liar.

'Your body tells a different story. No doubt because it is well trained to react to my sex in a way that flatters it.'

He was being brutally insulting, but Keira wasn't going to give him the satisfaction of seeing that he had upset her. Instead she told him coolly, 'It's amazing how often what we think we recognise in other people is merely what we have already decided we *want* to recognise.'

The look he gave her made her heart thud and then race with the fear of the hunted for the hunter. Within seconds she knew why.

'Are you saying that the telltale hardness of your nipples was caused specifically by me and for me?'

His challenge had caught her in a trap of her own making, and there was nothing she could do now other than look straight ahead and tell him in a betrayingly constricted voice, 'I think we should change the subject.'

This was a new variation on an old game, Jay acknowledged, and it was certainly an unexpectedly excitingly erotic one. She was good. She was very good. She could turn him from pride to anger, and from that to sexual heat and desire, all within the space of a few minutes and a handful of words. If she was as good in bed…

Half an hour later the four-by-four was parked in the city car park and they were being welcomed back into the very grand entrance hall Keira remembered from the previous day.

The scale model of the new city and its planned surrounding development was displayed on a large table under glass in an otherwise almost empty room, down the corridor and past Jay's office.

A man who had the ambition and the wealth to underwrite this kind of project had to have a determined and even a ruthless side to his nature, Keira acknowledged. He would certainly make a very formidable opponent, and one who would never willingly accept defeat or being denied something he wanted.

Without any orders seeming to be given, a houseboy had appeared with tea, and Keira drank the hot reviving liquid gratefully.

'We'll eat in the old town whilst we're out,' Jay told her. 'There are several good restaurants there. Meanwhile, if you want to freshen up, Kunal here will show you to your quarters.' He raised his wrist to look at his watch, and unwittingly Keira looked too.

His forearm was firmly muscled, its olive skin darkened with body hair. A feeling that was a volatile mix of weakness and heat flipped her heart against her ribs and tightened her lower stomach muscles. What was happening to her? How could just looking at a man's wrist do something like this to her? Have her imagining him pinning her down against the softness of a voile-curtained bed with the weight of that arm over her naked body?

'I've got a couple of phone calls to make, so I'll meet you downstairs in half an hour.'

Keira was glad that all she needed to do was nod her head and then turn to follow the houseboy, because she simply didn't trust herself to speak.

The guest wing must originally have been the women's quarters of the palace, Keira guessed. It had its own enclosed courtyard garden, complete with a fountain and a pool which she could see and hear through the open arched windows from the enormous bedroom Kunal had shown her to.

'You like?' Kunal asked her shyly. 'This palace was

built many many years ago by the Maharaja. Ralapur has many palaces—all very beautiful.'

'Ralapur reminds me of Jaipur,' Keira told him.

'No,' Kunal told her vehemently, immediately shaking his head. 'Ralapur is better than Jaipur. Much better.' He was laughing now, inviting her to share in his joke and his loyalty to his home.

Keira waited until Kunal had gone before exploring her new quarters. The bedroom had a hugely ornate French empire-style bed, which looked as though it had been built and decorated specifically for the room, and the bathroom, reached via a door to one side of the bed was virtually the same size as the whole of her open-plan living space in her London apartment, decadently opulent with a sunken bath and mirrored walls.

These rooms had been created for a sexually active and sensual woman, Keira decided—a woman who had been a courtesan, surely, rather than a consort? Was that why he had given her this suite? As a reminder of what he considered her to be?

She washed and changed quickly into a cotton top with short sleeves and a softly pleated skirt, and then made her way back along the corridor and down the stairs to the hallway, where Jay was standing waiting for her.

'I thought we would eat here,' Jay announced, indicating the fretted arched doorway of a restaurant just off the city's main street.

'They serve traditional local food, and I should warn you that it is quite spicy. If you would prefer to eat somewhere else…?'

Keira hadn't thought that she was hungry, but just the smell of food wafting through the door was enough to make her mouth water.

'No—here is fine,' she assured him.

The restaurant was busy, with waiters wearing brightly coloured traditional clothes and intricately folded turbans that gave them a fierce warrior-like air, and diners seated on large cushions on the floor around low-level tables.

Everyone turned to look at Jay, no doubt because of his status as a member of the royal family. The waiters bowed low to him, and the restaurant owner, who was dressed in a European business suit, came hurrying forward to welcome them, offering them a higher table with chairs when he saw Keira.

But Keira shook her head. 'Unless, of course, you would prefer that?' she asked Jay.

His dismissive shrug said that it wasn't a matter of any great concern to him how they sat, and he certainly had no trouble whatsoever adopting the traditional almost yoga-type pose she had assumed herself, with her legs and feet covered by her skirt.

'We serve traditional smoked *sule kebas* here,' the owner informed her, 'and the vegetarian food of the Maheshwari of the Marwaris. But if I may, I would recommend our *dal baati,* which is a house speciality.'

'Yes, please,' Keira accepted with a smile.

She was certainly at ease with traditional Indian customs and food, Jay acknowledged, as he watched Keira eating her meal with obvious enjoyment.

The shops were just reopening after the heat of the day when they stepped back out into the wide tree-shaded avenue, just over an hour later.

Jay explained to her that the water supply came from artesian wells deep down in the earth, below the rocky plateau on which the city was built and that the seventeenth-century poet prince who had created the city had

had underground storage systems built to provide water not just for his palace and his city but also for his gardens.

Listening to Jay, Keira could hear in his voice the pride in his ancestor. Their backgrounds were so very different. He could take pride in his parents and his upbringing, where all she could feel was shame. He was the son of a Maharaja; she was the daughter of a prostitute and a drug addict. He was a man and she was a woman, and when he touched her. But, no—she must not think like that.

Children in uniform were filing out of their school, walking together in pairs in a sedate crocodile.

'My brother has instituted several reforms since he came to power,' Jay told Keira as they watched the children. 'One of which is to ensure that every child receives a good education. He says it's the best investment there can be, as these children will be the future not just of our city but of India itself.'

They had reached the entrance to the bazaar and Keira stood still, its sights and scents enveloping her. Bright silks hung in the doorway of one shop, whilst intricately hand-beaten metalware lay heaped on the pavement outside another. A jeweller was throwing back his shutters to reveal the brightness of his gold to the late-afternoon sunshine. From inside a herbalist's shop the pungent smell of his goods drifted out into the heat.

Children released from their crocodile darted up the narrow passageways, laughing to one another, whilst three young Hindu initiates passed by in their orange robes, their voices raised in chanting joy.

Several hours later, when they were in the shop of a fabric merchant, Keira had to admit that Jay had sourced his contacts well. The merchant had told them that he had cousins who owned and ran a factory in a small town, south-east of the city, a town Keira already knew was famous for its block-printed cotton. The town owed its success to the fact that a local stream possessed certain minerals in its water that set dye.

The merchant had produced pattern books, showing some classic floral and pineapple designs originating from the eighteenth century, and others showing fabrics in indigo and madder, as well as assuring her that his cousins would be pleased to make up samples of fabrics for her in her own choice of colours.

The merchant's daughter-in-law came through from the living quarters at the rear of the shop, bringing tea for them to drink, with two young children clinging to her sari. The younger of them, a little girl with huge dark-brown eyes and soft curls, was only just learning to walk, and when she lost her balance Keira reacted immediately, catching her in her arms to steady her. Was there anything quite as wonderful as holding a child? Keira wondered tenderly as the little girl looked up and smiled shyly at her. A sense of loss filled her. There wouldn't ever be any children of her own for her.

Jay watched Keira with the fabric merchant's grandchild, and, seeing the look on her face, wondered what had caused it. Why was he so curious about her? She meant nothing to him, and that was the way he intended things to stay.

The fabric merchant was telling Keira that if she were to let him have some drawings and details of what she wanted he could arrange to have some sample patterns made up for her. Keira handed the little girl back to her mother and reached for her notebook and the samples, swiftly selecting colours and patterns in the combinations she thought she would need, her manner now businesslike and focused.

She had an easy rapport with people and a natural way of communicating with them, Jay observed. She respected their professionalism, and he could see that they in turn respected hers.

It was very important to him that this new venture was not just a success, but that it achieved an almost iconic status as a leader in its field. His heritage and his blood demanded that from him, as much as his own nature and pride.

Jay knew that there were those who envied him his success and would like to see him fail, but they never would. He was determined about that. He never lost—at anything. And this woman was going to learn that just as his business rivals had had to learn it.

And yet, despite the fact that on a personal level Keira pushed all the wrong buttons for him, as a designer he couldn't fault her. Somehow, without him being able to analyse just how she was doing it, she was creating an image for the properties that truly was cosmopolitan and yet at the same time very much of India. He had almost been able to see it taking shape in front of him as she talked to suppliers and merchants, her slender fingers reaching for small pots of paint and dye, or pieces of fabric, her quick mind picking up ideas and then translating them to those with whom she was dealing.

Professionally she was, as Sayeed had said, perfect for this commission.

Keira thanked the fabric merchant for his help, and got up from the cushion on which she had been seated whilst they talked with the single fluid movement she had learned from Shalini, ignoring the hand Jay had stretched out to help her. The last thing she wanted was to risk any physical contact with him, even if by doing so she was causing his mouth to tighten and earning herself a grim look. She couldn't think of a commission she would enjoy more than the one he had given her—it was a dream come true, and

all the more so now that she had met the suppliers he had
already sourced—but Jay's presence made that dream a
nightmare.

He was going away tomorrow, she reminded herself,
and she was going to be working so hard that she simply
wouldn't have time to think about him, much less worry
about her vulnerability to him.

It had grown dark whilst they had been in the shop, and
now the street outside was illuminated with pretty glass
lamps. The street opened into a small square where several
men sat at a table enjoying *shiska* pipes, the bright colours
of their turbans glowing under the light from the lanterns.

A group of young female dancers wearing traditional
dress, followed by several musicians, swirled through the
square, on their way to one of the restaurants to dance for
the diners, Keira guessed.

The evening air was vibrant with the scents, sights and
sounds of India. They throbbed and pulsed in the warm
air, taking on their own life form—a life form that was
softened and gentled by the nature of the people.

Jay had stopped to talk to a tall man in a western suit
who had hailed him. Whilst they were talking Keira spotted an antique shop on the other side of the square and
quickly headed towards it. Antiques and bric-a-brac were
something she just couldn't resist.

A tall boy, a teenager, dark-eyed and with the promise
of handsomeness to come—was obviously minding the
shop for someone else, and welcomed her in shyly. He
couldn't be more than seventeen or eighteen at the most,
Keira assessed, and whilst he was looking at her with curiosity, she didn't feel offended or threatened. He probably wasn't used to seeing Western women, and she knew
he meant no harm.

The shop contained mainly bric-a-brac, and she was

on the point of leaving when she saw a box full of black and white photographs on one of the shelves. She went to pick it up but the boy beat her to it, standing very close to her as he reached for the box for her.

Taking it from him, Keira looked through the photographs, her excitement growing as she did so. The box contained a mix of postcard pictures of maharajas and palaces, and so far as she was concerned was a terrific find. Properly framed they would make wonderful and highly individual wall art for the properties.

'How much for all of these?' she asked the boy, gesturing to the box.

'For you, lovely lady, is one thousand rupees,' he told her.

Keira knew the rules of trade here, and so she shook her head and told him firmly, 'Too much.' Then she offered him less than half of what he had asked for.

'No—is a good price I give you,' the boy told her earnestly, moving closer to her as though to reinforce his point. 'Because I like you. You are very pretty. Are you here on holiday?' he asked her. 'Do you have a boyfriend?'

Keira's heart sank. Oh, dear. Perhaps she should have been prepared for this, but she hadn't been.

'Perhaps I should come back later—' she began, but to her consternation the boy grabbed hold of her arm.

'No, please stay,' he begged her. 'I will give you the photographs if you like them.'

This was even worse, and Keira didn't know what she would have done if a man Keira assumed must be the boy's father and Jay hadn't arrived in the shop at the same time, neither of them looking very pleased.

'What's going on?' Jay demanded.

'I was just trying to buy these photographs,' Keira told him, unwilling to get the boy into trouble.

Very quickly Jay concluded the sale and handed over the necessary rupees, before hustling her out into the street, rich now with the smell of cooking food from the stalls that had been set up around the square.

Keira could tell that he was angry, but she wasn't prepared for the storm that broke over her the minute they were back inside the palace.

'You just can't resist, can you?' he challenged her savagely. 'Not even with a boy who's still wet behind the ears. The way you were flirting with him was—'

The lanterns illuminating the hallway threw long dark shadows across it. Keira would have given a great deal to hide herself in those shadows, and so escape from the tension between them, but she couldn't let his accusation stand.

'I wasn't flirting with him,' she told him truthfully, defending herself.

'Of course you were. You were leading him on. Just like you—' Jay stopped abruptly, but Keira knew what he had been about to say. He had been about to say just like she had led *him* on.

Shame burned its hot brand on her pale skin, making her cheeks sting.

She could not defend herself against that accusation. Her shame intensified.

'I expect the people who work for me and with me to reflect a proper professional attitude.'

'I *was* being professional,' Keira insisted.

'Yes, and it was perfectly obvious which profession it was you were representing.'

Keira could feel nausea burning her throat, and angry fear flooding her heart. She knew exactly what he was accusing her of being, and which profession he was alluding to: the oldest profession in the world, the profession whereby a woman sold her body to a man for his sexual gratification. Her mother's profession. The profession she had always sworn she would rather die a virgin than risk following.

'I was simply trying to buy the photographs, that was all,' she told Jay fiercely.

Her teeth had started to chatter, despite the fact that it was warm. The sickening fear she had never been able to subdue surged through her, smothering logic and reason. Somewhere deep inside herself the child who had heard her mother's words as though they were a curse on her still cowered under the burden of those words.

The present slipped away from her, leaving her vulnerable to the past and its pain. She could feel it gripping her and refusing to let her go.

The way the colour suddenly left her face and the bruised darkness of her eyes caught Jay off guard. She was looking at him as though he had tried to destroy her. Looking at him and yet somehow past him, as though he simply wasn't there, he recognised. He had never seen such an expression of tormented anguish.

He took a step towards her, but immediately she turned and almost ran up the stairs, fleeing from him as though he was the devil incarnate. Unwanted male guilt mingled with his anger as that very maleness made it a matter of honour for him to let her go, rather than pursue her and demand an explanation for her behaviour.

CHAPTER SIX

SHE HAD WORKED like someone possessed from the minute she had closed the door of the guest wing behind her, focusing all her energy on what had to be achieved and deliberately leaving nothing to spare that might trap her with the ghosts Jay's accusation had raised.

But they were still there, pushing against the tight lid of the coffin she had sealed them into like the undead, denied true oblivion and existing in a half world that made them desperate to escape. And it was Jay's words to her that had fed them and given them the strength to try to overpower her.

She looked down at her laptop and at the work she had just completed. Images of room layouts lay printed off and neatly stacked to one side of the laptop—rooms with walls painted in traditionally made paint in subtly different but toning shades of white. In the main she'd opted for modern, stylish furniture in black, chrome and natural wood, accenting the rooms with fabrics in colour palettes that went from acid lemon and lime through to hot sizzling pinks and reds, and from cool greys and blues through to creams and browns. Modern lighting and the use of mirrors opened up the smaller spaces and highlighted features. It was, Keira knew, probably the most complex portfolio she had ever produced at such short notice.

It was late—nearly three o'clock in the morning. She ought to go to bed, but she knew she wasn't relaxed enough to sleep.

Outside, the courtyard garden was bathed in the light from the almost full moon. Keira got up and opened the door that led to it.

The night air was softly warm, without the stifling heat that would come later in the year at the height of summer.

A mosaic-tiled path led to a square pool in the centre of the garden, and surrounded it, and Keira paused to look down at it, studying it more closely.

Jay couldn't sleep.

He threw back the bedclothes and stood up. He should have followed his initial feeling and brought in another designer—preferably one who was male.

He walked over to the high-arched windows of his room, which he'd left open to the fresh air. Beyond them was an enclosed balcony that ran the whole length of the suite of rooms that had belonged to the Maharaja for whom this palace had originally been built.

This was the only place in the palace from which it was possible to look down not only into his own private courtyard garden but also into that attached to the old women's quarters. Naturally only the Maharaja himself had been allowed to look on the beauty of his wives and concubines. For any other man to do so would have been an offence for which at one time he would have had to pay with his sight and probably his life.

Now no modern man would dream of thinking that no one else should look upon the face of a woman with whom he was involved. A woman was a human being of equal status, not a possession, and the very idea was barbaric— and yet within every man there was still a fierce need to keep to himself the woman he desired, and an equally fierce anger when that need was crossed.

As his had been earlier, when he had seen the way the young shop boy had looked at Keira and the way she had smiled back at him?

That was ridiculous. She meant nothing to him. Just because she had aroused him physically… He stepped out onto the veranda and frowned as he saw a movement in the women's courtyard.

Keira. What was she doing out there at three o'clock in the morning? And why was she crouching on the ground?

Snakes sometimes slid into these gardens.

It only took him a handful of seconds to pull on his underwear and a pair of jeans. The tiles beneath his bare feet still held the warmth of the day's sun as he padded down the private staircase that led into the courtyards. It wasn't until he had opened the gate between his own courtyard and the women's courtyard that Jay realised that what had brought him here had been an age-old in-built male protective concern, which he had not even realised he possessed until now, and which if he had known he possessed, he would not have thought would be activated by or for Keira…

The sight of Jay walking towards her through the shadows was so unexpected that it shocked Keira into immobility for a few seconds, before she struggled to her feet. His terse, 'What are you doing?' didn't help.

'I wanted a closer look at the pattern on these tiles,' she told him, indicating the tiles forming the narrow footpath. 'And if you've come to find out if I've finished the layouts you wanted, then the answer is yes. At least in draft form. They'll be on your desk before you leave tomorrow.'

The words were a staccato burst of edgy defensiveness that fell away into sharp silence when Jay stepped out of the shadows. Automatically she looked at him, and then couldn't look away, her breath locking in her throat, her stomach tightening in response to what she could see. His torso and his feet were bare, as though... as though he had been in bed. Naked? Why was she thinking that? He could just have been relaxing. But something told her that Jay wasn't the kind of man who relaxed by taking off his clothes and lounging around semi-nude.

'If they're ready I may as well have them now,' Jay told her.

'I was going to polish them a bit more.'

'There's no need. It's understood that these are preliminary drafts. If I have them now it will give me more time to consider them. I'll walk back with you and collect them.'

Keira wished she hadn't said anything about the layouts. She'd wanted to look them over again before handing them to him, but now if she refused to let him take them he was bound to think that she'd been boasting, and that they weren't finished at all.

'Very well,' she agreed.

She'd closed her door when she came out. As they approached it Jay stepped in front of her—intending, she realised too late, to open the door for her. But the practical whys and wherefores of how she had come to be touching him hardly mattered. Because when she'd reached out to stop herself from colliding with him he had reached out too, and now his hand was on her shoulder, and her senses were filled by the feel of his warm flesh beneath her hand and the scent of his skin in her nostrils.

She could have moved away. She certainly should have done so. But instead she was looking up at him, and he was looking back at her. A dangerous tension stretched the silence. Her fingers curled into his arm, the breath shuddering from her lungs.

Danger crackled through her senses like static electricity. Abruptly she removed her hand from his arm, but it was too late. Without knowing that she was doing so she had moved closer to him, as though in mute invitation, and he had responded to that invitation.

She had thought that people only kissed like this in films—briefly, testing, tasting. Two people who were both trying desperately not to give in to the fierce undertow of a desire that neither of them really wanted, only to be swamped by it as their lips met and they were overwhelmed by a hunger that leapt from nerve-ending to nerve-ending, binding them together as their mouths and hands and bodies meshed, plundered and pleaded.

It was like being possessed by a universal force that could not be controlled, Keira thought dizzily, her lips clinging to Jay's. His hand was spread across the back of her head beneath her hair, keeping her mouth close to his own whilst his tongue probed the soft willingness of her mouth, possessing it in the same way that her desire for him was possessing her.

Each intimacy between them only fed her desire for more, as though some powerful spell had been cast upon her ability to resist what was happening to her.

The hunger he had unleashed within her was enslaving her. He was enslaving her, Keira realised as she tried desperately to pull back from the chasm awaiting her and the darkness she knew it held. Only to fail when Jay touched her breast, cupping it within the hold of his hand so that her nipple rose tightly and eagerly to press against his flesh. Keira knew that it was her own response that had incited the explicitly erotic pluck of his fingertips against her nipple as he teased it into an even more blatantly hungry demand for more.

It was like being savaged by two opposing forces. No—it was like being fought over by them, Keira thought frantically. The one surging through her, taking her up to the heights of sexual excitement and need, and the other dragging her down to that place when the demons of her childhood lay in wait for her. Between them they could so easily tear her apart and destroy her. She must stop this. But she couldn't.

Jay was kissing the side of her neck, sending wild, wanton shivers of irreversible arousal racking her. She could hear herself moaning as she collapsed into him, letting him take the weight of her body, letting him know without words of her need for him to possess it and her completely.

He was hard and ready against her softness. Automatically she reached down between them to touch him, driven now by nature, which guided her movements so that her fingertips fluttered helplessly against the thick hard ridge of his erection.

His smothered groan into her skin followed by the sharply sexual nip of his teeth would have been enough to melt any resistance she might have had, even without the sudden fierce sweep of his free hand down the length of her body, pressing her into him before closing on the soft curve of her buttock.

She was lost, Keira admitted to herself. There could be no going back from this.

In the moonlight she could see the darkness of Jay's hand against her top. As though it was happening in slow motion she watched as his fingers curled into the fabric and pulled it away from her breast. Her heart was thumping slowly and heavily as she silently willed him not to stop, but instead to hurry, hurry... Because the need inside her could not be contained for much longer.

As though he had sensed that need Jay bent his head, taking her nipple into his mouth with fierce impatience and drawing on it, so that she could feel the sharp pangs of her own desire seizing her whole body, causing it to convulse with longing.

She was his. Jay could sense her body open to his, could already imagine what it would be like when she closed down on him as her orgasm possessed her and took him to his own pleasure. Just thinking about it made him ache so badly. Jay's hand went to the fastening of his jeans. He wanted her so much, was so out of control with longing for her that he doubted he would have time to make it to the bed, never mind anything else.

Anything else? What the hell was happening to him? Jay never allowed himself to be out of control, and he certainly never had unprotected sex. But he had been about to do so.

Had been.

At first when Jay pushed her away Keira couldn't understand or accept what was happening. She cried out in protest, her eyes wild with longing and incomprehension, until she was jerked back to reality by the stillness of Jay's stance and the look she saw in his eyes before he turned on his heel and walked away from her.

Shame, her familiar and hated companion, slid its dark shadow next to her and smiled its mocking triumph at her.

Somehow Keira managed to stumble inside her room, where she showered in darkness, unable to bear the sight of her own body. Her mother and her great-aunt had been right about her after all.

After an hour of lying rigidly in her bed, unable to sleep, she got up and switched on her laptop. But for once her work did not bring its normal comfort, pushing everything and everyone else out of her thoughts. Instead images of Jay—his face, his eyes, his hands—came between her and the screen to torment her.

It was close to dawn when she eventually fell into an exhausted and troubled sleep.

It was just gone six in the morning. Jay was showered and dressed and drinking the tea his manservant had brought him. The morning sun was bathing everything in primrose-gold light, the clear blue of the sky on the horizon turning darker where it met the pink walls of the buildings.

He could admire the city's beauty, but he could not feel entirely a part of it, Jay acknowledged. His self-imposed exile had broadened his horizons too much. The city would always hold a very special place in his heart, but he did not envy his elder brother his inheritance or his position. The status of second son—second best, as his father's mistress had so often taunted him in the past—brought with it a freedom Rao could never have, and in a variety of different ways. He had lost count of the number of approaches he had received in recent years from families desperate to secure him as a husband for their daughters, but unlike Rao he did not have to marry and secure the succession. He was free to remain free, and that was exactly what he intended to do.

He would be leaving within the hour by helicopter to his private jet and his journey to Mumbai.

On the table in front of him were Keira's plans. He had ordered a servant to retrieve them from her room. There were a couple of points he wanted to query with her before he left. The excellence of what she had done had caught him off guard. Like his loss of control and his reaction to her last night?

He had not lost control. Maybe not completely, but the extent to which he had come dangerously close to doing so had been a first for him. Irritated by the mocking tone of his inner voice, Jay put down his teacup.

The courtyard beneath his window looked so tranquil this morning it was hard to imagine that last night it had contained so much dark passion. A passion instigated by her, when she had taken that inviting step towards him. Maybe—but it was an invitation he could have refused.

He looked at his watch. It was still early, but there were a couple of questions he needed to ask Keira about her plans before he left.

As he stepped outside, the morning sunlight burnished the olive warmth of his skin, throwing into relief the strength of his facial bone structure.

The door to Keira's quarters opened easily. Jay could hear the quiet hum of her laptop and smell the scent of her sleep and her skin. Through the open doorway he could see the bed, and Keira herself, lying on top of it and quite obviously still asleep.

Jay turned back to the door, only to stop and turn again, to walk slowly towards the bed as through drawn there against his will.

Keira was lying on her side, clad in a pair of pyjamas that looked more suitable in design for a girl than a woman, and he could see quite clearly the tracks of her dried tears on her face, below telltale mascara smudges.

She'd been crying? Because of him?

Deep down within himself Jay could feel something, a sensation of emotional tightness and tension, as though something was breaking apart to reveal something else so sensitive and raw that he couldn't bear to feel it.

What was it? Compassion? Pity? Regret? Why should he feel pain for her vulnerability and her tears?

Angry with himself, Jay turned away from the bed and left as silently as he had arrived.

Women used their tears in exactly the same way as they used their bodies: to get what they wanted. He wasn't about to be taken in by such tactics.

Jay had gone and she was safe. Because without his presence she could not be tormented and tempted as she had been last night.

But Jay would come back, and when he did…

When he did things would be different, Keira promised herself grimly. She would have found a way to protect herself from her own weakness. It wasn't her pride that was insisting that she did that. Given the chance, she'd have preferred to run from what Jay aroused in her rather than battle with it. But she simply did not have that freedom. Her contract tied her to the work she had taken on and through that to Jay, and she was not in a position to risk the financial implications of breaking that contract.

CHAPTER SEVEN

IT WAS THREE days since Keira had last seen Jay—three days in which she had had time to focus on her work and rebalance her own sense of self.

Where another woman might have found it galling and humiliating to have a man walk away, having started to make love to her, Keira could only feel relieved that Jay had done so. She had been given a second chance to protect herself from her own weakness, and for that she could only be profoundly grateful.

But being grateful wasn't doing anything to ease the ache that had woken her from her sleep last night—and the night before, and the night before that. Keira stared grimly at her laptop screen, battling determinedly to will away such potentially dangerous thoughts. Was this the way her mother had felt about the married man she had once told Keira was her father, whose desertion she claimed had pushed her into the arms of a series of other men?

But then her mother had told her so many different stories, changing with her mood and her need for the drugs on which she'd been dependent. Keira pushed her laptop away from her with an awkward panic-stricken movement that betrayed what she was feeling.

She was not like her mother. She was her own self—an individual who had the power of authority and choice over what she did. No man could make her choose to want him against her will. No man—but what about her own emotions? Emotions? What Jay had aroused within her had nothing to do with emotions. Her desire for him had been sexual, that was all. Nothing more. That was impossible. Just like desiring him in the first place had also been impossible?

Keira's panic increased. She got up and went to the window, but looking down into the courtyard was a mistake. It might be bathed in sunlight now, but inside her head she could still picture it shadowed by moonlight, with Jay's body and her own shadowed along with it. In those shadows they had touched and kissed, and she had—but, no— she must not think of that.

She had an appointment in half an hour, to meet up with the fabric merchant, who had telephoned her to tell her that her samples had arrived. He had offered to bring them to the palace, but Keira had told him that she would go to him.

She had fallen in love with the city, and readily used any excuse to see more of it. She felt so at home here, so at peace—or rather she would have if she hadn't been dreading Jay's return.

The city had been laid out in a geometric grid of streets and squares. From the main square, opposite the palace, a network of narrow pedestrian streets branched out from the straight ceremonial main road that led to the city's main gates, along which in previous centuries the formal processions of maharajas and other dignitaries had passed.

It was these streets, with their stalls and artisan workshops, that fascinated Keira even more than the elegant palaces of the rich. Behind them lay the *bavelis*, the townhouses of the city's original eminent citizens, each of them an individual work of art in its own right.

As always, the rich mingling of scents and sounds absorbed Keira's attention. The sound of temple bells mingled with the laughter of children and the urgent cries of shopkeepers wanting to sell their merchandise.

Knowing she had time in hand, Keira made a detour from her destination that took her past the bazaar, famous for selling rose, almond, saffron and vetiver-flavoured sherbets. In the flower market workers were busy weaving garlands and making floral offerings for templegoers, and when she cut through the jewellery quarter of the bazaar Keira had to force herself not to be tempted to linger outside the shops of the *lac* bangle sellers.

These were the sights and sounds of Jay's home—the place where he had been born, the place where his family had ruled for so many generations. Where his family still ruled. Jay wasn't merely a successful and wealthy entrepreneur, he was also a member of one of India's royal families. His brother was the Maharaja. It was no wonder that he had that air of arrogance and pride about him. No wonder that he believed he could command others to his will.

But it wasn't the command of his royal status that she feared. Rather, it was the command of his essential sensuality—and he would have had that no matter what rank he had been born to, she suspected.

The merchant greeted her with great ceremony, bowing his head so much that Keira momentarily feared for the fate of his ornate turban. His daughter-in-law brought them tea, her sweet, shy smile echoing those of her children. She looked outstandingly pretty in her crimson and blue embroidered *ghaghara* gathered skirt, her *odhni* tucked into the waist of her skirt. She pulled the *odhni* round to drape it modestly over her head, her movements delicate and graceful, her hands and feet carefully patterned with henna.

When Keira saw the fabrics the merchant was spreading out on the floor in front of her she felt her heart skip a beat in delight. She studied the samples that were so excellently in tune with her own ideas, combining as they did tradition with a certain stylish modern twist.

'My cousin would like to invite you to visit his factory, so that you can see more of their work,' the merchant told her.

'Go to his town?' Keira queried excitedly 'Oh, yes. I would love to.'

'My cousin has a new designer, a man from your own country. He would like you to meet him so that you can discuss your requirements with him.'

Before Keira left the shop it was arranged that the merchant would contact his cousin, accepting his invitation on her behalf, whilst Keira would make arrangements via Jay's servants for a car and a driver to be put at her disposal to take her to the fabric town.

If when Jay returned she had proper samples of the fabrics she wanted to use, having consulted directly with the designer and producer, it would surely prove to him that whilst he had been away she had been far too busy working to have any time to waste on thinking about him.

Keira was still desperately trying to convince herself that it was India itself that was responsible for the overwhelming of her defences: India, with its potent mystery and sensuality that thrummed in the air and filled the senses, stealing away reality and resistance. It was India that was responsible for the fact that she lay awake in her bed at night, trying to deny the ache spreading through her in slow waves of heat and need. India that somehow, like a magician, conjured up those unwanted and forbidden images inside her head, created those secret private mental films in which she and Jay lay together, their naked bodies veiled only by the sheer voile bed-hangings enclosing them in their own intimate world.

Yes, it was India that had the power to touch her senses and break through her defences. Not Jay himself, Keira reassured herself.

Mumbai was its normal highly charged cosmopolitan self, Jay acknowledged. With meetings overrunning into cocktail and dinner parties that went on into the early hours of the morning as the socialites of the city mingled with its movers and shakers.

Tonight he was dining with a fellow entrepreneur, an Indian in his early fifties, originally educated in England, who had returned to Mumbai to take over a family business. Amongst the guests was a Bollywood actress who was currently trying to engage Jay's interest in something more intimate than dinner table conversation by asking him if he had yet visited the city's latest exclusive nightclub.

She was very beautiful, with the kind of figure that could make a grown man cry, and her fingertips rested lightly on Jay's suit-clad arm as she leaned closer to him to envelop him in a cloud of scent. Her movements were designed to be sensual and discreetly erotic, but for some reason they failed to stir his pulses. Her scent wasn't the scent he wanted to breathe in, her eyes weren't amber but dark brown, and whilst her touch did nothing whatsoever for him, he only had to think about Keira's touch for his body to react.

What nonsense was this? That one woman could quite easily be replaced by another was Jay's personal mantra—one he adhered to strictly. Jay moved restlessly in his chair, oblivious to the disappointment of his companion as she recognised his lack of interest in her. There was only one explanation he was willing to accept for Keira's unwanted intrusion into his thoughts, and that was quite simply that he ached for her because he had not brought their intimacy to its natural conclusion. If he had done so then he would not still be wanting her. That was all there was to it. Nothing more. Nothing more at all.

Jay was still repeating those words to himself several hours later, as he lay alone and sleepless in his bed in his hotel suite, the business documents he had intended to study left ignored on the bedside table.

Keira.

Jay closed his eyes, only realising his mistake when immediately his memory furnished him with a mental image of her in which her eyes burned dark gold with desire for him and her breath came in swift, unsteady little gasps of escalating arousal.

His own heartbeat picked up, hammering its message of need through his body.

He had been a fool not to take what had been on offer. She had probably had condoms to hand—women like her were always prepared.

The Bollywood actress had insisted on writing down her mobile number for him. He had two more days in Mumbai—could spend longer there if he chose. Longer? Since when did it take more than one night in bed with any woman to satisfy his desire for her? Wasn't that why he had grown bored with the ritual of pretending to have to seduce a woman who had already made it plain that she was up for sex with him, taking her shopping for the present she had made it clear she expected, then finding that, like a tiger fed on tame game instead of having to hunt, his belly was full in the sexual sense, but his appetite was somehow not satisfied. It was no wonder that he had actually welcomed the celibacy that had become his only sleeping partner these last few months.

And wasn't it in reality that very celibacy that was responsible for the white heat of his desire for Keira?

Keira. His thoughts had turned full circle, and his body now ached like hell. Jay threw back the bedcovers. Picking up the documents from the bedside table, he strode naked to the desk. He pulled on a robe and switched on his laptop, and proceeded to do what he could to blot Keira out of his thoughts by engrossing himself in some work...

'Oh, I love this toile,' Keira enthused as she studied the fabric sample in front of her, with its design of Indian palaces, monkeys, elephants and howdas printed in traditional single colours against the creamy white of the cotton background.

'I designed it myself,' Alex Jardine told her with a smile. 'I had some original copperplate rollers for toile fabric I was lucky enough to pick up in an antique market in France years ago, and when I showed them to Arjun, here, and explained what I wanted to do, he was able to find me a craftsman to copy the rollers for us so we could create this toile. It's one of four we've been experimenting with: two traditional, of which this is one, and two very contemporary designs.'

Keira nodded her head, fascinated by the designs.

'We're experimenting at the moment with charcoal, to black-dye the modern toile and give it a more edgy look,' he continued.

From the moment she had stepped into the fabric factory Keira had felt as though she had stepped into her own private Aladdin's cave. Bolts of fabrics of every hue imaginable were stacked to the ceiling, mouthwatering acid sherbet colours, rich traditional colours of crimson ruby, jade and emerald embellished with gold thread, sea and sky colours, and even pale creamy naturals. Her senses had fed on them as greedily as a child let loose in a sweet shop, and now she was every bit as giddy and dizzy as that child might have been, from consuming too many additives. She was on a high with the sheer intensity of her own rush of delight. And that delight was compounded by her sense of having met someone so much in tune with her own way of thinking in Alex.

At first sight she had felt slightly put off by him. Over six foot tall, with thick curly hair that reached down to his shoulders, he was dressed in white linen trousers, a loose linen shirt and with his feet bare. His voice was a languid 'okay yah' upper crust London drawl, and Keira had felt initially that there was rather too much of the *faux* hippie about him—so much so, in fact, that it was almost a theatrical affectation.

But then he had shown her his fabrics, his large hands as tender on them as though they were small children, his voice softening as he told her about their provenance and his own desire to keep his designs true to tradition whilst bringing in something unique and modern that was still 'of India', and Keira had been entranced and captivated.

'I am hoping that we'll be able to design something that has a bit of a Bollywood twist to it, but Arjun, here, thinks I'm being over-confident.' Alex laughed as he smiled at the factory owner.

'I just love what you're doing,' Keira told him. 'And if it was up to me I'd be buying up everything for this new venture, but I don't have that authority.'

'We can supply you with samples and you can show them to His Highness Prince Jayesh,' the factory owner was assuring her eagerly.

'Arjun won't let you leave until he's heaped you with samples,' Alex warned her, with a warm smile, reaching out to pluck a stray thread of cotton that had attached itself to the sleeve of her top as the factory owner hurried away for more samples.

Keira smiled back at him, unaware of the fact that Jay had just walked into the building and was standing watching the byplay between them with a glacier cold look in his eyes.

It was Alex who saw Jay first, his own gaze sharpening in recognition of what he could see in Jay's eyes as he strode towards them.

'There's a very angry-looking alpha male heading this way,' he told Keira drolly. 'And he looks very much as though he thinks I've been trespassing on his private property.'

'What?' Puzzled, Keira turned round and then gave a small 'oh' of mixed comprehension and surprise as Jay bore down on them, her stomach churning out its message of acute physical awareness of him as her heart pounded erratically.

He was wearing light linen, apparently oblivious to the heat in the factory, with no sign of perspiration dampening his skin in the way Keira knew it was dampening her own—although she could see the dark shadow along his jaw where he needed to shave. It gave him an extra edge of raw masculinity that touched her own femaleness as directly as though he himself had touched her—very intimately.

A giddy, nerve-tingling feeling had somehow taken hold of her, reminiscent of the way she felt after drinking champagne. Bubbles of sensation fizzed through her veins, heightening her awareness of him and her sensitivity to him. Her gaze was somehow drawn to his face, and refused to be moved. It was as though she had been possessed by the greed of a hedonist with an insatiable appetite, Keira decided shakily, unable to stop herself from visually gorging herself on the pleasure of looking at him.

Jay—here! What an extraordinary coincidence that he should have business here himself. Not that he looked at all pleased to have found her here, she noticed.

'Jay,' she greeted him weakly. 'You've come back early from Mumbai. I'm so glad you're here. I've just seen the most wonderful fabrics. You're going to love them, I know…' She was gabbling like an idiot, unable to stop herself as she plucked sample after sample from the pile Arjun had just returned with, wafting them before Jay's totally immobile gaze.

He hadn't spoken or moved, hadn't so much as acknowledged her in any way, and yet he filled her senses. All she could see, all she knew, was him.

'You must meet Alex,' Keira gabbled on. 'He's got the most wonderful ideas—'

She broke off as she physically felt the increase in tension, as clearly as though someone had actually tightened the air and removed oxygen from it. Jay's lips had thinned, his gaze icing over her before being directed past her to Alex.

'Arjun's got all the samples Keira and I have discussed,' Keira heard Alex saying easily. 'But you'll want to check them out for yourself, and as Keira knows I'm open to whatever input she wants to give me. Next time you come to visit, if you let me know beforehand, Keira, I'll book you into that boutique hotel I was telling you about and we can do dinner,' Alex offered, giving Keira another smile. 'And then I'll have time to show you what I can really do.'

When he winked at her and grinned, Keira couldn't help but laugh. Alex was a tease, but harmless, and she didn't in any way object to his mild social flirting, knowing it for what it was—which was nothing more than something to oil the wheels of business.

She would have liked to stay a bit longer, to share her enthusiasm and excitement for what she had seen with Jay, but he was making it very plain that he was not in the mood to look at fabrics and was clearly waiting to leave. He was also making it very obvious that he was expecting her to leave with him. Presumably he had completed his own business, whatever it had been, and so Keira thanked Arjun and allowed Jay to escort her out of the factory, whilst two young boys carried her precious samples over to the car and handed them to her driver.

However, when Keira made to follow them to her car, Jay stopped her.

'You're travelling back with me,' he told her abruptly.

She could have objected—perhaps she should have objected, given his dictatorial manner—but for some reason she remained strangely silent. Not because she actually wanted to travel back with him, of course, Keira insisted to herself as Jay opened the passenger door of his Mercedes and then stood beside it, waiting for her to get inside more in the manner of a gaoler than anything else. Keira winced when he closed the door with a definite thud.

It was late in the day and the town was busy with traffic, filling its narrow streets. All too conscious of the hazards presented by small children darting out into the road, plus old people, cyclists, bullock carts, the highly decorated trucks that were so much a part of India's road culture, not to mention stray cows and other cars, Keira didn't venture to speak for fear of distracting Jay's attention from his driving.

Once clear of the town, though, when Jay himself made no attempt to engage her in conversation, Keira found that despite the oppressive atmosphere caused by his silence she didn't feel brave enough to break it.

With the sun setting over the dusty plain she focused instead on the view beyond the window, and she couldn't stop herself from exclaiming aloud in delight when they passed a herd of camels being made ready to travel as they took advantage of the evening coolness.

'We're so close to the desert that I'd love to take the opportunity to see the annual Cattle Fair,' she told Jay enthusiastically. 'Have you seen it?' she asked him.

'Of course,' Jay told her shortly.

Of course he would have. This was his country, after all, Keira reminded herself. His manner was so European that she tended to forget that at times.

It made her feel uncomfortable and on edge to recognise that just the fact of seeing Jay when she hadn't expected to do so had had such a dramatic effect on her mood, changing her from an in-control businesswoman into someone whose every reaction was controlled by her awareness of him: a smile from him sent her heart soaring upwards, and a frown had it plunging downwards.

No one had affected her like this before, and knowing that he could and did made her feel on edge and vulnerable. She wanted to reject completely the pull he had on her senses, and yet at the same time she was drawn helplessly to check over and over again the intensity of it—like a moth drawn to the light that would ultimately destroy it, she thought with a small shiver, witnessing the helpless suicide of the soft-winged creatures as they flew into the beam of the car's headlights, switched on now that darkness had fallen.

The lights of the city broke the stark emptiness of the plain as they drove closer to it.

Jay was still struggling within himself to justify his in-

tense and uncharacteristic reaction to the fact that Keira
had been absent from the palace on his return.

That he had automatically expected she would be there
and had been so infuriated when she was not had been
bad enough, but he might have dismissed those feelings
as being caused by the ongoing sexual challenge she represented to him. However, explaining his own sense of
aloneness and the emptiness of the building without her
in it was something else again, and something for which
he could not find any logical reason.

In short, it had infuriated him to return and find her
gone. It had infuriated him even more to have to admit
to his own reaction to her absence. And it had infuriated
him most of all to have to endure his own inner sense of
desolation and the emptiness of the palace without her.

Why on earth should the absence of one woman—a
woman he barely knew—affect him to such an extent that
he had been driven to set out in pursuit of her? It was simply not logical. And it was most definitely not acceptable.

Jay considered himself to be a man who had overcome
the human weakness of being held hostage to emotion.
Everything he did was governed and motivated by reason and rationality. Of course he permitted himself to be
pleased when his goals and objectives were achieved, but
it was a controlled and disciplined satisfaction. Not for Jay
the pantomiming, posturing foolishness of the type who
found it necessary to trumpet their success to the world
in ridiculous displays of conspicuous consumption, which
invariably involved magnums of champagne, flashy mod-
els and equally flashy so-called 'boys' toys'.

Yes, he *had* celebrated his successes—with a carefully
chosen piece of art, or an addition to his worldwide property portfolio, and always a generous anonymous donation
to those charities he supported. These were charities in

the main that provided for orphaned children in the poorest of the world's countries, but this was a private matter.

What he had experienced today came dangerously close to challenging everything he believed about himself. That must not be allowed to happen. The enormity of what it might mean was too much. It wasn't the intimacy he had witnessed between Keira and her fellow countryman that had affected him. Rather it was his anger at her behaviour and the effect it might have on his own business reputation. Indians placed a great deal of importance on good moral behaviour, and he had no wish to see the reputation of his business tarnished by Keira's flirtatious and unprofessional manner. *That* was the cause of his anger, and it was perfectly logical. It had nothing whatsoever to do with emotion—and certainly not an emotion like jealousy.

They had reached the palace car park. Without a word to Keira Jay stopped the car, got out, and then went round to open the passenger door for her.

They were back inside the palace before Keira could find the courage to break the crushing silence Jay had imposed, telling him brightly, 'I'd better go and thank my driver, and retrieve the samples...'

'Wait,' Jay demanded curtly. 'There's something I wish to discuss with you first. We'll go to my office,' he told her, gesturing towards the stairs.

Whatever he wanted to say to her it wasn't going to be something she wanted to hear, Keira recognised as she took in the grim set of his mouth and the way he distanced himself from her as they walked up the stairs.

Once they were inside his office Jay closed the door with the same controlled ferocity with which he had closed the car door earlier, the small but definite thud of that closure causing Keira's heart to jolt uneasily into her ribs.

Keira could sense that a storm was brewing as clearly as

though she had seen thunderclouds building up and growling ominously on the horizon. It swept into the room without warning or ceremony, feeding on the oxygen in the air and leaving her chest tight as she struggled to breathe in the air that was left.

When Jay spoke, his words were like sheet lightning, slicing through the stifling silence.

'You had no business travelling so far out of the city without advising me of your plans beforehand.'

'You weren't here, and—'

'And you couldn't wait?' Jay challenged her coldly.

Keira gulped in air, bewildered by his anger.

'You were the one who introduced me to the fabric merchant so that I could obtain some samples,' she reminded him.

'The merchant, yes. But I most certainly did not suggest that you, a woman on your own, should travel anywhere unescorted, and that once having done so—'

'I was not unescorted,' Keira protested. 'I was with my driver. I'd gone there on business to—'

'To flirt with one of your own countrymen?'

'No!'

'Yes. Since that is most certainly what you were doing when I saw you.'

'What? That's ridiculous,' Keira defended herself.

'But you knew that he would be there?' Jay queried.

'Well, yes,' Keira admitted. 'But—'

'And immediately you knew that, you decided to go and check him out?'

'No! This is crazy. It was the fabric merchant who suggested that I might want to meet the designer and see his work at first hand.'

'Was it? Or did you suggest it yourself? Was it his work

you wanted to inspect at first hand or the man himself? A fellow European...'

What he was insinuating was as insulting as it was incorrect, Keira thought angrily.

'I went to check out fabric—Indian fabric. Not a European man, or indeed any kind of man,' Keira told him fiercely. 'I'm not interested in checking out men.'

Too late she realised her mistake. The look Jay slanted her was as steely sharp as a new blade.

'No? That's not the impression you've been giving me,' he taunted her.

Another minute and he'd be reminding her of her response to him. Keira tensed herself inwardly for the expected verbal blow, but to her relief instead he accused her coldly.

'You were flirting with him—you can't deny that.'

Relief washed through her, chilling the heat of her earlier anger.

'Yes, I can—and I do.'

Ignoring her protest, Jay insisted grimly, 'Admit it. You were coming on to him so hard that you were oblivious to anyone and everything else—not that he was objecting. He was as eager to get you into his bed as you were to be there. That was patently obvious.'

'That is *not* true, and I was *not* coming on to him,' Keira denied truthfully again. 'We were simply both being polite to one another.' She was getting her courage back now that she had escaped the humiliation of him reminding her how passionately she responded to him. 'Good manners are a highly valued trait in Indian society—something that Indian children are taught at their mother's knee. As I should have thought you would know.'

The silence was suddenly alive with the kind of danger that brought up the small hairs on the back of her neck.

'So you maintain that you were simply being polite, do you?'

'Yes,' Keira insisted.

'By offering yourself to him?'

'I was *not* doing that.'

'Yes, you were. Just like you've been offering yourself to me from the first moment we met.'

'That's not true!' Keira had had enough. She had to get out of this room and away from this man.

Shaking her head, she made for the door—only Jay got there ahead of her, barring her way with his body so that she virtually ran full-tilt into him.

She could feel the heat of his breath on her skin and the bite of his fingers into her upper arms. Her only means of escape was to close her eyes and try desperately to shut down her senses. But it was too late. Jay was swinging her round to imprison her against the wall, his mouth plundering hers. It was pointless trying to resist when her own body was in revolt and had turned traitor on her, joining Jay instead and offering itself up to him.

How could she want such an emotionally humiliating intimacy? How could she not reject the hot pouring tide of a sensuality she knew to be corrupted with the poison of contempt and lust? How could she moan and soften within the hardness of Jay's hold, seeking to give all of herself up to him?

She didn't know. But then she was past knowing anything other than the intensity of her need for Jay.

Her own arms were wrapped tightly around him now, her breasts sensitised by the movement of her body against his. Inside her head she could already see his hands covering their nakedness, feel the fierce tug of his mouth against her nipples.

She shuddered violently in reaction to her own thoughts.

A sharp spike of shock pierced through her, only to be overwhelmed by a fresh wave of aching longing as Jay pressed her even more closely to him, his hands moving up over her body to her breasts, cupping them, urging them free of their covering. Lamplight stroked the pale alabaster of her skin, latticed with the darker shadows of Jay's hands, and her nipples were desire-engorged and tight as she pressed into the cup of his palms. Just the simple act of his palms brushing against their tenderness was enough to make Keira shudder with need.

She couldn't bear there to be any barriers between them. She wanted his hands on her body. She wanted the freedom to explore and caress his body. She wanted to touch and taste him, know him and know his knowing of her, his full possession of her. Those feelings were like a form of madness in her blood that she couldn't withstand. They filled her head with images of them together and turned her body into an aching mass of yearning nerve-endings and willing flesh, created only for this man and this moment.

He felt hard and erect, ready for her in the same openly sexual way in which she knew her own body was ready for him. She could feel the damp softness between her legs, and the quick fierce pulse that went with it. She wanted desperately for him to touch her there, for him to caress her there. A small moan bubbled in her throat, followed by a shuddering gasp in acknowledgement of his accuracy in reading her mind when his hand dropped from her breast to her belly and then slid lower over her thigh, beneath her skirt, his fingers probing the edge of her thin silky knickers.

His kiss matched the intimate possession of his fingers. The very fact that the deliberate thrust of his tongue was more demanding than the delicate questing of the fingertip he rubbed against the wetness of her clitoris told her more clearly than any words that he was holding back—just as her own shudder of response and acceptance told him that she was eager to answer that demand.

But instead of taking things further Jay's mouth left hers, to move slowly along her jaw and towards her ear.

Keira didn't know which she wanted most…what he was doing or what he had been doing. Just the whisper of his breath…his lips against her skin…was sending her crazy.

Not that he was exactly immune to the reaction he was arousing in her either, by the way he was gripping her hips and pulling her tightly against his body, Keira recognised, with a fierce thrill of female pleasure.

Now it was her turn to groan aloud with delight as his hand moved back up her body and cupped her breast. Just the feel of his thumb tip rubbing sensuously across her tight aching nipple made her moan out loud.

She had to bite on her bottom lip to stop herself from begging him to take off her top and expose her breast to his gaze, his touch, to the hot hard caress of his mouth.

Frantically she tensed her muscles, squeezing her thighs together as she felt a surge of longing rocket through her.

As though he guessed what was happening to her Jay cupped her hip, his fingers kneading her rhythmically. She was leaning fully against the wall now, whilst Jay's hands caressed every inch of her, making her quiver from head to foot in open longing.

Was this something he had learned from the *Kama Sutra*?

When he took her hand and placed it against his own body she almost sobbed with pleasure. Her hands were long and slender, but the hard swollen length of him extended beyond her outstretched fingertips. Keira closed her eyes, pleasure a dark velvet blanket of sensuality behind her closed eyelids. She ached as though she had a fever for the feel of him inside her. She had had no idea there could be desire like this—instant, immediate, hot and hungry, a need that burned everything else into oblivion and drove a person on relentlessly until it was sated.

No doubt if Jay knew the truth about her he would think her very unworldly not to have experienced something like this before. Unlike him!

How many times…? How many women…? That thought burned through her in a hot agony of molten jealousy that stabbed through her, stiffening her body into rigid rejection of what she was feeling and thinking.

Abruptly she was shocked back into reality, her desire chilling into sick self-disgust. What was she thinking of? How could she be behaving like this when she knew…?

Panic twisted and speared inside her.

She had to get away from him—now. Before it was too late and she became one of those women, a woman like her mother, who loved the wrong man and made the wrong choices.

Loved…

Keira started to tremble violently with reaction. Jay's hands were still on her body but she pushed them away, taking him by surprise and opening the door before he could stop her.

Once free of his office she started to walk faster, finally breaking into a run so that by the time she had reached the sanctuary of her room her heart was thudding against her chest wall. From exertion, or from the fear she had brought from Jay's office with her? The fear that she might be falling in love with him.

Keira sank down onto her bed, her head in her hands.

Jay could feel beads of sweat forming on his skin and then chilling as he fought to regain his self-control. He could hear the sound of his own breathing, shallow and strained, whilst his heart thudded and pounded accusingly against his ribs. His body ached and raged against its denial, but Jay was more concerned with his inability to control his emotions rather than any inability to control his flesh.

How could it have happened? How could he have allowed his physical desire for a woman to lead him into the kind of behaviour he had exhibited today? Pursuing her, burning up with fury because he had seen her smiling at another man, wanting to physically stamp his possession on her and deny that same opportunity to any other man.

Jay strode across the room and threw open the shutters to let in the night air. But nothing could rid his senses of the scent of Keira, and of his own arousal. They clung together, wrapped around one another as though they belonged together, filling his head with tormenting images. How *could* they belong together?

Sex was an act that took place between two separate people who returned to that separateness. If Keira hadn't run from him he would have taken her to bed…

But she had, ignoring both her own arousal and his. And she *had* been aroused. Jay knew that. He moved awkwardly, forced to tense his body against the still far too potent memory of how she had reacted when he had touched her, her lips clinging to his, her nipples swelling tightly into his palm, her sex soft and wet.

Irritably Jay speedily shut down the too easily conjured up mental pleasure his senses were giving him. He was a fool if he couldn't recognise that a good part of the reason he wanted her was the fact that she was playing a game that meant he couldn't have her. A game in which she offered and then withdrew that offer. A game that was one of the oldest in the world.

He took a deep breath of the cool air. It was totally illogical that he should continue to want her, knowing what she was. But a feeling he didn't want to admit to twisted his belly. Jealousy? Savagely he dismissed the mocking inner voice he didn't want to hear. It was impossible for him to feel jealous. Jealousy was an emotion, and he simply did not 'do' emotions. Not ever—not with anyone.

If he had any sense he would terminate her contract immediately and send her back to England with a compensation payment. He would negotiate with her to buy her designs and put a new team in place to put them into practice. That way if, by some impossible to imagine chance, he *had* somehow become vulnerable to some kind of hitherto never experienced male folly, then it would be brought to a swift end.

Yes, that was what he must do. Just as soon as he got back from Mumbai.

CHAPTER EIGHT

HER HEAD ON one side, Keira carefully studied the newly painted walls of the show house. She had chosen the paint from over a dozen different samples, all of which had been applied in square patches to the wall so that she could assess the effect on the room's light and size.

'Yes,' she told the waiting painter with a pleased smile. 'That's perfect.'

Someone else might not consider it worthwhile on such a tight schedule to spend time finding exactly the right shade of off-white, but to Keira such niceties were an essential part of the way she worked. The right paint would provide the foundations of her scheme, and thus in her opinion was vitally important. Combining both Jay's wishes and Alex's advice, she had sourced her paint locally, and the supplier had been marvellously patient about fine-tuning the pigment to get the shade she wanted.

The painter was smiling broadly himself now, a huge watermelon grin stretching across his face as he promised her that he would have the paint mixed and delivered to her ready for the decorators to start work in the morning.

It was a month since the evening she had fled—not just from Jay, but more tellingly from her own response to him—to spend virtually the whole night curled up on her bed, agonising over what she should do.

The discovery in the morning that Jay had returned to Mumbai had given her a breathing space that had enabled her to think logically and practically about her situation and her options. She had reasoned that financially she could not afford to break her contract, whilst emotionally and sexually she could not afford to mirror her mother's folly in falling in love with the wrong man and going to bed with him.

Jay inhabited a world in which the super-rich called nowhere home. It was unlikely that their paths would ever cross again once she had finished her work here. Reasonably, therefore, all she had to do was keep her distance from him until life put an even greater distance between them. Once it had she could ache all she wanted for him, in the secure knowledge that all she *could* do was ache. Better to burn with unappeased longing than to be destroyed be the acid corrosion of shame and self-disgust.

And anyway, now she was alert to her own danger she had herself properly under control, Keira assured herself firmly.

Really? So why, then, was her stomach now twisting itself in knots just because she could see Jay walking towards her?

He was here, and her world had tilted on its axis. But she could act naturally and keep things on a professional footing, Keira decided, and she told him briskly, 'Jamil has been very patient with me, and we've finally got the right paint colour. The decorators should be able to start work tomorrow, and by the time they've finished the furniture and soft furnishings should be starting to arrive.'

Jay nodded his head.

'You haven't given me a decision yet on the toile fabric I discussed with you,' Keira reminded him. 'So if you've got time…'

'You mean your fellow countryman's designs?' Jay stopped her.

'Yes,' Keira agreed, telling him enthusiastically, 'I thought his contemporary designs were fun and quirky and would appeal to buyers—especially if we move away from the traditional French colours into something more dramatic and modern. Black on hot pink or bright yellow would make a real statement if we used it on cushions, for instance.'

'And of course if I agree to buy your countryman's designs then naturally he's going to want to show his gratitude—probably in a private suite at that hotel he was discussing with you.' The sardonic tone of Jay's voice coupled with the innuendo of his words made Keira's heart plummet downwards.

'That is grossly unfair and insulting,' she told him furiously. 'There is only one reason I would ever recommend anyone to a client, and that is because, in my professional opinion, they or their product are right for the job. That is the way I do business. You, of course, may have other methods.'

'You *dare* to accuse me of your own low moral standards?'

Jay looked so angry as he took a step towards her and stood almost menacingly over her, filling the air with the heat of his fury, that Keira wasn't sure what would have happened if the site manager hadn't come and interrupted them, explaining that there were some papers he needed Jay to sign.

The sooner this commission was completed and she could end her association with Jay the better, Keira told herself fiercely.

She had an appointment to meet with one of the manufacturers who was providing some of the furniture for the show homes tomorrow. His factory was several hours' drive away, in a small town close to the border of the desert. Remembering what had happened when she had gone to visit the fabric factory, this time Keira had sent a message first to Jay, explaining what she intended to do and requesting his approval. He had not said anything about it just now.

Keira's heart slid heavily into her ribs. It was no use trying to lie to herself. Each time she saw him she might promise herself that this time she would not permit herself to endure that surge of sick, aching need that made her long to be in his arms even though she knew that that was the worst place she could ever be, but she knew that in reality it was a promise she would never be able to keep.

Take today. It was just over four weeks since she had last seen him—four weeks, two days and ten minutes, to be exact. Well, twenty minutes if she counted the extra ten minutes she had spent concealed behind the fretwork of the latticed *jails,* designed to keep the women of the harem from public view whilst enabling them to look down into the street below, watching Jay walk away from the palace.

Four weeks during which she had resolutely focused on her work, filling every heartbeat of time with a feverish busyness designed to deny her the ability to give in to the temptation to think about Jay. She had even taken to reading books on Indian culture and crafts when she went to bed, until her eyes became too heavy to stay open.

And yet earlier today, the minute she had looked up and seen him, every rule she had made to protect herself had been ignored and forgotten.

It had taken his insulting remark about Alex to force her to recognise reality.

In that regard at least she was most certainly not her mother's daughter, Keira recognised tiredly. She felt no quickening of her senses at all where other men were concerned.

Which made her danger greater rather than less. Loving the wrong man could be every bit as destructive as loving too many wrong men—especially when that wrong man was a man like Jay.

Jay leaned against one of the pillars supporting the vaulted ceiling of the palace's main reception room. The walls and the pillars were decorated with a traditional form of plasterwork that had been hand polished with a piece of agate, to create a marble finish, but of course that finish was a fake, false—just like Keira. Did she really think he had been deceived by that protest of hers about her fabric designer friend?

Jay paced the room restlessly. He had gone to Mumbai to escape from the ache of wanting her that being here with her gave him. He had even sworn that he would ease that ache in the arms of the actress who had been so delighted to hear from him. So why hadn't he done exactly that? And why had he cut short his visit and returned here ahead of schedule?

He wasn't going to answer that question. Why should he, when he had so many far more important matters to concern himself with?

Keira's heart sank as she stood in the main entrance hall to the palace. Her driver had just brought her the unwelcome news that he was not going to be driving her to her appointment but that instead Jay was going to take her, and that he would join her shortly.

Up above her was the gallery she had just walked along, which separated the main part of the palace from the women's quarters, where once they had lived in Purdah.

Purdah! The concealment of a woman's face and body from the eyes of all men except those of her immediate family. To some a protection, but to others a form of imprisonment. As a Western woman the very thought of enduring Purdah was beyond comprehension.

But wasn't the reality that what she herself was enduring, and had endured for most of her life, was in its own way an inner form of Purdah, imposed on her by her own fears? Her Purdah meant that her emotions and desires must always remain hidden away, denied the light of day for her own protection.

Keira tensed as she heard Jay's now familiar footsteps crossing the hallway.

'I'm sorry to have kept you waiting.'

How formal he sounded—and looked, Keira thought, contrasting his immaculate appearance in a perfectly fitting lightweight neutral-coloured suit worn over a pale blue shirt with her own jeans and shirt. But then she had dressed for the bumpy, dusty ride she had been anticipating. Her driver tended to keep the windows of the car open rather than use the air-conditioning, so that he could engage in conversation with other drivers.

They were in the car before Jay spoke to her again.

'Remind me again what the purpose of your visit to this manufacturer is?'

The sarcastic tone of his voice made Keira wish even more that he had not chosen to accompany her.

'I want to see the finished furniture before it is delivered, to make sure that it will work. He's making some special shelving units for the larger properties. They're to go into the studies and the children's rooms, and I wanted to see how he's getting on with them. If my idea works I thought they could be adapted to various age groups if they were given different paint finishes. I also wanted to make sure that he understands that all the paint used must be lead-free. I'm trying where possible to ensure that all the raw materials used come from sustainable sources. Green issues are just as big here in India with the middle classes as they are in Europe, of course.'

Jay had been driving fast, but now he had slowed down to allow for the leisurely progress of several camel carts.

'I see. And can I be confident that this designer is not another of your countrymen, looking for what you are so obviously eager to give?'

He was hateful, horrible, making accusations without any justification to back them up. Except that in his arms she *had* been eager to give, hadn't she? And she could hardly tell him that he was the first, the last and the only man to whom she had wanted to give herself. Even if she did he wouldn't believe her, and if he ever got to know about her background and her mother, he'd think he had even more reason for his accusations.

'I am not the one who controls what you do or don't think,' was the only thing she could think of to say to him to show her feelings about his comment.

But it was no use. He swooped on her words as swiftly as a predatory bird of prey to the lure—so much so, in fact, that she could almost feel the verbal bite of his sharp talons as he countered, 'But you are the one whose behaviour gives rise to my thoughts.'

Keira had had enough.

'If you choose to think that a simple lighthearted exchange of words between a man and a woman is tantamount to an offer of sex then I feel sorry for you—or rather I feel sorry for the women who are the victims of your prejudice, should they happen to indulge in what they think is lighthearted conversation with you.'

'Your sex does not indulge in lighthearted conversation. It plans the course of its words with military precision—from the minute a woman makes an approach to a man to the minute he hands over to her the reward she has already decided he will give her in exchange for the pleasure of her company.'

'That is just cynical and unfair. There may be some women who do do that, but—'

'Some women—of which you are one, as we both already know.'

Keira knew there was nothing she could say that would make him accept that he was wrong about her. And why should she care if he did? What benefit would it be to her? It would simply make her even more vulnerable to him. At least this way she had his contempt of her to strengthen her determination not to allow her feelings for him to betray her.

The furniture factory was outside a small, dusty and very busy town on the caravan route where the plain met the desert.

Henna painters sat cross-legged on the roadside, hoping for passing custom; up ahead of them a farmer was unloading cackling chickens onto a stall ready to sell, whilst hot food was already on sale at another stall, filling the air with the scent of spices and cinnamon. A group of temple musicians walked past, their brightly coloured turbans contrasting with their white clothes.

'The factory is over there,' she told Jay, pointing in the direction of a two-storey building set apart from the others.

The desert heat hit Keira the minute she stepped out of the air-conditioned car. It was post-monsoon now, and she couldn't imagine what it must be like in the oppressive heat before the rains came.

The air was sharp with the smell of glue and paint, stinging her nostrils and making her catch her breath.

Their arrival had obviously been noticed, because the door to the factory owner's office had opened and the owner himself was hurrying towards them. Keira saw the anxious look he gave Jay, and felt sorry for him. Jay was an extraordinarily formidable man, especially when his mouth was compressed and he was frowning, as he was doing now.

'Hello, Mr Singh,' Keira greeted the factory owner. 'Please let me introduce His Highness Prince Jayesh to you.'

Keira could see how awed the factory owner was by Jay—which was hardly surprising. Jay dwarfed the other man, physically and materially, and poor Mr Singh was looking more anxious by the second.

They were ushered towards the office with many bows and a great deal of ceremony. The factory owner was plainly on edge, but no more than Keira was herself. This was a big test of her ability not just to locate and order furniture, but also to ensure that what she had ordered worked with the whole scheme.

She sensed that Jay had accompanied her not just to check up on her, but in the hope that she might fail—and that, of course, added to her anxiety.

'And now, Miss, if you will come, please, and see your shelves?' Mr Singh invited once they had gone through the formality of drinking tea.

Mr Singh led them into an anteroom of the factory, where Keira's shelving had been put on display.

To her relief it was exactly what she had wanted: constructed in sections so that it could be put together in different combinations, to cover an entire wall or merely part of it, either low or high on the wall. These particular shelves had been painted black and then rubbed down for a modern look.

Keira went up to them to inspect them properly, checking the quality of the paintwork and then testing the shelves themselves for stability.

'They are good, yes?' the factory owner asked eagerly.

'Yes,' Keira confirmed.

The factory owner's mobile phone rang. As he turned aside to answer it Keira ran her hand along the underside of one of the shelves, wincing when her finger was pierced by a small splinter of wood and quickly withdrawing her hand to inspect the damage.

'Let me see,' Jay demanded peremptorily

The factory owner had excused himself to deal with his call, and suddenly the small room felt very claustrophobic now that she was alone in it with Jay.

'It's only a splinter,' Keira told him. But he was ignoring her, reaching for her hand and taking hold of it before she could stop him whilst he frowned over the splinter and then expertly removed it.

A single small drop of bright red blood had formed at the exit to the wound, but Keira barely noticed it. All her attention was concentrated on the fact that Jay's fingers were still curled around her wrist, and that he was standing close enough to her for her to hear the sound of his heartbeat.

Her own heartbeat increased in speed. The drop of blood quivered in response to it. Jay looked down at it, and then lifted her hand to his mouth.

Keira drew in a sharp breath and then discovered that she couldn't release it. She started to tremble.

The slow curl of Jay's tongue around her finger felt like rough velvet stroking her skin. Molten heat invaded her body. She wanted to close her eyes and stay with him, savouring this feeling for ever. She wanted... The sound of footsteps outside the door as the factory owner returned jerked her back to reality. She pulled her hand free and exhaled unsteadily.

The factory owner was saying something, but she couldn't concentrate, so it was Jay who responded to him.

How could something so simple be responsible for the sensations and emotions tearing her apart?

CHAPTER NINE

THEY WERE JUST over halfway back to the city when Keira happened to glance in the passenger-side wing mirror and notice the stormclouds that were rapidly darkening the sky behind them, piling on top of one another in a leaden grey and densely packed mass.

Jay had obviously seen them too, because he depressed the accelerator and told her crisply, 'Looks like we could be in for a downpour.'

'I thought the monsoon season was over,' Keira told him. The clouds were toppling over one another now, spilling out to cover the sky in a billowing rolling wall that was moving speedily towards them.

'It is,' Jay agreed. 'This is obviously a freak storm of some sort. It can happen. Hold on,' he warned her, as he pressed the accelerator even further and the car surged forward at a speed that sent them bouncing over the poor-quality road.

'I wouldn't normally want to travel at this speed on a road like this, but I'd rather not be caught out here in the open if the storm catches up with us. If a deluge starts this road could all too easily be turned into a river.'

Keira nodded her head, recognising the truth of what he was saying.

The sky was almost purple-black behind them now, and

the branches of the scrubby sparse trees were bending and twisting in the ferocity of the wind that was pushing the storm towards them. Flocks of birds rose from the trees, wheeling and screeching before turning to flee. Eerily electric yellow-white lightning flashed behind them, followed by crashes of thunder that made Keira wince and cling to her seat.

She no longer wanted to look in the wing mirror, but of course she couldn't stop herself from doing so. The storm was catching up with them.

'Watch out.'

Jay swung the car to avoid hitting a cow that had strayed into the road, throwing Keira hard against both her seat belt and the arm he had flung across to protect her. Her own immediate instinct was to hold tightly to his arm, as much for comfort as anything else.

'Sorry about that.'

His voice was clipped, and Keira could feel him tensing his arm, ready to pull away from her as though he was keen to break their physical contact. Just as she should be.

'I'm just glad you managed to avoid the cow,' Keira told him shakily, trying to make some effort at normal conversation to distract herself from the dangerous direction of her thoughts. She released him, and then had to fight not to grab hold of him again as another bolt of lightning lit up the bruised tungsten-dark sky.

Large fat drops of rain hammered down on the car's roof and hit the windscreen, mingling with the dust to turn it into muddy rivulets.

'I'm going to have to slow down,' Jay warned her. 'Otherwise we'll risk aquaplaning off the road.'

Keira nodded her head. She was grateful to him for keeping her informed of what he was doing and why, but she didn't want to distract him from his driving by talking to him.

Not that she could talk to him now and be heard—not over the noise of the thunder and the rain that was engulfing them.

Sheet lightning illuminated a torrent of rain so powerful that it was as though they were driving under a waterfall. In the car's headlights Keira could see the muddy froth of boiling water where the road used to be.

Jay had cut the car's speed, but Keira could still feel the dangerous suck and pull of the flooding water as it seethed beneath their tyres, threatening to wash them off the road.

Strangely, she didn't feel as afraid as she knew she should. Because she was with Jay? Keira glanced briefly towards him. He was staring ahead, concentrating on his driving, his hands on the steering wheel careful and controlled rather than white-knuckled with anxiety. Somehow she knew that Jay would not let the storm beat him.

'Ralapur's up ahead,' Jay told her, and sure enough, as Keira peered through the windscreen, she could see here and there the glimmer of lights.

Jay picked up speed again, leaving the storm behind, and they came to the new Tarmac road—commissioned and paid for, she had learned, by Jay's brother, who was proving to be a forward-thinking and caring figurehead. The Tarmac gleamed wet under the drum of the rain, but at least it was free of any surface water.

By the time they reached the city car park the rain had actually almost stopped, but the storm was obviously following them.

'If you want to stay here whilst I go and get you a raincoat and an umbrella—?' Jay offered, as he switched off the engine.

Keira shook her head. 'No, I'll come with you,' she

told him. She'd rather risk getting a bit wet and having the safety of his presence than remaining dry and staying in the car on her own.

'Come on, then.'

They were only yards from the square in front of the palace when the storm caught up with them, drenching them with a deluge of rainfall that soaked them through to the skin, hammering down so hard that Keira felt as though she could hardly breathe.

When Jay took hold of her hand, shouting to her above the noise of the rain, 'We'll go this way—it's quicker!' as he half-pulled her down a narrow passageway and through a high gate in the wall that took them into his own private courtyard, she didn't have the breath to object, even if she had wanted to do so. Far easier and safer to simply let Jay lead her up the flight of stone stairs that led from his courtyard to his door, which he opened speedily, pushing Keira inside ahead of him, and then slammed closed behind them, enclosing them both in the welcome dry protection of the room beyond it.

The thought occurred to Keira that not once during the storm had she felt anything less than complete faith in Jay, and complete trust in his judgement as he had made decisions she knew she would not have had the confidence to make. But what she would remember most of all about the storm was the warmth of his hand holding hers. It was pointless telling herself that the sense of intimacy she had felt and the joy it had brought her were completely out of proportion to his actions, and therefore a warning sign of how dangerously out of her depth she was getting. It was too late. She suspected that somehow, somewhere along the journey from their first meeting to being here in this room, she had fallen in love with him.

Out of breath and soaking wet, Keira pushed her realisation aside and looked round the room. A bedroom. Jay's bedroom? Her heart lurched and crashed into her ribs—and not out of fear, she recognized, as Jay strode across the room to switch on the lights.

She was shivering now, and not just because of her body's reaction to the intimacy of their surroundings. Her wet clothes were plastered to her body, just as Jay's were plastered to his. Jay's shirt was clinging to his torso, so sodden that it had become virtually opaque. Her heart was skittering around inside her ribcage now, her mouth was dry and a dangerous and unwanted pulse was aching deep inside her. Keira dragged her gaze away from its hungry focus on Jay and made herself study her surroundings instead.

A large modern bed dominated the room, with crisp white bedlinen turned down over a richly embroidered silk coverlet. Art Deco lamps with Tiffany shades threw soft shadows across the dark silk-rug-covered floor, repeating the 1930s theme of the women's quarters and reminding Keira that it had been a habit of the fabulously wealthy Maharajas of that era to build themselves new palaces, decorated and furnished in the fashion of the times.

Outside the sky had turned dark, and the only sound was that of the rain hammering down. Keira lifted her hand to brush her wet hair out of her eyes and then nearly jumped out of her skin as suddenly there was a flash of lightning so intense it seared the sky, followed almost immediately by the most deafening crash of thunder. As she cried out, more in shock than fear, the lights went out, plunging the room and the city beyond it into darkness.

Keira took a step forward and then came to an abrupt halt as she collided with Jay. His fingers curled round her upper arms—to steady her or to hold her off? She didn't know. All she did know was that the mere act of him touching her was setting off a storm of its own inside her body that she knew she would not be able to contain. Desire zig-zagged through her like the lightning outside, burning from nerve-ending to nerve-ending, leaving her a mass of aching, volatile need. Her heart crashed into her ribs. The threat of her longing was causing her far more fear than what was happening outside. Instinctively and immediately Keira tried to protect herself, but it was too late. Her body had other ideas. As she had done before she leaned towards him, the stifled urgent sound of her breathing tattooing onto the silence a sensuality that spoke openly of her desire.

Jay heard the message and recognised it. He should turn her down. But in the electric tension of the darkened room her quickened breathing was suddenly a conduit for the desire he had been fighting to keep at bay from the moment he had first seen her. It ran like fire over gunpowder along his veins and through his senses, blowing apart his control over not just his reactions, but over something he had thought no woman could ever influence—his emotions.

Rejection burned into need; need—that was all, Jay told himself fiercely. The feeling growing within him that she had some kind of unique magnetic pull on his senses was just his imagination.

Ignoring the warnings his brain was trying to give him, he reached for Keira, demanding softly, 'What is it? What do you want? Tell me.'

The ragged catch in her breath quickened his own arousal. He could feel her trembling, smell the scent of her skin, hear the ache in her low moan of longing.

'Is it this?'

He had drawn her to him with one strong, sinuous movement that brought her up tightly against his body.

'Tell me,' he repeated. 'Tell me that you want me.'

This was madness—a madness she would regret. Yet somehow she no longer cared.

'I want you,' Keira whispered. And as though the admission had released her from all constraint, she could feel the wild, wanton rush of her own hot desire as it stormed through her body, overpowering everything that stood in its way. 'I want you,' she repeated unsteadily, but more loudly. 'I want you…'

'How? How do you want me? Tell me. Show me. Show me your desire. Show me the way you want me to please you. Talk to me in words and tell me your pleasure.'

What he was asking of her was impossible, but that didn't stop his words from exciting her almost unbearably.

Their bodies gave off a mutual heat of need through the wet fabric of their clothes. She could smell it, feel it, and breathing it in was like breathing in something headily intoxicating.

Thunder roared overhead, and lightning spat and forked— and Keira's heartbeat went into overdrive.

She registered the rise and fall of Jay's chest with a small shuddering breath. In the dim light his eyes shone molten like mercury, his gaze quicksilver, loaded with promise and danger.

The hot, almost feral scent of Jay's arousal mingling with that of his skin charged a feeling within her so sharp it was almost a pain, and longing leached from her blood into her flesh.

She should not be feeling like this, but it was too late to tell herself that now.

She was torn between her longing for him and her fear because she did so; torn between arousal and animosity, between the intensity of her need to drive him over the edge that would result in him possessing her and the equal intensity of her need to escape from that darkness within herself.

Almost as though he sensed the battle taking place inside her, Jay tightened his hold on her, warning her without words that it was too late now for her to try to escape.

Keira shivered and made a small sound of protest against her own arousal, whispering, 'No...'

'*Yes.*' Jay overruled her. 'Yes.'

His mouth was explosively demanding on her own, but Keira didn't care. His passion was overwhelming her half-hearted attempt at dutiful resistance, and she was more than glad to let it. She had to respond to him. There was no other choice, and nor did she wish for one. This was what she had been yearning and aching for. This was what she had been born for.

The storm had engulfed them both, and Keira was swamped by it. In the warm darkness of the room the sounds of their increasingly aroused breathing, of hands against flesh, shaping, touching, caressing, of mouth against mouth, of tongues twining and seeking, were an erotic counterpoint to the uneven thud of their heartbeats.

Layer upon layer the passion built between them, with each breath, each unsteady pulse-beat taking her higher, Keira recognised. And Jay's touch fed its heat as his hands shaped her body and his mouth commanded her response.

Outside the storm still raged ignored—until a fiercely bright bolt of lightning flashed outside, briefly filling the room with a brilliant white light.

Keira tensed, dragging her mouth away from Jay's to look uncertainly towards the window. Jay's gaze fastened on the rise and fall of Keira's breasts. The rapid movement of her chest dragged the wet fabric of her blouse against her skin, so that he could see her flesh beneath it. Keira wasn't looking at the window now. She was looking at him, her nipples dark and hard and straining as tightly against the wet silk of her bra as his erection was straining against his trousers.

The brilliance of the lightning faded, but the accuracy with which Jay found the place where the aureole of her nipple met the curve of her breast caused Keira to gasp out loud, her nipple hardening under the erotic touch of his thumb and forefinger.

'Look at me,' Jay commanded. He wanted to see her desire for him as well as feel it. He wanted to watch whilst the touch of his hands brought her pleasure. He wanted to see in her eyes what could not be hidden or denied by any verbal rejection.

In the shadowy semi-light Keira gave herself over to the flood of pleasure storming through her, her eyes liquid gold with arousal and her lips stung soft and swollen from his kisses as she looked up at Jay.

Just the heat engendered by the way Jay was looking back at her should surely have been enough to melt the clothes from her flesh, leaving her naked and open to his touch in all the ways she wanted it to be, Keira thought helplessly.

The lightning might have faded, softening the room back into darkness, but its brief life had lasted long enough for Jay to be able to reach unerringly for the buttons on Keira's blouse.

He heard her whimper, then felt her shudder when he tugged the wet fabric away from her skin, allowing her to sway closer to him, her naked breasts openly ready for the possession of his hands.

Could this really be her? Moaning, wantonly arching her back, pushing her body hungrily and rhythmically against Jay's touch? Keira wondered dizzily. Fierce spasms of pleasure surged through her, urging her to demand more.

The caress of his hands on her breasts was making her ache unbearably for the touch of his lips against them, for the stroke of his tongue, the possessive, sensual suckling of her flesh that she knew would ignite a need in her that would change her for ever. Just thinking about it was making the pulse deep inside her grow, wanting the stroke of his fingers.

'Does this pleasure you? Do you want more?'

She was beyond speech—beyond anything other than giving herself over to him completely.

Keira didn't know whether or not she had spoken, but she did know that a message had been given and understood. And now they were both tugging at one another's clothes, interspersing their actions with kisses and caresses and, in her case, soft, fevered, delighted little moans of pleasure as she discovered some new bit of him to touch.

Who could have known that rain-wet flesh could feel so erotic, or that such an intensity of urgency could possess her?

Jay's hands were shaping her naked body, stroking down to her thighs and then up over her. His fingertips, spanning the smoothness of her bottom and then lifting her so that he could press her into his arousal, had her raking her nails down the length of his upper arm, whilst she sobbed her sexual heat into the wet flesh of his throat.

Had she parted her own thighs in open willingness, soliciting his long and deliberately erotic exploration of her intimate flesh, or had Jay parted them himself?

Keira had no idea, and she cared even less. She couldn't think or exist beyond the sensual stroke of his fingertip backwards and forwards over her clitoris.

Possessed by the desire that had materialised as quickly as the storm, Keira tugged and tore at Jay's clothes, shuddering with blatant sexual pleasure at each touch of his hands on her naked rain-sleek skin, moaning her delight and inciting more intimacy as each touch fuelled her hunger for more.

Here in this room, filled with the heat they themselves had generated, it felt almost as though the storm had ripped from her all her inhibitions.

Jay wasn't touching her any more; he wasn't giving her that almost too intense pleasure, and its loss was making her tremble and ache. But before Keira could voice her loss Jay was picking her up and carrying her to the wide bed.

Keira clung to him as he lowered her onto the mattress, pressing passionate kisses on his throat and then his chest, her golden eyes brilliant with what it meant to be the woman he had aroused within her.

The storm had laid bare her feelings, both physical and emotional. She couldn't hide from them any more She had fallen in love with Jay.

He pushed her back on the bed and then kissed her mouth, slowly and deeply, until her senses swam and her nipples stiffened achingly into the palms of his hands. She welcomed the heat of his mouth as he kissed his way along the curve of her breast to circle first one nipple and then the other with the tip of his tongue.

The pulse deep inside her turned into a thudding, knowing, gnawing ache that leapt to the touch of Jay's fingers and responded rhythmically to their caress.

He moved back down the bed, circling her slim ankle with his hand and lifting her leg so that he could string kisses from the inside of her ankle bone all the way along her leg to her knee, and then beyond, up over her thigh, whilst she trembled violently with a pleasure her body could not contain.

The thunder and lightning was inside her, possessing her, tossing her from one peak of pleasure to the next.

Somehow her feet were on his shoulders. Somehow her body lay open to him to explore and enjoy as he wished. Keira gasped as his fingertips stroked through the parted wetness of the inner lips of her sex and her clitoris over and over again, slowly, then faster, moving over her and within her, taking her up so high, so fast, that she could barely draw breath between her shocked gasp of recognition and the sob of pleasure that convulsed her throat muscles at exactly the same time as Jay's caresses convulsed her body into the sharp intense spasm of her orgasm.

The pleasure, so swift and savage, clung to her in an aftermath of intense sweetness and emotional sensitivity that left her trembling, and Jay looked down at her. Her body felt weightless and boneless, and yet at the same time so heavy with exhaustion that she couldn't move. Overcome by her emotions, Keira reached for Jay's hand and pressed it fervently to her lips in an age-old gesture of intense love.

She was good—even better than he had expected. Taking her pleasure with a direct simplicity that had acted on him like a powerful aphrodisiac. He wanted to see that pleasure again. He wanted to watch whilst he gave it to her and she took it. He wanted her legs wrapped around him whilst he took her, stroking slowly and deeply into her, until she begged him to move faster and deeper, until she took him with her to that place she had just been... But, unexpectedly, she was practically falling asleep as he held her.

Frowning, Jay lowered her onto the bed and watched as her eyes closed.

It was the sound of running water that woke Keira—that, and a sense of loss because even in sleep she had known that Jay had left her.

The room was still dark, although the storm had gone.

A shaft of oblong light from the half-open bathroom door coupled with the sound of the shower told her where Jay had gone.

She got up out of bed and padded naked towards the bathroom. Black marble covered the floor, its richness reflected in the ornately panelled mirrored walls. One half of the bathroom was almost filled with a large rectangular bath, sunk into the floor and reached via a set of marble steps. The other side of the room had been turned into the equivalent of a modern wet room, separated from the bathing area by a vanity unit and a glass screen. Jay was standing beneath the shower in the wet-room area, with his back to her.

Soapsuds and water glistened on his skin. Keira's heart and body contracted on a surge of love for him. She watched him for as long as she could bear to be apart from him, and then ran to him.

Jay turned as she reached the shower, looking at her and then taking her in his arms, kissing her slowly and sweetly, and then less slowly as she pressed herself closer to him.

Keira scooped some of the lather off his body and rubbed it against her own, watching the way the colour of his eyes burned from grey to silver as he poured shower gel into his palm and then slowly applied it to her body.

Ten minutes later, when the foam had disappeared along with the shower water, Keira knew that the desire Jay's touch had aroused in her was nowhere close to disappearing. Quite the opposite.

Slowly and wonderingly she reached out to touch him, running her fingertips along his breastbone and then down his body, through the soft dark hair that thickened around the base of his hardness.

Her chest rose and then fell sharply as her senses responded to the intimacy of her exploration, and uncertainly she stroked delicately along the rigid shaft.

Jay shuddered. What Keira was doing to him was sheer torment, and she must know it. He wanted to be enclosed by her, to be held firm, to feel her body embracing and caressing him. He wanted to take her and hold her and thrust deep into her. He wanted to feel her body's desire for his. He wanted to lose himself in her. He wanted...

Keira could feel the heavy, uneven thud of Jay's heartbeat, could taste the unique hot salt of his skin. 'I want you,' she told him, breathing the words out against his skin, the raw uneven huskiness of her voice matching the unsteadiness of her heartbeat. 'Make love to me, Jay.'

Her hands flat against the hard muscles of his six-pack, she placed a line of kisses down his body, her lips moving lower until finally she placed a kiss of love and longing against the smooth, rigid hardness of the flesh that pulsed beneath the hold of her hand.

At last she had done it—had begged him as he had sworn that she would. His pride was appeased. And only just in time, Jay acknowledged. He wasn't prepared to admit even to himself just how very few seconds more he would have lasted before his desire for her overwhelmed him and he had been the one begging her.

Now Jay couldn't wait any longer. He swept her up into his arms and carried her back to the bed.

His desire to finish what they had begun drove through the barriers he normally imposed on himself, so that his lovemaking wasn't confined to the mere physical skill he normally used to ensure his partner's pleasure whilst he himself remained emotionally detached. That detachment was replaced with something he could neither control nor reject, that swept and burned through him, taking possession of him.

Keira herself was lost—totally and completely. All that mattered was Jay and what she was feeling. There was no room for anything else. Together they filled her senses and her thoughts. His lovemaking had taken her to the heights already tonight. Now he was showing her that there were heights beyond those heights—unimaginable peak after peak of such exquisite sensual pleasures that they burned her senses like a brand. Jay's brand, she thought dizzily.

Keira was oblivious to the rustle of foil as Jay fought to control himself long enough to practise safe sex, knowing only that he had moved away from her. Wantonly she urged him back to her, with soft pleas interspersed with hungry kisses and caresses.

The return of the hard weight of him between her thighs made her shudder and arch up against him, her hands gripping his shoulders as he moved against her, thrusting slowly into her.

How could there be such an intensity of pleasure? It was driving her forward to meet it, to meet him, as he filled her body, possessing it—possessing her. It grew and sharpened, and an urgent, compelling need rushed through her, refusing to be checked, matching its pace to Jay's deepening thrusts.

The world—no, the universe, *his* universe, Jay acknowledged, had become the feel of Keira's flesh enclosing him, the feel of being with her and within her. This was all that mattered—the only thing that mattered. He thrust deeper, and felt the barrier that barred his way. The *barrier?* She was a *virgin?* How could she possibly be a virgin? Disbelief, followed by anger, followed by outrage, burned through him.

Why had Jay gone so still? That wasn't what she wanted. Keira moved eagerly against him, covering his mouth with her own, showing him with the hot, urgent thrust of her tongue just what she did want.

Caught totally off guard by his discovery, and by the way it changed the dynamics of what was happening, Jay wanted to withdraw from Keira. But both her body and his own were conspiring to prevent him from doing so. Her flesh clung wantonly to his, enclosing and possessing him in its soft moist heat, overwhelming what his brain wanted his body to do. His body had very different ideas. He moved, intending to pull back, but Keira moved with him, and within the space of one sharp indrawn breath it was too late for him to stop—too late for him to do anything but submit to the demands of their shared desire.

This time the pleasure was different, Keira recognized: deeper, stronger, its convulsions tightening around Jay's flesh and holding him there until her orgasm became his, and his hers. Until she was stormed, swept, elevated to a place beyond any place she had ever thought could exist, to a depth of intensity that shocked her as much as it pleasured her.

CHAPTER TEN

A VIRGIN—HOW COULD she have been a virgin? Jay stared grimly into the darkness whilst Keira slept at his side. It angered and disturbed him that all his preconceptions about her had been so very wrong, and that as a virgin she had been so far from his original assessment of her. It angered him that his judgement of her had been so glaringly wrong. He felt betrayed by his own inability to assess her correctly, and further angered by the belief that she would now have expectations and ambitions that he had no intention of fulfilling. Had he known the truth about her he would have warned her off, making sure that they did not have sex. By concealing her true sexual experience from him, or rather her lack of it, she had allowed him to go on believing what he had, putting him in an untenable situation. Deliberately?

Twenty-something virgins had by definition to have a pretty heavy agenda going on. Either they had sexual hang-ups or problems—which patently she most certainly did not—or there was another reason. And the only logical reason Jay could think of was that Keira had remained a virgin because she expected to exchange her virginity for commitment. That was never going to happen. He had no intention of making a commitment to any woman—ever. During the years of their estrangement his father had let him know many times via his courtiers that he wanted to make plans to arrange a suitable marriage for him, but in that both he and Rao had withstood their parent, refusing to submit to a marriage of tradition and royal necessity.

Rao would, of course, ultimately have to marry, and his wife would have to be someone worthy of being his Maharani. For himself, Jay knew that it would be expected if he did marry that he too would marry a suitable bride. But he had no intention of marrying—not anyone, not ever. So Keira had wasted her virginity on him and he would have to tell her so. There must not be any more errors of judgement or aspiration.

Slowly, like wisps of fine cloud, memories of the night drifted back to him. Keira whispering his name to him, thanking him for her pleasure, her eyes huge with emotion.

Emotion. Jay's mouth compressed. What had happened between them had nothing to do with emotion—at least not on his part—and the sooner he told her that the better. Both for her sake as well as his own. The last thing he wanted was to have her start building some ridiculous fantasy out of what had quite simply been a single night of sex—and one that he had no intention of repeating. He would have to speak to her before the situation got even more out of hand than it was already.

Keira had been awake for some time, lying in bed and marvelling at the difference between the woman she had been and the woman she was now. Her body glowed still with the aftermath of her pleasure. *Their* pleasure, she reminded herself. Jay would know now that he had been wrong about her, and that what she felt for him was unique, something she had never shared with anyone else. She was still on a physical and emotional high from last night, in a blissed-out state where the world felt like a fairytale come true and she its heroine princess. And all because of Jay.

Jay! Where was he? What would he say to her? What would she say to him? Her heart was thumping unsteadily. Already she missed him. Already she ached for him and wanted to be with him. Already the effect of the night's sexual intimacy had changed her and their relationship, and her heart was speeding on wings into a magical world where everything and anything was possible.

It was Jay himself who brought her back down to earth, arriving with a tray of tea and an expression that had her giddy heart's headlong race brought to an abrupt halt.

Something was wrong. Something was more than wrong. Jay was looking autocratic and distant. He was fully dressed. He didn't come to her, or even sit down on the bed beside her, instead he walked over to the window and then turned to face her so that its light fell on her face but obscured his.

'I owe you an apology. And I'm afraid it will have to be accompanied by a warning.'

He was speaking to her as though he was addressing a business meeting, Keira recognised, his whole manner cool and distant. Her heart was pounding again—but not this time with elation. Instead what she felt was dread.

'I want to be frank with you, Keira. Had I known you were a virgin I would never have had sex with you. Were you a girl of eighteen or so, I would add here that I understand you might have had rosy romantic delusions about men falling passionately in love with sweet innocent virgins, and throwing their heart and an offer of marriage at their feet having taken that virginity. But you are not eighteen. You are twenty-seven. Women of twenty-seven do not remain virgins by accident or out of some romantic delusion. To have chosen virginity when yours is such a sensual and passionate nature can't have been easy.'

Keira's mouth had gone dry. She might not have been expecting quite the eighteen-year-old's scenario he had described with such sparing and cruel accuracy, but to be addressed as Jay was addressing her now was a horrible shock and very hurtful.

'My assumption has to be that you chose virginity because you saw it as, shall we say, a good business decision—an insurance policy that would mature with handsome dividends when it was offered to your chosen recipient: your exclusivity sexually, both past and future, in exchange for the right kind of marriage. I do not doubt that there are men, wealthy men, who are willing to make such a barter in return for the security that comes from knowing that their wife is indeed a model of virtue. However, I am not one of those men. To be blunt, I have no intention of making a commitment to any woman ever, either inside marriage or outside it, and had you told me the truth about yourself first, I would have suggested that you retained your virginity to bestow on someone else. Sexually, what we shared last night was very enjoyable, but that was all it was for me. A fleeting enjoyment which is now over and will be quickly forgotten. I am sorry if my words offend or upset you, but it is better that you know the truth. It would be cruel of me indeed to allow you to hope for something I have no intention of giving you or anyone else.'

Keira felt each word like a blow to her heart and her pride. He was both wrong about her and right. She had not set out to use her virginity to force him into a commitment, but she *had* given it up to him because she herself had made an emotional commitment to him. He must never know that, though. Not now. For her pride's sake she had to salvage what she could of the situation and her self-respect.

It did not help that she was lying naked under the bed-clothes whilst he was fully dressed. Didn't it tell her all she really needed to know about him that even now, when he was humiliating her, he had taken for himself every advantage there was to be had in order to give himself more power than her. He was dressed; she wasn't. He had the light behind him; she had it on her. He had had time to plan and rehearse what he intended to say; she had not. Well, luckily for her, living with her great-aunt had taught her a great deal about how to defend herself when she was the weaker party.

She pulled the bedclothes securely around her body and sat up.

'I appreciate what you're saying,' she told him, trying to keep her voice as cool and focused as his had been, 'but I must tell you that once again you've reached a conclusion about me that isn't correct.'

There was a telling silence during which Keira waited, praying that he wouldn't tell her outright that he didn't believe her.

His assessing, 'Meaning?' had her exhaling unsteadily.

'Meaning that, yes, I had chosen to remain a virgin, but the reason I did so had nothing whatsoever to do with any desire on my part to get married. Far from it.'

He had moved slightly, but she still could not see his face.

'You remained a virgin because you don't want to get married? Forgive me, but I have to say that I don't...'

Any minute now he was going to start asking questions she could not answer. She had to head him off with something plausible.

'I wanted a career and my own independence, and as a teenager it seemed to me that as soon as a girl fell in love she stopped wanting those things. So I vowed not to fall in love. It was far too dangerous. Remaining a virgin was a by-product of my decision not to fall in love.'

She gave what she hoped was a convincingly careless small shrug.

'Obviously as I've grown older I've been able to recognise that it is possible to have sex and remain emotionally independent, and I had begun to wonder what I might be missing because of a decision made when I was very immature.'

'And you've been looking round for someone to experience sex with? Is that what you're trying to say?'

Keira actually managed to laugh.

'I hadn't got as far as that, and if I had done there would have been the embarrassment of my virginity to deal with. I'm old enough to understand that what happened between us was something that neither of us expected to happen and that both of us would probably have preferred not to have happened.'

There had been the clear ring of truth in her voice when she had spoken about her vow not to fall in love and her fear of doing so, Jay acknowledged. He had already misjudged her once. His pride didn't want him doing so a second time. It made sense for him to accept what she was saying, but at the same time he still intended to reinforce his own message to her by putting things on a strictly business footing.

'It might be best in the circumstances if we terminated our contract,' Keira told him. She couldn't afford to break it herself, but she was hoping desperately now that *he* would terminate it. How on earth was she going to be able to work for him now feeling as she did about him? *Feeling* as she did about him? What did that mean?

'I do not wish to terminate our contract,' Jay was telling her sharply. 'It would be too costly and disruptive to find another interior designer at this stage. That is in part why I am speaking with you as I am. I don't want there to be any misunderstandings—any hopes or aspirations, shall we say, that cannot be met.'

Keira permitted herself a small, bitter inward smile as she imagined what he would think if he knew the truth about her.

'All my hopes and aspirations are focused on my business.'

'As mine are on mine,' Jay responded.

Jay had gone. She was on her own, but even now Keira did not dare to give way to her emotions—just as she had never dared to do so when she had lived with her great-aunt.

To allow anyone to see her pain was to risk having it used against her, to hurt her even more. She had learned that lesson very young. But the pain she had experienced then was nothing compared to what she must somehow find a way to live through now.

The unthinkable, the unbearable, the most cruel of all cruelties had infiltrated her defences and overpowered her. She had fallen in love with Jay. But he must never know that. She would die before she would humiliate herself by letting him see what a fool she had been.

Last night she had broken the most important promise she had ever made to herself. Now she must face the consequences, she told herself bleakly.

CHAPTER ELEVEN

HER WORK ON the first three of the show houses was finished, and there was no real need for her to be here at this hour of the morning, straightening cushions, checking on the arrangement of flowers and the drape of curtains, but Keira was desperate to keep herself busy. Jay was due back from Mumbai today.

Was she going to be strong enough not to betray any reaction to his return? He had, after all, made the situation plain enough to her. From the moment he had questioned her about her virginity to the moment he had left for Mumbai he had treated her with clinical detachment. She, meanwhile, had gone through hurt to anger and back to hurt again, and it had been a relief of sorts when he had actually left.

At least with him gone she had been able to get on with her work without the fear of what his proximity might do to her self-control.

But soon he would be back. And last night her dreams had been filled with her longing for him—so much so, in fact, that her body now ached physically and tormentingly for him.

He had emailed her to tell her that he was bringing with him the art director of a new swish homes magazine, with a view to the magazine doing a feature on the development— complete with photographs of her interiors and an interview with her on modern interior design and décor.

Keira had dressed appropriately for the interview in one of her favourite silk linen outfits, a softly styled cream skirt teamed with a toning strappy top under a wrap cardigan. She had completed her outfit with a pair of designer sunglasses and a fashionably large leather bag—a gift from an up-and-coming young designer whose apartment she had once styled for a photoshoot.

She had read recently in *Vogue* that the handbag was now a top 'must have' fashion item.

Would Jay be pleased with the work she had done? She tried to see the rooms through his eyes instead of her own. Her hands were trembling slightly as she straightened the piece of polished wood artwork she had placed on the glass-topped coffee table. What was she going to do if he didn't like it? Burst into tears? Hardly.

What she wanted him to see was his in-control interior designer, not a needy, over-emotional woman who had fallen in love with him.

She couldn't stay here all day. She needed to return to the palace. Jay hadn't been specific in his email as to the timing of his return.

She was just on the point of leaving the show house when a four-wheel-drive drew up outside, and Jay and another man climbed out of it.

Keira felt as though her heart had physically stopped beating, as though the earth itself had stopped moving— because, like her, it was so focused on this one man that nothing else could exist.

The ache that had taken possession of her heart now spread to the rest of her body, so that every part of her that had touched him or been touched by him longed violently for that physical contact once more.

He was coming towards her, turning his head so that he could look at her. To make sure that she still understood what he had told her? Keira forced her lips into a professional smile, no different for Jay than it was for the man to whom he was introducing her, who was now smiling at her with male warmth and interest that threw into sharp relief Jay's coldness towards her.

'My friends call me Bas,' he told her, 'and I hope that you will do the same. I have heard a great many complimentary things about your work, and I am looking forward to featuring it in our magazine.'

'I expect Jay has already told you that part of his remit was that he wanted me to use local products as much as possible?' Keira asked him as she stepped to one side to allow the two men to enter the show house.

'Do you feel that interfered with your own creativity?'

'No, not at all. Using local products and focusing on the nature of the land around the development was very much in keeping with my own way of working. I enjoyed finding different ways to stick to Jay's remit, but at the same time ensure that the houses reflect the lifestyles and tastes of the people who will buy the properties.'

Keira stopped speaking to allow the art director to look at the décor and inspect what she had done.

'I'm impressed,' he told her. 'Very impressed. This toile, for instance...'

'Locally made and designed.'

'Jay, with your permission I'd like to make Keira and the work she's done here a lead feature in our magazine. In fact I'd love to devote an entire magazine to what's going on here, with interviews with the local craftsmen, articles on the history of those crafts, that kind of thing. What's happening here really is revolutionary. Now that I've seen what Keira's done I'm really blown away.'

Jay was frowning, and Keira wondered if perhaps he wasn't as pleased with the interiors as she had hoped.

'What I need to do is get a crew up here and some interviews set up. I know you want the feature to coincide with the launch of the development via your own advertising. You said you'd be launching officially at the World Trade Fair in six months' time? Keira, I'll want to do an in-depth interview with you, and I'd like to get an idea of how you work. Would it be okay with you if I attached myself to you and followed you around for the next couple of days?'

Jay was frowning even more now.

'Well, if Jay doesn't mind...' she told Bas helplessly.

'Of course he doesn't mind. That's what he's brought me down here for—isn't it, Jay?'

Ignoring the other man, Jay turned to Keira and said tersely, 'Come and see me in my office at the palace in an hour's time. I want to go through a few things with you. I'll take you to your hotel now, Bas, and leave you there to get yourself settled in.'

The art director smiled warmly at Keira.

'It's only a flying visit for me this time, but I'm already looking forward to coming back and getting to spend more time with you.'

At least someone had admired the work she had done, even if that someone wasn't Jay, Keira thought sadly as she waited for the houseboy to come back from telling Jay that she was here to see him.

She had arrived early for their appointment, and now she was feeling slightly sick and very nervous. The only thing that was keeping her going was her pride—and her determination to prove to Jay that she could be utterly professional.

Rakesh had returned and was asking her to follow him.

With every step that took her closer to Jay's office and Jay himself her apprehension increased, until she would have given anything to turn and run away. What if he told her that he knew how she felt about him? What would she do then? How would she survive that humiliation?

Rakesh had knocked on the door and was pushing it open for her. It was too late now for her to run away. Keira stepped into the room, and then froze as she realised that Jay was standing so near to the door that she had virtually walked straight into him. When he reached past her to shut the door she felt close to dizziness with the effort of not allowing her body to react to his proximity. It was like depriving her lungs of oxygen, leaving her feeling dangerously weak and off balance. She had missed him so much. She ached for him so much. But she must not feel like this—she must not *be* like this.

'Has Bas asked you to go to bed with him yet?'

The words, delivered in a harsh, flat and yet distinctly antagonistic voice, shocked her out of her painful thoughts.

'No, of course not.'

'There is no *of course not* about it,' Jay told her. 'He wants you. He made that perfectly obvious.'

This kind of discussion was the last thing she had expected, and she had no idea how to deal with it.

'If you're concerned that I might prejudice the success of your development by behaving unprofessionally—' she began, but Jay cut ruthlessly across what she was saying.

'You don't want him, then?' he demanded.

'No, I don't.'

'Do you want me?'

It was several betraying seconds before she could find the breath to speak.

'No.'

'Do you want me to *make* you want me?'

Now she was panicking. 'I'm not staying here to listen to any more of this.'

He reached the door before her, blocking her escape, leaving her with nowhere to go other than into his arms.

His kiss was fiercely possessive and even more fiercely sexual, with the tip of his tongue as it probed the soft line of her lips mirroring the hard urgency of his erection. His hands were caressing her breasts, shaping her body to his own. A few more heartbeats and she would be totally lost, not caring one bit about the promises she had made to herself.

'I want you in my bed.'

Keira made herself resist the lure of his words.

'Because you think another man wants me?' she challenged him.

'No—although I admit seeing him looking at you the way he was made me decide that I'd better not waste any time putting my proposition to you.'

The word 'proposition' struck a chill note against Keira's heart and her overheated senses.

Jay had released her now, and was telling her bluntly, 'Sex in my office has never had much appeal for me, but if I don't put some distance between us I can't promise you that it isn't going to happen. The next time you and I have sex I want to have the time and the privacy to ensure that it's a very special and memorable experience—and for all the right reasons.'

Her heart was thumping unsteadily now, her body reacting to the promise contained in his words in a way that made total nonsense of her vow to herself to remain in control.

'You as good as said that you aren't into virgins,' she reminded him.

'You aren't a virgin any more. Look, the reality is that

whether we like it or not there's a sexual attraction between us that I'm prepared to admit is far stronger than
I'd allowed for. It's certainly strong enough to have kept
me awake at night wanting you whilst I've been away—
wanting only you. We both know the score: no long-term
relationship, no commitment, no emotional trauma. But
that doesn't mean that we can't be bed partners. My guess
is that you want me every bit as much as I want you, and
my proposition to you is that we give ourselves a break
and ride the wave together rather than fight against it. The
kind of intense sexual hunger we're experiencing burns
itself out quickly once its satisfied. Right now by resist-
ing it all we're doing is feeding it. Far better to enjoy it,
and one another, for the short duration of its lifetime—
don't you agree?'

Oh, yes, she agreed. She'd always loved living dangerously— *not*! Keira couldn't think of anything more calculated to destroy her than becoming Jay's 'bed partner'.
She knew that as soon as he stopped wanting her physically he would want her out of his life. She knew that he
felt nothing whatsoever emotionally for her, that all he
wanted from her was sex. And yet, shamefully, she was
desperately tempted to agree—just to have the pleasure
he was offering her and the memories it would give her.

If she refused, how was she going to feel ten years from
now? Twenty years from now and more? Knowing that she
could have had this time with him but had refused it out
of fear of the emotional pain she knew must come with it.
And wasn't there another concern she ought to consider?
a sly inner voice pointed out to her. If she refused mightn't
Jay start to suspect that she was refusing because she had
fallen in love with him?

'Have dinner with me tonight,' Jay suggested. 'You can
give me your answer then.'

'Very well.'

Keira marvelled that she could sound so calm and matter of fact.

'We'll have dinner in my private quarters, here at the palace.'

Now she was panicking—and excited, and aroused...

What did one wear to have dinner with a man when that dinner was a prelude to that man taking you to bed? It wasn't a situation Keira had ever been in before. She had never had cause to dress for seduction. Images of low-cut balcony bras trimmed with lace and itsy-bitsy pieces of silk and lace masquerading as knickers floated through her head. Her underwear was of the smooth, no-VPL nude colour variety, far more functional than it was sexy.

She remembered that she had seen a shop in the bazaar, selling ethereally delicate and diaphanous harem pants and beaded bra tops. Would Jay appreciate her dressing up like a Bollywood dancing girl? Somehow she thought he was too sophisticated for that kind of obvious 'bedroom' outfit. So what did a woman who was going to be a man's non-permanent sexual partner wear pre-foreplay? Was there a set 'uniform'? Tailored clothes and no underwear *à la* Sharon Stone, perhaps? Keira didn't think she was quite ready to be quite so 'up front', as it were.

In the end, having decided that for her own sense of self-respect she should be herself—or at least as much herself as she could be given that Jay must not know how she felt about him—Keira opted for a simple loose-fitting cream dress and a pair of cream sandals. Her skin gleamed silkily with the light tan it had developed, and since this was definitely not a business meeting Keira left her hair down, to swing softly on her shoulders. She wasn't a fan of excessive make-up, using only a light touch of mascara and lipstick, and she was glad that she had opted for a simple casual appearance when unexpectedly Jay himself came to escort her to dinner. She discovered, on opening the door to him, that he too was dressed casually, wearing an unstructured linen shirt open at the throat and a pair of jeans.

It was hard not to show what she was feeling, and even harder to look as relaxed as Jay himself obviously was as he smiled at her and told her, 'I thought we'd walk back through the gardens.' He looked down at her feet as he spoke, presumably to check that she was wearing suitable garden-walking footwear, and yet Keira felt the most intense surge of sensual heat flood through her as he focused on her bare toes with their pale pink–polished nails.

He couldn't possibly know that she had been reading the *Kama Sutra* since he had mentioned it to her—any more than he could know how much her sexual senses had been awakened by what she had read and the realisation of the many opportunities the human body provided for shared sexual pleasure. It had been a painful learning curve in many ways, reinforcing for her both how much she loved and wanted Jay and how much it hurt knowing that she would never share those pleasures with him.

Only now she would. Her spirits soared and flew. When Jay reached for her hand she put her own into his and smiled at him. Immediately his hand tightened on hers.

'Do you realise how much you are tempting me when you smile like that?'

'Like what?'

'Like you can't wait to be in my arms.'

'I…' Keira paused There were a hundred and more smart, sassy responses she could give him, but only one of them really mattered. There were so many reasons why she should not be honest with him. But she couldn't help herself. 'I can't,' she told him simply.

He had been stroking her fingers, but now he stopped. Keira could feel the heat they were both generating pressing in on them, wrapping them in an invisible cloak of sensual longing.

'Rakesh will have brought our dinner.'

'Then we'd better go and eat it.'

Simple words, and yet the messages their other senses were exchanging went far deeper and were far more intimate.

Dusk was stealing the light and the heat from the gardens, cloaking them in soft shadows. Keira didn't know whether to be relieved or disappointed when Jay didn't pause to kiss her as he guided her to the steps that led up to his private quarters and took her into a traditionally styled salon with low-lying divans drawn up around a table. Jewel-coloured glass lamps illuminated the room in rich reds and ambers, and scented smoke perfumed the air. The strains of soft music echoed softly through the scented darkness, brushing against Keira's senses like a physical touch. This was foreplay *Kama Sutra*-style, and already she was captivated and entranced.

When Jay led her to one of the divans and took the one adjacent to it himself she lay as he had done, so that their heads were almost touching. But she still wasn't prepared for it when he reached for one of the bowls on the table and dipped into it, feeding her a small ball of rice flavoured with saffron and stuffed with plump sultanas. It was all so shockingly erotic: the intimacy of being fed by him, the touch of his fingers against her lips, the scent of his body as he leaned closer to her. All of it—and most of all when he suggested softly to her, 'Why don't you feed me?'

Her fingers were trembling when she lifted the rice to his lips, and her whole body was trembling by the time he had taken it from her, his fingers closing round her wrist to hold her as he licked her fingers, slowly and deliberately.

After that Keira had an appetite for only one thing. Although she did manage to eat the small juicy strawberries Jay fed her before finally losing her self-control and pressing her lips to his fingers and then his palm.

As though it was a signal he had been waiting for, Jay stood up and held out his hand to her. Silently Keira took it. Her heart was thumping heavily. In the jewelled shadows of the scented room Jay pulled her closer, and then traced the shape of her face with his fingertips. When he reached her mouth Keira's lips parted automatically, her tongue-tip caressing his flesh before she sucked his fingers into her mouth.

Jay's free hand was on her breast, his fingers stroking her nipple, and when she sucked on his fingers he reciprocated by plucking erotically at her nipple. Keira sucked harder and was rewarded in kind. She stroked her tongue over his fingertips and then shuddered in wild delight when Jay bent his head and placed his mouth over her fabric-covered breast, his tongue probing the hard jut of her nipple. How could something so simple arouse her to such intense pleasure?

She could feel her heat beating impatiently inside her body. She could feel her body pulsing, softening, opening in eager liquid longing. It was too late now to regret her prim decision not to take the shameless step of abandoning her underwear, too late to wish that she had done exactly that so all Jay had to do to satisfy the hungry ache inside her was slide his hand inside her dress and then—Keira shuddered wildly when, just as though she had spoken her wanton longing out loud, Jay put his hand on her thigh. Not, as she quickly discovered, to touch her intimately, but instead so that he could pick her up and carry her into the bedroom, where he placed her down on his bed.

Now his fingertip tracing of her flesh began again— but not this time on her face. Instead it was her body he was touching, tracing, with those light, delicate touches that somehow inflamed her senses far more than anything more heavy-handed could have done.

Long before he was kneeling beside her, cupping her now bare foot in his hand, Keira had lost the fight to retain her self-control and had given herself over completely to his keeping. Her body was an instrument, tuned only to respond to his touch, and from it he was now drawing a pleasure so intense that it verged on pain. If he were to stop touching her now she would fall into an abyss of unsatisfied longing that would burn through her for ever, she decided wildly when his tongue tip traced the inner arch of her bare foot, sending fierce strobes of pleasure right up to the heart of her sex.

She had no memory of them removing their clothes, but they must have done since they were both now naked. Jay's body was lean and superbly muscled, its scent and taste given over into her possession as she touched and kissed him as intimately as she dared, stroking her fingertips over his rigidly erect sex and marvelling at its sensitivity to her touch and its capacity for response.

Jay was caressing the inside of her thighs, encouraging them to fall open and offer him the hidden mystery of her body. Like the petals of a lily, opening to the heat of the sun, the lips of her sex curved and swelled open at his touch, slick against her body's eager, ready wetness. The pulse deep inside her that had begun what felt like an eternity ago quickened and deepened into an urgent ache. Jay's deliberate caress against her clitoris provoked a low moan from her throat, and an agonized, *'Don't...'* causing Jay to frown.

'You want me to stop?' he asked her.

'Only because I want you inside me, and I'm afraid that if you don't stop it's going to be too late.'

That was as close as she could get to telling him that she suspected she was about to orgasm, but it was obvious that he knew what she was trying to say. He covered the whole of her sex with his hand and then repositioned himself, bending his head to kiss her and then sliding his hands beneath her to lift her, so that her legs were on his shoulders. He moved slowly and deliberately into her, with carefully paced thrusts that took him deeper and deeper and had Keira crying out with fierce pleasure as she rose to meet him, picking up his rhythm until she was the one taking him deeper, holding him there so that her body could take its pleasure of him, tightening around him to caress and enjoy him before eagerly urging him further.

'Faster,' she told him. 'Deeper—deeper, Jay.' Her voice trembled, like her, on the edge of the precipice as Jay gathered himself and waited until Keira's cries told him that she could wait no longer.

As the world swung on its axis and a million darts of pleasure exploded inside her like so many fireworks, Keira clung desperately to Jay.

Her face wet with tears of completion, she told him brokenly, 'That was wonderful.'

'That is just the start,' Jay told her as he wiped away her tears with his thumb-pad. 'There will be many, many wonderful times for us, and many wonders for us to explore together and share.'

CHAPTER TWELVE

JAY HAD BEEN right. As the days had turned into weeks and the weeks into months—three of them, to be exact—there had been many wonderful times. There had been night after night during which she had thought she had climbed the heights, only to discover those heights had been mere foothills of pleasure.

Jay was an expertly sensual teacher, and Keira admitted she was a very eager pupil—his pleasure her own and hers his.

There had been nights when they had lain on the divans and Jay had shown her the beautifully illustrated plates in the ancient copy of the *Kama Sutra* he had told her he had bought as a young man in a bazaar. It had originally been the property of a maharaja whose library had been sold, he had explained to her, and was of immense cultural and financial value.

He had read the text to her, his voice sensually soft and erotic as he stroked the words as delicately as he stroked her skin. Uncertainly at first, but then with growing confidence, Keira had studied the illustrated plates whilst Jay encouraged her to choose a position she found erotically exciting so that they could experience it together. Jay had teased her that they should go through the alphabet, that every night they should pick a different letter and a different position. But some nights they would have run through half a dozen letters before dawn had streaked the sky, and others they would have enjoyed only one, taking their pleasure over and over again.

Against all her expectations—and Keira suspected Jay's as well—his desire for her, far from burning itself out, had actually increased.

When he had to be away from her on business, his return often resulted in him breaking his rule of not having sex in his office, such was the intensity of his physical desire for her.

His *physical* desire for her, Keira reminded herself sadly. Because that was all he felt for her. Physical desire.

There had been pleasure beyond any pleasure she could ever have imagined between them, but for her—hand in hand with that pleasure, measuring it step by step and now finally outweighing it—there had also been terrible pain. It was a pain that came not just from knowing that Jay would never return her feelings, but increasingly from her own unexpected and dangerous feelings of mingled guilt and pain about her past. Guilt because she had withheld the truth about it from Jay, and pain because she could never be her true self with him—because she couldn't ever know the kind of security that came from being accepted as she was.

The reality was that she was living not just one lie but several, and that could not go on. It was destroying her. She lived in fear of letting slip to Jay in the heat of their intimacy the fact that she loved him. She lived in fear of the ultimate ending of their relationship when he grew tired of her. And yet at the same time a part of her longed for the peace of mind that would come from knowing she would no longer need to lie by default.

She couldn't bear the thought of the rejection and contempt she would see in his eyes once he knew the truth about her. And she would see them. She knew that. She hadn't forgotten his attitude towards her when they had first met and he had mistakenly believed that she was the kind of woman willing to offer her body in return for material benefits.

Like mother, like daughter. How often had she heard those words from her great-aunt? They were branded into her—a curse that she carried with her, and a fear that would always haunt her.

She had given in to her own longing to be Jay's lover believing his desire for her would burn itself out in a matter of days—no more than a couple of weeks at most. She had judged that that was something she could survive for the sake of the pleasure it would give her and the memories she would have. But now it had been three months, and with each passing day her longing for what she could not have was growing stronger. Soon it would overwhelm her. Before that happened she had to leave.

Her work on the houses was finished. Jay had been away in Mumbai for the last three days, and in his absence she had forced herself to think about her own situation and to make the decision she knew she must make for her own sake.

Her bags were packed and her ticket for her flight home bought. In just over an hour's time she would be leaving for the airport in the taxi she had already booked. All she had to do was write the letter she had to leave for Jay, telling him that she had completed the work he had commissioned her to do, that she had enjoyed their time together, but that it was time for her to return to London and her own life and career.

He would soon find someone new to replace her in his bed.

* * *

Jay looked out of the window of his private yet as it touched down on the runway. He had no idea why he had felt this compulsion to conclude his business in Mumbai ahead of schedule. It wasn't, after all, the first time he had been apart from Keira during their relationship. His absences had served to increase their desire for one another, and his returns had brought new heights of pleasure for them both. Keira had never reacted to his absence with sulks or demands—nor had she ever indicated that she had missed him, or would have liked to have gone with him. There was no logical reason for him to feel this almost driven urgency to get back to her. She would be there, waiting to welcome him with the sensual eagerness of her body for his possession and her open delight in the pleasure he gave her.

She was the ideal bed partner: sensual and spirited, taking and giving pleasure in equal measure. It had surprised him how much, given the fact that she had been so inexperienced, and yet her acceptance of his terms for their relationship and its lack of any commitment had allowed him to let down his guard with her and show her his passion for her, safe in the knowledge that she came to him out of her own desire for him rather than any desire for what he could give her.

Maybe that was why he continued to want her so intensely long after he had expected to have had his fill of her.

He no longer read the *Kama Sutra* to her because now they had created their own personal repertoire of intimate pleasures—pleasures she had taken eagerly and adapted inventively to her own needs and to his, making them special and personal by the way she had put her own mark on them.

And on him?

Jay frowned. His thoughts were fast-tracking down a route that was becoming all too familiar. No commitment, he had said, and he had meant it. He still meant it.

His car was waiting for him. He preferred to drive himself. He removed his suit jacket, throwing it into the back of the car along with his laptop and his case.

He had seen Bas whilst he had been in Mumbai, and the art director was pressuring him to set up an interview with Keira. The advertising was booked for the launch of the development, and he had seen the photographs of the interiors and understood why the agency he had hired to market the development had been so enthusiastic about its success.

Keira had excelled his remit and produced something that was iconically stylish in concept and yet at the same time extremely liveable. Looking at the photographs, he had caught himself wondering what she might do with his London apartment, had even mentally visualised her living there in it with him. He pressed his foot down on the accelerator. In his pocket was a leather case from one of Mumbai's most exclusive jewellers, containing a pair of antique diamond wrist-cuffs. He had known the moment he had seen them that Keira would love them. They were unique. Just like her.

It was time for her to leave. She could put the letter on Jay's desk on her way out. Keira picked up her bag and reached for the handle of her trolley case.

Her bedroom door opened.

She swung round, the colour leaving her face as she saw Jay standing in the doorway, looking from her to the case and then back again.

His curt, 'What's going on?' didn't do anything to steady her nerves.

Keira knew that her voice was trembling as she told him unsteadily, 'My work here is finished...'

'Your work may be finished, but what about us?'

This was so much worse than she had expected. She must stay focused and be practical, not give in to her longing to beg him to make her stay.

'I have to earn my living, Jay.'

So he had been right all along. It had all been an elaborate set-up—a trick to bring him to this point. A sickening rush of bitter anger seized him. But it wasn't strong enough to stop him giving in and telling her harshly, 'Don't worry. I'll make it worth your while to stay. How much did you have in mind? Ten thousand a month?'

Keira couldn't speak or move. The ferocity of her pain gripped her. It was no good telling herself that she had known what he really thought of her, and that she had no one to blame but herself for the humiliation and anguish she was now suffering. She was, after all, her mother's daughter—wasn't she?

'Not enough? Well, how about if I throw this in as a sweetener?'

Jay reached into his jacket pocket and removed the jeweller's box, which he threw onto the chair close to where Keira was standing.

'Go ahead and open it,' he told her.

Keira felt as though her heart was shrivelling inside her chest, as if she was, in all the ways that really mattered, going through a form of emotional death. It was pointless reminding herself that she had known she would suffer. Knowing had not prepared her for the reality of that pain.

'I'm not for sale, Jay,' she told him. She felt leached of

life and hope, her voice mirroring her feelings and recording her sense of emptiness and loss.

'No?'

'No.'

She thought that he was physically going to stop her from going. And to her shame a part of her actually hoped that he might, despite what he had just said and done. But, although he started to move towards her, he stopped short of reaching her.

She had to walk so close to him that she could almost feel and hear the angry thud of his heartbeat. That same heartbeat she had felt so many times against her own body, and wishing that it might match the love that filled her own heart for him.

Well, she knew now how impossible that was. All Jay wanted was to buy her for as long as he wanted her. That knowledge made her feel acutely sick.

The day she returned home Keira checked her accounts online and found that a very large sum of money indeed had been paid into her business account. Far more than was due to her from Jay on completion of the contract.

Keira emailed him, pointing out his error, and received an email in return saying that the extra was 'for services rendered'. It would not be accepted if it was returned as he always paid his dues.

After she had finished crying Keira made out a cheque for the extra amount and gave it to a charity that helped rescue young women from prostitution, informing them that the money was a gift from Jay.

It was over. It should never have existed in the first place. But now it was over and she had to find a way to get on with her life.

CHAPTER THIRTEEN

SHE JUST HOPED that her potential client kept their appointment, Keira thought as she walked through the entrance of the expensive and very exclusive boutique hotel suggested by the client as a meeting place. Far too exclusive and discreet to have anything as commercial as a foyer, its entrance hall was more like the entrance to a private home.

An elegantly dressed woman wearing what Keira suspected might be Chanel greeted her and suggested that she might like to wait in a private sitting room, overlooking their equally private garden.

The hotel had been designed by a very well-known design team and showed all their hallmark touches. Keira was impressed and envious.

It had been six weeks since she had left India, and each one of them had felt like its own special version of hell.

Things had to get better. *She* had to get better. And she had to get over Jay. She had to stop loving him and wanting him. She had to.

'Hello, Keira.'

Jay! She stood up, and then had to sit down again as her legs refused to support her.

He looked thinner, with lines running from his nose to his mouth that were surely new—unless they were a trick of the light.

'I apologise for tricking you into coming here, but I couldn't think of any other way to get you to see me.' He put down the briefcase he was carrying. 'I've brought some press cuttings to show you, just in case you haven't already seen them. Your work on the houses has attracted rave reviews.'

'I'm glad the development has been a success.' How wooden and stilted her voice sounded—nothing like the voice in which she had told him of the pleasure he was giving her, the pleasure she had wanted him to go on giving her when they had been in bed together. The pain breaking inside her was unbearable, but it had to be borne. She could not escape from it.

'I owe you an apology.'

Could this really be Jay, actually sounding almost humble, actually attempting to be a penitent? Or was she simply imagining it?

'I've missed you, Keira.'

Now she *knew* she was imagining things.

Never in a hundred lifetimes would the Jay she knew have admitted to missing her.

He was looking at her patiently, waiting for her to say something.

'If you are trying to say that you want me back—' she began, only to have him shake his head.

'No, that isn't what I'm trying to say,' he told her crisply.

The hopes she had tried to pretend she didn't have crashed in on her. Why, why, *why* had she let herself hope so stupidly? Because she was a fool and she loved him, that was why.

'What I'm trying to say is that what I thought I wanted from life is not what I want at all. I've changed, Keira. You have changed me. From being a man who didn't want to commit to a woman at any price, I've become a man who would give every penny he possessed for the chance to make a commitment to one very special woman. And that woman is you. I've come to ask if you will give me a chance to show you how special what we've already shared is, and how much more special it can be. I want you—not just in my bed, Keira, but in my life, as my partner, my love, my one and only for all time. I want you to marry me.'

It was a dream. It had to be. This could not be Jay standing here saying these things to her. But it was.

'You can't mean it,' was all she could say.

'I *do* mean it. Perhaps the blow to my head that concussed me brought me to my senses—I don't know. I only know that when I came round in hospital all I wanted was to have you there with me.'

'Hospital? You've been hurt?'

Jay shrugged dismissively.

'A minor car collision—nothing serious. I was driving too fast, trying to escape the demons who were telling me I had just ruined my life, having driven away the one thing that made it worth living.'

The bitter-sweetness of it all tore at Keira's heart. Would it be so very wrong to allow herself the joy of playing make-believe for a few precious minutes before she told him the truth and had to watch him recoil from her? Why not? She had nothing left to lose, after all.

'If you're trying to tell me you love me…' she suggested, with great daring.

'Yes?'

'It might be easier to convince me if you showed me instead.'

It was just a game, just make-believe. And that was the reason, the only reason, she was able to make such a provocative appeal.

'Like this, you mean?'

He had crossed the room in a few strides to take her in his arms.

'You'll never know how much I've missed you,' he told her emotionally, before he kissed her.

This was heaven and hell all rolled into one—pleasure and pain, joy and guilt—and she could not bear to relinquish either Jay or her make-believe dream that somehow there could be a happy-ever-after for them. But she knew that she must. She could not live a lie. She could not and would not deceive him a second time.

'I love you, Keira. I never thought I'd ever want to say those words to any woman, but now not only do I want to say them to you, I want to go on saying them, and not just saying them but living them. I want to hear you saying them to me. Is there any chance that you might do that, do you think?'

'I do love you, Jay.' It was the truth, after all.

His kiss was so sweet and tender, so loving and giving— so very precious when she knew it could be their last.

'I recently opened a letter thanking me for my substantial gift. I take it that donating money to a charity that aids prostitutes was your way of underlining my offence, firstly in misjudging you and secondly in thinking I could buy you?'

It would be easy to be a coward and agree, but her conscience wouldn't let her. She took a deep breath and stepped out of the protection of his arms, fixing her gaze on the wall and not on Jay.

'Actually, I donated your money to that particular charity because of my mother. She was a prostitute, you see, and a drug addict.'

Silence.

'She's dead now. She died when I was twelve. Like mother, like daughter—that's what the great-aunt who took me in after her death used to say to me. It's what people think, isn't it? I feared at one stage that I could grow to be like her myself. She often said to me herself that I would.'

Still silence.

'You're shocked, of course. And disgusted. People are— it's only natural. What kind of responsible parent would want their child playing with a child whose mother sold her body to buy drugs? Certainly the parents of the children I was at school with didn't, and who could blame them? And what kind of man would want to take the risk of having a relationship with a woman whose mother had sex with men for money? You won't want me now, Jay. I know that. You have a responsibility, after all, to your name and to your position.'

'Was that why you stayed a virgin? Because of your mother?'

His question surprised her into looking at him. The silver-grey gaze was filled with something that looked close to pity. Pity? Shouldn't he be regarding her with contempt?

'Yes.'

'Tell me about it.'

Keira wanted to refuse, but somehow she discovered that instead she was telling him how she had felt—the pain of her childhood with its conflicting and confusing feelings, the love for her mother that had sometimes been more like anger and sometimes filled with despair.

'Once I was old enough to understand, I hated what she did,' she told him. 'And sometimes I hated her too, for being what she was. As I grew up we would quarrel about it. During one of our quarrels I told her that I was ashamed of her, and that I would never let myself end up like her. I probably hurt her, although I couldn't see that at the time. She laughed at me and told me that I wouldn't have a choice. She said that since I was her daughter I had inherited her promiscuous nature and that sooner or later, as she put it, some lad would come along and I'd open my legs for him. She said it would be expected of me, and that—like her—I'd love the wrong kind of men for the wrong kind of reasons.'

Keira had to stop talking to swallow against her own sadness. Her mother must have felt so alone and unloved, but she had never seen that before. She had been too young and too emotionally immature herself then to see it. If nothing else, loving Jay had taught her to view her mother in a different and surely a fairer light.

'What she said left me feeling both frightened and angry. I swore to myself that if I had her nature then I would make sure I controlled it.'

'By never having sex?' Jay guessed.

Keira nodded her head.

'Yes. It was easy until I met you. I never guessed...I had no idea...'

'I made you feel that you were like your mother?'

Keira shook her head.

'At first, yes. But then later, once we were lovers, my physical hunger for you showed me that I could never be like my mother. I wanted you so passionately, so exclusively, that I knew I could never give, never mind sell to another man, what I only wanted to give to you. I thank you for that, Jay—because knowing that has freed me from my fear of my own sexuality. My great-aunt and my mother both warned me that I would end up like my mother, but I know now that that will never happen. You won't want me now, of course.'

'On the contrary. If anything, what you have just told me makes me love you even more.'

Keira couldn't believe her ears.

'You can't love me now. I'm not good enough for you, Jay.'

'I am the one who isn't good enough for you. You are worth a hundred—no, a thousand of me, Keira. You humble me with your honesty and your compassion, your generosity of spirit and heart and your loyalty. I am not good enough for you, but that will not prevent me from having the arrogance to beg you to be my wife.'

'Your *wife?*'

'Of course.' Now the look he was giving her was indeed haughty.

'Do you think I would shame our love by not proclaiming it to the world in the most potent way the world recognises? And besides...' both his voice and his expression softened '...I refuse to let there be any chance of me losing you. Once you have committed yourself to me you will stay with me, and with our children. I know you well enough for that. You will be like my mother—faithful and loving. She would have liked you.'

'Jay, you cannot marry me. Your brother won't allow it. You are his heir.'

'Rao is my brother, not my keeper. I make my own decisions about my life. I have already told him of my desire to make you my wife, and he said that he had every sympathy for you.'

He laughed ruefully, and then shook his head.

'I do understand why you have thought the way you have. You have had much to bear and endure that I wish I could have spared you. But our happiness together will be all the sweeter because of the past pain we have both endured. I promise you that there is not a single thought or doubt in my heart or my head about the strength of my love for you. I promise you too that if you refuse me now I shall pursue you and plead with you until you give in and agree to marry me.'

Keira searched his expression, her heart lifting with joy when she saw that he was speaking the truth.

A little unsteadily, but with a heart filled with love, she went into his arms, lifting her face for his kiss.

EPILOGUE

KEIRA WATCHED THE busy preparations for the wedding ceremony from the shadows in the garden beyond the courtyard.

The sun was going down, and on the stillness of the lake the palace seemed to float as ethereally and delicately as the lilies.

In the courtyard the Mandap was being assembled; those wedding guests who had already arrived for tomorrow's ceremony were pausing to watch.

Keira saw the man emerging from the shadows to watch her. He was as male and formidable as the desert lion, and her heart lifted and thudded into her ribs, her breath catching on a swift stab of desire.

'Jay.'

'I thought I might find you here.'

They had been married in a civil ceremony in London earlier in the week, before flying back here to Jay's home to celebrate their marriage with a traditional marriage ceremony.

Last night Rao had held a formal dinner to welcome her into the family, but this was the first time she and Jay had really been alone since their arrival.

'You're wearing the bracelets,' Jay commented as he drew Keira into his arms.

'I couldn't resist,' Keira admitted.

He had given her the Cartier bangles on their first night together, after they had declared their love for one another in a very private celebration.

'What *I* can't resist is loving you,' Jay told her softly. 'Now and for ever.'

'Now and for ever,' Keira agreed, before she reached up to draw him down to her so that she could kiss him.

* * * * *

To my editor for her patience.

THE TYCOON'S VIRGIN

CHAPTER ONE

'Mmm.' Jodi could not resist sneaking a second apprecia-tive look at the man crossing the hotel lobby.

Tall, well over six feet, somewhere in his mid-thirties, dark-suited and even darker-haired, he had an unmistak-able air about him of male sexuality. Jodi had been aware of it the minute she saw him walking towards the hotel exit. His effect on her was strong enough to make her pulse race and her body react to him in a most unusual and un-Jodi-like manner, and just for a second she allowed her thoughts to wander dreamily in a dangerous and sensual direction.

He turned his head and for a shocking breath of time it was almost as though he was looking straight at her; as though some kind of highly intense, personal communi-cation was taking place!

What was happening to her?

Jodi's heart, and with it her whole world, rocked pre-cariously on its oh-so-sturdy axis; an axis constructed of things such as common sense and practicality and doing things by the book, which had suddenly flung her into an alien world. A world where traitorous words such as 'love at first sight' had taken on a meaning.

Love at first sight? Her? Never. Stalwartly, Jodi dragged her world and her emotions back to where they belonged.

It must be the stress she was under that was causing her to somehow emotionally hallucinate!

'Haven't you got enough to worry about?' Jodi scolded herself, far more firmly than she would ever have scolded one of her small pupils. Not that she was given to scolding them very much. No, Jodi loved her job as the headmistress and senior teacher of the area's small junior school with a passion that some of her friends felt ought more properly to be given to her own love life—or rather the lack of it.

And it was because of the school and her small pupils that she was here this evening, waiting anxiously in the foyer of the area's most luxurious hotel for the arrival of her cousin and co-conspirator.

'Jodi.'

She gave a small sigh of relief as she finally saw her cousin Nigel hurrying towards her. Nigel worked several miles away in the local county-council offices and it had been through him that she had first learned of the threat to her precious school.

When he had told her that the largest employer in the area, a factory producing electronic components, had been taken over by one of its competitors and could be closed down her initial reaction had been one of disbelief.

The village where Jodi taught had worked desperately hard to attract new business, and to prevent itself from becoming yet another small, dying community. When the factory had opened some years earlier it had brought not just new wealth to the area, but also an influx of younger people. It was the children of these people who now filled Jodi's classrooms. Without them, the small village school would have to close. Jodi felt passionately about the benefits her kind of school could give young children. But the local authority had to take a wider view; if the school's

pupils fell below a certain number then the school would
be closed.

Having already had to work hard to persuade parents
to support the school, Jodi was simply not prepared to sit
back whilst some arrogant, uncaring asset-stripper of a
manufacturing megalomaniac closed the factory in the
name of profit and ripped the heart out of their community!

Which was why she was here with Nigel.

'What have you found out?' she asked her cousin anxiously, shaking her head as he asked her if she wanted anything to drink. Jodi was not a drinker; in fact she was, as
her friends were very fond of telling her, a little bit old-
fashioned for someone who had gone through several years
at university and teacher-training college. She had even
worked abroad, before deciding that the place she really
wanted to be was the quiet rural heart of her own country.

'Well, I know that he's booked into the hotel. The best
suite, no less, although apparently he isn't in it at the moment.'

When Jodi exhaled in relief Nigel gave her a wry look.
'You were the one who wanted to see him,' he reminded
her. 'If you've changed your mind...?'

'No,' Jodi denied. 'I have to do something. It's all over
the village that he intends to close down the factory. I've
already had parents coming to see me to say that they're
probably going to have to move away, and asking me to
recommend good local schools for them when they do.
I'm already only just over the acceptable pupil number as
it is, Nigel. If I were to lose even five per cent of my pupils...' She gave a small groan. 'And the worst of it is that
if we can only hang on for a couple more years I've got a
new influx due that will take us well into a good safety
margin, providing, that is, the factory is still operational.
That's why I've got to see this...this...'

'Leo Jefferson,' Nigel supplied for her. 'I've managed to talk the receptionist into letting me have a key to his suite.' He grinned when he saw Jodi's expression. 'It's OK, I know her, and I've explained that you've got an appointment with him but that you've arrived early. So I reckon the best thing is for you to get up there and lie in wait to pounce on him when he gets back.'

'I shall be doing no such thing,' Jodi told him indignantly. 'What I want to do is make sure he understands just how much damage he will be doing to this village if he goes ahead and closes the factory. And try to persuade him to change his mind.'

Nigel watched her ruefully as she spoke. Her high-minded ideals were all very well, but totally out of step with the mindset of a man with Leo Jefferson's reputation. Nigel was tempted to suggest to Jodi that a warm smile and a generous helping of feminine flirtation might do more good than the kind of discussion she was obviously bent on having, but he knew just how that kind of suggestion would be received by her. It would be totally against her principles.

Which was rather a shame in Nigel's opinion, because Jodi certainly had the assets to bemuse and beguile any red-blooded man. She was stunningly attractive, with the kind of lushly curved body that made men ache just to look at her, even if she did tend to cover its sexy female shape with dull, practical clothes.

Her hair was thick and glossily curly, her eyes a deep, deliciously dark-fringed, vibrant blue above her delicately high cheekbones. If she hadn't been his cousin and if they hadn't known one another since they had been in their prams he would have found her very fanciable himself. Except that Nigel liked his girlfriends to treat flirtation and sex as an enjoyable game. And Jodi was far too serious for that.

At twenty-seven, she hadn't, so far as Nigel knew, ever had a serious relationship, preferring to dedicate herself to her work. Nigel knew that there were more than a handful of men who considered that dedication to be a total waste.

As she took the key card her cousin was handing her Jodi hoped that she was doing the right thing.

Her throat suddenly felt nervously dry, and when she admitted as much to Nigel he told her that he'd arrange to have something sent up to the suite for her to drink.

'Can't have you driven so mad by thirst that you raid the mini-bar, can we?' he teased her, chuckling at his own joke.

'That's not funny,' Jodi immediately reproved him.

She still felt guilty about the underhanded means by which she was gaining access to Leo Jefferson's presence, but according to Nigel this was the only way to get the opportunity to speak personally with him.

She had originally hoped to be able to make an appointment, but Nigel had quickly disabused her of this idea, telling her wryly that a corporate mogul such as Leo Jefferson would never deign to meet a humble village schoolteacher.

And that was why this unpleasant subterfuge was necessary.

Ten minutes later, as she let herself into his hotel suite, Jodi hoped that it wouldn't be too long before Leo Jefferson returned. She had been up at six that morning, working on a project for her older pupils, who would be moving on to 'big' school at the end of their current year.

It was almost seven o'clock, past Jodi's normal evening-meal time, and she felt both tired and hungry. She stiffened nervously as she heard the suite door opening, but it was only a waiter bringing her the drink Nigel had promised her. She eyed the large jug of brightly coloured fruit juice he had put down on the coffee-table in front of her a little ruefully as the door closed behind the departing waiter. Good old plain water would have been fine. Her mouth felt dry with nervous tension and she poured herself a glass, drinking it quickly. It had an unfamiliar but not unpleasant taste, which for some odd reason seemed to make her feel that she wanted some more. Her hand wobbled slightly as she poured herself a second glass.

She read the newspaper she had found on the coffee-table, and rehearsed her speech several times. Where was Leo Jefferson? Tiredly she started to yawn, gasping with shock as she stood up and swayed dizzily.

Heavens, but she felt so light-headed! Suspiciously she focused on the jug of fruit juice. That unfamiliar taste couldn't possibly have been alcohol, could it? Nigel knew that she wasn't a drinker.

Muzzily she looked round the suite for the bathroom. Leo Jefferson was bound to arrive soon, and she wanted to be looking neat and tidy and strictly businesslike when he did. First impressions, especially in a situation like this, were very important!

The bathroom was obviously off the bedroom. Which she could see through the half-open door that connected it to the suite's sitting room.

A little unsteadily she made her way towards it. What on earth had been in that drink?

In the suite's huge all-white bathroom, Jodi washed her hands, dabbing cold water on her pulse points as she gazed uncertainly at her flushed face in the mirror above the basin before turning to leave.

In the bedroom she stopped to stare longingly at the huge, comfortable-looking bed. She just felt so tired. How much longer was this wretched man going to be?

Another yawn started to overwhelm her. Her eyelids felt heavy. She just had to lie down. Just for a little while. Just until she felt less light-headed.

But first…

With the careful concentration of the inebriated, Jodi removed her clothes with meticulous movements and folded them neatly before sliding into the heavenly bliss of the waiting bed.

As Leo Jefferson unlocked the door to his hotel suite he looked grimly at his watch. It was half-past ten in the evening and he had just returned to the hotel, having been to inspect one of the two factories he had just acquired. Prior to that, earlier in the day, he had spent most of the afternoon locked in a furious argument with the now ex-owner of his latest acquisition, or rather the ex-owner's unbelievably idiotic son-in-law, who had done everything he could at first to bully and then bribe Leo into releasing them from their contract.

'Look, my father-in-law made a mistake. We all make them,' he had told Leo with fake affability. 'We've changed our minds and we no longer want to sell the business.'

'It's a bit late for that,' Leo had replied crisply. 'The deal has already gone through; the contract's been signed.'

But Jeremy Driscoll continued to try to browbeat Leo into changing his mind.

'I'm sure we can find some way to persuade you,' he told Leo, giving him a knowing leer as he added, 'One of those new lap-dancing clubs has opened up in town, and I've heard they cater really well for the needs of lonely businessmen. How about we pay it a visit? My treat, we can talk later, when we're both feeling more relaxed.'

'No way,' was Leo's grim rejection.

The gossip he had heard on the business grapevine

about Jeremy Driscoll had suggested that he was a seedy character—apparently it wasn't unknown for him to try to get his own way by underhanded means. At first Leo had been prepared to give him the benefit of the doubt—until he met him and recognised that Jeremy Driscoll's detractors had erred on the side of generosity.

A more thoroughly unpleasant person Leo had yet to meet, and his obvious air of false bonhomie offended Leo almost as much as his totally unwarranted and unwanted offer of bought sex.

The kind of place, any kind of place, where human beings had to sell themselves for other people's pleasure had no appeal for Leo, and he made little attempt to conceal his contempt for the other man's suggestion.

Jeremy Driscoll, though, it seemed, had a skin of impenetrable thickness. Refusing to take a hint, he continued jovially, 'No? You prefer to have your fun in private on a one-to-one basis, perhaps? Well, I'm sure that something can be arranged—'

Leo's cold, 'Forget it,' brought an ugly look of dislike to Jeremy's too pale blue eyes.

'There's a lot of antagonism around here about the fact that you're planning to close down one or other of the factories. A man with your reputation...'

'Oh, I think my reputation can stand the heat,' Leo replied grittily.

He could see that his confidence had increased Jeremy's dislike of him, just as he had seen the envy in the other man's eyes when he had driven up in his top-of-the-range Mercedes.

Out of the corner of his eye he caught sight of the newspaper that Jeremy had rudely continued to read after Leo's arrival. There was an article on the page that was open detailing the downfall of a politician who had tried unsuc-

cessfully to sue those who had exposed certain tawdry
aspects of his private life, including his visits to a mas-
sage parlour. The fact that the politician had claimed that
he had been set up had not convinced the jury who had
found against him.

'I wouldn't be so sure about your reputation if I were
you,' Jeremy warned Leo nastily, glancing towards the
paper as he spoke.

Giving him a dismissive look, Leo left.

Leo frowned as he walked into his suite. There was no
way in a thousand years he was going to change his plans.
He had worked too hard and for too long, building up his
business from nothing...less than nothing, slowly, pains-
takingly clawing his way up from his own one-man band,
first overtaking and then taking over his competition as
he grew more and more successful.

The Driscoll family company was in direct competition to Leo's. Since their business duplicated his own, it
was only natural that he should have to close down some
of their four factories. As yet Leo had not decided which
out of the four. But as for Jeremy Driscoll's attempt to get
him to back out of the deal...!

Tired, Leo strode into the suite without bothering to
switch on the lights. At this time on a June evening there
was still enough light in the sky for him not to need to
do so, even without the additional glow of the almost full
moon.

The bedroom wasn't quite as well-lit; someone—the
maid, he imagined—had closed the curtains, but the bathroom light was on and the door open. Frowning over such
sloppiness, he headed towards the bathroom, closing the
door behind him once he was inside.

Giving his own reflection a brief glance in the mirror,

he paused to rub a lean hand over his stubble-darkened jaw before reaching for his razor.

Jeremy Driscoll's bombastic arrogance had irritated him to an extent that warned him that those amongst his family and friends who cautioned that he was driving himself too hard might have something of a point.

Narrowing the silver-grey eyes that were an inheritance from his father's side, and for whose piercingly analytical and defence-stripping qualities they were rightly feared by anyone who sought to deceive him, he grimaced slightly. He badly needed a haircut; his dark hair curled over the collar of his shirt. Taking time out for anything in his life that wasn't work right now simply wasn't an option.

His parents professed not to understand just where he got his single-minded determination to succeed from. They had been happy with their small newsagent's business.

His parents were retired now, and living in his mother's family's native Italy. He had bought them a villa outside Florence as a ruby-wedding present.

Leo had visited them, very briefly, early in May for his mother's birthday.

He put down his razor, remembering the look he had seen them exchange when his mother had asked wistfully if there was yet 'anyone special' in his life.

He had told her with dry humour that not only did his negative response to her maternal question relate to his present, but that it could also be applied indefinitely to his future.

With unusual asperity she had returned that if that was the case then it was perhaps time she paid a visit to the village's local wise woman and herbalist, who, according to rumour, had an absolutely foolproof recipe for a love potion!

Leo had laughed outright at that. After all, it was not

that he couldn't have a partner, a lover, if he so wished. Any number of stunningly attractive young women had made it plain to him both discreetly and rather more obviously that they would like to share his life and his bed, and, of course, his bank account... But Leo could still remember how at the upmarket public school he had won a scholarship to the female pupils had been scornfully dismissive of the boy whose school uniform was so obviously bought secondhand and whose only source of money came from helping out in his parents' small business.

That experience had taught Leo a lesson he was determined never to forget. Yes, there had been women in his life, but no doubt rather idiotically by some people's standards, he had discovered that he possessed an unexpected aversion to the idea of casual sex. Which meant...

Unwantedly Leo remembered his body's sharply explicit reaction to the woman he had seen in the hotel foyer as he had crossed it on his way to his meeting earlier.

Small and curvy, or so he had suspected, beneath the abominable clothes she had been wearing.

Leo's mother did not have Italian blood for nothing, and, like all her countrywomen, she possessed a strong sense of personal style, which made it impossible for Leo not to recognise when a woman was dressing to maximum effect. This woman had most certainly not been doing that at all. She had not even really been his type. If he was prepared to admit to a preference it was for cool, elegant blondes. Most definitely not for delectably sexy, tousled and touchable types of women, who turned his loins to hotly savage lust and even distracted his mind to the extent that he had almost found himself deviating from his set course and thinking about walking towards her.

Leo never deviated from any course he set himself—ever—especially not on account of a woman.

With an indrawn breath of self-disgust, Leo stripped off his clothes and stepped into the shower.

As a teenager he had played sports for his school, which, ironically, had done wonders to increase his 'pulling power' with his female schoolmates, and he still had the powerful muscle structure of a natural athlete. Impatiently he lathered his body and then rinsed off the foam before reaching for a towel.

Once dry, he opened the bathroom door and headed for the bed. It was darker now, but still light enough, thanks to the moonlight glinting through the curtains, for him not to need to switch on the light.

Flipping back the bedclothes, Leo got into the bed, reaching automatically for the duvet, and then froze as he realised that the bed—*his* bed—was already occupied.

Switching on the bedside lamp, he stared in angry disbelief at the tousled head of curly hair on the pillow next to his own—a decidedly female head, he recognised, just like the slender naked arm and softly rounded shoulder he could now see in the lamplight.

The nostrils of the proudly aquiline nose he had inherited from his mother's Italian forebears flared fastidiously as they picked up the smell of alcohol on the softly exhaled breath of the oblivious sleeping form.

Another scent—a mixture of warm fresh air, lavender and a certain shockingly earthy sensuality that was Jodi's alone—his senses reacted to in a very different way.

It was the girl from the foyer. Leo would have recognised her anywhere, or, rather, his body would.

Automatically his brain passed him another piece of information. Jeremy Driscoll's oily-voiced suggestiveness as he had tried to persuade Leo to go back on their contract. Was this...this girl the inducement he'd had in mind? She had to be. Leo could not think of any other reason for her presence here in his bed!

Well, if Jeremy Driscoll dared to think that he, Leo, was the kind of man who…

Angrily he reached out to grasp Jodi's bare arm in strong fingers as he leaned across her to shake her into wakefulness.

Jodi was fathoms-deep asleep, sleeping the sleep of the pure of heart—and the alcohol-assisted—and she was having the most delicious dream in which she was, by some means her sleeping state wasn't inclined to question, wrapped in the embrace of the most gorgeous, sexy man. He was tall, dark-haired and silver-eyed, with features re-assuringly familiar to Jodi, but his body, his touch, were wonderfully and excitingly new.

They were lying together, body to body, on a huge bed in a room with a panoramic view of a private tropical beach, and as he leaned towards her and stroked strong fingers along her forearm he whispered to her, 'What the hell are you doing in my bed?'

Her brain still under the influence of her 'fruit cocktail' Jodi opened bemused, adoring eyes.

Why was her wonderful lover looking so angry? Smiling sleepily up at him, she was about to ask him, but somehow her attention became focused on how downright desirable he actually was.

That wonderful naked golden-brown body. Naked. Yummy! More than yummy! Jodi closed her eyes on a sigh of female appreciation and then quickly opened them again, anxious not to miss anything. She watched the way the muscles in his neck corded as he leaned over her, and the sinewy strength of his solid forearms, so very male that she just had to reach out and run an explorative fingertip

down the one nearest to her, marvelling at the difference
between it and her own so much softer female flesh.

Leo couldn't believe his eyes—or his body. She, the
uninvited interloper in his bed, was brazenly ignoring his
angry question and was actually daring to touch him. No,
not just touch, he acknowledged as his body reacted to her
with a teeth-clenching jerk that gave an immediate lie to
his previous mental use of the word 'unwanted'. What she
was doing—dammit—was outright stroking him, caressing him!

Torn between a cerebral desire to reject what was happening and a visceral surge of agonisingly intense desire
to embrace it, and with it the woman who was tormenting
him with such devastating effectiveness, Leo made a val-
iant struggle to cling to the tenets of discipline and self-
control that were the twin bastions of his life. To his shock,
he lost. And not just the campaign but the whole war!

Jodi, though, fuelled now by something far more subtle than alcohol, and far stronger, was totally oblivious
to everything but the delicious dream she had found her
way into.

Imagine. When she touched him, like so, the most extraordinary tremors ran right through his whole body—
and not just his, she acknowledged as she considered the
awesome fact that her own body was so highly responsive,
so reactive to every movement of his.

She was so lucky to be here with him on this wonderful private island of love and pleasure. Tenderly she leaned
forward and flicked her tongue-tip delicately against the
hollow at the base of his throat, revelling in the sensation
of his damp skin against her tongue, its texture, its taste,
the way that fierce male pulse thudded to life at her touch.

Leo couldn't believe what was happening. What she
was doing; what he was letting her do. He found himself

lying back against the pillow as she was the one to arch provocatively over him, whilst her tongue busily and far too erotically laved his skin.

Even in the less than half-light of the shadowy bedroom he could see the naked outline of her body with its narrow waist and softly flaring hips; her legs were delectably shaped, her ankles tiny and delicate, the shadowy triangle of hair between her thighs so soft and tempting that...

His throat dry with angry tension and gut-wrenching longing, Leo felt his whole body shudder.

He could see her breasts, soft, rounded, creamy-skinned, with darkly tender crests and tormentingly erect nipples.

Unable to stop himself, he lifted his hands carefully, cupping them. He could feel their warm weight, and he could feel, too, the tight hardness of those wanton peaks, tauntingly challenging him to...

Jodi gasped and then shivered in delight as she felt the rough pressure of her lover's tongue against her nipple.

'Oh, it feels so good,' she whispered to him, closing her eyes as she gave herself up to the sensations he was arousing. Her hand slipped distractedly from his arm to her own body, flattening betrayingly against her belly as she drew in a juddering breath of delirious pleasure.

Leo could scarcely believe the sheer wantonness of her reaction to his touch. He tried to remind himself that she was there for a purpose, doing the job she had been hired for, but his senses were too drugged to allow him to think rationally.

He had known then, in that fleeting second he had seen her in the hotel foyer, that she could affect him like this; that he would want her like this, no matter what the stern voice of his conscience was trying to tell him.

His hand slid to the curve of her waist and flared possessively over her hip, which fitted as perfectly into his grip as though they had been made for each other.

Her hands were on his body, their touch somehow innocently explorative, as though he was the first man she had ever been so intimate with—which was a ludicrous thought!

The soft whispers of female praise she was giving him had to be deliberately calculated to have the maximum effect on a man's ego—any man's ego—he tried to remind himself. But somehow he couldn't stop touching her— couldn't stop *wanting* her!

Jodi sighed blissfully in a sensual heaven. He seemed to know instinctively just how and where to caress her, how to arouse and please her. Her body soared and melted with each wonderful wave of erotic pleasure. Voluptuously she snuggled closer to him shivering in heady excitement as she let her hands wander at will over his body—so excitingly different from her own.

The bedclothes, which she had pushed away an aeon ago so that she could look at the powerful nakedness of the male body she was now so hungry for, lay in a tangled heap at the bottom of the bed. Moonlight silvered her own body, whilst it turned the larger and more muscular shape of her lover's into a dark-hued steel.

She ached so much for him. Her hands moved downwards over him, her gaze drawn to his taut, powerful magnificence.

Deliberately she drew her fingertips along the hard length of his erection, closing her eyes and shuddering as a deep thrill twisted through her.

Leo couldn't understand how he was letting this happen! It went totally against everything he believed in! Never before in his life had he experienced such intense and overwhelmingly mindless desire, nor been so driven

by the fierce pulse of it to take what he was being so
openly offered.

Every single one of his senses was responding to her
with an uncheckable urgency that left his brain flounder-
ing.

The scent, the sight, the feel of her, her touch against his
body, even the soft, increasingly incoherent sound of her
husky, pleading moans, seemed to strike at a vulnerability
inside him that he had never dreamed existed.

He reached out for her, giving in to the need burning
through him to kiss every delicious woman-scented inch
of her, and then to do so all over again, slowly and thoroughly, until the unsteadiness of her breathing was a torment to his senses. He finally allowed himself the pleasure
of sliding his fingers through the soft, warm tangle of curls
concealing her sex, stroking the flesh that lay beneath and
slowly parting the outer covering of her to caress her with
full intimacy.

She felt soft, hot, moist and so unbelievably delicate
that, ignoring the agonised urging of her voice against
his ear, he forced himself to love her slowly and carefully.

He could feel her body rising up to reach his touch as
she writhed frantically against him, telling him in broken
words of open pleasure that jolted like electricity through
his senses just what she wanted from him and how. She
somehow managed to manoeuvre both of them so that he
was pushing urgently against her and then inside her, as
though the intimacy was beyond his own physical control.

She felt. She felt...

Jodi heard the low, visceral male sound he made as he
entered her, filled her, and sharp spirals of intense pleasure flooded her body.

Just hearing that sound, knowing his need, was almost
as erotically exciting as feeling him move inside her. Long,

slow, powerful thrusts lifted and carried her and caused her to reach out for him, drawing him deep inside her. The pleasure of feeling her body expand to accommodate him was so indescribably precious that she cried out aloud her joy in it and in him. She loved this feeling of being wrapped around him, embracing him, holding him, somehow nurturing and protecting his essential male essence.

Somewhere on the periphery of his awareness, Leo recognised that there was something that his mind should be aware of, something important his body was trying to tell him, something about both the intensity of what he was experiencing and the special, close-fitting intimacy of the tender female body wrapped around his own. But the age-old urgency of the need now driving him was short-circuiting his ability to question anything.

All he knew was how good she felt, how right, how essential it was that he reciprocate the wonderful gift she was giving him by taking them both to that special place that lay so tantalisingly almost within reach…another second, another stroke, another heartbeat.

He felt her orgasm gripping her; spasm after spasm of such vibrant intensity that its sheer strength brought him to his own completion.

As she lay in his arms, her body trembling in the aftershock of her pleasure, her damp curls a wild tangle of soft silk against his chest, he heard her gasping shakily, 'That was wonderful, my wonderful, wonderful lover.'

And then as he looked down into her eyes she closed them and fell asleep, with all the speed and innocence of a child.

Broodingly Leo studied her. There was no doubt in his mind that she was a plant, bought and paid for with Jeremy Driscoll's money.

And he, idiotic fool that he was, had fallen straight into

the trap that had been set for him. And he suspected, now that he had time to think things through properly, that this was something more than Jeremy Driscoll supplying him with a bedmate for the night.

Jeremy was simply not that altruistic. Not altruistic in any way, shape or form, and Leo knew that he had not mistaken the dislike and envy in the other man's eyes earlier in the day. Jeremy knew that he, Leo, was not about to change his mind. Not unless Jeremy Driscoll believed he had some means of forcing him to do so.

Now, when it was too late, Leo remembered the newspaper article Jeremy Driscoll had been reading,

For a man in his position, an unmarried man, the effect of a public exposé, a woman selling her kiss-and-tell story to one of the national newspapers, would not be devastating. But Leo would be pilloried as a laughing stock for being so gullible and, as a result, would lose respect in the business world. If that happened he would not be able to count on the support and belief he was used to. No businessman, not even one as successful as Leo, wanted that.

He got out of bed, giving Jodi a bitter look as he did so. How could she lie there sleeping so peacefully? As though…as though… Unable to stop himself, Leo felt his glance slide to her mouth, still curved in a warmly satisfied smile. Even in her sleep she was somehow managing to maintain the fiction that what had happened between them was something special. But then no doubt she was a skilled actress. She would have to be.

The reality of what he had done pushed relentlessly through his thoughts. His behaviour had been so totally alien that even now he couldn't imagine what had possessed him. Or, at least, he could, but he couldn't understand how he had allowed it to get so out of control.

Or why he was standing beside the bed and continuing

to look at her, when surely his strongest urge ought to be to go and have a shower as hot and strong as he could stand until he had washed the feel, the scent, the taste of her off his body and out of his senses. But for some incomprehensible reason that was the last thing he wanted to do...

Just in time he managed to stop himself from reaching out to touch her, to stroke a gentle fingertip along that tender cheekbone and touch those unbelievably long, dark lashes, that small, straight nose, those soft, full lips.

As though somehow she sensed what he was thinking, her lips parted on a sweetly sensual sigh, her mouth curling back into another smile of remembered pleasure.

What the hell was he doing, letting her sleep there like that? By rights he ought to wake her up and throw her out. He glanced at the alarm clock supplied by the hotel. It was two o'clock in the morning, and he told himself that it was because of his inbred sense of responsibility that he could not bring himself to do so.

It just wasn't safe for a woman—any woman, even a woman like her—to wander about on her own so late at night; anything could happen to her!

But he wasn't going to get back in that bed with her. No way!

Going into the bathroom, he pulled on the complimentary robe provided by the hotel and then made his way into the sitting room, closing the bedroom door behind him as he did so and snapping on the light.

The first thing he saw was the almost empty cocktail jug and the glass Jodi had drunk from.

Grimacing, he pushed it to one side. She had even had the audacity to order a drink on Room Service. Because she had needed the courage it would give her to go to bed with him?

He warned himself against falling into the trap of feeling sorry for her, making excuses for her. She had known exactly what she was doing... Exactly... He frowned as he moved a little uncomfortably in his chair.

He was wide awake now and he had some work he could be doing. When his would-be seducer woke up they were going to need to have a short, sharp talk.

There was no way he was going to allow Jeremy Driscoll to blackmail him into backing out of the contract he had made with his father-in-law.

Still frowning, he reached for his briefcase.

CHAPTER TWO

RUBBING HER EYES, Jodi grimaced in disgust at the sour taste in her mouth. Her head ached, and her body did too, but they were different sorts of aches; the ache in her body had a subtle but quite distinctly pleasurable undertone to it, whilst the one in her head…

Cautiously she moved it and then wished she had not as a fierce, throbbing pain banged through her temples.

Instinctively she reached across, expecting to find her own familiar bedside table, and then realised that she was not in her own bed.

So where exactly was she? Like wisps of mist, certain vague memories, sounds, images, drifted dangerously across her mind. But no, surely she couldn't have? Hadn't! Frantically she looked to the other side of the large bed, the sledgehammer thuds of her heart easing as she saw to her relief that it was empty.

It had been a dream, that was all, a shocking and unacceptable dream. And she couldn't imagine how or why… But… She froze as she saw the quite unmistakable imprint of another head on the pillow next to her own.

Shivering, she leaned closer to it, stiffening as she caught the alien but somehow all-too-familiar scent of soap and man rising from the pillow.

What had been vague memories were becoming sharper and clearer with every anxious beat of her heart.

It was true! Here in this room. In this bed! She had. Where was he? She looked nervously towards the bathroom door, her attention momentarily distracted by the sight of her own clothes neatly folded on a chair.

Without pausing for logical thought she scrambled out of the bed and hurried towards them, dressing with urgency whilst she kept her gaze fixed on the closed bathroom door.

She longed to be able to shower and clean her teeth, brush her hair, but she simply did not dare to do so. Appallingly explicit memories were now forcing themselves past the splitting pain of her alcohol-induced headache. She couldn't comprehend how on earth she could have behaved in such a way.

She had been drinking, she reminded herself with disgusted self-contempt. She had been drinking, and whatever had been in that potent cocktail Room Service had sent up to the suite had somehow turned her from the prim and proper virginal woman she was into a...an amorous, sexually aggressive female, who...

Virginal! Jodi's body froze. Well, she certainly wasn't that any more! Not that it mattered except for the fact that, driven by her desire, she hadn't taken any steps to protect her health or to prevent...

Jodi begged fate not to punish her foolishness, praying that there would be no consequences to what she had done other than her own shocked humiliation.

Picking up her handbag, she tiptoed quietly towards the bedroom door.

Leo was just wondering how long his unwanted guest intended to continue to sleep in *his* bed, and whether or not

five a.m. was too early to ring for a room-service breakfast, when Jodi reached for the bedroom door.

Even though his body ached for sleep, he had been furiously determined not to get back into his bed whilst she
was in it. One experience of just how vulnerable he was
to her particularly effective method of seduction was more
than enough.

Even now, having had the best part of three hours of sol-
itude to analyse what had happened, he was still no closer
to understanding why he had been unable to stop himself
from responding to her, unable to control his desire.

Yes, he had felt that bittersweet pang of attraction when
he had first seen her in the hotel foyer, but knowing what
she was ought surely to have destroyed that completely.

He tensed as he saw the bedroom door opening.

At first, intent on making her escape, Jodi didn't see
him standing motionlessly in front of the window.

It was light now, the clear, fresh light of an early summer morning, and when she did realise that he was there
her face flushed as sweetly pink as the sun-warmed feath-
ers of clouds in the sky beyond the window.

Leo heard her involuntary gasp and saw the quick, de-
spairing glance she gave the main door, her only exit from
the suite. Anticipating her actions, he moved towards the
door, reaching it before her and standing in front of it,
blocking her escape.

As she saw him properly Jodi felt the embarrassed heat
possessing her body deepen to a burning, soul-scorching
intensity. It was him, the man she had seen in the foyer,
the man she had thought so very attractive, the man who
had made her have the most extraordinarily uncharacteristic thoughts!

Out of the corner of her eye Jodi could see the coffee-
table and the telltale cocktail jug.

'Yes,' Leo agreed urbanely. 'Not only have you illegally entered my suite, but you also had the gall to run up a room-service bill. Do you intend to pay personally for the use of my bed and the bar, or would you prefer me to send the bills to Jeremy Driscoll?'

Jodi, who had been staring in mute distress at the cocktail jug, turned her head automatically to look at him as she heard the familiar name of her least favourite fellow villager.

'Jeremy?' she questioned uncertainly.

Jeremy Driscoll's father-in-law might own the local factory, and Jeremy himself might run it, but that did not make him well-liked in the locale. He had a reputation for underhand behaviour, and for attempting to bring in certain cost-cutting and potentially dangerous practices, which thankfully had been blocked by the workers' union and the health and safety authority.

But what he had to do with her present humiliating situation Jodi had no idea at all.

'Yes. Jeremy,' Leo confirmed, unkindly imitating the anxious tremor in her voice. 'I know exactly what's going on,' he continued acidly. 'And why you're here. But if you think for one minute that I'm going to allow myself to be blackmailed into giving in...'

Jodi swallowed uncomfortably against the tight ball of self-recrimination and shame that was lodged in her throat.

Did Leo Jefferson—it had to be him—really think that she was the kind of person who would behave in such a way? His use of the word 'blackmail' had particularly shocked her. But was the truth any easier for her to bear, never mind admit to someone else? Was it really any more palatable to have to say that she had been so drunk—albeit by accident—that she simply had not known what she was doing?

To have gone to bed with a complete stranger, to have done the things she had done with him, and, even worse, wanted the things she had wanted with him... A woman in her position, responsible for the shaping and guiding of young minds...

Jodi shuddered to think of how some of the parents of her pupils, not to mention the school's board of governors, might view her behaviour.

'Well, you can go back to your paymaster,' Leo Jefferson was telling her with cold venom, 'and you can tell him, whilst you might have given me good value for his money, it makes not one jot of difference to my plans. I still have no intention of cancelling the contract and allowing him to buy back the business.

'I have no idea what he hoped to achieve by paying you to have sex with me,' Leo continued grimly and untruthfully. 'But all he gave me was a night of passably good if somewhat over-professionalised sex. If he thinks he can use that against me in some way...' Leo shrugged to underline his indifference whilst discreetly watching Jodi to see how she was reacting to his fabricated insouciance.

She had gone very pale, and there was a look in her eyes that under other circumstances Leo might almost have described as haunted.

Jodi fought to control her spiralling confusion and to make sense out of what Leo Jefferson was saying. She was going to avoid thinking about his cruelly insulting personal comments right now. They were the kind of thing she could only allow herself to examine in private. But his references to Jeremy Driscoll and her own supposed connection with him were totally baffling.

She opened her mouth to say as much, but before she could do so Leo was exclaiming tersely, 'I don't know who you are or why you can't find a less self-destructive way of earning a living.'

Ignoring the latter part of his comment, Jodi pounced with shaky relief on his 'I don't know who you are'.

If he didn't know who she was, she certainly wasn't going to enlighten him. With any luck she might, please fate, be able to salvage her pride and her public reputation with a damage-limitation exercise that meant no one other than the two of them need ever know what had happened.

She had abandoned any thought of pursuing her real purpose in seeking him out. How on earth could she plead with him for her school's future now? Another burden of sickening guilt joined the one already oppressing her. She had not just let herself down, and her standards, she had let the school and her pupils down as well. And she still couldn't fully understand how it had all happened. Yes, she had had too much to drink, but surely that alone...

Cringing, she reflected on her reaction to Leo Jefferson when she had seen him walking across the hotel foyer the previous evening. Then, of course, she had not known who he was. Only that...only that she found him attractive...

She felt numbed by the sheer unacceptability of what she had done, shamed and filled with the bleakest sense of disbelief and despair.

Her lack of any response and her continued silence were just a ploy she was using as a form of gamesmanship, Leo decided as he watched her, and as for that anguished shock he had seen earlier in her eyes, well, as he had good cause to know, she was an extremely accomplished performer!

'I have to go. Please let me past.'

The soft huskiness of her voice reminded Leo of the way she had moaned her desire to him during the night.

What the hell was the matter with him? He couldn't possibly still want her!

Even though he had made no move to stand away from the door, Jodi walked towards it as determinedly as she could. She had, she reminded herself, faced a whole roomful of disruptive teenage pupils of both sexes during her teacher training without betraying her inner fear. Surely she could outface one mere man? Only somehow the use of the word 'mere' in connection with this particular man brought a mirthless bubble of painful laughter to her throat.

This man could never be a 'mere' anything. This man...

She had guts, Leo acknowledged as she stared calmly past him, but then no doubt her chosen profession would mean that she was no stranger to the art of making a judicious exit.

It went against everything he believed in to forcibly constrain her, even though he was loath to let her go without reinforcing just what he thought of her and the man who was paying her.

Another second and she would have been so close to him that they would almost have been body to body, Jodi recognised on a mute shudder of distress as Leo finally allowed her access to the door. Expelling a shaky, pent-up breath of relief, she reached for the handle.

Leo waited until she had turned it before reminding her grimly, 'Driscoll might think this was a clever move, but you can tell him from me that it wasn't. Oh, and just a word of warning for you personally: any attempt to publicise what happened between us last night and I can promise you that any ridicule I suffer you will suffer ten times more.'

Jodi didn't speak. She couldn't. This was the most painful, the most shameful experience she had ever had or ever wanted to have.

But it seemed that Leo Jefferson still hadn't finished

with her, because as she stepped out into the hotel corridor he took hold of the door, placing his hand over hers in a grip that was like a volt of savage male electricity burning through her body.

'Of course, if you'd been really clever you could have sold your story where it would have gained you the highest price already.'

Jodi couldn't help herself; even though it was the last thing she wanted to do, she heard herself demanding gruffly, 'What…what do you mean?'

The cynically satisfied smile he gave her made her shudder.

'What I mean is that I'm surprised you haven't tried to bargain a higher price for your silence from me than the price Driscoll paid you for your services.'

Jodi couldn't believe what she was hearing.

'I don't…I didn't…' She began to defend herself instinctively, before shaking her head and telling him fiercely, 'There isn't any amount of money that could compensate me for what…what I experienced last night.' And then, before he could say or do anything more to hurt her, she managed to wrench her hand from his and run down the corridor towards the waiting lift.

A girl wearing the uniform of a member of the hotel staff paused to look at her as Jodi left Leo's suite, but Jodi was too engrossed in her thoughts to notice her.

Leo watched her go in furious disbelief. Just how much of a fool did she take him for, throwing out a bad Victorian line like that? And as for what she had implied, well, his body had certain very telltale marks on it that told a very different story indeed!

To Jodi's relief, no one gave her a second glance as she hurried through the hotel foyer, heading for the exit. No doubt they were used to guests coming and going all the time.

'Stop thinking about it,' she advised herself as she stepped out into the bright morning sunlight, blinking a little in its brilliance.

The first thing she was going to do when she got home, Jodi decided as she drove out onto the main road, was have a shower, and the second was to compose the letter she would send to Leo Jefferson, putting to him the case for allowing the factory to remain open—there was no way she was going to try to make any kind of personal contact with him now!

And the third: the third was to go to bed and catch up on her sleep, and very firmly put what had happened between them out of her mind, consign it to a locked and deeply buried part of her memory that could never be accessed again by anyone!

Jodi opened the front door to her small cottage, one of a row of eight, built in the eighteenth century, with tiny, picturesque front gardens overlooking the village street and much longer lawns at the rear. After carefully locking up behind her she made her way upstairs.

It was the sound of her telephone ringing that finally woke her; groggily she reached for the receiver, appalled to see from her watch that it was gone ten o'clock. Normally at this time on a Saturday morning she would be in their local town, doing her weekly supermarket shop before meeting up with friends for lunch.

As luck would have it, she had made no such arrangement for today, as most of her friends were away on holiday with their families.

As her fingers curled round the telephone receiver her stomach muscles tensed, despite the fact that she knew it was impossible that her caller could be Leo Jefferson; after all, he didn't even know who she was, thank goodness! A small *frisson* of nervous excitement tingled through her body, quickly followed by a strong surge of something she would not allow herself to acknowledge as disappointment when she recognised her cousin Nigel's voice.

It was no wonder, after all she had been through, that her emotions should be so traumatised that they had difficulty in relaying appropriate reactions to her.

'At last,' she could hear Nigel saying cheerfully to her. 'This is the third time I've rung. How did it go with Leo Jefferson? I'm dying to know.'

Jodi took a deep breath; she could feel her heart starting to pound as shame and guilt filled her. The hand holding the receiver felt sticky. She had never been a good liar; never been even a vaguely adequate one.

'It didn't,' she admitted huskily.

'You chickened out?' Nigel guessed.

Jodi let out a sigh of relief; Nigel had just given her the perfect answer to her dilemma.

'I...I was tired and I started to have second thoughts. And—'

Before she could tell Nigel that she had decided to write to Leo Jefferson rather than speak with him her cousin had cut across her to say tolerantly, 'I thought you wouldn't go through with it. Never mind. Uncle Nigel has ridden to the rescue for you. My boss has invited me over to dinner tonight, and I've asked him if I can take you along with me. He'll be speaking to Leo Jefferson himself next week, and if you put your case to him I'm sure he'll incorporate the plight of the school into his own discussion.'

'Oh, Nigel, that's very kind of you, but I don't think...' Jodi began to demur. She just wasn't in the mood for a dinner party, and as for the idea of putting the school's case to Nigel's boss, who was the chief planning officer for the area, Jodi's opinion of her own credibility had been so undermined that she just didn't feel good enough about herself to do so.

Nigel, though, made it clear that he was not prepared to take no for an answer.

'You've got to come,' he insisted. 'Graham really does want to meet you. His grandson is one of your pupils, apparently, and he's a big fan of yours. The grandson, not Graham. Although…'

'Nigel, I can't go,' Jodi protested.

'Of course you can. You must. Think of your school,' he teased her before adding, 'I'm picking you up at half-past seven, and you'd better be ready.'

He had rung off before Jodi could protest any further.

Wearily Jodi studied the screen of her computer. She had spent most of the afternoon trying to compose a letter to send to Leo Jefferson. The headache she had woken up with had, thankfully, finally abated, but every time she tried to concentrate on what she was supposed to be doing a totally unwanted mental picture of Leo Jefferson kept forming inside her head. And it wasn't just his face that her memory was portraying to her in intimate detail, she acknowledged as she felt herself turning as pink as the cascading petunias in her next-door neighbour's window boxes. Mrs Fields, at eighty, was still a keen gardener, and as she had ruefully explained to Jodi she liked the strong, bright colours because she could see them.

Jodi's own lovingly planted boxes were a more subtle combination of soft greens, white and silver, the same silver as Leo Jefferson's sexy eyes.

Jodi's face flamed even hotter as she stared at her screen

and realised that she had begun her letter, 'Dear Sexy Eyes'.

Quickly she deleted the words and began again, reminding herself of how important it was that she impress on Leo Jefferson the effect the closure of the factory would have not just on her school but also on the whole community.

All over the country small villages were dying or becoming weekend dormitories for city workers, although everyone here in their local community had worked hard to make theirs a living, working village.

If she could get Nigel's boss on her side it was bound to help their case. Frowning slightly, she pushed her chair away from her computer. She ought to be used to fighting to keep the school going now. When she had first been appointed as its head teacher she had been told by the education authority that it would only be for an interim period, as, with the school's numbers falling, it would ultimately have to be closed.

Even though she had known she would get better promotion and higher pay by transferring to a bigger school, as soon as Jodi had realised the effect that losing their school would have she had begun to canvass determinedly for new pupils, even to the extent of persuading parents who had previously been considering private education to give their local primary a chance.

Her efforts had paid off in more ways than one, and Jodi knew she would never forget the pride she had felt when their school had received an excellent report following an inspection visit.

Her pride wasn't so much for herself, though, as for the efforts of the pupils and everyone else who had supported the school; to have to stand back and see all the ground they had gained lost, the sense of teamwork and community she had so determinedly fostered amongst the pupils destroyed, was more than she wanted to have to bear.

She had proved just how well the children thrived and learned in an atmosphere of security and love, in a school where they were known and valued as individuals, and Jodi was convinced that the self-confidence such a start gave them was something that would benefit them through their academic lives. But somehow, trying to explain all of this to Leo Jefferson was far harder than she had expected.

Perhaps it was because she suspected that he had already made up his mind, that, so far as he was concerned, the small community he would be destroying simply didn't matter when compared with his profits. Or perhaps it was because all she could think about, all she could see, was last night and the way they had been together...

With every hour that distanced her from the intimacy they had shared it became harder for her to acknowledge what she had done. It just wasn't like her to behave in such a way, and the proof of that, had she needed any, was the fact that he, Leo Jefferson, had been her first and only lover!

Too overwrought to concentrate, Jodi stood up and started to pace the floor of her small sitting room in emotional agitation.

Shocking though her behaviour had been, she knew and could not deny that she had enjoyed Leo Jefferson's touch, his lovemaking, his possession.

But that was because she had been half-drunk and half-asleep, she tried to defend herself, before her strong sense of honesty ruthlessly reminded her of the way she had reacted to him when she had first seen him, when she had quite definitely been both sober and awake!

It was nearly six o'clock. Her letter wasn't finished,

but she would have to leave it now and go and get ready for the evening.

Nigel was going to a lot of trouble on her behalf and she ought to feel grateful to him. Instead, all she wanted was to stay at home and hide from the world until she had come to terms with what she had done.

CHAPTER THREE

LEO GRIMACED AS he ran a hand over his newly shaven jaw. There was no way he felt like going out to dinner, but when Graham Johnson, the chief planning officer for the area, had rung to invite him to his home Leo had not felt he could refuse.

It made good business sense to establish an amicable arrangement with the local authority. Leo had already met Graham and liked him, and when Graham had explained that there was someone he would find it interesting to meet on an informal basis Leo had sensed that Graham would not be very impressed were he to turn him down. And besides, at least if he went out it would stop him from thinking about last night, and that wretched, unforgettably sexy woman who had got so dangerously under his skin.

As yet, Jeremy Driscoll had made no attempt to contact him, and Leo was hoping that he had the sense to recognise that Leo was not to be coerced—in any way—but somehow he doubted that Jeremy had actually given up. He wasn't that type, and, since he had gone as far as paying his accomplice to play her part, Leo suspected that he was going to want value for his money.

Did Driscoll avail himself of Leo's tousle-haired tormentor's sexual skills? It shocked Leo to discover just how unpalatable he found that thought! Was he crazy, feeling possessive about a woman like that, a woman any man could have? Unwantedly Leo found himself remembering the way her body had claimed him, tightening around him almost as though it had known no other man. Now he *was* going crazy, he told himself angrily as he peered at the approaching signpost to check that he was driving in the right direction.

'Jodi, you aren't listening to me.'

Jodi gave her cousin an apologetic look as he brought his car to a halt outside his boss's house.

'Come to think of it, you're not exactly looking your normal, chirpy self.' He gave her a concerned look. 'Worrying about that school of yours, I expect?'

Ignoring his question, Jodi drew a deep breath, determined to tackle him about an issue that had been weighing very heavily on her mind.

'Nigel, what on earth possessed you to order that cocktail for me last night? You know I don't drink, and because it never occurred to me that it was alcoholic…well, there was so much fruit in it…'

'Hey, hang on a minute,' Nigel protested in bewilderment. 'I never ordered you anything alcoholic.'

'Well, whatever the waiter brought to Leo Jefferson's suite definitely was,' Jodi informed him grittily.

'They must have misunderstood me,' Nigel told her. 'I asked them to send you up a fruit cocktail. I thought it seemed expensive—what a waste; I bet you didn't touch it after the first swallow, did you?'

Fortunately, before she was obliged to lie to him, he took hold of Jodi's arm and walked her firmly towards the front door, which opened as they reached it to reveal their host, Graham Johnson, a tall grey-haired man with a warm smile.

'You must be Jodi.' He shook Jodi's hand, and introduced himself. 'I've heard an awful lot about you!'

When Jodi gave Nigel a wry look their host shook his head and laughed.

'No, not from Nigel, although he has mentioned you. I was referring to our grandson, Henry. He's one of your pupils and an ardent admirer. With just reason, too, according to his parents. Our daughter, Charlotte, is most impressed with the dramatic improvement the school has achieved in Henry's reading skills.'

Jodi smiled her appreciation of his compliments and a little of the tension started to leave her body as they followed Graham into the house.

Mary Johnson was as welcoming as her husband, informing Jodi that she had trained as a teacher herself, although it had been many years since she had last taught.

'My daughter was a little concerned at first when she heard that you were an advocate of a mixture of traditional teaching methods and educational play, but she's a total convert now. She can't stop telling us how much Henry's spatial skills have improved along with his reading ability.'

'We like to encourage the children to become good all-rounders,' Jodi acknowledged, explaining, 'We feel that it helps overall morale if we can encourage every child to discover a field in which they can do well.'

'I understand from our daughter that you've actually got parents putting their children's names down for the school almost as soon as they are born.'

'Well, perhaps not quite that,' Jodi laughed, 'but certainly we are finding that our reputation has been spread by word of mouth. We're above the safety limit we need to satisfy the education authority as regards pupil numbers and likely to stay that way, unless, of course, the factory is closed down.'

Jodi gave Graham Johnson an uncertain look as she saw his expression.

'The final decision with regard to that rests with Leo Jefferson,' he told her gently, 'which is why I've invited him to join us for dinner tonight. It was Nigel's idea, and a good one. It might help matters if the two of you were to meet in an informal setting. I suspect that from a businessman's point of view Leo Jefferson hasn't really considered the effect a closure of the factory would have on the village school. And, of course, it isn't inevitable that he will close down our factory. As I understand it, of the four he has taken over he only intends to close two.'

Jodi wasn't really listening to him. She had stopped listening properly the moment he had said those dreadful words, 'I've invited him to join us for dinner tonight'.

Leo Jefferson was coming here. For dinner. She was going to be forced to sit in the same room with him, perhaps even across the table from him.

She felt sick, faint, paralysed with fear, she recognised as the doorbell rang and Graham went to answer it.

Frantically she looked at the French windows, aching to make her escape through them, but it was already too late, Graham was walking back into the room accompanied by Leo Jefferson. The man she had spent the night with... Her lover!

Leo had been listening politely to his host as Graham showed him the way to the sitting room, opened the door and ushered Leo inside. He proceeded to introduce Leo to the other occupants of the room, but the moment he had stepped through the door Leo stopped hearing a single word that Graham was saying as he stared in furious disbelief at Jodi.

She was standing by the French windows, looking for

all the world like some martyr about to be taken away for beheading, her eyes huge with anguish and fear as she stared mutely at him.

What was going on? What was she doing here? And then Leo realised that Graham was introducing her to him as the local school's head teacher.

He felt as though he had somehow strayed into some kind of farce. He accepted that things were different in the country, but surely not so damned different that a village headmistress moonlighted as a professional harlot!

The surge of furious jealousy that burst over the banks of his normal self-control bewildered him, as did the immediate antipathy he felt towards the man standing at her side.

'And this is Nigel Marsh, my assistant and Jodi's cousin,' Graham Johnson was explaining.

Her cousin. To his own relief Leo felt himself easing back on his ridiculous emotions.

'A little surprise for you!' Nigel whispered to Jodi whilst Mary was talking to Leo.

Jodi gave him a wan smile.

'Jodi, can I get you a drink?' Graham was asking jovially.

'I don't usually drink, thank you,' Jodi responded automatically, and then flushed a deep, rich pink as she saw the look that Leo Jefferson was giving her.

'She's always been strait-laced, even before she qualified as a teacher,' Nigel informed Graham humorously. 'Can't think how we came to share the same gene pool. I'm always telling her that she ought to loosen up a little, enjoy life, let herself go.'

Jodi didn't want to look at Leo Jefferson again, but somehow she couldn't stop herself from doing so. To her shock he had moved closer to her, and whilst Nigel re-

sponded to something Mary was saying he leaned forward
and whispered cynically to Jodi, 'That's quite a person-
ality change you've managed to accomplish in less than
twenty-four hours.'

'Please,' Jodi implored him, desperately afraid that he
might be overheard, but to her relief the others had moved
out of earshot.

'Please... I seem to remember you said something like
that to me last night,' Leo reminded her silkily.

'Stop it,' Jodi begged in torment. 'You don't understand.'

'You're damned right I don't!' Leo agreed acerbically,
adding, 'Tell me something; do your school governors
know that you're moonlighting as a hooker? I accept that
schoolteachers may not be overly well-paid, but somehow
I've never imagined them supplementing their income with
those sort of private lessons.'

'No, you...'

Jodi meant to continue and tell Leo he had it all wrong,
but her vehement tone caused Nigel to break off his conversation with Mary Johnson and give her a concerned look.
He knew how passionate she was about her school, but he
hadn't expected to hear her arguing with Leo Jefferson so
early in the evening. It did not augur well. However, before
Nigel could step in with some diplomatic calming mea-
sures Mary was announcing that she was ready for them
to sit down for dinner.

'That was absolutely delicious.' Nigel sighed appreciatively
as he ate the last morsel of his pudding. 'Living on your
own is all very well, but microwave meals can't take the
place of home cooking. I keep saying as much to Jodi,' he
continued plaintively to Mary, giving Jodi a teasing glance.
'But she doesn't seem to take the hint.'

'If you want home cooking you should learn to cook yourself,' Jodi returned firmly. 'I insist that all the children at school, boys and girls, learn the basics.'

'And I think it's wonderful that they do,' Mary supported her, turning to Leo to tell him, 'Jodi has done wonders for her school. When she first took over they had so few pupils that it was about to be closed down, but now parents are putting down their children's names at birth to ensure that they get a place.'

Jodi could feel herself starting to colour up as Leo turned to look at her.

The whole evening had been a nightmare, and so far as she was concerned it couldn't come to an end fast enough.

'Oh, yes, Jodi is passionate about her school,' Nigel chimed in supportively.

'Passionate?'

Jodi could feel the anxiety tensing her already over-stretched nervous system as Leo drawled the word with an undertone of cynical dislike that she hoped only she could hear. Was he going to give her away?

To her relief, Leo went on, 'Oh, yes, I'm sure she is.'

'I think,' Graham began to say calmly, with a kind smile in Jodi's direction, 'that she is also concerned about the potential effect it would have on the school if you were to close down the Frampton factory.'

When Leo gave him a sharp look Graham gave a small shrug and told him, 'It's no secret that you intend to close one and possibly two of the factories—the financial Press have quoted you on it.'

'It's a decision I haven't made as yet,' Leo responded tersely.

'So are you considering closing down our factory?' Jodi couldn't resist demanding.

Leo frowned as he listened to her. She had hardly spo-

ken directly to him all night. In fact, she had barely even
looked at him, but he could feel both her tension and her
hostility as keenly as he could feel his own reaction to her.

It infuriated him, in a way that was a whole new experience for him, that she should be able to play so well and
so deceitfully the role of a dedicated schoolteacher when
he knew what she really was.

She must be completely without conscience! And she
was in charge of the growth and development of burgeon-
ing young minds and emotions. How clever she must be
to be able to dupe everyone around her so successfully;
to be able to win their trust and merit their admiration
and respect.

Leo told himself that the intensity of his own emotions
was a completely natural reaction to the discovery of her
duplicity. If he was to reveal the truth about her—but, of
course, he couldn't, after all he wasn't exactly proud of
his own behaviour.

But why had she done it? For money, as he had originally assumed? Because she enjoyed flirting with danger?
Because she wanted to help Driscoll? For some reason, it
was this last option that he found the least palatable.

Jodi could feel Leo's bitterly contemptuous gaze burning the distance between them. If he should mention last
night…! If Nigel had given her the slightest indication
that Leo was going to be a fellow guest no power on earth
would have been able to get her within a mile of Mary
and Graham's.

She had cringed inwardly, listening to the others sing-
ing her praises, hardly daring to breathe in case Leo said
anything. But of course last night's events did not reflect
much more creditably on him than they did on her. Although he, as a man, at least had the age-old excuse of

claiming, as so many of his sex had done throughout history, that the woman had tempted him.

Soon their current school term would be over. Normally she experienced a certain sadness when this happened, especially at the end of the summer term, since their eldest pupils would be moving on to 'big' school. Right now she felt she couldn't wait for the freedom to quietly disappear out of public view.

A couple of friends from university had invited her to join them on a walking holiday in the Andes and she wished that she had agreed to go with them. Instead, she had said she wanted to spend some time decorating her small house and working on her garden, as well as planning ways to make the school even better than it already was—something which in Jodi's eyes was more of a pleasure than a chore.

Now, thanks to Leo Jefferson, all the small pleasures she had been looking forward to had been obscured by the dark cloud of her own guilt.

'Well, we shall certainly be very disappointed if you choose to close down our factory,' she could hear Graham saying to Leo. 'We're a small country area and replacing so many lost jobs isn't going to be easy. Although logically I can understand that the Newham factory does have the advantage of being much closer to the motorway network.'

'Unfortunately, it is all a question of economics,' Leo was replying. 'The market simply isn't big enough to support so many different factories all producing the same thing...'

Suddenly Jodi had heard enough. Her passionate desire to protect her school overwhelmed the fear and shame that had kept her silent throughout the evening and, turning towards Leo, she told him angrily, 'It managed to support them well enough before your takeover, and it seems to me that it would be more truthful to say that the economics in question are those that affect your profits—not to mention the tax advantages you will no doubt stand to gain. Have you no idea of the hardship it's going to cause? The people it will put out of work, the lives and families it will destroy? I've got children at school whose whole family are dependent on that factory—fathers, mothers, grandparents, aunts, uncles. Don't you care about anything except making money?'

Jodi could feel the small, shocked silence her outburst had caused. Across the table, Nigel was giving her a warning look, whilst Graham Johnson was frowning slightly.

'We all understand how you feel, Jodi.' he told her calmly. 'But I'm afraid that economics, profits, can't just be ignored. Leo is competing in a worldwide market-place, and for his business to remain successful—'

'There are far more important things in life than profits,' Jodi interrupted him, unable to stop herself from stemming the intensity of her feelings now that she had started to speak.

'Such as what?' Leo checked her sharply. 'Such as you keeping enough pupils in your school to impress the school inspectorate? Aren't you just as keen to show a profit on your pupil numbers in return for Education Authority funding as I am on my financial investment in my business?'

'How dare you say that?' Jodi breathed furiously. 'It is the children themselves, their education, their futures, their lives, that concern me. What you are doing—'

'What I am doing is trying to run a profitable business.' Leo silenced her acidly. 'You, I'm afraid, are blinkered by your own parochial outlook. I have to see the bigger picture. If I was to keep all the factories operating inevitably none of them would be profitable and I would then be out of business, with the loss of far more jobs than there will be if I simply close down two of them.'

'You just don't care, do you?' Jodi challenged him. 'You don't care about what you're doing; about the misery you will be causing.'

She knew that she was going too far, and that both Nigel and the Johnsons were watching her with concern and dismay, but something was driving her on. The tension she had been feeling all evening had somehow overwhelmed the rational parts of her brain and she was in the hands of a self-destructive, unstoppable urge she couldn't control.

'What I care about is keeping my business at the top of its field,' Leo told her grimly.

'Precisely,' Jodi threw at him, curling her lip in contempt as she tossed her head. 'Profit... Don't you care that what you are doing is totally immoral?'

Jodi tensed as she heard the sharp hiss of collective indrawn breath as she and Leo confronted one another in bitter hostility.

'*You* dare to accuse me of immorality!'

Had the others heard, as she had, the way he had emphasised the word 'you'? Jodi wondered in sick shock as she tried to withstand the icy contempt of the look he was giving her.

'Jodi, my dear.' Graham finally intervened a little uncomfortably. 'I'm sure we all appreciate how strongly you feel about everything, but Leo does have a point. Naturally his business has to be competitive.'

'Oh, naturally,' Jodi agreed bitingly, throwing Leo a caustic look.

Nigel was standing up, saying that it was time that they left, but as Graham pulled out Jodi's chair for her she still couldn't resist turning to Leo to challenge, 'In the end everything comes down to money, doesn't it?'

As he, too, stood up he looked straight at her and told her softly, 'As you should know.'

Jodi could feel her face burning.

'Oh, and by the way,' Leo added under cover of Mary going to fetch them all their coats, 'you can tell your friend Driscoll—'

Jodi didn't let him get any further.

'Jeremy Driscoll is no friend of mine,' she told him immediately. 'In fact, if you want the truth, I loathe and detest him almost as much as I do you.'

She was shaking as she thanked Mary and slipped on her coat, hurrying out into the warmth of the summer night ahead of Nigel, who had turned back to say something to their host.

As she waited for him beside the car, her back towards the house, she was seething with anger. At the same time she began to feel the effects of the shock of seeing Leo Jefferson and the way she had argued with him so publicly.

As she heard Nigel come crunching over the gravel towards her, without turning to look at him, she begged fiercely, 'Just take me out of here...'

'Where exactly is it you want me to take you? Or can I guess?'

Whirling round, Jodi expelled her breath on a hissing gasp as she realised that it wasn't Nigel who was standing next to her in the shadow of the trees but Leo Jefferson.

'Keep away from me,' she warned him furiously, inadvertently backing into the shadows as she strove to put more distance between them.

Her reaction, so totally overplayed and unwarranted, was the last straw so far as Leo was concerned.

'Oh, come on,' he snarled. 'You haven't got an audience now!'

'You don't know anything,' Jodi spat back shakily.

'That wasn't what you were telling me last night,' Leo couldn't stop himself from reminding her savagely. 'Last night—'

'Last night I didn't know what I was doing,' Jodi retaliated bitterly. 'If I had done I would never...' She was so overwrought now that her voice and her body both trembled. 'You are the last man I would have wanted to share what should have been one of the most special experiences of my life.'

Jodi was beyond thinking logically about what she was revealing; instead she was carried along, flung headlong into the powerful vortex of her own overwhelming emotions.

Leo could hear what she was saying, but, like her, his emotions were too savagely aroused for him to take on board the meaning of her words. Instead he held out to her the handbag she had unknowingly left behind in the house, telling her coldly, 'You forgot this. Your cousin is still talking with Graham and Mary and he asked me to bring it to you. I think he probably wanted to give you the opportunity to apologise to me in private for your appalling rudeness over dinner...'

'*My* rudeness.' Jodi reached angrily for her handbag and then froze as her fingertips brushed against Leo's outstretched hand.

Just the feel of his skin against her own sent a shower of sharp electric shocks, of unwanted sensation, slicing through her body.

'Don't touch me,' she protested, and then moaned a soft, tormented sound of helpless need, dropping her handbag and swaying towards him in exactly the same breath as he reached for her. He dragged her against his body and the feel of him was so savagely, shockingly familiar that her body reacted instantly. She looked up into his face, her lips parting. His mouth burned against hers like a brand, punishing, taking, possessing. She felt him shudder as his fingers bit into the tender flesh of her upper arms. But then as his tongue-tip probed her lips he seemed to change his mind. He released her abruptly and, turning on his heel, walked away.

It was several seconds before she could stop shaking enough to bend down and pick up her bag. Whilst she was doing so she heard Nigel saying her name.

'Sorry about the delay,' he apologised as she stood up and he unlocked the car. 'Feeling better now that you've got all that off your chest?' he asked her wryly.

'Better?' Jodi demanded sharply as they both got into his car. 'How could I possibly be feeling better after having to spend an evening with that…that…?'

'OK, OK, I get the picture,' Nigel told her, adding, 'In fact, I think we all did. I do understand how you feel, Jodi, but ripping up at Leo Jefferson isn't going to help. He's a businessman and you've got to try to see things from his point of view.'

'Why should I see things from his point of view? He doesn't seem to be prepared to see them from mine,' Jodi challenged her cousin.

Nigel gave her a wry look.

'There is a very apt saying about catching more flies with honey than vinegar,' he reminded her, 'although something tells me you aren't in the mood to hear that.'

Jodi could feel her face starting to burn.

'No, I'm not,' she said tersely.

'Why couldn't things have just stayed the way they were?' she moaned to Nigel as he drove her home. 'Everything was all right when the Driscolls owned the factory.'

'Not totally,' Nigel told her quietly, but shook his head when Jodi looked at him. He had already said too much, and he wasn't yet free to tell her about the fraudulent practices that Jeremy Driscoll was suspected of having operated within the business.

Jodi didn't push him further on that point; instead she burst out, 'Leo Jefferson is the most hateful, horrid, arrogant, impossible man I have ever met and I wish...I wish...'

Unable to specify just exactly what she wished, and why, Jodi bit her lip and looked out of the car window, glad to see that they were already in the village and that she would soon be home.

Leo grimaced as he paced the sitting-room floor of his suite. He had a good mind to ring down to Reception and ask them to transfer him to a different set of rooms; these reminded him too much of last night and her—Jodi Marsh!

That infuriating woman who had by some alchemic means turned herself from the wanton, sensual creature who had shared his bed last night into the furious, spiky opponent who had had the gall tonight to sit there and accuse *him* of immoral behaviour! How he had stopped himself from challenging her there and then to justify herself Leo really didn't know. And she was a schoolteacher! Perhaps he was being unduly naïve, but he just couldn't get his head around it at all.

And as for her comments about his plans for the factory and the effect it would have on other people's lives if he was to close it down...!

Leo frowned. Did she think he enjoyed having to put people out of work? Of course he didn't, but economic factors were economic factors and could not simply be ignored.

Well, he just hoped that she didn't get it into her head to come back tonight and pay him a second visit, because if she did she would find there was no way he was going to be as idiotically vulnerable to her as he had been last night. No way at all!

CHAPTER FOUR

'YOU PUSHED ME.'

'No, I didn't.'

With gentle firmness Jodi sorted out the dispute caused by one of her most problematic pupils on her way across the school yard.

Left to his own devices, she suspected, seven-year-old Ben Fanshawe might have been a happy, sociable child, but, thanks to the efforts of his social-climbing mother, Ben was a little boy with an attitude that was driving the other children away.

Jodi had tried tactfully to discuss the situation with his mother, but Ben's problems were compounded by the fact that Myra Fanshawe was not just a parent, but also on the school's board of governors. It was a position she had single-mindedly set her sights on from the minute she and her husband had moved into the village.

A close friend of Jeremy Driscoll and his wife, Myra had made it plain to Jodi that she would have preferred to send her son to an exclusive prep school. It was only because her in-laws were refusing to pay their grandson's school fees until he was old enough to attend the same school as the previous six generations of male Fanshawes that Ben was having to attend the village primary school.

Having bullied and badgered her way into the position

of Chair of the Board of Governors, Myra had continually bombarded both the board and Jodi herself with her opinions on how the school might be improved.

Having lost her most recent battle to impose a system of teaching maths that she had decided would be enormously beneficial for Ben, Myra had made it abundantly clear to Jodi that she had made a bad enemy.

For Ben's sake, Jodi had tried tactfully to suggest that he might benefit from being encouraged to make more friends amongst his schoolmates. But her gentle hints had been met with fury and hostility by Myra, who had told Jodi that there was no way she wanted her son mixing with 'common village children'.

'Once Benjamin leaves here he will be meeting a very different class of child. He already knows that, and knows too that I would have preferred him to be attending a proper prep school. I do wish I could make his grandparents understand how much better it would be if he was already in private education. Jeremy and Alison were totally appalled that we could even think of allowing him to come here. At least now that I'm Chair of the Board of Governors I shall be able to make sure that he is receiving the rudiments of a decent education.

'The vicar's wife commented to me only the other day how much better the school has been doing since I became involved.' She had preened herself, leaving Jodi torn between pity for her little boy and amazement at Myra's total lack of awareness of other people's feelings.

As it happened, Anna Leslie, the vicar's wife, had actually told Jodi herself how unbearable she found Myra and how much she loathed her patronising attitude.

With only such a short time to go before the end of term, it was perhaps only natural that the children should be in such a high-spirited mood, Jodi acknowledged as she made her way to her office.

By the time the school bell rang to summon the children to their classes she was so engrossed in her work that she had almost managed to put Leo Jefferson right out of her mind.

Almost…

Leo tensed as his mobile phone rang. He was in his car, on his way to meet with his accountant at the Frampton factory that had been the subject of his heated exchange of views with Jodi on Saturday night.

He frowned as he registered the unavailable number of his caller. If Jodi was ringing him in an attempt to… Reaching out, he answered the call using the car's hands-free unit, but the voice speaking his name was not Jodi's and was not, in fact, even female, but belonged instead to Jeremy Driscoll.

'Look, old boy, I just thought I'd give you a ring to see if the two of us couldn't get together. The word is that you're going to have to close down at least a couple of the factories and I'm prepared to make you a good offer to buy Frampton back from you.'

Leo frowned as he listened.

'Buy it?' he challenged him curtly, waiting for Jeremy to threaten to blackmail him into agreeing, but, to his surprise, Jeremy made no reference whatsoever to either Jodi or her visit to his bed.

'Look, we're both businessmen—and we both know there are ways and means of you selling the business back to me that would benefit us both financially…'

Leo didn't respond.

Jeremy Driscoll had been away on holiday in the Caribbean with his wife when his father-in-law had accepted

Leo's offer to buy out the business, and it was becoming increasingly obvious to Leo that for some reason he did not wish to see the sale go through.

'I haven't made my mind up which factories I intend to close as yet,' Leo informed him. It was, after all, the truth.

'Frampton is the obvious choice. Anyone can see that,' Jeremy Driscoll was insisting. Beneath the hectoring tone of his voice Leo could hear a sharper note of anxiety.

Leo had almost reached the factory. Reaching out to end the call, he told Jeremy Driscoll crisply, 'I'll call you once I've made up my mind.'

As he cancelled the call Leo's frown deepened. It disturbed him that Jeremy Driscoll hadn't said a single word about Jodi. Somehow that seemed out of character. Driscoll wasn't the sort of man to miss an opportunity to maximise on his advantage and, even though Leo knew he wouldn't allow himself to be blackmailed, he was still in a potentially vulnerable position.

But nowhere near as delicate and vulnerable as the one Jodi herself was in, he acknowledged grimly. What on earth had possessed her?

'So what you're saying is that I should close this factory down?' Leo asked his accountant as they finished their tour of the Frampton site.

'Well, it does seem to be the obvious choice. Newham has the benefit of being much closer to the motorway system.'

'Which means that it would be relatively easy to sell off as a base for a haulage contractor,' Leo interrupted him wryly. 'That would then allow me to consolidate production at Frampton, and use the Newham site solely for distribution, or if that proved to be uneconomical to sell it off.'

'Well, yes, that could be an option,' the accountant acknowledged.

'Frampton also has the benefit of having recently had a new production line,' Leo continued.

'Yes, I know. It seems there was a fire, that destroyed the old one, which brings me to something else,' the accountant told him carefully. 'There are one or two things here that just don't tie up.'

'Such as?' Leo challenged him curiously.

'Such as two fires in a very short space of time, and certain anomalies in the accounting system. It seems that this factory has been run by the owners' son-in-law, who prior to working in the business gained a reputation for favouring practices which, shall we say, are not entirely in line with those approved of by the Revenue.'

'So what we are actually talking about here is fraud,' Leo stated sharply.

'I don't know, and certainly I haven't found anything fraudulent in the accounts that were submitted to us on takeover. However, it may be that those accounts are not the only ones the business produced. Just call it a gut feeling, but something tells me that things are not totally as they should be.'

Had his accountant unwittingly hit on the reason why Jeremy Driscoll was so anxious to retain ownership of this particular factory? Leo wondered.

'If you're serious about finding a haulier buyer for the Newham land,' his accountant continued, 'I might know of someone.'

Leo stopped him. 'I might well opt to set up my own distribution network. With distribution costs rising the way they are, it makes good economic sense to be able to control that aspect of the business.'

'Mmm...'

What the hell was he doing? Leo asked himself in inner
exasperation. He was finding arguments to keep Frampton
open! Surely he wasn't allowing himself to be influenced
by the emotional opinions of a woman who knew nothing
about business? Although she did know everything about
how to please a man. This man! How to infuriate and drive
him insane was more like it, Leo decided in furious, angry
rejection of his own weak thoughts.

He and the accountant parted company at the factory
gate. It was almost lunchtime, and Leo recalled that there
was a pub in the village where he could no doubt get something to eat.

If he was to change his plans and retain the Frampton
factory it would mean spending a good deal of time in
the area; several months at least. He would have to rent
somewhere to live.

Perhaps predictably the pub was almost opposite the
church, and separated from the church by the graveyard
and a small paddock was the school.

Her school!

Since it was lunchtime, the school yard was filled with
children.

Turning into the pub car park, Leo parked and then got
out to walk round to the main entrance to the dining room.

As he did so his attention was caught by a small group
of children clustering around a familiar figure.

Jodi's curls were burnished a deep, rich colour by the
sunlight. She was wearing a cotton skirt and a toning
blouse, her legs bare beneath the hem of her skirt.

She hadn't seen him, Leo acknowledged, and she was
laughing at something one of her pupils had said, her head
thrown back to reveal the taut line of her throat, with its
creamy smooth skin, the same skin he had caressed and
kissed.

Leo could feel the sensual reaction filling his body. He still wanted her!

She looked completely at home in her chosen role and Leo could see that the children were equally relaxed with her. And then, as though somehow she had sensed his presence, she looked towards him, her whole body freezing and the joy dying abruptly from her face as their gazes battled silently across the distance that separated them.

As though they sensed her hostility the children too had become still and silent, and as he watched Leo saw her ushering them away from the school boundary out of sight.

The pub dining room was surprisingly busy, but Leo barely paid any attention to his fellow diners. His thoughts were taken up with Jodi, a fact which caused him to wonder grimly yet again just what the hell was happening to him.

He ate his meal quickly without really being aware of it. In his mind's eye he could still see Jodi surrounded by her pupils. She had looked...

He shook his head, trying to dismiss her image from his thoughts, and caused the waitress who had served him to give a tiny little shiver and reflect on how dangerous and exciting he looked—and how very different from her boyfriend!

Having finished his meal and refused a second cup of coffee, much to the waitress's secret disappointment, Leo got up, oblivious to her interest in him.

On his way back to the car he noticed that the school playground was now empty, the children no doubt back at their desks.

For God's sake, he derided himself as he drove back towards the town, didn't he have enough to think about at the moment without being obsessed by a schoolteacher?

* * *

'Well, we don't normally have many rental properties,' the agent in the local town was informing Leo. 'But it just so happens that we've been asked to find a tenant for a thoroughly charming Georgian house, just outside Frampton. I don't know if you know the village.'

'Yes, I know it,' Leo confirmed a little grimly.

'I live there myself.' The agent smiled. 'I don't know if you have children, but if you do I can thoroughly recommend the village school. Jodi Marsh, the head teacher, is wonderful—'

'I know Jodi,' Leo interrupted him brusquely.

'You do?' The agent gave him a discreetly speculative look. 'Well, if you're a friend of Jodi's you'll find you get a very warm welcome in the village. She's as popular with the parents as she is with the children, and deservedly so.

'My wife dreads the thought of her leaving; she says the school just wouldn't be the same without her. We all admire the way she campaigned so tirelessly to keep the school open and to raise enough money to buy the playing field adjacent to it to stop Jeremy Driscoll from acquiring it as building land. That didn't make her popular with Jeremy at all, but Jodi has never been a fan of his, as you'll probably know...'

Again he gave Leo a speculative look, but Leo discovered that he was strangely reluctant to correct the other man's misconceptions. For one thing he was too busy analysing the agent's surprising comments about Jodi's antipathy towards Jeremy Driscoll to notice.

'If you'd like to view Ashton House?' the agent continued questioningly.

Leo told himself that he should refuse, that deliberately choosing to live anywhere within a hundred-mile radius of Jodi Marsh was complete madness, but for some reason he heard himself agreeing to see the house, and accepting the agent's suggestion that they should drive over to view it immediately.

'I rather get the impression that Jeremy Driscoll isn't the most popular of people around here?' Leo commented to the agent half an hour later as they stood together in front of the pretty Georgian property.

'Well, no, he isn't,' the agent agreed. 'And, despite the fact that he's married, Jeremy fancies himself as something of a ladies' man. Of course Jodi, in particular, is well known for her strict moral code, so I suppose it was almost inevitable that she should make it very plain to him that his advances were unwelcome.'

Leo struggled to absorb this new information as the agent changed tack to tell him about the house. 'It was built originally for the younger son of a local landowner; it's listed, of course, and with all its original internal decorative features—a real gem. If I had the money I would be very tempted to put in an offer for it. The elderly lady who owned it died a few weeks ago, and the beneficiaries under her will ultimately want to sell it, but until the estate is sorted out they need to find a tenant for it so that it doesn't fall into disrepair. Shall we go inside?'

The house was undoubtedly, as the agent had said, a 'gem', and had he been looking for a permanent home Leo knew that he too would have been tempted to acquire it. As it was, he was more than happy to meet the relatively modest rent the owners were requesting.

However, as Leo followed the agent back to his office, so that they could complete the paperwork for the rental, it wasn't so much the new temporary home he had acquired that was occupying his thoughts as the agent's revelations about Jodi.

Just why was it that everyone seemed to think that Jodi

was a paragon of all the virtues? There was no way that
he could be wrong about her, was there?

But later on in the day as he drove back to his hotel he
was aware of a small and very unwanted niggling doubt
that somehow just would not be silenced. Was it realistic
for him to believe that so many other people were wrong
and that he was right? Common sense told him that it
wasn't!

But nothing changed the fact that Jodi had still, most
definitely, been in his bed!

Jodi forced herself to smile at the group of fathers gathered in a huddle outside the school gates, talking to one
another whilst they kept a protective eye on their children.

The factory operated a shift system, which meant that
quite a large proportion of the families where both parents worked split the task of delivering and collecting their
offspring from school. Fathers for some reason seemed to
favour afternoon school runs, and if Jodi hadn't still been
preoccupied with her thoughts of Leo Jefferson she would
have stopped for a chat.

As it was, whilst walking past she registered the fact
that the men were discussing the possible closure of the
factory, and how they intended to make their objections
known.

'We should do something to stop the closure!' someone protested angrily. 'We can't just stand by and lose our
jobs, our livelihood.'

'What we need to do is to stage a demonstration,' another man was insisting.

A demonstration! Well, Jodi couldn't blame them
for wanting to make their feelings public; she would be
tempted to do exactly the same thing if anyone was to
threaten to close her beloved school.

A tiny frown creased her forehead. These parents were the very ones who had supported her unstintingly in her determination to keep the school open, and in her fund-raising to make sure that the school retained its adjacent playing field. The very least she could do, surely, was to support them in turn now. And her feelings about Leo Jefferson had nothing to do with it...

Retracing her footsteps, she walked back towards the small group.

'I couldn't help overhearing what you were just saying about demonstrating against the closure of the factory,' she began. 'If you do—' she took a deep breath '—you can certainly count on my support.'

'What, publicly?' one of them challenged her.

'Publicly!' Jodi confirmed firmly. As she spoke she had the clearest mental image of Leo Jefferson, watching her with icy-eyed contempt across Mary and Graham's dinner-table...

'Leo... Have you got a moment?'

Halfway across the hotel foyer, Leo stopped as Nigel Marsh came hurrying towards him.

'Look, I was wondering if we might have a word?'

Leo frowned as he looked at Jodi's cousin. The younger man looked both slightly uncomfortable and at the same time very determined.

Shooting back the cuff of his jacket, Leo glanced at his watch before telling him crisply, 'I can give you ten minutes.'

Nigel looked relieved.

'Thanks. I just wanted to have a word with you about Jodi...my cousin...you met her the other evening.'

He was speaking as though Leo might have forgotten just who Jodi was, Leo recognised, wondering just what

Nigel Marsh would say if Leo was to tell him that Jodi was someone he would never be able to forget.

However, Leo had no intention of revealing any such thing. Instead he replied with dry irony, 'You mean the schoolteacher.'

Nigel gave him a relieved look.

'Yes. Look, I know she must have come across to you as…as having a bit of a bee in her bonnet about your take-over—'

'She certainly has plenty of attitude,' Leo cut in coolly, causing Nigel to check himself. 'And a very hostile attitude where I'm concerned,' Leo continued crisply.

'It isn't anything personal,' Nigel denied immediately. 'It's just that the school means so much to her. She's worked damned hard to make it successful, and she's always been the kind of person who is attracted to lame dogs, lost causes… I remember when we were kids, she was always mothering something or someone. I know she went a little bit over-the-top the other night. But she wasn't expecting to see you there, and I suppose having hyped herself up to put her case to you at the hotel the night before and then having chickened out…'

He stopped suddenly, looking uncomfortably self-conscious, realising that he had said more than he should, but it was too late; Leo was already demanding sharply, 'Would you mind explaining that last comment, please?'

Even more uncomfortably Nigel did as he had been requested.

Leo waited until he had finished before asking him incredulously, 'You're saying that Jodi, your cousin, planned to approach me in person in my suite so that she could put the school's position to me and ask me to reconsider closing down the factory?'

'I know that technically I shouldn't have encouraged

or helped her,' Nigel acknowledged, 'and Graham will probably read me the Riot Act if he finds out, but I just couldn't not do something. If you really knew her you'd understand that.'

Leo did, and he understood a hell of a lot more now too. Like just why Jodi had been in his room. His room, but not his bed! Had she ordered that nauseating alcoholic concoction to give herself some false courage? And then perhaps over-indulged in it? If so...

Nigel was still speaking and he forced himself to listen to what he was saying.

'Jodi deserves a break. She's battled so hard for the school. First to improve the teaching standards enough to get in more pupils, and then more recently against Jeremy Driscoll, to prevent him from acquiring the school's playing field.'

'I'd heard something about that,' Leo acknowledged.

'Jeremy wasn't at all pleased about the fact that he lost that piece of land. And, as I've already warned Jodi, she's made a dangerous enemy in him. It's no secret that he isn't at all well-liked locally.' Nigel gave a small grimace of distaste. 'Jodi can't stand him and I don't blame her.'

Leo started to frown, silently digesting what he was hearing. Nigel Marsh was the second person to tell him that Jodi didn't like Jeremy Driscoll.

Which meant...which meant that he had—perhaps—misjudged her on two counts. Yes, but that didn't explain away her extraordinary sensuality towards him in bed.

If he was to accept everyone else's opinion, such behaviour was totally out of character. As was his own, Leo was forced to acknowledge.

'I know that Jodi went a bit too far the other night,' Nigel was continuing, 'But in her defence I feel I have to say that she does have a point; without the factory—'

'Her precious school would be in danger of being closed down,' Leo interjected for him.

'We're a rural area, and it would be very hard to replace so many lost jobs,' Nigel said. 'That would mean that for people to find work they would have to move away, and so yes, ultimately the school could potentially be reduced to the position it was in when Jodi took over. But she's the kind of person who has always been sensitive to the feelings of others, and it is her concern for them that is motivating her far more than any concern she might have for her own career.'

He gave Leo a wry look.

'As a matter of fact, I happen to know that she's already been approached by a private school who are willing to pay her very well to go to them, and to include a package of perks that would include free education for her children were she to have any.'

'She isn't involved in a relationship with anyone, though, is she?' Leo couldn't stop himself from asking.

Fortunately Nigel did not seem to find anything odd in Leo's sudden question, shaking his head and informing him openly, 'Oh, no. She's one very picky lady, is my cousin. Casual relationships are just not her style, and as yet she hasn't met anyone she wants to become seriously involved with.'

'A career woman?' Leo hazarded.

'Well, she certainly loves her work,' Nigel conceded, then changed the subject to tell Leo apologetically, 'Look, I've taken up enough of your time. I hope you don't mind me bending your ear on Jodi's behalf.'

'I'm half-Italian,' Leo responded with a brief shrug. 'Family loyalty is part of my heritage.'

It was the truth, and if he was honest Leo knew he would have to admit that he admired Nigel Marsh for his spirited defence of his cousin. But their conversation had left Leo with some questions only one person could answer—Jodi herself. But would she answer them? And would it really be wise of him to ask them and to risk becoming more involved with her?

More involved? Just how much more involved was it possible for two people to actually be? Leo wondered ironically.

Jodi closed her eyes and took a deep breath, filling her lungs with the soft, warm evening air. It was three days since she had last seen Leo Jefferson but he had never been far from her thoughts, even when she should, by rights, have been concentrating on other things. The committee meeting for the school's sports day, which she had attended two nights ago, for instance, and the impromptu and far less organised meeting she had attended last night to discuss the proposed demonstration outside the factory.

Feelings were running very high indeed with regard to the possible closure and, although Jodi had spoken to Nigel about it, he had not been able to tell her anything.

'Leo Jefferson has been in London, tied up in various meetings,' he had explained to her.

What he couldn't tell her, for professional reasons, was that they had been informed there was a very real possibility that Jeremy Driscoll was going to be investigated with regard to anomalies in the stock records and accounts. It seemed there were considerable discrepancies involved for which no rational explanation had as yet been forthcoming.

Nigel had heard on the grapevine that Jeremy Driscoll was claiming the discrepancies had been caused by employee theft, and it was true that he had made insurance claims for such losses. However, the authorities were by no means convinced by his explanation, and it seemed that Leo Jefferson too was now questioning the validity of the accounts he had been provided with prior to buying the business.

Overhead, as Jodi climbed the narrow footpath that led to one of her favourite places, Ashton House—the beautiful Georgian manor house set in its own grounds outside the village—she could hear a blackbird trilling.

It had been agreed at last night's meeting that the workforce would start the demonstration tomorrow morning. Jodi was planning to join the demonstrators after school had finished for the day. As a student she had done her fair share of demonstrating, for both human- and animal-rights groups, and then, as now, as she had firmly explained to the committee, she was vehemently opposed to any kind of violence being used.

'I think we're all agreed on that point,' one of the mothers of Jodi's pupils had confirmed. 'I just wish it didn't have to come to this. We've tried to initiate talks with this Leo Jefferson, but he says that he doesn't consider it appropriate to meet with us at the moment.'

Leo!

Jodi closed her eyes and released her breath on a sigh.

She might not have seen him for three days, but that did not mean… Hastily she opened her eyes. She wasn't going to think about those dreams she kept on having night after night, or what they might mean. Dreams in which she was back in his hotel suite…his bed…his arms. They were just dreams, that was all. They didn't mean that she wanted a repetition of what had happened between them. The fact that she had woken up last night just in time to hear herself moaning his name meant nothing at all…and neither did the shockingly physical ache that seemed to be constantly tormenting her body whenever she forgot to control it.

And as for those shockingly savage kisses she kept dreaming about... Well, those just had to be a product of her own fevered imagination, didn't they?

CHAPTER FIVE

Leo frowned as he heard the sound of someone walking along the footpath that skirted round the boundary to Ashton House. He had moved in officially that morning, having organised a cleaning team to go through the house ahead of him. He was now exploring the garden and coming to the conclusion that it was going to take a dedicated team of gardeners to restore it to anything like its former glory.

He had spent the last few days in London, locked in a variety of meetings concerning both his acquisition of the factories and their future. And now it seemed the authorities wanted to open enquiries into the financial workings of the Frampton factory, in particular whilst it had been under Jeremy Driscoll's management.

If he did decide to keep the factory going he would first of all need to make a decision about what to do with the other sites.

One of them housed the oldest factory, with an out-of-date production line and a depleted workforce, and was a natural choice to be closed down.

Of the other three…if he opted to keep Frampton in production he would have to either sell off the factory adjacent to the motorway system or change its usage to that of a distribution unit.

If he did that… Leo tensed as the walker drew level with the gate in his walled garden that gave on to the path, and he had a clear view of her.

Jodi Marsh!

Jodi saw Leo at exactly the same time as he saw her. The sight of him froze her in her tracks. What was Leo Jefferson doing in the garden of Ashton House? Her house. The house she had secretly wanted from the first minute she had seen it!

Before she could gather herself together and hurry past he was opening the gate and coming towards her. He stood in front of her, blocking her path.

'I'd like to talk to you,' she heard him telling her coolly.

Jodi glared at him, praying that he couldn't hear the furious, racing thud of her heart or guess just what kind of effect he was having on her.

'Well, I certainly would not like to talk to you,' she retaliated.

Liar. Liar! her conscience tormented her silently. And you don't just want to talk to him either…

Horrified that he might somehow sense what she was feeling, Jodi tried to walk away, but he had already masterfully taken hold of her arm, and as she battled against the dizzying sensation of his touch somehow or other she found that she was being gently but firmly propelled through the gate and into the garden beyond.

She had been in the garden before—at the invitation of the old lady who had lived there who, like Leo, had happened to see her on the path one day.

She had ached then with sadness to see its neglect, and longed to be the one to restore both it and the house to their former glory. Of course that was an impossible dream. Jodi dreaded to imagine just how much money it would take to restore such a large house and so overgrown a garden. Far too much for her, but not, it seemed, too much for Leo Jefferson.

'Will you please stop manhandling me?' she demanded angrily as Leo closed the gate, and then her face burned a deep, betraying pink as she saw the way he was looking at her.

If he dared to say one word about anything she might have said to him under the influence of alcohol and desire she would... But to her relief he simply looked at her for several heart-stopping seconds before asking her quietly, 'What were you doing in my suite?'

Jodi gaped at him. It took her several precious moments to recover from the directness of his question, but finally she did so, rallying admirably to remind him firmly, 'Well, according to you, I was there because...' She stopped as he started to shake his head.

'I don't want you to tell me what I believed you were doing there, Jodi, I want to hear your version of events.'

Her version. Now he had surprised her. Stubbornly she looked away from him.

'It doesn't matter now, does it?' she challenged him.

'Doesn't it? According to your cousin, you were there to ask me to reconsider closing down the factory.'

Flustered, Jodi looked at him before demanding worriedly, 'You've been speaking to Nigel?'

Leo could tell that he had caught her off guard.

'I told him right from the start that it was a crazy idea, but he wouldn't listen.' Barely pausing for breath, she continued, 'I thought at first he meant that I should talk to you in the hotel foyer, but then he told me that he'd managed to borrow a key card.'

'And so you went up to the suite to wait for me and whilst you were there you ordered yourself a drink,' Leo supplied helpfully.

Jodi stared at him.

'No,' she denied vehemently, so vehemently that Leo knew immediately she was speaking the truth. Shaking her head, she told him angrily, 'I would never have ordered a drink without paying for it. No, I asked Nigel to arrange it for me. Nigel thought he'd ordered a soft drink, not—' She stopped abruptly, clamping her lips together and glowering at Leo.

'I can't see what possible relevance any of this has now,' she began, but Leo was determined to establish exactly what had happened—and why!

'So whilst you were waiting for me you drank the fruit punch, which was alcoholic, and then...'

Jodi had had enough.

'I don't want to talk about it,' she told him fiercely, 'and you can't make me.'

'You went to bed with me,' Leo reminded her softly. 'And from what I've learned about you, Jodi Marsh, that is something—'

'It was nothing,' Jodi denied sharply. 'And, anyway, you were the one who went to bed with me. I was already there, asleep.'

'In my bed...and you—' Leo stopped abruptly. This wasn't getting them anywhere and it wasn't what he wanted to say.

'Look,' he told her quietly, 'it seems that I misjudged the situation...made an error about the reasons for you being there,' he corrected himself. 'And, that being the case, I really think that we should discuss—'

'There isn't anything I want or need to discuss with you,' Jodi jumped in tensely.

The fact that he might have mistaken her reason for being in his suite, and even the fact that he was prepared

to acknowledge as much, made no difference to what she
had done or how she felt about it.

'What happened just isn't important enough to warrant
discussing,' she added, determined to bring their conversation to an end, but to her consternation Leo was refusing to let the subject drop.

'Maybe not to you, but I happen to feel rather differently,' he said curtly. 'It is not, let me tell you, my habit
to indulge in casual sex with a succession of unknown
partners.'

Casual sex! Jodi had to struggle to prevent herself from
physically cringing. Was there to be no end to the humiliation her behaviour was forcing her to suffer?

Before she could stop herself she was retorting passionately, 'For your information, I have not had a succession
of partners, and in fact…'

Abruptly she fell silent, her face flushing. No, she must
not tell him that! If she did he was bound to start asking
even more questions than he already had, and there was
absolutely no way she was going to tell him about that idiotic foolishness she had experienced when she had first
seen him in the hotel foyer.

No doubt some might claim that she had fallen in love
with him at first sight, and that was why…but she, Jodi,
was made of sterner and far more realistic stuff. She was
a modern-thinking woman and would not contemplate
such nonsense!

What was it about her that infuriated him to the point
where he itched to take hold of her and make her listen to
him? Leo wondered distractedly, unable to stop himself
from focusing on her mouth and remembering how hot
and sweet it had tasted. He wanted to kiss her again now,
right here. But she was already turning back towards the

gate, and a sudden surge of common sense warned him against the folly of going after her and begging her to stay when it so plainly wasn't what she wanted. But she had wanted him that night. She had wanted him and he had wanted her right back. And for him the problem was that he still did.

'Jodi?' he began, making a last attempt to talk to her, but, as he had already known she would, she shook her head.

'No, I...'

She barely had time to give a disbelieving and indignant gasp before she was dragged unceremoniously and ruthlessly into Leo's arms, and held there tightly.

Against his ardent seeking mouth she tried to make a protest, but it was smothered immediately by the hot passion of his kiss...dizzying her, bemusing her, confusing her, so that somehow instead of repudiating him she was actually moving closer, reaching out to him...

Somewhere deep in her brain a warning bell started to ring, but Jodi ignored it, Leo was kissing her and there was no way she wanted anything, least of all some silly old warning bell, to come between her and the sheer intensity and excitement, the total bliss, of feeling his mouth moving possessively and passionately against her own.

'Mmm...'

Leo could feel the heavy, crazy thud of his heartbeat as Jodi suddenly dropped her defensive attitude and became so soft, so pliable, so bewitchingly and adorably warm in his arms that he was sorely tempted to pick her up and carry her straight to his bed.

But a bird calling overhead suddenly brought Jodi to her senses; white-faced and shaking, she pulled away from him. How on earth could she have allowed that to happen? Her mouth stung slightly and she had to resist the temptation to run her tongue-tip over it—to comfort it because it was missing the touch of Leo's? She ached from head to foot and she had started to tremble. Shocked to her heart by her lack of self-control, she cried out to him in a low tortured voice, 'Don't you ever touch me again...ever!'

And then she was gone, turning on her heel to flee in wretchedness, her heart throbbing with pain and self-contempt, refusing to stop as she heard Leo calling after her.

Jodi was still trembling when she reached the security of her own home. She had heard a rumour in the village that Ashton House had a tenant, but it had never occurred to her that it might be Leo Jefferson. Nigel had warned her that Leo had said that the negotiations over which of the factories he intended to close were likely to be protracted, but why did he have to move here to Frampton?

She felt as though there wasn't a single aspect of her life he hadn't now somehow penetrated and invaded.

Or a single aspect of herself?

Hurriedly she walked into her small kitchen and started to prepare her supper. Nigel had rung earlier and suggested they have dinner together, but Jodi had told him she was too busy, worried that if she saw him she might inadvertently betray the plans for the demonstration the following day.

Not that they were doing anything illegal, but she knew that Nigel would not entirely approve of her involvement in what was going to happen and would try his best to dissuade her.

She loved her cousin very much, they were in many ways as close as if they had been brother and sister, and she knew how shocked he would be if he was to learn how she had behaved with Leo Jefferson. She felt ashamed her-

self…but what was making her feel even worse were the
dreadful dreams she kept having in which she relived what
had happened—and enjoyed it.

Swallowing hard, Jodi tried to concentrate on what she
was doing, but somehow she had lost her appetite. For
food, that was. Standing in the garden earlier with Leo,
there had been a moment when she had looked up at him,
at his mouth, and she had never felt so hungry in her life…

Leo woke up with a start, wondering where he was at
first, in the unfamiliarity of his new bedroom at Ashton
House. He had been dreaming about Jodi and not for the
first time. Reaching for the bedside lamp, he switched it
on. The house had been repainted prior to being let and the
smell of fresh paint still hung faintly on the air. Leo got
out of bed and padded over to the window, pushing back
the curtains to stare into the moonlit garden.

In his sleep he had remembered something about Jodi
that disturbed him. Something he had not previously properly registered, but something that, knowing what he did
now, made perfect sense!

Was it merely his imagination or had there really been
a certain something about Jodi's body that might mean he
had in fact been her first lover?

No, it was absurd that he should think any such thing.
Totally absurd. She had been so uninhibited, so passionate…

But what if he was right? What if, in addition to having unwittingly drunk the alcoholic concoction supplied
by her cousin and fallen asleep, she had been totally inexperienced?

Leo swallowed hard, aware of how very difficult he was
finding it to use the word 'virgin', even in the privacy of
his own thoughts.

But surely if that had been the case she would have said something.

Such as what? he derided himself. *Oh, by the way, before I went to bed with you I was a virgin.*

No, that would not be her style at all. She was far too independent, had far too much pride.

But if she had been a virgin...

At no point in the proceedings had she suggested that they should be thinking in terms of having safe sex, and he had certainly not been prepared either emotionally or practically to take on that responsibility, which meant...

There was no way Leo could sleep now. So far as Jodi's sexual health was concerned, and his own, if he was right and she had been a virgin, he knew he need have no worries, but when it came to the risk of an unplanned pregnancy—that was a very different matter. And one surely that must be concerning Jodi herself.

He would very definitely have to talk to her now, and insist that she give him the answers to his questions.

Closing his eyes, he forced himself to recall every single second of the hours they had spent together—not that there was really any force involved, after all, his body and his senses had done precious little else other than relive the event ever since it had happened. But this time it was different, this time he was looking for clues, signs that he might have previously missed.

There had been that sweetly wonderful closeness between them in their most intimate moments, the feeling of her body being tightly wrapped around him. But she had said nothing. Given no indication that... What in hell's name had she been doing? he wondered, suddenly as angry for her as though she were his personal responsibility.

She was a schoolteacher, for heaven's sake. She was supposed to behave responsibly!

If she had been a virgin it put a completely different complexion on the whole situation. He was perhaps more Italian than he had ever previously realised, Leo recognised wryly as he felt an atavistic sense of male protectiveness engulf him, and with it an even more unexpected sense of pride. Because he had been her first lover? Because she might have accidentally conceived his child? Just how chauvinistic was he?

His mother, of course, would be overjoyed. A grandchild, and the kind of daughter-in-law she would wholly approve of and love showing off to her Italian relatives.

Whoa...Leo cautioned himself. These were very dangerous and foolish thoughts that had no business whatsoever clogging up his head.

For one insane moment he actually wondered if his mother might have gone ahead and got her village wise woman to put some kind of a love spell on him. Then reality resurfaced.

There was only one person to blame for the situation he was in and that one person was himself. He could, after all, have resisted Jodi. She was a woman, small and slender, weighing, he guessed, something around a hundred and twenty pounds, whilst he was a man, taller, heavier, and perfectly capable of having stopped her had he so wanted to.

Only he hadn't...

Have a heart, he protested to himself; she was there, warm, wanton, beddable, and totally and completely irresistible. It made him ache right through to the soles of his feet right now just to think about it.

Leo grimaced as he felt his body's unmistakable reaction to his thoughts.

He wanted her in a way that was totally alien to anything he had ever experienced before.

He wanted her. He wanted her. Oh, heavens, how he wanted her!

Jodi gave a tiny moan in her sleep, her lips forming Leo's name, and then abruptly she was awake, the reality of her situation blotting out the delicious pleasure of her lost dream.

She had felt so much safer when Leo Jefferson had not known who she was, when he had for some incomprehensible reason believed she was in cahoots with Jeremy Driscoll. Jeremy Driscoll! Jodi gave a brief shudder. Loathsome man!

One of the women who was going to be demonstrating had said at their committee meeting that she had seen Jeremy at the factory, coming out of a disused storeroom. He hadn't seen her and she had said that he had been behaving very furtively.

None of the workers liked Jeremy, and Jodi had wondered just exactly what he had been doing at the factory when it now belonged to Leo. Not that it was any concern of hers. No, her concern was much closer to home.

She had come so close to betraying herself this evening when Leo had been questioning her. The last thing she wanted was for him to realise that, far from being the experienced sensualist he obviously thought she was, she had, in fact, been a virgin before she had taken it into her idiotic head to go to bed with him.

And the reason she didn't want him to know the truth was because she was terrified that if he did he might start questioning just why she had been so compulsively attracted to him, so totally unable to resist the temptation he had represented.

She could, of course, always claim that, as a woman in her twenties, she had begun to see her virginity as a burden she wanted to free herself from, but somehow she doubted that he would believe her. He was too shrewd, too perceptive for that.

If he should ever find out just how she had felt about him when she had seen him in the hotel foyer Jodi knew that she would just die of embarrassment and humiliation.

But of course it was totally impossible that he should find out, wasn't it? Because only she knew.

And only she was going to know.

And only she knew that until she had met him she had been a virgin, and this evening she had as good as told him. That had been a mistake, yes, she allowed judiciously, but it was a mistake she had learned from. A mistake she most certainly was not going to be repeating.

She pulled the covers up more closely around herself. In the dream she had just woken from Leo had been wrapping her in his arms whilst he tenderly stroked her skin and even more tenderly kissed her lips...

What on earth was she? A born-again teenager indulging in a fantasy? She was not going to dream about him again, she told herself sternly. She was not!

The first Leo knew about the demonstration was when he received a phone call from a local radio station asking if he would like to comment on the situation.

Several other calls later he had elicited the information that the demonstration was non-violent, protesting against the factory being closed down.

Meetings he had already arranged with a large haulage group who were interested in potentially acquiring the site of the motorway-based factory meant that Leo was unable to go to Frampton himself until later on in the day, but he did speak with the leader of the group to set up a meeting with them to discuss the situation.

Although he was not prepared to say so at this stage, Leo had virtually made up his mind that he would keep the Frampton factory open. This decision had nothing whatsoever to do with Jodi Marsh, of course.

Later in the day, when the police rang him to inform him that they intended to monitor the situation at the demonstration, Leo told them that he had every confidence that things would be resolved peacefully.

It was four o'clock, and there was no way he could leave London until at least five. His mind started to wander. What was Jodi doing now? He really did need to talk to her; if there was the remotest chance that she might have conceived his child then he needed to know about it.

Jodi glanced a little anxiously over her shoulder. She had joined the demo an hour ago, straight from school. At first things had been quiet and peaceful, and the leader had told her that Leo Jefferson had been in touch with him to organise a meeting for the following day. But then to everyone's surprise, half an hour ago Jeremy Driscoll had arrived. At first he had demanded that they open the factory gates to allow him access and when they had refused Jeremy had got out of the car. A small scuffle had ensued, but ultimately Jeremy had been allowed to walk into the office block.

He was still inside it, but ten minutes ago a police car had drawn up several yards away from the demonstrators, quickly followed by a reporter and a photographer from the local paper.

Now the original peaceful mood of the picketers had changed to one of hostile aggression as Jeremy emerged from the building, and one of the demonstrators to whom

Jeremy had been particularly verbally abusive on his way into the factory caught sight of him.

'You don't really think that this is going to make any difference to Jefferson's decision to close this place down, do you?' Jodi could hear Driscoll challenging her fellow demonstrator contemptuously.

'He's agreed to meet with us in the morning,' the other man was retaliating.

'And you think that means he's going to listen to what you have to say! More fool you. He's already decided that this place isn't viable and who can blame him, with a lazy, good-for-nothing workforce like you lot? It's because of you that we've had to sell the place. Everyone knows that...'

Jodi gave a small indignant gasp as she heard him.

'That's not true,' she interjected firmly, causing Jeremy to turn to look at her.

'My God, you!' he breathed. 'I suppose I should have guessed,' he sneered as he gave Jodi's jeans and T-shirt-clad body a deliberately lascivious stare. 'This isn't going to do you any favours with the school board, is it? But then, of course, your precious school will end up being closed down along with the factory, won't it? Looks as if I shall be getting my building land after all.' He smirked as he started to walk purposefully towards Jodi. People tried to stop him, but he was too quick for them.

As he moved towards Jodi one of the men started to step protectively between them. He was only a young man, nowhere near as heavily built as Jeremy, and Jodi winced as she saw the force with which Jeremy thrust him to one side.

The young man retaliated, and suddenly it seemed to Jodi as though all hell had broken loose; people were shouting, shoving, the police car doors were opening, and then before she could move, to her shock, Jeremy had suddenly taken hold of her and was dragging her across the factory forecourt.

Instinctively she tried to resist him, hitting out at him as he deliberately manhandled her; her panic was that of any woman fearing a man she knew to be her enemy, and had nothing whatsoever to do with her role in the demonstration. Jeremy dragged her towards one of the advancing police officers, claiming to them that she had deliberately assaulted him.

'I insist that you arrest her, Officer,' Jodi could hear him saying as he gave her a nastily victorious look. 'I shall probably press charges for assault.'

Jodi tried to protest her innocence, but she was already being bundled towards the police van that had screamed to a halt alongside the car.

Jodi blinked in the light from the flashbulb as the hovering photographer took their picture.

The police station was busy. Jodi couldn't believe what was happening to her. A stern-looking sergeant she didn't recognise was beginning to charge them all. Jodi was feeling sick. Her head ached; she felt grubby and frightened. There was a bruise on her arm where Jeremy Driscoll had manhandled her.

'Name...'

Jodi flinched as she realised that the sergeant was speaking to her.

'Er—Jodi Marsh,' she began. Supporting the workforce by taking part in a peaceful demonstration was one thing. Ending up being charged and possibly thrown into a police cell was quite definitely another. She couldn't bear to think about what the more conservative parents of her pupils were going to say, never mind the school governors or the education authority.

'Excuse me, Officer.'

She was quite definitely going to faint, Jodi decided as she heard the unmistakable sound of Leo Jefferson's voice coming from immediately behind her.

Something about Leo's calm manner captured the sergeant's attention. Putting down his pen, he looked at him.

Leo had arrived at the factory gates just in time to hear from those who were still there what had happened.

'Yes, and they even took the schoolteacher away,' one of the onlookers had informed Leo with relish, wondering why on earth his comment should have caused his listener to turn round and head straight back to his car with such a grim look on his face.

'I'm Leo Jefferson,' Leo introduced himself to the sergeant. 'I own the factory.'

'You own it.' The sergeant was frowning now. 'According to our records, it was a Mr Jeremy Driscoll who reported that there was a problem.'

'Maybe he did, but I am quite definitely the owner of the factory,' Leo reiterated firmly. 'Can you tell me exactly what's happened, Officer. Only, as I understand it, the demonstrators were peaceful and I had in fact arranged to meet with them in the morning.'

'Well, that's as maybe, sir, but we were telephoned from the factory by Mr Driscoll who said that he was not being allowed to leave and that both he and the property had been threatened with violence. Once we got there a bit of a scuffle broke out and this young lady here...' he indicated Jodi '...actually attempted to assault Mr Driscoll.'

Jodi could feel her face crimsoning with mortification as she leapt immediately to her own defence, denying it. 'I did no such thing. He was the one who attacked me...'

To her horror, she could actually feel her eyes filling with childish tears.

'I think there must have been a mistake,' Leo Jefferson was saying. Although she couldn't bring herself to turn round and look at him, Jodi could feel him moving closer to her, and for some insane reason she felt that instinctively her body sought the warmth and protection of his.

'I happen to know Miss Marsh very well indeed. In fact she was at the factory on my behalf, as my representative,' Leo lied coolly. 'I cannot imagine for a second that she would have assaulted Mr Driscoll.'

The sergeant was frowning.

'Well, my officers have informed me that he was most insistent she be arrested,' he told Leo. 'He said that he intended to press charges against her for assault.'

Jodi gave a small, stifled sob.

'Indeed. Well, in that case I shall have to press charges against him for trespass,' Leo informed the sergeant. 'He quite definitely did not have my permission to enter the factory, and I rather imagine that the revenue authorities will be very interested to know what he was doing there. There are some account books missing that they are very anxious to see.'

Jodi gave a small start as she listened to him, impulsively turning round to tell Leo quickly, 'The mother of one of my pupils mentioned that she saw him coming out of one of the unused storerooms.' Her voice started to fade away as she saw the way Leo was looking at her arm.

'Is Driscoll responsible for that?' he demanded dangerously.

Without waiting for her to reply he turned to the desk sergeant and said with determined authority, 'I understand that you may have to charge Miss Marsh, but in the meantime, Officer, I wonder if you would be prepared to release her into my care. I promise that I won't let her out of my sight.'

The desk sergeant studied them both. He had a full custody suite and no spare cells, and he could see no real reason why Jodi shouldn't be allowed to leave if Leo Jefferson was prepared to vouch for her.

'Very well,' he acknowledged. 'But you will have to take full responsibility for her, and for ensuring that she returns here in the morning to be formally charged if Mr Driscoll insists on going ahead.'

'You have my word on it,' Leo responded promptly, and then before Jodi could say anything he had turned her round and was gently ushering her out into the summer night.

To her own chagrin, Jodi discovered that she was actually crying.

'It's the shock,' she heard Leo saying to her as he guided her towards his car. 'Don't worry, you'll be OK once we get you home.'

'I want a bath...and some clean clothes,' Jodi told him in a voice she barely recognised as her own.

'The bath I can provide; the clothes we shall have to collect from your house on the way to mine,' Leo replied promptly.

'Yours!' Jodi's forehead creased as she allowed Leo to fasten the passenger seat belt around her. 'But I want to go to my own home.'

'You can't, I'm afraid,' Leo told her. 'The sergeant released you into my care, remember, and I have to produce you at the station in the morning.'

'But I can't stay with you,' Jodi protested.

'I'm sorry, Jodi.' Leo's voice was unexpectedly kind. 'You have to.'

'I didn't really assault Jeremy.' Jodi tried to defend herself. 'He was the one...' She stopped and bit her lip, her stomach clenching on a leap of nervous shock as she saw the ferocity in Leo's eyes as he turned to study her.

'If he hurt you... Did he, Jodi?'

When she looked away from him Leo cursed himself for the intensity of his own reaction. He had quite plainly shocked and frightened her, and she had already been frightened more than enough for one night.

'I thought the demonstration was supposed to be a peaceful one,' he commented as he drove back towards the village.

'It was,' Jodi acknowledged. 'But Jeremy was very confrontational and somehow things got out of hand. Is it true that he's being investigated?'

'Yes,' Leo told her briefly, 'but I shouldn't really have said so, I don't suppose.'

When they reached her cottage he insisted on going inside with her and waiting until she had packed a small case of necessities, and Jodi felt too disorientated to be able to have the strength to resist.

Jeremy Driscoll's manner towards her had left her feeling vulnerable, and she couldn't help remembering how when she had won her battle with him to retain the playing field for the school he had threatened to get even with her. He was a vengeful and dangerous man, and for tonight at least, loath though she was to admit it, she knew she would feel far safer sleeping under Leo Jefferson's roof than under her own.

CHAPTER SIX

'WHEN WAS THE last time you had something to eat?'

Leo's prosaic question as he unlocked his front door and ushered Jodi into the hallway of the house made her give him an uncertain look.

She had been steeling herself for, if not his hostility, then certainly some sharply incisive questions. The fact that he seemed more worried about her personal welfare than anything else was thoroughly disconcerting—but nowhere near as disconcerting as the relief and sense of security it had given her to have him take charge in the way that he had done.

'Lunchtime.' She answered his question on autopilot, whilst most of her attention was given to what she was feeling at a much deeper level. 'But I'm not hungry.'

'That's because you're still in shock,' Leo told her gently. 'The kitchen is this way.'

At any other time Jodi knew that she would have been fascinated to see the inside of the house she had admired so much, but right now she felt as though her ability to take in anything was overwhelmed by the events of the evening.

As Leo had suggested, she suspected that she was suffering from shock. Otherwise, why would she be so apathetically allowing Leo to make all her decisions for her? She let him guide her firmly to a kitchen chair and urge her into it, whilst he busied himself opening cupboards and then the fridge door, insisting that the light supper he was going to make them both would help her to sleep.

'Which reminds me,' he added several minutes later as he served her with an impressively light plate of scrambled eggs, 'I'm afraid that you will have to sleep in my bed-room, since it's the only one that's properly furnished at the moment; I can sleep downstairs on a sofa.'

'No,' Jodi protested immediately, praying that he wouldn't guess the reason for the hot colour suddenly burning her face. The very thought of sleeping in his bed was bringing back memories she had no wish to have surfacing at any time, but most especially when the man responsible for them was seated opposite her.

To her consternation, Leo shook his head at her instinctive refusal, telling her calmly, 'It's all right, I can guess what you must be thinking, but you don't need to worry.'

Jodi tensed. How could he possibly know what she was thinking? And if he really did then how dared he treat it and her as though…?

As she tried to gather her thoughts into a logical enough order to challenge him she heard him continuing, 'The cleaning team came today, and they will have changed the bed linen.'

Jodi almost choked on her scrambled eggs as relief flooded through her. He hadn't realised what she was thinking after all; hadn't realised just what piercingly sensual and shocking images the mention of his bed had aroused for her.

But at least his comments had given her time to gain some control of her thoughts, and for her to remember that she was supposed to be a sensible, mature adult.

'I can't possibly take your bed,' she informed Leo in what she hoped was a cool and businesslike voice.

'Why not?' Leo demanded, giving her a quizzical look, and then threw her into complete turmoil as he reminded her softly, 'After all, it isn't as though you haven't done so before.'

As the blood left her face and then rushed back to it in a wave of bright pink Jodi felt her hand trembling so much that she had to grip the mug of tea Leo had given her with both hands to prevent herself from spilling its contents.

She knew that she was overreacting, but somehow she just couldn't stop herself.

Leo's teasing comment had not just embarrassed her, it had left her feeling humiliated as well, Jodi recognised as she felt the unwanted prick of her tears threatening to expose her vulnerability to him.

But even as she struggled fiercely to blink them away, Leo was already apologising.

'I'm sorry,' he offered. 'I shouldn't have said that.' Leo paused, watching her, mentally berating himself for offending her. It amazed him how much discovering that he had been wrong in his earlier assessment of the situation had changed what he felt about her.

The last thing he wanted to do was to hurt her in any way, but there were still certain issues they needed to address—together—and, although he had not deliberately tried to lead up to them, now that the subject had been introduced perhaps he should seize the opportunity to discuss his concerns with her.

'I know that this perhaps isn't the best time in the world to say this,' he began quietly, 'but we really do need to talk, Jodi…'

Unsteadily Jodi put her mug down on the table.

'Is that why you brought me here?' she demanded as fiercely as she could. 'So that you could cross-examine me? If you think for one minute that just because you saved me from a night in prison I am going to repay you by betraying the others involved in the demonstration, I'm afraid you'd better take me back to the station right now—'

'Jodi.' Leo interrupted her passionate tirade as gently as he could. 'I don't want to talk to you about the problems at the factory, or the demonstration.'

As he watched her eyes shadow with suspicion Leo wondered what she would say if he was to tell her that right now there was only one person and one problem on his mind, and that was her!

'I've already arranged a meeting with representatives of the factory workforce for tomorrow, when I intend to discuss my proposals for the future of the factory with them,' he told her calmly.

'Yes, I heard.' Jodi suddenly felt totally exhausted, drained to the point where simply to think was a superhuman effort. 'Then what did you want to talk to me about?' she asked him warily.

Leo could see how tired she looked and he berated himself for his selfishness. She was still in shock. She needed to rest and recuperate, not be plagued by questions.

'It doesn't matter,' he told her gently. 'Look, why don't you go to bed? You look completely done in...' Leo reached out to help her out of the chair.

Sensing that he was about to touch her, Jodi felt her defences leap into action, knowing all too well just how vulnerable she was likely to be to any kind of physical contact with him right now. She sprang up out of the chair, almost stumbling in her haste to avoid contact with him, and in doing so precipitated the very thing she had been so desperate to prevent. As Leo reached out to steady her his hands grasped her arms. As he took the weight of her fall against his body he closed the distance between them.

It was just a week since she had first seen him, a handful

of days, that was all, so how on earth could it be that she was reacting to him as though she was starving for physical contact as though the sudden feel of him against her answered a craving that nothing else could hope to appease?

It was as if just the act of leaning against him fulfilled and completed her, made her feel whole again, made her feel both incredibly strong and helplessly weak. She felt that she had found the purpose in life for which she had been created and yet at the same time she hated herself for her neediness.

Mutely she pushed against his chest, demanding her release. Leo obeyed the demand of her body language, asking her gruffly, 'Are you OK?'

'Yes, I'm fine,' Jodi responded as she stepped back from him and turned away, ducking into the shadows so that he couldn't see the aching hunger in her expression.

How had things possibly come to this? How had she come to this? Where had her feelings come from? They were totally alien in their intensity and their ferocity.

Leo held the kitchen door open for her. Shakily she walked out into the hallway.

Leo accompanied her to the bottom of the stairs. Jodi began to climb them, her heart bumping heavily against the wall of her chest. She dared not look at Leo, dared not do anything that might betray to him how she was feeling.

'It's the second door on the left along the landing,' she could hear him telling her. 'You'll find clean towels and everything in the bathroom. I'll go and get your bag for you and leave it outside the bedroom door.'

He was telling her as plainly as though he had used the words themselves that she need not fear a repetition of what had happened in his hotel bedroom, Jodi recognised. Which was surely very thoughtful and gentlemanly of him. So why wasn't she feeling more appreciative, more relieved? Why was she, to be blunt about it, actually feeling disappointed?

Wearily Jodi made her way to the top of the stairs.

As he stood watching the tiredness with which she moved Leo ached to be able to go after her, gather her up protectively in his arms. He deliberately forced himself to turn round and go out to the car to bring in Jodi's bag.

The look of confusion and despair he had seen on her face in the police station had prompted him into a course of action he now recognised as riven with potential hazards.

When he returned with Jodi's bag he took it upstairs, knocked briefly outside his closed bedroom door and went straight back downstairs again, shutting himself in the sitting room.

Jodi was standing staring out of the bedroom window when she heard Leo's knock. She deliberately made herself count to ten—very slowly—before going to open the door, and then told herself that she was relieved and not disappointed to find that the landing was empty and there was no sign of Leo.

Both the bedroom and the bathroom adjoining it were furnished so impersonally that they might almost have been hotel rooms; but thinking of hotel rooms in connection with Leo aroused thoughts and feelings for her that were far from impersonal. Jodi hastily tried to divert her thoughts to less dangerous channels as she went into the bathroom and prepared for bed.

Now that she was on her own she knew that she ought to be thinking about the morning and the possibility of having to face the charges that Jeremy Driscoll had threatened to bring against her—a daunting prospect indeed, but somehow nowhere near as daunting as having to acknowledge just how strong her feelings for Leo were.

That comment he had made to her earlier about her previous appropriation of his bed!

It had made her feel embarrassed and even humiliated, yes, but it had made her remember how wildly wonderful it had felt—she had felt—to be there in his arms. In his life? But she wasn't in his life, and he wasn't in hers, not really. All they had done was have sex together, and every woman—even a schoolteacher—knew that for men the act of sex could be enjoyed with less emotional involvement than they might feel consuming a bar of chocolate—nice at the time but quickly forgotten.

She crawled into Leo's bed—totally sober this time! The bed smelled of clean, fresh linen, as anonymous and bereft of any tangible sign of Leo as the room itself. Curling up in the centre of the large bed, she closed her eyes, but despite her exhaustion sleep evaded her.

She was almost too overtired to sleep, she recognised, the anxieties filling her thoughts, refusing to allow her to relax. She closed her eyes and started to breathe slowly and deeply.

Downstairs, Leo was finding sleep equally hard to come by. He had work to do that could have occupied his time and his thoughts, but instead he found that he was pacing the sitting-room floor, thinking about Jodi. Worrying about Jodi, and not just because he had now realised just what an awkward situation they could both be in because of their shared night together.

That bruise on her arm caused by Jeremy Driscoll had made him feel as though he could quite happily have torn the other man limb from limb and disposed of his carcass to the nearest hungry carnivore. The mere thought of him even touching Jodi...

Abruptly he stopped pacing. What the devil was happening to him? Did he really need to ask that? he mocked himself inwardly. He was in love. This was love. He was transformed into a man he could barely recognise. A man who behaved and thought illogically, a man driven by his emotions, a man who right now…

He froze as he heard a sound from upstairs, and then strode towards the door, wrenching it open just in time to hear it again, a high-pitched sound of female misery.

Leo took the stairs two at a time, flinging open the bedroom door and striding across the floor to where Jodi lay in the middle of the bed.

She was awake; in the darkness he could see her eyes shining, but she was lying as silently still as though she dared not breathe, never mind move.

'Jodi, what is it?' he demanded.

A wash of shaky relief sluiced through Jodi as she heard and recognised Leo's voice. She had been dreaming about Jeremy Driscoll. A most awful dream, full of appalling and nameless nightmare terrors. It had been the sound of her own muffled scream of sheer panic that had woken her, and for a couple of heartbeats after Leo had thrown open the bedroom door she had actually believed that he was Jeremy.

Now, though, the sound of his voice had reassured her, banishing the nightmare completely.

Too relieved to think of anything else other than the fact that he had rescued her from the terror which had been pursuing her, she turned towards him, telling him, 'I was having the most horrid dream…about Jeremy Driscoll…'

Just saying his name was still enough to make her shudder violently as she struggled to sit up so that she could talk properly to Leo, who was now leaning over the bed towards her.

She could see the anxiety in his eyes now that her own

had accustomed themselves to the night-time shadows of
the room, their darkness softened by the summer moonlight outside.

'I'm sorry if I disturbed you.' She began to apologise
and then checked as she saw that he was still fully dressed.

Was the sitting-room sofa so uncomfortable that he
hadn't even bothered trying to sleep on it, or did the fact
that he still had his clothes on have something to do with
her presence here in his house? Was she afraid that she
might try to seduce him a second time?

'What is it? What's wrong?'

The speed with which he had read her expression caught
Jodi off guard. Her defences, already overloaded by the
events of the day, gave up on her completely.

'You're still dressed,' she told him in a low voice. 'You
haven't been to bed; if that's because—'

But before she could voice her fears Leo was inter-
rupting her.

'It's because right now the only bed I want to be in is
already occupied, and denied to me,' he told her huskily.
'Unless, of course, you're prepared to change your mind
and share it with me?'

Leo knew that he was doing exactly what he had told
himself he must not do under any kind of circumstances;
that he was behaving like a predator, taking advantage of
both Jodi's vulnerability and her current dependence on
him, but he still couldn't stop himself. Just the sight of her
sitting there in his bed, her slim bare arms wrapped around
her hunched-up knees as she looked uncertainly up at him,
was enough to make him know that he was prepared to be
damned for this eternity and every eternity beyond it just
to have her in his arms again, to be granted the opportunity to hold her, touch her, kiss her, caress her.

He wasn't still dressed because he didn't want her, Jodi

realised, or because he was afraid that she might embarrass them both by coming on to him. She could feel her whole body starting to tremble beneath the onrush of wild excitement that was roaring through her.

Leo groaned her name, unable to hold back his longing for her. He reached for her, wrapping her in his arms, his mouth so passionately urgent that the sound of her name was lost beneath his kiss.

Jodi knew that she should resist him, that she should insist that he release her, so why instead of doing so was she clinging shamelessly to him? She opened her mouth eagerly to the demanding probe of his tongue, her whole body racked with a raw, aching hunger for him.

She had almost begun to convince herself that their previous lovemaking couldn't possibly have been as good as she remembered, that she had exaggerated it, romanticised it, turning it in her mind into an implausible state of perfection that was total fantasy. Now, shockingly, she knew her memory *had* been at fault, although not in the way that she expected!

Leo's lovemaking had not been as wonderful as she had remembered—it had been even better! More pleasurable, more intoxicating...

As her body relived the pleasure his had given her Jodi knew that there was no point in trying to stop herself from responding to him, no way she could stop herself from wanting him.

She heard the small, tortured groan that filled her own throat as she feasted greedily on his kiss. The touch of his mouth against hers was like receiving a life-giving transfusion, she told herself dizzily as Leo cupped her face in his hands and held her a willing captive and kissed her with an intimacy that almost stopped her heart.

Jodi trembled and then shuddered as the pleasure of

THE TYCOON'S VIRGIN

being so close to him filled her, running through her nervous system like pure adrenalin.

'We shouldn't be doing this.' Jodi could hear the total lack of conviction in the longing-filled softness of her voice.

'I know,' Leo responded rawly. 'But I just can't stop myself.'

'I don't want you to stop!'

Had she really said that? Jodi was shocked by her own wanton lack of restraint, and shocked too by the discovery that somehow or other she had already managed to unfasten half of the buttons of Leo's shirt.

Beneath her explorative fingertips she could feel the soft silkiness of his body hair.

She leaned forward, breathing in the scent of his skin with deliberate sensuality.

A rush of sensation flooded her, a dizzying kaleidoscope of emotions, recognition—she would recognise his scent anywhere—exaltation, just to have the freedom to be so intimate, so possessively womanly with him. Inhaling his scent only served to remind her of just how many other ached-for intimacies she could enjoy with him. She felt a surge of power, of female strength, knowing that she was responsible for the acceleration of his breathing.

Leo felt himself shudder from top to toe, totally unable to control the fierceness of his response to Jodi. It felt as if every sensation he had ever experienced had just been intensified a thousandfold. Even the simple act of breathing seemed to fill his whole body, his every sense with a heart-rocking awareness of her and longing for her.

This wasn't, he recognised, mere lust, this was the big one; *the* one. She, Jodi, was his one and only. But, he knew instinctively, he couldn't tell her so, not now, not yet; what they were building between them was still too fragile.

He groaned out loud again as Jodi kissed his bared torso. His desire for her ran like fire through his body, the sweetest form of torture.

Swiftly Leo removed the rest of his clothes, never once losing eye contact with Jodi whilst he did so.

He warned himself that she might see in his eyes his love for her, but he couldn't make himself break the contact between them that seemed to be binding them so intimately close together.

In her eyes he could see wonderment, uncertainty, longing, and even a little old-fashioned female shock. Her body clenched when he cupped the tender ball of her shoulder with one hand whilst tugging off the last of his clothes with the other, but she didn't make any attempt to break the gaze that was locking them together.

Somehow the silent visual bonding between them was as sensually charged as touching.

His body ached intolerably for her, and so too did his heart, his entire being.

'Jodi.' He whispered her name again as he gathered her closer, finally breaking their eye contact to look down at her mouth and then up into her eyes again before slowly brushing his mouth against hers.

Jodi felt as though she was going to explode with the sheer force of the sensual tension building up inside her.

It was a good job she was not some impressionable teenager, she told herself, otherwise she would be in danger of deceiving herself that the way Leo was looking at her, as though he wanted to communicate something deeply meaningful, meant that he really cared about her.

She knew that she ought to bring what was happening between them to an end now, before things went any further, but Leo was taking hold of her, brushing his mouth against hers once more in a way that aroused in her such a sweetly aching desire.

Beneath his mouth Leo could feel Jodi's parting; he could taste the sweet exhaled breath, feel the soft little tremor that ran through her body as she nestled closer to him.

Leo was stroking her skin with his hands, making her ache and quiver, his mouth leaving hers to caress the vulnerable place where her shoulder joined her throat, nuzzling little kisses up to her ear whilst his tongue-tip investigated its delicate whorls. Each small sensation co-alesced, melded together until she was on fire with the heat of the need he was creating inside her.

Her breasts, swelling, peaking, ached for the touch of his hands. As though he seemed to know it he shaped them, stroking the pads of his thumbs over the erect crests of her nipples.

Jodi trembled and moaned, closed her eyes, welcoming the velvet darkness that lapped protectively around her, and then opened them again on a gasp of piercingly sweet pleasure as she felt Leo's mouth against first one breast and then the other.

Her fingers dug into the hard muscles of his back, her body arching in an irresistible mixture of supplication and temptation.

Leo was kissing her belly, rimming her navel with his tongue. Her fingers clenched in his thick, dark hair. Her intention had been to push him away, but helplessly her hands stilled as he moved lower and then lower still.

Such intimacy was surely only for the most beloved of lovers, but Jodi couldn't find the strength to resist or deny what he was giving her; her body, like her emotions, clenched first against what was happening, and then gave in.

As he moved his body over hers and entered her Leo immediately felt the first fierce contraction of her release. His own body leapt to meet and complete it, his emotions as well as his senses taking hotly satisfying pleasure in knowing they were sharing this moment together.

Jodi cried out Leo's name, wrapping herself around him, holding him deep inside her, where she had so much wanted him to be. It felt so wondrously right to have him there, a part of her, now and for always.

'Leo.'

She sighed his name in exhausted pleasure as tears of fulfilment washed her eyes and flowed onto her face, to be tenderly licked away by Leo, before he reached out to wrap her in his arms.

She was asleep before they closed fully around her.

CHAPTER SEVEN

LEO ALLOWED HIMSELF a small smile of satisfaction when he finally replaced the telephone receiver at the end of what had been a long half-hour of diplomatic discussion with the police.

He had earlier spent a very terse and determined five minutes on the telephone to Jeremy, informing him of the fact that he would most certainly be placing charges against *him* for unlawfully being on the company's premises if he was to go ahead and try to accuse Jodi of anything. Did he, Jeremy, Leo had asked grimly, possess the same physical evidence of this supposed assault that Jodi did of his unwarranted manhandling of her? Jeremy had blustered and tried to counter-threaten, but in the end he had given way.

The police had been rather less easy to negotiate with; for a start, as the superintendent had told Leo coolly, they did not take too kindly to the demands the demonstration at the factory had placed on their very limited financial budget, and they were certainly not about to give out a message to the public that acts of violence were something they were prepared to permit.

Leo had protested that the demonstration had been intended to be a peaceful one, citing the fact that he, as the owner of the factory, did not feel it necessary to make any kind of complaint against his workforce, so then surely the matter could be allowed to rest. As it transpired, Leo discovered that in the end none of the protesters had actually been held overnight at the police station, and that Jodi would have been the only one of them who might have faced the prospect of charges, and that only because of the assault incident claimed by Jeremy.

Ultimately the police had agreed, that since Jeremy was prepared to drop his accusation, there was no real case against her and she did not need to return to the station.

He had, Leo recognised, barely an hour left to go before he was due to talk with the factory's workforce, and there was still that vitally important and delicate issue he needed to discuss with Jodi!

Showered and dressed, Jodi hesitated at the top of staircase. Although she had pretended to be asleep, she had been fully aware of Leo getting out of bed and leaving her.

How was it possible for a supposedly intelligent woman to make the same mistake twice?

As anxious as she was about what might lie ahead of her when she returned to the police station, she was even more concerned about her feelings for Leo. Her feelings? When was she going to have the courage to give them their proper name?

Her love!

A tiny sound somewhere between a denial and a moan bubbled in her throat. If only last night hadn't been so...so perfect. So everything she had ever wanted the intimacy she shared with the man she loved to be. If only Leo had been different, if only he had done something, anything, that had made her want to distance herself from him.

As she started to make her way down the stairs Leo suddenly appeared in the hallway, standing watching her, making her feel breathless and shaky, weak with the sheer power of her love for him.

'I've just finished speaking with the police,' Leo began.

'Yes, I haven't forgotten that I've got to go back,' Jodi informed him quickly. Somehow she managed to force herself to give him a tight proud look, which she hoped would tell him that she was completely unfazed by the prospect. 'I'm not sure just what the formalities will be.' Her voice startled to wobble slightly, despite her efforts to control it. 'Presumably I shall have to contact a lawyer.'

'There wouldn't be any point in you doing that,' Leo began to inform her, and then stopped as he saw the look of white-faced anxiety she was trying so valiantly to conceal from him. 'Jodi. It's all right,' he told her urgently. 'I—that is, the police have decided that there's no need for you to go back.'

Leo wasn't entirely sure why he had decided not to tell Jodi of the role he had played in that decision; it just seemed like the right choice to make.

'I don't have to go back?'

It wasn't just her voice that was trembling now, Leo recognised as he watched the relief shake her body. The urge to go to her and wrap her in his arms whilst he told her that he would never allow anything to hurt or frighten her ever again was so powerful that he had taken several steps towards her before he managed to pull himself back.

Jodi was convinced she must have misunderstood what Leo was telling her.

'You mean I don't have to go right now, today?' she questioned him uncertainly.

'I mean you don't have to go back ever,' Leo corrected her. Adding in a softly liquid voice, 'It's over, Jodi. There isn't anything for you to worry about.'

'But what about Jeremy Driscoll?' Jodi protested.

'Apparently he's changed his mind,' Leo told her carelessly, turning away from her as he did so.

There was no way he wanted Jodi to feel that she was under any kind of obligation to him for speaking to Jeremy.

He was still aware that last night he had to some extent coerced her into making love with him, at least emotionally. And when the time came for him to tell her how he felt about her he didn't want her to feel pressured in any way at all.

He had a right, he believed, to explain how he felt now and how his own fight against his feelings had led, in part, to his original misjudgement of her. But he was not going to use any kind of emotional blackmail to compel Jodi into saying she felt the same.

When it came to whether or not they had created a new life together; well, that was a very different matter. Leo would use any means possible to make sure he would be a presence in that child's life.

'Look, Jodi, I have to go out shortly,' he told her. 'But before I do, there's something we have to discuss.'

Jodi felt her stomach lurch, a cold feeling of dread swilling through her veins.

She knew what was coming, of course; what he was going to say to her...

'Last night was a mistake. I'm sorry. But I hope you understand...'

Mentally she steeled herself for the blow she knew was about to fall.

'Let's go into the kitchen,' Leo began unexpectedly. 'I've made some coffee, and you must be hungry.'

Hungry!

'I thought you were in a rush to go out,' Jodi tried to protest as Leo ushered her towards the kitchen.

'I've got an appointment I have to keep,' Leo agreed, 'but I can talk whilst you eat.'

Eat! Jodi knew there was no way she could do that, but still she allowed Leo to fill her a bowl of cereal, and pour them both a mug of coffee before he began quietly, 'The first time we met I made a grave misjudgement, not just of the situation, Jodi, but of you as well.'

Leo paused, as though he was searching for the right words, and Jodi began to stiffen defensively.

'I'm concerned, Jodi, that because of the…the circumstances surrounding the intimacy we've shared we may both be guilty of having neglected to—er—think through the consequences of our actions and do something to ensure…' Leo stopped and shook his head.

'Look, what I'm trying to say, Jodi, is that if there's any chance that you might be pregnant…well, then something will have to be arranged. I wouldn't want you to…'

Pregnant. Jodi's heart bumped and thudded against her ribcage as she stared at Leo in mute shock. *'Something will have to be arranged…'* She tried to absorb the meaning of his words. Did he think for one minute that if she was carrying his child she would allow that precious new life to be 'arranged' away? She would never agree to anything like that. Never!

Her blood ran cold. She had been expecting him to tell her that last night had been a mistake, an impulse he now regretted, a mere sexual encounter which she wasn't to take seriously nor read anything meaningful into. But to know that he had already thought as far ahead as wanting to dispose of any possible consequences of their intimacy hurt her more than she felt able to cope with and, at the same time, made her more angry than anything else he had either said or done.

What was it he was really worried about? Fathering a

child he didn't want, or having her make any kind of financial or emotional claims on him on behalf of that child? What sort of a woman did he think she was?

Before she could even think about what she was saying she told him quickly and sharply, 'There is no chance of me being...of anything like that.'

Her heart was still thumping as she spoke, but her reactions were instinctive and immediate. How could she possibly continue to love him after this?

Jodi sounded so coldly positive that Leo started to frown. Had he been wrong to presume that just because she wasn't experienced that meant that she was unprotected from the risk of pregnancy?

Before he could stop himself Leo heard himself insisting fiercely, 'But that night in my suite was your first time, and—'

'How could you possibly know that?' she demanded, oblivious in her anger of the fact that she herself had just confirmed his gut feelings. Without waiting for him to answer her she continued emotionally, 'Well, just because I happened to be...because you were my first...' she amended hurriedly, 'that does not mean that I am going to get pregnant!'

As she spoke Jodi was getting up from the table and storming out of the kitchen, telling Leo acidly as she did so, 'I'm going to get my things and then I'm going home right now. And I never want to see you again! From the moment you arrived in Frampton you've caused misery and made life impossible for everyone. And just let me tell you that there's absolutely no way I would ever want to inflict on my child the burden of having you for a father.'

'Are you sure you'll be all right?'

Jodi glowered at Leo as he reached out to open the pas-

senger door of his car. It had been galling in the extreme
after her outburst to be forced to accept his offer of a lift
home.

'Well, I shall certainly be far better here in my own
home than I was last night in yours, won't I?' she demanded with pointed iciness as Leo insisted on carrying
her bag to her front door for her and waiting to see her
safely inside.

As she gave in to the unwanted temptation to watch
him drive away Jodi felt sick with fear for her future, and
anger against herself.

She was surely too adult, too mature for this kind of
emotional folly!

As he drove away from Jodi's cottage Leo discovered that
he was actually grinding his teeth. The last thing he felt
like doing right now was sitting down at the negotiating
table. The only thing he wanted to do was to take hold of
Jodi Marsh and tell her in no uncertain terms just how
he felt about her, and what his life was going to be without her...

So much for his earlier high-minded promise to himself
not to use any kind of emotional blackmail to press his
suit, Leo reflected grimly. But those comments Jodi had
made about not wanting him as a father for her child had
hurt—and badly—and he had been within a breath of telling her in no uncertain terms that if her body was allowed
to speak for itself it might have a very different story to
tell. 'Because make no mistake about it, Jodi Marsh, your
body damned well wanted me!'

To Leo's consternation he suddenly realised as the
sound of his own voice filled the car that he was talking to himself! No wonder they called love a form of
madness!

* * *

More drained by everything that had happened than she wanted to admit, Jodi suddenly discovered that she was craving the escape of sleep. She normally had buckets of energy, but these last couple of days she had felt physically drained. On her return home she went upstairs, intending to collect some washing, and then she saw her bed, and one thing led to another and...

It was the sound of her doorbell ringing that finally woke her. Realising that she had fallen deeply asleep, still fully dressed, she made her way groggily downstairs, her heart leaping frantically as she wondered if her visitor was Leo.

It had hurt her so badly this morning, after the wonderful night they had spent together, to know how desperate he was to distance himself from her and to make sure she knew that he didn't want her.

However, her visitor wasn't Leo, but Nigel her cousin. As she let him in he was waving a newspaper in front of her.

'You're on the front page,' he told her. 'Have you seen the paper yet?'

The front page! Jodi took the newspaper from him and studied it, her face burning with consternation and embarrassment as she studied the photograph of the previous evening's arrests.

'I was half expecting I was going to have to bail my strait-laced cousin out of prison,' Nigel joked as he made his way towards her small kitchen.

'Only, as I understand it, Leo got there before me.'

He shot Jodi a wry look as she demanded, 'Who told you that?'

'I rang the police station,' Nigel informed her. 'Reading between the lines, it sounds as if Leo must have put one hell of a lot of pressure on Jeremy Driscoll to get him to back off from charging you.'

To back off? Jodi began to frown.

'But Leo said that Jeremy had changed his mind,' she protested shakily.

'Yeah, but probably only after Leo had told him that if he didn't he would change it for him, if my guess is correct,' Nigel agreed derisively. 'Apparently Leo was on the phone to the police for nearly half an hour this morning, insisting that he did not want charges pressed against you, or any of the workforce. It seems to me that Leo must think an awful lot of you, little cousin, to go to so much trouble on your behalf,' Nigel teased her. 'This wouldn't be the beginning of a classic tale of romance between two adversaries, would it?' He grinned, his smile fading when he saw the look of white-faced despair Jodi was giving him. 'Are you OK?' he asked in concern.

'I'm fine,' Jodi lied.

'Feel like going out for a meal tonight?' Nigel suggested.

Jodi shook her head. 'No; I've got some work I need to prepare for school on Monday,' she told him, 'but thanks for asking.'

Nigel was almost at the front door, when he turned round and told her, 'Leo was meeting with the representatives of the factory this morning. Did he drop any hints about what he was going to say to them?'

'No, why should he?' she asked Nigel primly.

He was, she could see, giving her a worried look.

'Something's wrong; you're not your normal self, Jodi. What—?'

'Nothing's wrong,' she lied grittily. 'I'm just tired, that's all.'

She felt guilty about lying to Nigel, who was practically

her best friend as well as her cousin, but what alternative did she really have?

A small, uncomfortable silence followed her denial, before Nigel turned to open the front door.

Jodi watched him go. She had been unfairly sharp with him, she knew, and ultimately she would have to apologise and explain, but not right now. Right now she just wasn't capable of doing anything so rational! All she really wanted to do was to think about Leo, and what Nigel had told her.

It had confused her to learn that Leo had intervened with the authorities on her behalf. After all, he had allowed her to believe that they had been the ones to contact him, and not, as Nigel had implied, the other way around.

It galled Jodi to know that she was in his debt—not that that made a single scrap of difference to what she felt about what he had said to her earlier. No way! Those words were words she would never forgive him for uttering. Still, she knew she would have to thank him for what he had done, and the sooner she got that onerous task over with the better! Gritting her teeth, she went upstairs to shower and get changed.

Leo saw Jodi as she walked up the drive towards the front door of Ashton House. He was standing in the room he was using as an office, having just completed a telephone call with his new partner in the haulage and distribution business he intended to site at the motorway-based factory.

As he had informed the representatives of the Frampton workforce earlier, he had now decided to keep that factory open, but it would be up to them to prove to him that he had made the right decision, with an increased output to ensure his business kept its competitive edge over its overseas rivals.

Despite the fact that it was a hot summer's day, Jodi was wearing a very formal-looking black trouser suit, its jacket open over a white T-shirt.

Leo, in contrast, had changed into a pair of casual chinos on his return from his meeting, but that did not prevent Jodi from thinking how formidable he looked as he opened the door just as she reached out to ring the bell.

Formidably male, that was, she admitted to herself as he invited her into the house.

Why, oh, why did she have to feel this way about him? Her pain at loving him was laced with her furious anger at his unbelievably callous words of the morning.

Perhaps to him, a high-powered businessman, an unplanned child was just a problem to be disposed of, but there was no way she could contemplate taking such an unemotional course.

If she thought for one moment that there was the slightest chance that she could be pregnant... After all, she had lied to Leo when she had intimated that she had taken precautions to ensure that she did not conceive.

Now she was deliberately trying to frighten herself, Jodi decided firmly, dismissing her uncomfortable anxiety. She was not pregnant. Totally, definitely not.

And, besides, didn't she have enough to worry about?

As she followed Leo inside the house she began with determination, 'Nigel's been to see me. He says that I have you to thank for the fact that I did not have to return to the police station this morning.'

The way she delivered the words, with an extremely militant look in her eyes, made Leo curse her cousin silently.

'Jodi—' he began, but she shook her head, refusing to let him continue.

'Is it true?' she demanded.

'The police agreed with me that there was no reason to take things any further with any of those concerned in what essentially had been a peaceful demonstration,' Leo palliated.

'So it is true,' Jodi announced baldly. 'Why did you do it?' she asked him bitterly.

'So that you could have me under some kind of obligation to you? Why would you want that, or can I guess?' she demanded sarcastically. 'So that you could demand that I—?'

'Stop right there.'

Now it was Jodi's turn to fall silent as Leo glared furiously at her. Did she really think that he would stoop so low as to try to demand that she make love with him?

Beneath his anger, running much, much deeper, Leo could feel the savage, ripping claws of pain.

Jodi told herself that she wasn't going to back down or allow him to make her feel she was in the wrong. After what he had said this morning it seemed perfectly logical to her that he would consider using the fact that he had negotiated her freedom to demand that she acquiesce to his demands over an accidental pregnancy.

All the anguish she was feeling welled up inside her. Ignoring the oxygen-destroying tension crackling between them, and the anger she could see glinting in Leo's eyes, Jodi protested, 'You just don't care, do you? Feelings, human life—they don't matter to you. You're quite happy to close down the factory and put people out of work...'

And quite happy, too, to deny his child the right to live, Jodi reflected inwardly, the pain of that knowledge twisting her insides like acid—not just for the child she was positive she had not conceived but also for the destruction of her own foolish dreams.

Somewhere deep down inside herself she had seen him

as a hero, a truly special man, imbued with all the virtues that women universally loved, especially the instinct to protect those weaker and more vulnerable than himself. It hurt to know just how wrong she had been.

Leo had had enough. How dared she accuse him of not having feelings? If he was as callous, as uncaring as she was accusing him of being, right now she would be lying under him on his bed whilst he...

As Leo fought to control the surging shock of his fierce desire he couldn't stop himself from retaliating savagely, 'If this is your way of trying to persuade me to keep the factory open, let me tell you the tactics you employed in my hotel suite would be far more effective.'

Leo knew the moment the words were out of his mouth that they were a mistake, but it was too late to recall them.

Jodi was looking at him with an expression of contemptuous loathing in her eyes, whilst her mouth...!

Leo had to swallow—hard—as he saw that small, betraying tremble of her firmly compressed lips. The same lips he had not such a very long time ago teased open with his tongue before...

Was that actually a groan Leo had just uttered? Jodi wondered with furious female anger. Well, he certainly deserved to be in pain after what he had just said to her!

It was only the sheer force of her anger that was keeping her from bursting into either incoherent speech or helpless emotional tears.

How could he have stooped so low as to throw that at her?

Well, he would quickly learn that she could be equally offensive!

'If I thought that such tactics would work—and that you would not renege on any deal made in the heat of the moment—I might almost be prepared to risk them,' she told him with pseudo-sweetness, her tone changing completely as she added in a much colder and more authoritative voice, 'But if I were in your shoes...'

'You'd do things differently?' Leo supplied for her.

'Well, if I were you I'd make sure of my facts before I started throwing accusations around.' Jodi turned round, giving him one last furious look as she told him, 'I'm not listening to any more of this.'

And then she was gone before Leo had the chance to stop her, leaving him mentally cursing both her and himself.

Why on earth hadn't he simply told her that he had found a way of keeping the factory open?

Why? Because his damned stupid male pride wouldn't let him, that was why!

By the time she had walked home, Jodi was feeling both queasy and slightly light-headed. It was because of the heat of the sun and the fact that she had not really had very much to eat, Jodi told herself firmly—to even think of allowing herself to imagine anything else was completely and utterly silly.

Silly, yes, but still somehow she couldn't stop herself from imagining, dreading that her foolish behaviour was now going to have dire consequences.

It wasn't that she didn't like children—she did, nor even that she didn't want to be a mother and have babies herself—she did. But not yet, and most certainly not like this.

No, she wanted her babies to be planned for with love, by two people equally committed to their relationship and their children's future.

She was, she told herself, panicking unnecessarily, deliberately blowing up a small feeling of nausea into something else. Easy to tell herself that, but far harder to believe it. Guilt was a terribly powerful force!

With her imagination running away from her at full speed and sending her harrowing images of single-parenthood, it was hard to think rationally.

Even if she was pregnant, it was far too soon for her to be suffering from morning sickness, surely, and if her nausea wasn't caused by that then how could she be pregnant?

But what if she was? What if? A woman in her position, a schoolteacher, pregnant after a one-night stand! She went cold at the thought, filled with repugnance for her own behaviour. Mentally she started counting the days until she could be sure that she was safe. And in the meantime... In the meantime she would just have to try not to panic!

CHAPTER EIGHT

JODI COULD FEEL the buzz of excitement being generated by the group of parents gathered outside the school gates. Puzzled, she looked at them. Normally on a Monday parental exchanges were slightly subdued, but this morning's mood was quite obviously very upbeat—unlike her own, Jodi recognised, pausing as one of the parents called out to her.

'Have you heard the news—isn't it wonderful? I could hardly believe it when John came home on Saturday and told me that Leo Jefferson had announced he intended to keep the factory open.'

Jodi stared at her.

Leo had done that? But he had told her... Before she could sort out her confused thoughts another mother was joining in the conversation, chuckling warmly as she congratulated Jodi on her part in the previous week's demonstration at the factory.

'We were all really surprised and impressed by the way Mr Jefferson spoke up for you to the police, telling them that he had no intention of taking things any further. And then to learn that he's going to keep the factory open after all. It totally changes the way we all think about him.' She beamed, giving Jodi a look she didn't understand before continuing, 'Of course, you must have known what was going to happen before the rest of us!'

Jodi's face started to burn.

The other parents were also looking at her with an un-expected degree of amused speculation, she recognised, although she had no idea why until suddenly she could hear Myra Fanshawe exclaiming vehemently, 'Well, per-sonally I think it's absolutely disgraceful. A person in her position…a schoolteacher. A head teacher…indulging in a liaison of that nature. I must say, though, I'm not totally surprised. I've never approved of some of her teaching methods!'

Myra was talking to one of the other parents, her back to Jodi. As Jodi approached the other woman whispered something urgently to Myra, her face flushing with em-barrassment.

But it seemed that her embarrassment was not shared by Myra, who tossed her head and then said even more loudly, 'Well, I'm sorry, but I don't really care if she does hear me. After all, she's the one at fault. Behaving like that… Openly spending the night in his hotel suite, and then try-ing to convince us all that she's Ms Virtue personified!'

Jodi felt her face burning even hotter as the group of parents surrounding Myra gave way and stood back as she approached.

Jodi's heart gave a sickening lurch as she saw the look of malicious triumph in the other woman's eyes. Myra had never liked her, she knew that. Jodi had to admit that she didn't particularly care for Myra either, but there was too much at stake here for her to be ruled by such feelings.

Reminding herself—not that she needed any remind-ing—of her position and her responsibilities as the school's head teacher, Jodi took a deep, calming breath and con-fronted the other woman.

'I assume that I am the subject of your discussion, and if that is the case—'

'You aren't going to try to deny it, I hope,' Myra interrupted her rudely before Jodi could finish speaking. 'It wouldn't do you any good if you did. Ellie, the receptionist who saw you at the hotel, both when you arrived and the next morning when you left, is my god-daughter, and she recognised you immediately from your photograph in the local paper. She couldn't believe it when she read that you had been demonstrating at the factory. Not when she knew that you'd spent the night with its owner.'

Jodi's heart sank. This was even worse than she had expected, and she could see from the varying expressions on the faces of the other parents that they were all shocked by Myra's disclosures.

What could she say in her own defence? What mitigating circumstances could she summon up to explain? Bleakly Jodi was aware that there was nothing she could say that would make the situation any better and, potentially, telling the truth would make things a whole lot worse!

'You do realise, don't you, that, given my position on the board of governors, it will be my duty to bring up the doubts your behaviour gives me as to your suitability to teach our children?'

'I haven't—'

Jodi tried to interrupt and defend herself, but Myra overrode her, stating loudly, 'And, on top of everything else, you were taken into custody by the police. It is my belief that the education authority should be told!' she said to Jodi with obvious relish. 'After all, as a parent, I have my child's moral welfare to think about,' Myra was continuing with a sanctimonious fervour that had some of the more impressionable parents watching her round-eyed. 'In your shoes...' she continued in an openly triumphant manner.

To Jodi's relief, the final bell summoning the children

to their classrooms started to ring, giving her the perfect opportunity to escape from her tormentor.

From her tormentor maybe, she allowed half an hour later as she stood motionlessly staring out of the window of her small office, but not from the torment itself.

She had seen the looks—from pity right through to very unpleasant salacious curiosity—on the faces of the parents as they'd watched her reaction to Myra's disclosures. She knew that Myra had the power to make life very difficult and uncomfortable for her and for her family. The other members of the board were naturally going to be concerned about the probity and the moral standing of their school's head teacher, and, although Jodi did not think that any legal disciplinary action would be taken against her, naturally she did not relish the thought of being at odds with the governors or indeed of having her lifestyle bring disrepute on the school.

And as for Myra's remark about the education authority, well, Jodi suspected that had just been so much hot air, but she also knew that her own conscience would not allow her to stay on at the school against the wishes of the parents, or in a situation where they felt that she was not the right person to have charge of their children. Jodi's heart sank. If that was to happen...! If she was to be put in a position where she felt honour bound to step down from her post, after everything she had done, all her hard work. But what could she say in her own defence? she reminded herself bleakly. And that jibe Myra had made about her maternal concern for the moral welfare of her son had really hit a raw nerve.

Jodi's head was starting to ache. She had deliberately made herself eat a heavy breakfast this morning, just to prove to herself—not that she had needed it—that she most certainly was not suffering from the nauseous early-morning tummy of a newly pregnant woman. The meal was taking its natural toll on her now.

She felt distinctly queasy, but surely because she was so tense with anxiety and misery? She tried to reassure and comfort herself, but harrowing tales of members of her sex who had found themselves in exactly the position she was dreading kept being dredged up by her conscience to torment her. And the unfortunate thing was that she was prone to having an erratic cycle, especially when she was under stress.

Myra's comments had all but obliterated the original discomfort she had felt on learning that, contrary to what he had told her, Leo had actually decided to keep the factory open. Why had he let her accuse him like that?

It was almost lunchtime before Leo learned what was happening to Jodi.

He had been tied up with his accountants most of the morning, swiftly renegotiating finance packages to accommodate the changes he had made to his business plans for the factories he had taken over.

His bankers had shaken their heads over the discovery that he intended to set up his own haulage and distribution business and then admitted ruefully that, being Leo, he was probably going to make a very profitable success of it.

But all morning what he'd really been thinking about, worrying about, had been Jodi and the row they had had the previous day. Why had he let her go like that?

He had a meeting at the factory, and when he arrived there he discovered that Jeremy Driscoll was waiting to see him.

Furiously angry, he confronted Leo, telling him, 'I want to collect some papers I left here, but the cretins you have left in charge have refused to allow me access to the store-room. God knows on whose instructions.'

'On mine,' Leo told him equably.

There was a copy of the local paper on the desk, and Leo frowned as he caught sight of it and saw Jodi's photograph on the front page.

Jeremy had obviously seen it too, and he sneered as he commented, 'Little Miss Goody Two Shoes. Well, everyone's going to know what she is soon enough now.'

'What do you mean?' Leo demanded tersely as he recognised the malice glinting in Jeremy's pale blue eyes.

'What do you think I mean?' Jeremy grinned. 'She was spotted leaving your suite, creeping out of the hotel in the early hours of the morning. Good, was she?

'Well, you might have been impressed but somehow I doubt the parents of the brats she teaches are going to be when they learn what she was up to. Their head teacher, tricking her way into a man's hotel suite and not leaving until the morning...' Jeremy started to shake his head disapprovingly. 'I shouldn't be surprised if they demand her resignation.'

As he listened to him Leo's heart sank. Jeremy was too sure of himself, swaggeringly so, in fact, to simply be making a shot in the dark. Someone obviously *had* seen Jodi leaving his suite.

Leo's brain went into overdrive as he sought furiously for a way to protect her. There was only one thing he could think of doing that might help.

Fixing Jeremy with a cool, bored look, he told him calmly, 'Oh, I hardly think so; after all, what's so wrong about an engaged couple spending the night together?'

'An engaged couple?' Jeremy was staring nonplussed at him, but to Leo's relief he didn't immediately reject

Leo's claim; instead he challenged, 'If that's true then why doesn't anyone know about it?'

'Because we've chosen to keep it to ourselves for the moment,' Leo responded distantly, 'not that it's any business of yours or anyone else's. Oh, and by the way,' he continued, giving Jeremy a nasty smile, 'I understand from my accountants that they've been approached by the tax authorities regarding some anomalies in the accounting system you put in place here after the fire that destroyed the previous records. Of course,' Leo continued smoothly, 'my accountants have assured the Revenue that we are prepared to give them all the help they might need.'

Miserably Jodi stared across her desk. As luck would have it, the school's parents had a meeting this evening at which she was supposed to be speaking about her plans to increase the range of extra-curricular activities provided for the children. Jodi gave a small shudder. She could guess what was going to be the hot topic of conversation at that meeting now!

And she could guess, too, just how much criticism and disapproval she was going to encounter—deservedly so, she told herself grimly.

Breaking into Leo's suite, getting drunk, falling asleep in his bed and then, as though all of that weren't enough…

She wasn't fit to be a teacher, or to hold the responsible position she did, Jodi decided wretchedly, and Myra Fanshawe had been right when she had warned Jodi that the parents would take a very dim view of what she had done.

If only that photograph of her had not appeared in the local paper. But it had, and— She tensed as she heard a soft knock on her door, her face colouring as Helen Riddings, the more senior of her co-teachers, popped her head round the door to ask uncertainly, 'Are you all right? Only…'

Only what? Jodi wondered defeatedly. Only you've heard the gossip and now you're wondering if it's true and, if it is, just what I'm going to do about it?

'I'm sorry, it's my turn for playground duty, isn't it?' Jodi answered her, avoiding the other woman's eyes, knowing perfectly well that her colleague had not really come to her office to remind her about that.

'Oh, but you haven't had any lunch,' Helen protested, obviously flustered. 'I can do the playground duty for you if you like.' She stopped and then looked acutely self-conscious as she told Jodi, 'Myra Fanshawe is in the playground with some of the other parents...'

'It's all right, Helen,' Jodi told her quietly when she broke off in embarrassment. 'I can guess what's going on. I expect that you and the other teachers will have heard the gossip by now...' Jodi could feel her courage starting to desert her.

'You don't look very well,' Helen commiserated, obviously genuinely concerned for her. 'Why don't you go home?'

Before the situation became so untenable that she had no option other than to retreat there—permanently? Was that what Helen meant? Jodi wondered bitterly.

'No, I can't do that,' she responded.

She was beginning to feel acutely ill. Gossip, especially this kind of gossip, spread like wildfire; she knew that. How long would it be before it reached the ears of her friends and family? Her cousin...his parents...her own parents...?

Jodi's stomach heaved. Her mother and father, enjoying their retirement, were on an extended trip around America, but they would not be away indefinitely. Her family were so proud of her. So proud of everything she had achieved for the school. What could she say to them when they asked her for an explanation? That she had seen Leo Jefferson in the hotel foyer and fallen immediately and helplessly in lust with him?

In lust. As Helen left her office and closed the door behind her Jodi made a small moan of self-disgust.

But it wasn't lust she felt for Leo Jefferson, was it? Lust did not affect the emotions the way her emotions had been affected. Lust did not bring a person out of their dreams at night, crying out in pain and loss because that person had discovered a cruel truth about the man they loved.

Her stomach churned even more fiercely.

She wasn't going to be sick, she wasn't. But suddenly, urgently, Jodi knew that she was!

It was tension, that was all, nothing else. Jodi assured herself later when she was on her way to take her first afternoon class.

She wondered if it was too soon to buy one of those test kits; that way she could be completely sure. Jodi flinched as she reflected on the effect it would have on the current gossip about her if she was to be observed buying a pregnancy-testing kit. No, she couldn't take such a risk!

Was it really only such a short time ago that she had been a model of virginal morality, basking in the approval of both the parents and the school authorities? And she'd been in receipt of an offer of employment from the area's most prestigious private school… She felt as though that Jodi belonged to another life! How could she have got herself into such a situation? She had heard that falling in love was akin to a form of madness.

Falling in love! Now she knew she was dangerously close to losing her grip on reality. No way did she still think she was in love with Leo Jefferson. No way!

Leo looked at his watch. He had been in meetings for the whole of the afternoon, but at last he was free.

He was acutely conscious of the fact that it might be politic for him to warn Jodi about their 'engagement', but after the way they had parted the last time they had met he doubted that trying to telephone her was going to be very successful.

School must be over for the day by now. He could drive over to the village and call on her at home, explain what had happened, tell her that once the furore had died down they could discreetly let it be known that the engagement was off.

Just the memory of the salacious look in Jeremy Driscoll's eyes when he had taunted Leo this morning about the gossip now circulating concerning Jodi was enough to make Leo feel murderous and to wish that he had the real right to protect Jodi in the way that he wanted to be able to protect her. And, so far as he was concerned, the best way to do that was for her to have his ring on her left hand—his wedding ring! He really was far more Italian than he had ever realised, he recognised grimly as he headed for his car, which reminded him—he ought to telephone his parents. The visit he had promised his mother he would make to see them again soon would have to be put back, at least until he was satisfied that Jodi was all right.

'I take it that you will be attending the meeting this evening?'

Jodi tensed warily as Myra Fanshawe stepped past the other parents grouped at the school gates to confront her.

'Only, now that you've got a wealthy fiancé to consider, I don't imagine you're going to be particularly concerned about the future of the school or its pupils, are you?'

A wealthy fiancé. Her? What on earth was Myra talking about? Jodi wondered wearily.

She couldn't remember ever feeling so drained at the

end of a school day, but of course this had been no ordinary day, which no doubt explained why all she wanted to do was to go to sleep, but not until after she had had some delicious anchovies... For some reason she had been longing for some all afternoon! Which was most peculiar because they were not normally something she was very keen on!

Myra was standing in front of her now, her cold little eyes narrowing with hostility as she continued, 'I hope you don't think that just because you're engaged to Leo Jefferson it means that certain questions aren't going to be asked—by the parents if not the education authority,' she sniffed prissily. 'And—'

'Just a minute,' Jodi stopped her sharply, 'what exactly do you mean about me being engaged to Leo Jefferson?'

She was starting to feel light-headed again, Jodi recognised, her face burning hot and then cold as she wondered how on earth Myra could possibly have got hold of such an outrageous idea—and quite obviously spread it around as fast and as far as she could, Jodi guessed despairingly as she saw the other parents watching them.

'It's a little too late for you to assume either discretion or innocence now,' Myra told her disdainfully. 'Although I must say that, as a parent, I do think that someone in your position should have made more of an attempt to employ them both instead of acting in a way that could bring the school into disrepute.'

'Myra...' Jodi began grimly, and then stopped as the small knot of parents in front of the gates fell back to allow the large Mercedes to pull to a halt outside them.

'Well, here comes your fiancé,' Myra announced bitchily as Leo got out of the car. 'I just hope he doesn't think because he's bought Frampton at a ridiculous, knock-down price—virtually tricking the family into selling the business to him against their will, from what Jeremy has told us—it means that he's got any kind of position or authority locally! Jeremy was very highly thought-of by his workforce,' she continued, with such a blatant disregard for the truth that Jodi could hardly believe her ears.

Leo had reached them now, and for a reason she certainly was not going to analyse, Jodi discovered that a small part of her actually felt pleased to have him there.

Not that he had any right to be here, making a bad situation even worse by putting his hand proprietorily on Jodi's arm, before bending his head to brush his lips lightly against her cheek as he murmured into her ear, 'I'll explain when we're on our own.' Then he moved slightly away from her to say in a louder voice, 'Sorry I'm late, darling; I got held up.'

And then, without giving her an opportunity to say a word, he was guiding her towards his car, tucking her solicitously into the passenger seat, and then getting in the driver's seat beside her.

Jodi waited until she was sure that they were safely out of sight of the gathered watchers, before demanding shakily, 'Would you mind explaining to me just what is going on, and why Myra Fanshawe seems to think that we are engaged?'

'Myra Fanshawe?' Leo queried, puzzled.

'The woman with me as you drove up,' Jodi explained impatiently.

She felt tired and cross and very hungry, and the ridiculous temptation to beg Leo to stop the car so that she could lay her head on his shoulder and wallow in the cathartic pleasure of a really good cry was so strong that it was threatening to completely overwhelm her.

'She's a close friend of Jeremy Driscoll,' she offered casually, 'and—'

'Oh, is she?' Leo growled. 'Well, no doubt that explains how she knows about our engagement.'

'Our engagement?' Jodi checked him angrily. 'What engagement? We are not engaged...'

'Not officially—'

'Not in any way,' Jodi interrupted him fiercely.

'Jodi, I had no choice,' Leo told her quietly. 'Driscoll told me about the fact that you'd been seen leaving my suite early in the morning. He was...' Leo paused, not wanting to tell her just how unpleasant Jeremy's attitude and assumptions had been. 'Apparently—'

'I know what you're going to say.' Jodi stopped him hotly. 'I was seen leaving your room, so I must be some kind of fallen woman, totally unfit to teach school, to be involved with innocent children. For heaven's sake, all I've done is to go bed with you twice; that doesn't mean...'

To her own consternation her eyes filled with emotional tears, her voice becoming suspended by the sheer intensity of what she was feeling...

'Jodi, I know exactly what it does mean and what it doesn't mean,' Leo tried to reassure her. 'But that knowledge belongs only to the two of us. You do know what I'm saying, don't you?' he asked her gently.

When she made no response and instead looked studiedly away from him out of the passenger window he could see the deep pink colour burning her skin and his heart ached for her.

'I didn't think you'd particularly care for it if I were to take out a full-page advert in the local paper announcing that you were a virgin until that night in my suite.'

'That doesn't mean you have to claim that we're engaged,' Jodi protested.

'I did it to protect you,' Leo told her.

To protect her! How could he sit there and claim to want

to protect her when he had already told her that he didn't want to keep their child? Or was that why he was doing this? Jodi wondered wretchedly. Was this just a cynical ploy to make her feel she could trust him, to keep her close enough to him for him to be able to control her, and act quickly, if necessary, to…?

'It isn't your responsibility to protect me.' Jodi told him fiercely.

'Maybe not in your eyes,' Leo retaliated, suddenly serious in a way that made her heart thud in pure female awareness of how very male and strong he was, and how she longed to be able to lean on that strength, and to feel she could turn to it and him for comfort and for protection and for love…

But of course she couldn't! Mustn't…

'But in mine, Jodi, I can assure you that I consider it very much my responsibility. You aren't the only one with a reputation to consider and protect, you know,' he told her. His voice was suddenly so hurtfully curt that Jodi turned to look at him—and then wished that she hadn't, as the mere sight of his profile caused a wave of helpless longing to pulse through her body, pushing every other emotion out of its way.

She must not feel like this about him, Jodi told herself in defensive panic. She must not want him, ache for him…love him…

A small sound somewhere between pain and despair constricted her throat.

'How do you think it is going to reflect on me once it becomes public knowledge that you and I—?'

'You mean, you're doing this for yourself and not for me?' Jodi challenged him.

This was more like it. Knowing that his behaviour was

motivated by selfishness would surely help her to control and ultimately conquer her love for him?

'I'm doing it because right now it is the only option we have,' Leo told her firmly.

Jodi could feel herself weakening. It would be such a relief to simply let Leo take charge, to let him stand between her and the disapproval of public opinion.

To let the world at large believe that he loved her and that...

No. She could not do it. Because if she did she would be in grave danger of allowing herself to believe the same thing!

'No!' she told him fiercely, shaking her head in rejection. 'I'm not going to hide behind you, Leo, or lie, or pretend... What I did might have been wrong. Immoral in some people's eyes. But in my own eyes what would be even worse would be to lie about it. If people want to criticise or condemn me then I shall just have to accept that and be judged by them; accept the consequences of my behaviour.'

As he watched her and saw the fear fighting with the pride in her eyes Leo was filled with a mixture of admiration for her honesty and a helpless, aching tenderness for her vulnerability. She was so innocent, so naïve. He had to protect her from herself as much as from others.

As he swung his car into the drive to Ashton House he told her bluntly, 'You'll be crucified. Do you really want to throw away everything you've worked for, Jodi? The school, everything you've achieved there? Because I promise you that is what could happen.'

'There are other schools,' Jodi told him whilst she struggled to contain the pain his words were causing her.

He brought the car to a standstill and Jodi suddenly realised just where they were.

'Why have you brought me here?' she demanded indignantly. 'I wanted to go home.'

'You're my fiancée,' Leo told her silkily. 'This is your home.'

'No,' Jodi protested furiously. 'No... I...' She stopped and shook her head. 'We can't be engaged,' she told him helplessly. 'It isn't... We don't...'

'We have to be, Jodi,' Leo responded, shattering what was left of her composure by telling her, 'We can't afford not to be.'

'Take me home,' Jodi demanded wretchedly. 'To my home.' She added insistently, 'I've got a meeting tonight and if I don't go Myra Fanshawe is going to have a field-day.'

Jodi sank down onto her small sofa. The meeting had been every bit as bad as she had dreaded, with Myra Fanshawe openly attempting to turn it into a debate on morality, plainly intent on embarrassing and humiliating Jodi just as much as she could.

Jodi had not been without her supporters, though; and several people had come up to her to congratulate her with genuine warmth on her engagement.

'It must have been very hard for both of you,' one of the parents had sympathised with her, 'with your fiancé potentially planning to close down the factory and you being committed to keeping it open. However,' she'd added with a smile, 'love, as they say, conquers all.'

Love might very well do so, Jodi reflected miserably now, but she was never likely to find out, since Leo quite plainly did not love her.

Her telephone rang, and this time, expecting Nigel, she picked up the receiver.

'You're a dark horse, aren't you?' were his opening words.

Jodi's heart sank.

'You've heard,' she guessed.

'Of course I've heard,' Nigel agreed wryly. 'The whole damned town has heard. Oh, and by the way, the parents have been on to me, wanting to know when they're going to get to meet your fiancé; I think my mother was on the phone to yours this afternoon.'

'What?' Jodi yelped in dismay. 'But I didn't want them to know...'

'What?' Nigel sounded confused.

'I mean I didn't want them to know yet,' Jodi hastily corrected herself. 'I mean I wanted to tell them myself and, what with everything happening so quickly...'

'Very quickly,' Nigel agreed with cousinly frankness as he told her, 'I must say, I got a bit of a shock to learn that you'd spent the night with Leo at his hotel, especially in view of the fact that you treated him like public enemy number one at the dinner party.'

'Oh, Nigel...' Jodi began, and then stopped. How on earth could she explain to her cousin just what had happened? And how on earth could she explain to anyone else if she couldn't explain to Nigel?

When she had told Leo that she didn't want to involve herself in any kind of deceit or hide behind him she had meant what she had said, but now suddenly she realised that things were not quite so simple as that and that there were other people in her life whose views and feelings she had to take into account.

For several minutes after she had finished her call with Nigel she sat nibbling on her bottom lip before finally reaching for the phone.

She dialled Leo's number while her fingers trembled betrayingly.

When he answered just the sound of his voice was
enough to make her stomach quiver in helpless reaction.

'It's Jodi,' she told him huskily. 'I've been thinking
about what you said about our...about us being engaged
and I...I agree...'

When Leo made no response her mouth went dry. What
if he had changed his mind? What if he no longer cared
about his own reputation or felt it was his responsibility,
as he had put it, to protect hers?

And then she heard the click as the receiver was suddenly replaced and her heart lurched sickeningly. He *had*
changed his mind!

Now what was she going to do?

Ten minutes later she curled herself up into her sofa in
a forlorn little ball and then frowned as her front doorbell
suddenly rang.

It would be Nigel again, no doubt, she decided wearily,
getting up and padding barefoot to the door.

Only it wasn't Nigel, it was Leo, and as she stepped into
her hallway she realised that he was carrying a bottle of
champagne and two glasses.

'There's only one real way in my book an engaged couple should celebrate their commitment to one another,' Leo
told her in a laconic drawl as she stared at him, 'and it in-
volves privacy and a bed. Preferably a very large bed, and
a very long period of privacy, but, since our engagement
is not of the committed-for-life variety, this will have to
be the alternative...'

As he finished speaking Leo looked at her, and Jodi
knew that her face was burning—not with embarrassment
or anger, she realised guiltily, but with the heat of the sheer
longing his words had conjured up inside her.

'Of course,' Leo was suggesting softly, 'if you would
prefer the first option...'

Jodi gave him an indignant look.

'What I'd prefer,' she told him, 'is not to be in this wretched situation at all.'

As she turned away from him Leo wondered what she would say if he told her just how dangerously close he was to picking her up in his arms and taking her somewhere very private and keeping her there until she was so full of the love he wanted to give her that...

That what? he asked himself in mental derision. That she would tell him that she loved him?

'How did the parents' meeting go?' he asked her gently as he opened the champagne and poured them both a glass.

'Our engagement opened to mixed reviews,' Jodi told him wryly.

She wasn't going to tell him that Myra had informed her before she had left that she had decided it was her moral duty to inform the education authority of the situation.

'It's only a storm in a teacup.' Leo told her gently. 'Six months from now all this will be forgotten.'

That wasn't what he'd said earlier, Jodi thought, when he'd insisted that the only way to protect her job was for them to be engaged. Jodi bit her lip. Still, in six months' time Leo might have forgotten her but she would never be able to forget him.

Leo handed Jodi one of the glasses of champagne. Shaking her head, she refused to take it.

'No, I can't,' she told Leo bleakly.

To her relief he didn't press her, simply putting the glass down before asking her quietly, 'Because of the effect the cocktail at the hotel had on you? Jodi, from the smell of the jug, it contained the most lethal mixture of alcohol...'

Before he could finish Jodi was shaking her head. Oddly perhaps, in the circumstances, that had not been her reason for refusing the champagne.

'It isn't that,' she told him hollowly. 'It's that I hate having to pretend like this,' she told him simply. 'I abhor the deceit, and it just seems wrong somehow to celebrate in such a traditional and romantic way what is, after all, just a pretence…a fiction—'

'Jodi!'

Her honesty, so direct and unexpected, had brought a dangerous lump of emotion to Leo's throat. She looked so sad, so grave-eyed, so infinitely lovable that he wanted to take hold of her and…

'It doesn't…'

'Please, I don't want to discuss it any more.' Jodi told him, getting up and moving restlessly around the room.

She knew what he had been going to say. He had been going to say that under the circumstances their dishonesty didn't matter, and perhaps it didn't—to him, but it mattered to her. Most of all because there was something unbearably hurtful…something that was almost a desecration, about them cynically using a custom that should be so special and meaningful, and reserved only for those who truly loved each other and believed in that love, for their own practical ends.

'I…I'd like you to go now,' she told him chokily.

For a moment Leo hesitated. She looked so vulnerable, so fragile that he wanted to stay with her, to be with her, and she looked pale and tired as well…

Frowningly Leo checked and studied her again.

'Jodi. I know we've already been through this, but…if there is any chance that you could be wrong and you are pregnant, then I—'

'I am not pregnant,' Jodi interrupted him sharply.

If she had been wondering if perhaps she had misjudged him, her defences weakened by his unexpected sensitivity towards her and the situation she was in, then he had just given her the proof that she had not, she recognised bitterly.

If, too, she had been foolishly reading some kind of selfless and caring emotion into his arrival at her house tonight, and the things he had said to her, then she was certainly being made sharply aware of her error.

Of course there was only one reason he was here, only one reason he was concerned, and only one person he was concerned for! And that person certainly wasn't her, or the child he quite obviously did not want her to have.

'I'm tired,' she told him flatly. 'And I want you to go...'

As she spoke she was already heading for the front door. Leo followed her.

As he got back in his car, he wondered what he had hoped to gain by his actions. Had he really thought that the simple act of calling to see her, bringing her champagne so that they could celebrate their fictitious engagement together, was in any way going to change her lack of love for him? How could it?

He might be a fool, he decided determinedly as he drove back to Ashton House, but he was still an honourable man and he damned well intended to make sure that both Jodi and her reputation were protected for just so long as they needed to be, whether she wanted it or not. As of now they were an engaged couple in the eyes of the outside world. And soon she would be wearing his ring to prove it!

CHAPTER NINE

UNABLE TO STOP herself, Jodi stared at the discreet, but flawlessly brilliant solitaire diamond engagement ring she was wearing.

She had protested long and loud against Leo's decision to buy her a ring, but he had refused to give in. In the end she had been the one to do that, partially out of sheer weariness and partially out of a cowardice she was loath to admit to.

Her aunt and uncle, Nigel's parents, had invited her and Leo to have dinner with them, and Jodi had known, as indeed Leo had warned her, that, being of an older generation, they would expect to see a newly engaged woman wearing a ring.

And it had been because of that and only because of that that she had allowed Leo to drive her to the city and buy her the diamond she was now wearing on her left hand.

At first she had tried to insist that she should wear something inexpensive and fake, but Leo had been so angered by her suggestion that she had been shocked into giving in.

She hadn't been allowed to know the price of the ring Leo had finally chosen for her. She had tried to opt for the smallest diamond the jeweller in the exclusive shop had shown her but Leo had simply insisted that she try on

several rings before announcing that the one he liked best
was the solitaire she was now wearing.

His choice had been another shock to Jodi, because it
was in fact the very ring she would have chosen herself—
under different circumstances. Now, as she sat next to him
in his car, she couldn't help touching it a little self-con-
sciously as the diamond caught the light and threw out a
dazzling sparkle.

She wasn't exactly looking forward to this evening's
dinner, much as she loved her aunt and uncle. They were
a very traditional couple, especially her aunt, who was
bound to ask all manner of difficult questions.

'You didn't have to do this,' she told Leo awkwardly as
she gave him directions to their home. 'I could have come
up with an excuse. After all, with the takeover...'

It was all over the village now that Jeremy Driscoll was
being investigated by the revenue authorities, but even that
gossip had not been enough to silence Myra Fanshawe's
repeated references to her concern over Jodi's behaviour.

'You want to speak to Mr Jefferson?' Leo's new secretary
at the factory asked the woman caller who had asked to
speak to Leo. The woman had explained that she hadn't
been able to get through to him on his mobile and that she
hadn't heard from him in several days.

'Oh, I'm sorry, but he isn't here at the moment. And I
expect he's switched off his mobile, because he's gone to
meet his fiancée.'

On the other end of the line, Leo's mother, Luisa Jefferson, almost dropped her receiver.

'His fiancée,' she repeated. 'Oh, well, yes...of course.'

'Shall I tell him you called?' Leo's secretary asked her
helpfully.

'Er—no...that won't be necessary,' Luisa informed her.

Replacing the receiver, she went in search of her husband, whom she found seated on a sun lounger beside their pool.

'I have to go to England to see Leonardo,' she informed him.

The evening had gone surprisingly well. Leo had laughed obligingly at her uncle's jokes and praised her aunt's cooking with such a genuineness that it was plain that they were both already ready to welcome him with open arms into the family.

Jodi, with the benefit of far more objectivity at her disposal, watched the proceedings with pardonable cynicism.

'So,' Jodi heard her aunt asking archly, once they were in her sitting room with their after-dinner coffee. 'what about the wedding? Have you made any plans as yet?'

'No—'

'Yes—'

As they both spoke at once her aunt looked from Leo's smiling face to Jodi's set one with an understandably baffled expression.

'We've only just got engaged,' Jodi defended her denial.

'I'd marry Jodi tomorrow if she'd agree,' Leo told her aunt with a wicked, glinting smile in Jodi's direction that made her want to scream. He was enjoying this. She could tell.

'Well, of course Jodi will want to wait until her parents return,' her aunt said lovingly, before asking, 'And what about your parents, Leo?'

'I want to take Jodi out to Italy to meet them just as soon as I can,' Leo responded truthfully, 'but I already know that they will love her as much as I do.' And then, before Jodi could guess what he intended to do, he leaned towards her, taking one of her hands and enfolding it tenderly between both of his before bending his head to brush his mouth against hers.

Jodi could feel the quivering, out-of-control wanting begin deep down inside her the moment he touched her; it shocked and frightened her, and it made her feel very angry as well. She felt angry with Leo for making her love him, and angry with herself too, and yet she still couldn't stop herself from closing her eyes and wishing that all of this was real; that he did love her; that their futures really lay together.

Jodi's aunt and uncle said goodbye to them at their front door. Leo had placed his arm around Jodi as they walked to the door, and he kept it there whilst they walked to the car, even though it was parked out of direct sight of the house.

'You can let go of me now,' Jodi told him as they reached the car. 'No one can see us.'

'What if I don't want to let go of you?' Leo demanded softly.

There was just enough moonlight for Jodi to be able to see the hot glint of desire that glittered in his eyes as he looked down at her.

Shakily she backed up against the car, her heart hammering against her ribs—but not with fear.

'Leo!' she protested, but he was already sliding his hands slowly up over the bare flesh of her arms. His touch made her tremble with desire, her emotions so tightly strung that she was afraid of what she might do. If just the casual caress of his hands could make her feel like this...

But she was so hungry for him. So very, very hungry!

'We're engaged,' Leo breathed against her ear. 'Remember...we're allowed to do this, expected to...and, God knows, I want to!' he told her, his voice suddenly changing and becoming so fiercely charged with sensuality that it made Jodi shiver all over again.

'But our engagement isn't real,' she told him.

'It may not be, but this most certainly is…' Leo growled

And then he was holding her, one large hand on her waist, whilst the other cupped her face, tilting it, holding it Jodi held her breath as she felt him looking at her, and then he was bending his head, and his mouth was on hers and…

When had she lifted her own hand towards his jaw? When had she parted her mouth for the hot, silent passion of his kiss? When had she closed that final tiny distance between them, her free hand gripping his arm, her fingers digging into its muscle as the ache inside her pounded down her defences?

'What is it about you that makes me feel like this?' Leo was demanding thickly, but Jodi knew that the words, raw with longing, helpless in the face of so much desire, might just as well have been her own.

She knew too that if Leo was to take her home with him now there was no way she would be able to resist the temptation he was offering her. Right now she wanted him more than she wanted her pride, her self-respect, or her sanity!

'Right now,' she heard Leo telling her thickly, 'I could…'

An owl hooted overhead, startling them both, and abruptly Leo was moving back from her, leaving her feeling cold and alone as he turned to unlock the car doors.

Jodi stared mutely at the package she was holding in her hand. She had bought it when she had been in the city with Leo, the day he had taken her there to get her engagement ring. She had seen the chemist's shop and had managed to slip away to get what she had begun to fear she needed.

That had been well over three weeks ago now and… Reluctantly she turned the package over and read the instructions. It was just a precaution, she told herself firmly, that was all.

It was practically impossible that her suspicions were anything more than simple guilty anxiety. Sometimes odd things happened to bodies, especially when their owners were under the kind of stress she was under right now.

Myra had informed her that her committee had felt that they had no option other than to report their concerns over her behaviour to the education authority, and that was exactly what they had done.

Jodi had already had to undergo an extremely difficult and worrying telephone interview, and now she was waiting to see what they were going to do.

At best, she would simply get a black mark against her for having been reported, and at worst... Jodi didn't want to think about what the worst-case scenario could be.

Jodi was under no delusions about the seriousness of the situation she was in, but right now...

She looked unhappily at the pregnancy-testing kit she was holding. She didn't really need to do it, did she? After all, it was only a matter of a few days late—well, a week or so—and she was one hundred per cent sure that that unwelcome feeling of nausea she had been experiencing recently was simply nerves and tension.

And the craving for anchovies?

She was careful about her health and followed a low-fat, low-salt diet. Her body had decided that it needed salt, obviously. Obviously!

Taking a deep breath, Jodi took the kit out of its packet. It was going to show negative, she knew that. She knew it.

Positive. Jodi stared at the testing kit, unable and unwilling to accept the result it was showing. Her hand shook as she picked it up for the tenth time and stared at it.

It must be wrong. A faulty kit, or she had done something wrong. Panic began to fill her. She couldn't be pregnant. She couldn't be!

Leo's baby! She was going to have Leo's baby! Why on earth was she smiling? Jodi wondered in disbelief as she saw her reflection in her bathroom mirror.

This was quite definitely not smiling territory...

Downstairs she heard her post coming through the letterbox. The school term had finally come to an end, so she did not have to rush to get to work. She finished dressing and went downstairs, collecting her letters on the way.

There was a card from her parents, and a whole bunch of unsolicited trash mail.

Jodi had to sit down before she could bring herself to look at it. Her parents. No need to ask herself how they would feel about what had happened. There would be gossip, there was bound to be, and she knew that life as an unmarried mother was not the life they had envisaged for her or for their grandchild. If she was honest it was not the life she had ever envisaged for herself either. Jodi's throat felt tight and dry.

She had asked her aunt and uncle not to say anything about her engagement to her parents if they spoke to them, explaining—quite truthfully—that she wanted to tell them herself, in person.

Then, knowing that they weren't due home for another two months at least, she had convinced herself that she had plenty of time to get her life back to some kind of normality before their return, but now...!

Her parents would love her and support her no matter what she did, she knew that, and her baby, their grandchild, no matter how unconventional its conception, would be welcomed and loved. But there would be gossip and disapproval, and, with Leo continuing to be a presence locally through the factory, Jodi knew there was no way that she could stay. How could she? How could she inflict such a situation on her family, and as for her baby…how could she allow him or her to grow up suffering the humiliation of knowing that he or she had been rejected by their father?

No, life would be much easier for all those she loved if she simply moved away.

After all, she decided proudly, it wasn't as though it was her teaching skills that were in question.

And as for the fact that she would be a single mother, well, a hundred or more miles away, just who was going to be concerned or interested in the malicious criticism of Myra Fanshawe?

'Mother!'

Stunned, Leo stared into the familiar face of his very unexpected visitor as he answered his front doorbell. He had told his parents that he had moved to a rented property in Frampton and that he would be living there until he had sorted out all the complications with the business. He knew he had not been able to keep his promise to go and visit his parents again, in Italy, but he had certainly not expected to have his mother turn up on his doorstep.

'Where's Dad?' he asked her, frowning as he watched her taxi disappearing down his drive.

'I have come on my own,' his mother told him. 'I cannot stay more than a few days,' she added, 'but I am sure if we apply ourselves that will be sufficient time for me to meet your fiancée.'

Leo, who had been in the act of picking up his mother's case, suddenly straightened up to look at her.

Several responses flashed son-like through his brain, but his mother was his mother, and one very astute woman, as he had had over thirty years to find out and appreciate.

'I think you'd better come inside,' he told her steadily as he took hold of her arm.

'I think I'd better,' his mother agreed wryly, pausing only to tell him, 'This house is a very good family house, Leonardo; it is well built and strong. Children will grow very well here, and I like the garden, although it needs much work. Is she a gardener, this fiancée of yours? I hope so, for a woman who nourishes her plants will nourish her husband and her children.'

His mother was the only person in the world who called him Leonardo with that particular emphasis on the second syllable of his name, Leo reflected as he ushered her into the hallway and saw her glance thoughtfully at the vase of flowers Jodi had arranged on the hall table earlier in the week.

Leo had taken her home with him prior to visiting her aunt and uncle so that he could drop off some business papers. His telephone had rung, and the consequent call had taken some time, and when he had finally rejoined her he had discovered that she had collected some wind-blown flowers from the garden and arranged them in a vase.

'It seems such a shame to just let them die unappreciated and unloved,' she had told him defensively.

'So, she is a home-maker, this fiancée of yours,' his mother pronounced, suddenly very Italian as she subjected Jodi's handiwork to a critical maternal examination. 'Does she cook for you?'

'Mamma!' Leo sighed, leading her into the kitchen. 'There is something that you need to know…and it is going to take quite some time for me to tell you.'

'There is,' Luisa Jefferson informed her son firmly, 'only one thing I need to know and it will take you very little time to tell me. Do you love her?'

For a moment she thought that he wasn't going to reply.

He was a man, after all, she reminded herself ruefully, not a boy, but then he grimaced and pushed his hair back off his face in a gesture that reminded her of her own husband before he admitted, 'Unfortunately, yes, I do.'

'Unfortunately?' she queried delicately.

'There is a problem,' Leo told her.

His mother's unexpected arrival was a complication he had not foreseen, but now that she was here he was discovering to his own amusement and with a certain sense of humility that he actually wanted to talk to her about Jodi, to share with her not just his discovery of his love for Jodi but also his confusion and concern.

'In love there is always a problem,' his mother responded humorously. 'If there is not then it is not love. So, tell me what your particular problem is… Her father does not like you? That is how a father is with his daughter. I remember my own father—'

'Mamma, I haven't met Jodi's father yet, and anyway…I have told you that I love Jodi, but what I have not told you yet is that she does not love me.'

'Not love you? But you are engaged, and I must say, Leonardo, that I did not enjoy learning of your engagement from your secretary; however—'

'Mamma please,' Leo interrupted her firmly. 'Let me explain.'

When he did Leo was careful to edit his story so that his mother would not, as he had initially done, jump to any unfair or judgemental conclusions about Jodi, but he could tell that she was not entirely satisfied with his circumspect rendition of events.

'You love her and she does not love you, but she has agreed to become engaged to you to protect her reputation, since by accident she fell asleep in your hotel suite and was seen leaving early in the morning?'

Her eyebrows lifted in a manner that conveyed a whole range of emotions, most of which made Leo's heart sink.

'I am very interested to meet this fiancée of yours, Leonardo.'

Leo drew in his breath.

'Well, as to that, I cannot promise that you will,' he began. 'I have to go to London on business this afternoon, and I had planned to stay there for several days. You could come with me if you wish and do some shopping,' he offered coaxingly.

His mother gave him an old-fashioned look.

'I live in Italy now, Leonardo. We have Milan. I do not need to shop. No, whilst you are in London I shall stay here and wait for you to return,' she pronounced. 'Where does she live, this fiancée of yours?' she asked determinedly.

Leo sighed.

'She lives here in Frampton. Mamma, I know you mean well,' he told her gently. 'But please, I would ask you not to…to…'

'To interfere?' she supplied drily for him. 'I am your mother, Leonardo, and I am Italian…'

'I understand,' Leo told her gently. 'But I hope you will understand that, since I know that Jodi does not love me, it can only cause me a great deal of humiliation and unwanted embarrassment if it was to be brought to her attention that I love her, and quite naturally I do not wish to subject either of us to those emotions, which means…' He took a deep breath. 'What I have told you, Mamma, is for your ears only, and I would ask that it remains so, and that you do not seek Jodi out to discuss any of this with her. I do not want her to be upset or embarrassed in any way, by anyone.'

For a moment he thought that she was going to refuse, and then she took a deep breath herself and agreed.

'I shall not seek her out.'

'Thank you.'

As he leaned forward to kiss her Leo heard his mother complaining, 'When I prayed that you would fall in love I did not mean for something like this to happen!'

'You want grandchildren, I know.' Leo smiled, struggling to lighten the mood of their conversation.

'I want grandchildren,' his mother agreed, 'but what I want even more is to see you sharing your life with the person you love; I want to see your life being enriched and made complete by the same kind of love your father and I have shared. I want for you what every mother wants for her child,' she told him fiercely, her eyes darkening with maternal protection and love. 'I want you to be happy.'

His mother couldn't want those things she had described to him any more than he wanted them for himself, Leo acknowledged a couple of hours later as he drove towards Frampton *en route* for London. He had left his mother busily dead-heading roses, whilst refusing to listen to any suggestion he tried to make that, since he could not say categorically when he would be back, she might as well return home to Italy.

In the village the temptation to turn the car towards Jodi's cottage was so strong that Leo found he was forced to grip the steering wheel to control it.

His life would never be happy now, he reflected morosely.

Not without Jodi in it. Not without her love, her presence, her warmth; not without her!

Jodi stared at her computer screen, carefully reading the resignation letter she had been working on for the last three hours. Now it was done, and there was nothing to stop her from printing it off and posting it, but somehow she could not bring herself to do so—not yet.

She got up and paced the floor, and then on a sudden impulse she picked up her keys and headed for the door.

It was a beautiful, warm summer's day, and the gardens of the cottages that lined her part of the village street overflowed with flowers, creating an idyllic scene.

Normally just the sight of them would have been enough to lift her spirits and make her think how fortunate she was to live where she did and to be the person she was, a person who had a job she loved, a family she loved, a life she loved.

But not a man she loved... The man she loved... And not the job she loved either—soon. But, though the school and her work were important to her, they did not come anywhere near matching the intensity of the love she had for Leo.

Leo. Busy with her thoughts, Jodi had walked automatically towards the school.

There was a bench opposite it, outside the church, and Jodi sat down on it, looking across at the place that meant so much to her and which she had worked so hard for.

She was not so vain that she imagined that there were no other teachers who could teach as ably, if not more so, as she had done herself, but would another teacher love the school the way she had done? Would another woman love Leo the way she did?

Her eyes filled with tears, and as she reached hurriedly into her bag for a tissue she was aware of a woman sitting down on the bench next to her.

'Are you all right, only I could not help but notice that you are crying?'

The woman's comment caught Jodi off guard. It was, not, after all, a British national characteristic to comment on a stranger's grief, no matter how sympathetic towards them and curious about them one might be.

Proudly Jodi lifted her head and turned to look at the woman.

'I'm fine, thank you,' she told her, striving to sound both cool and dismissive, but to her horror fresh tears were filling her eyes, spilling down over her cheeks, and her voice had begun to wobble alarmingly. Jodi knew that any moment now she was going to start howling like a child with a skinned knee.

'No, you aren't. You are very upset and you are also very angry with me for saying so, but sometimes it can help to talk to a stranger,' the other woman was telling her gently, before adding, 'I saw you looking at the school...'

'Yes,' Jodi acknowledged. 'I...I teach there. At least, I did...but now...' She bit her lip.

'You have decided to leave,' her interlocuter guessed. 'You have perhaps fallen in love and are to move away and you are crying because you know you will miss this very beautiful place.'

Although her English was perfect, Jodi sensed that there was something about her questioner that said that she was not completely English. She must be a visitor, someone who was passing through the area, someone she, Jodi, would never, ever see again.

Suddenly, for some inexplicable reason Jodi discovered that she did want to talk to her, to unburden herself, and to seek if not an explanation for what was happening to her, then at least the understanding of another human being. Something told her that this woman would be understanding. It was written in the warmth of her eyes and the encouragement of her smile.

'I am in love,' Jodi admitted, 'but it is not... He...the man I love...he doesn't love me.'

'No? Then he is a fool,' the other woman pronounced firmly. 'Any man who does not love a woman who loves him is a fool.' She gave Jodi another smile and Jodi realised that she was older than she had first imagined from her elegant appearance, probably somewhere in her late fifties.

'Why does he not love you? Has he told you?'

Jodi found herself starting to smile.

'Sort of… He has indicated that…'

'But you are lovers?' the woman pressed Jodi with a shrewdness and perspicacity that took Jodi's breath away.

She could feel her colour starting to rise as she admitted, 'Yes, but…but he didn't… It was at my instigation… I…' She stopped and bit her lip again. There were some things she could just not bring herself to put into words, but her companion, it seemed, had no such hang-ups.

'You seduced him!'

She sounded more amused than shocked, and when Jodi looked at her she could actually see that there was laughter in the other woman's dark eyes.

'Well…I…sort of took him by surprise. I'd fallen asleep in his bed, you see, and he didn't know I was there, and when I woke up and realised that he was and…' Jodi paused. There was something cathartic about what she was doing, about being able to confide in another person, being able to explain for the first time just what she had felt and why she had felt it.

'I'd seen him earlier in the hotel foyer,' she began in a low voice. 'I didn't know who he was, not then, but I…'

She stopped.

'You were attracted to him?' the other woman offered helpfully.

Gratefully Jodi nodded.

'Yes,' she agreed vehemently. 'He affected me in a way that no other man had ever done. I just sort of looked at

him and...' Her voice became low and strained. 'I know
it sounds foolish, but I believe I fell in love with him there
and then at first sight...and I suppose when I woke up and
found myself in bed with him my...my body must have
remembered how I'd felt then, earlier, and.... But he...
well, he thought that I was there because... And then later,
when he realised the truth, he told me... He asked me...'
Her voice tailed off. 'I should never have done what I did,
and I felt so ashamed.'

'For falling in love?' the older woman asked her, giving a small shrug. 'Why should you be ashamed of that?
It is the most natural thing in the world.'

'Falling in love might be,' Jodi agreed, 'but my behaviour, the way I...' Jodi shook her head primly and had to
swallow hard as she tried to blink away her threatening
tears.

Her companion, though, was not deterred by her silence and demanded determinedly, 'So, you have met a
man with whom you have fallen in love. You say he does
not love you, but are you so sure?'

'Positive,' Jodi insisted equally determinedly.

'And now you sit here weeping because you cannot bear
the thought of your life without him,' the older woman
guessed.

'Yes, because of that, and...and for other reasons,' Jodi
admitted.

'Other reasons?'

Jodi drew an unsteady breath.

'When...after...after he had realised that I was not as he
had first imagined, well, when he realised the truth about
me he warned me that if...if by some mischance I...there
should be...repercussions from our intimacy then he would
expect me to...to...'

Jodi bit down on her lip and looked away as fresh tears welled in her eyes.

'I told myself that it was impossible for me to love a man like that, a man who would callously destroy the life of his child. How could I love him?'

She shook her head in bewilderment, whilst her companion demanded in a disbelieving voice, 'I cannot believe what you are saying. It is impossible; unthinkable...'

'I can assure you that it is the truth,' Jodi insisted shakily. 'I didn't want to believe it myself, but he told me. He said categorically that something would have to be arranged. Of course, then I really did believe that it was impossible that I could be—but now...'

As Jodi wrapped her arms protectively around her still slender body her companion questioned sharply, 'You are pregnant? You are to have...this man's child?'

Numbly Jodi nodded. 'Yes. And I am also facing an enquiry because I was seen leaving his hotel suite, and other things. And, as a head teacher, it is of course expected that I should... That was why he said we should get engaged, because of the gossip and to protect me.'

As she spoke Jodi raised her left hand, where Leo's diamond glistened in the sunlight nearly as brightly as Jodi's own falling tears. 'But how can he offer to protect me and yet want to destroy his own child?'

'What will you do?' the other woman was asking her quietly.

Jodi drew a deep breath.

'I plan to move away and start a fresh life somewhere else.'

'Without telling your lover about his child?'

After everything she, Jodi, had told her, how could she sound so disapproving? Jodi wondered.

'How can I tell him when he has already told me that he

doesn't want it? "Something will have to be arranged"—
that is what he said to me, and I can imagine what kind of
arrangement he meant. But I would rather die myself than
do anything to hurt my baby.' Jodi was getting angry now,
all her protective maternal instincts coming to the fore.

She had no idea how long she had been sitting on the
bench confiding in this stranger, but now she felt so tired
and drained that she longed to go home and lie down.

As she got up she gave her unknown companion a tired
smile.

'Thank you for listening to me.' She turned to go, but
as she did so the other woman stood up too, and to Jodi's
shock took hold of her in a warm embrace, hugging her
almost tenderly.

'Have courage,' she told her. 'All will be well. I am
sure of it.'

As she smiled comfortingly at her, Jodi had the oddest
feeling that there was something about the woman that was
somehow familiar, but that, of course, was ridiculous. Jodi
knew that she had never seen her before.

CHAPTER TEN

'LEONARDO, YOU ARE to drive back to Frampton right now.'

'Mamma,' Leo protested.

'Right now, Leonardo!' Luisa Jefferson insisted. 'And before you do, could you please explain to me how it is that poor Jodi believes that you wish not only to deny yourself as a father the child you have created with her, but that you wish to deny it the right to life as well?'

'What...what child? Jodi told me there would be no child.'

'And she told me that there will be, not that I needed telling; I could see it in her eyes...her face. You have hurt her very badly. She truly believes that you do not love her and she is hurting because she thinks she loves a man who would destroy her child.'

'I cannot understand how she could possibly think that!' Leo protested. 'I would never—'

'I know that, of course,' his mother interrupted him, 'but your Jodi, it seems, does not. "Something will have to be arranged", is apparently what you told her.'

'What...? Yes...of course...but I meant...I meant that if she was pregnant we would have to get married,' Leo told his mother grimly. 'How on earth could she interpret that as...?'

'She is the one you should be speaking to, Leonardo,

and not me. And you had better be quick. She plans to leave, and once she does…'

'I'm on my way,' Leo announced. 'If you dare to say anything to her until I get there you will be banned from seeing your grandchild until he or she is at least a day old.'

When she replaced her telephone receiver Luisa Jefferson was smiling beatifically.

Picking it up again, she dialled the number of her home in Italy. When her husband, Leo's father, answered she greeted him, 'Hello, Grandpapa!'

'Oh, come on, Jodi, I'm starving and I hate going out for dinner on my own.'

'But, Nigel, I'm tired,' Jodi had protested when Nigel had rung her unexpectedly, demanding that she go out to eat with him, 'and surely you could ask one of your many girlfriends.'

But in the end she had given in and she had even managed not to protest when, having picked her up in his car, he had suddenly realised that he must have dropped his wallet on her footpath and gone back to pick it up.

Now, though, at barely ten o'clock, she was exhausted, and yawning, and she couldn't blame Nigel for glancing surreptitiously at his watch.

She hadn't been the most entertaining of companions.

Even so, his brisk, 'Right, let's go,' after he had checked his watch a second time made her blink a little.

'Don't you want to finish your coffee?' she asked him.

'What? Oh, no…I can see you're tired,' he offered.

He had been in an odd mood all evening, Jodi recognised, on edge and avoiding looking directly at her. But she was too tired to ask him what was wrong, instead allowing him to bustle her out into the car park and into his car.

Once they reached her house, Jodi asked him if he

wanted to come in, but rather to her surprise he shook his head.

As she heard him drive away Jodi decided that she might as well go straight upstairs to bed.

In Jodi's sitting room the light from her computer screen lit up the small space around it, but Jodi was too exhausted to bother glancing into the room, and so she didn't see the smiling babies tumbling in somersaults all over her computer screen around the large typed message that read, 'I love ya, baby, and your mamma too!'

Once upstairs, she went straight to the bathroom, cleaning off her make-up and showering before padding naked into the darkened bedroom she was too familiar with to need to switch on the light.

She was already virtually asleep before she even pulled back the duvet and crawled into the longed-for comfort of her bed—the good old-fashioned king-size bed that almost filled the room and which Nigel had wickedly insisted on buying her as a cousinly moving-in gift. It was a bed that no one other than her had ever slept in—though someone was quite definitely sleeping in it now!

It was a someone she would have known anywhere, even without the benefit of being able to see his face. She would have known him simply by his scent, by the subtle air of Leo-ness that enfolded her whenever she was in his presence.

Leo! Leo was here, fast asleep in her bed! No, that just wasn't possible! She was going mad. She was daydreaming…fantasising!

'Mmm.' Jodi gasped as a decidedly realistic pair of warm arms wrapped themselves firmly around her body, imprisoning it against their owner's wonderfully familiar maleness.

'Leo!' Jodi whispered his name weakly, her voice shot through with the rainbow colours of what she was feeling.

'How could you possibly believe that I don't love you?' she heard him demanding thickly. 'I'm mad about you! Crazily, insanely, irredeemably and forever in love with you. I thought you were the one who didn't love me. But then they do say that pregnancy affects a woman's ability to reason logically...'

'Leo!' Jodi protested, her voice even weaker. She couldn't take in what was happening and, even more importantly, had no idea how it had come about. 'How? What?' she began, but Leo was in no mood to answer questions.

His lips were feathering distracting little kisses all along her jaw, her throat, her neck. He was whispering words of love and praise in her ear; he was smoothing a tender hand over the still flat plane of her belly, whilst his voice thickened openly with emotion as he whispered to her, 'How could you think I didn't want our child, Jodi?'

She tried to answer him but the seeking urgency of his mouth on hers prevented her, and, anyway, what did questions, words matter when there was this, and Leo, and the wonderful private world of tender loving they were creating between them?

'The first time we met you stole your way into my bed and my heart,' Leo said to her as he touched her with gentle, adoring hands, the true extent of his passion only burning through when he kissed her mouth. 'And there hasn't been a single day, a single hour since then when I haven't ached for you, longed for you,' he groaned. 'Not a single minute when my love for you hasn't tormented and tortured me!'

Jodi could see as well as feel the tension pulsing through his nerve-endings as he reined in his sensual hunger for her.

'Now it's my turn,' he told her. 'Thanks to Nigel, I have stolen my way into your bed, and I warn you, Jodi, I do not intend to leave it until I have stolen my way into your heart as well, and heard from your own lips that you intend to let me stay there, in your heart, in your life and the life of our child—for ever!'

'For ever,' Jodi whispered back in wonder as she touched the damp stains on his face that betrayed the intensity of his emotions.

'I might have thought that loving you was torture,' Leo told her rawly, 'but now I know that real torture would be to lose you. Do you know what it was like finding you in my bed, having you reach out and touch me, love me?' Leo was groaning achingly. 'Shall I show you?'

Hadn't her mother always warned her against the danger of playing with fire?

Right now, did she care?

'Show me!' she encouraged him boldly.

She could hear the maleness in his voice as well as feel it in his body as he told her triumphantly, 'Right.'

They made love softly and gently, aware of and awed by their role as new parents-to-be, and then fiercely and passionately as they claimed for themselves the right to be lovers for themselves.

They made love in all the ways Jodi had dreamed in her most private and secret thoughts—and then in some ways she had never imagined.

And then, as it started to become light, after Leo had told her over and over how much he loved her, how much he loved both of them, and insisted that she tell him that she returned his feelings, Jodi demanded, 'Explain to me what has happened… How…?' She stopped and shook her head in mute bewilderment. 'It's almost as though a fairy godmother has waved her wand and…'

Propping himself up one elbow, Leo looked tenderly down at her.

'That was no fairy godmother,' he quipped ruefully. 'That was my mother!'

'What?' Jodi sat bolt upright in bed, taking the duvet with her, only momentarily diverted by the magnificent sight of Leo's naked body. Long enough, though, to heave a blissful sigh of pleasure and run her fingertip lazily down the length of him, before finally playfully teasing it through the silky thickness of his body hair whilst watching with awed fascination as his body showed an unexpectedly vigorous response to her attentions.

'Don't go there,' Leo warned her humorously. 'Not unless you mean it.'

Hastily removing her hand, Jodi insisted, 'I want to hear what's been going on.'

Leo heaved a sigh of mock-disappointment.

'My mother flew over from Italy to see me. She'd heard about our engagement from my new secretary and not unnaturally, I suppose, given the nature of mothers, she decided that she wanted to meet my fiancée—the girl who had answered her prayers and those of the village wise woman, whose skills she had commissioned on my behalf. No, don't ask, not yet,' he warned Jodi, shaking his head.

'She wanted to know all about you, and I naturally obliged—well, up to a point. I told her that I'd fallen totally and completely in love with you,' he admitted to Jodi, his voice and demeanour suddenly wholly serious. 'And I told her too that you did not return my feelings. As you know, I had to go to London on business, so I invited her to go with me but she refused. She said she preferred to stay where she was until she was due to take up her return flight. I had my suspicions then, knowing her as I do, and so I made her promise that she would not under any circumstances attempt to seek you out—and she promised me that she wouldn't, but it seems from what she has told me that fate intervened.

'She had gone for a walk in the village, when, as she put it, she saw a young woman in distress. Naturally she wanted to help, so she sat down beside you and—'

'That was your mother?' Jodi interrupted. Now she began to understand!

'I felt that there was something familiar about her,' she admitted, 'but I just couldn't put my finger on what it was.

'Mmm.' She smiled lovingly as Leo broke off from his explanations to kiss her with slow thoroughness. 'Mmm...' she repeated. 'Go on.'

'With what?' Leo teased her. 'The kisses or the explanation?'

'Both!' Jodi answered him promptly.

'But the rest of the explanation first, please, otherwise...'

Laughing, Leo continued, 'Just as soon as she had left you she rang me in London, demanding to know what on earth I had said to you to give you the impression that I wouldn't want our child! Jodi...' Gravely Leo looked at her, his eyes dark with pain. 'How could you have thought that I...?'

'You said something would have to be arranged,' Jodi defended herself firmly.

'Yes, but the arrangement I had in mind was not a visit to—' He broke off, so patently unable to even say the words that Jodi instinctively wrapped her arms tightly around him, as filled with a desire to protect him as she had been to protect their unborn child.

'The place I had in mind for you to visit was a church so that we could be married,' Leo told her hoarsely. 'That was what I was talking about. Even if I had not loved you

I could never, would never... Thank heavens my mother knows me better than you seem to! Still, at least that puts us on an equal footing now. I originally misjudged you and now you have misjudged me, and, that being the case, I suggest that we draw a line beneath it and start again.'

He took a deep breath. 'I love you, Jodi Marsh, and I want to marry you.'

Jodi began to smile.

'I love you too, Leo Jefferson,' she responded, 'and I want to marry you...'

'Now, getting back to the matter of those kisses...' Leo told her wickedly as he drew her back down against his body, and rolled her gently beneath him.

Several hours later, Jodi smiled a very special smile to herself. 'And so Nigel left his key for you to find under the flowerpot by the front door?' she questioned Leo as she licked the jam from her toast off her fingers and looked across the bedroom at him as he walked out of the bathroom, freshly showered, smiling as he watched her eating her toast hungrily.

'Yes; he took a considerable amount of persuading, though, and he was terrified that you might suspect that something was going on.'

'I probably would have done if I hadn't been so tired,' Jodi admitted.

Watching her, Leo could feel his love for her filling him. It had been a tremendous risk, short-circuiting things by installing himself in her bed, but thankfully it had worked, allowing them to talk openly and honestly to one another.

As Jodi finished her late breakfast he reached for her again, drawing her towards him, burying his face against her body before wrapping his arms around her and kissing her tenderly.

When his mobile rang he cursed and reached for it, starting to switch it off and then stopping as he murmured to Jodi, 'It's my mother.'

'Hello, Mamma.' He answered the call and from where she was standing Jodi could hear his mother quite plainly, 'Leonardo, it is not you I wish to speak to but my daughter-in-law-to-be, your delightful Jodi. You have had her to yourself for quite long enough. Put her on the phone to me this minute, if you please, whilst I tell her about this wonderful shop for all things *bambino* in Milan.'

EPILOGUE

'AND YOU STILL intend to teach at your school?'

Over her mother-in-law's head Jodi smiled into Leo's eyes as Luisa Jefferson cooed ecstatically over the bundle that was her baby grandson.

It was Leo and Jodi's wedding anniversary and they had flown out to Italy to stay with Leo's parents.

'For the time being, but only on a part-time basis,' Jodi replied.

All the letters of support she had received from her pupils' parents had thrilled Jodi, and, as she and Leo had agreed, she owed it to everyone who had supported her to stay on at the school until the right kind of replacement for her had been found.

'After all,' she had smiled to Leo, 'our own children will be going there.'

Leo had bought Ashton House, and Jodi had spent all her free time in the months before baby Nicholas Lorenzo's birth organising its renovation and redecoration.

Leo's parents had flown over to Frampton from Italy for the baby's birth, and a special extra guest had been invited to the large family christening, much to Leo's wry amusement and his mother's open delight.

'Her name is Maria, and she says that she will make a special potion for you to drink that will guarantee the happiness of you and Leonardo and your children,' Luisa Jefferson had whispered to Jodi when she had introduced her village's wise woman to her.

'My happiness is already guaranteed,' Jodi had responded with a shining smile of trust and love in her husband's direction. 'Just so long as I have Leo!'

* * * * *

REQUEST YOUR
FREE BOOKS!

2 FREE NOVELS PLUS
2 FREE GIFTS!

YES! Please send me 2 FREE Harlequin Presents® novels and my 2 FREE gifts (gifts are worth about $10). After receiving them, if I don't wish to receive any more books, I can return the shipping statement marked "cancel." If I don't cancel, I will receive 6 brand-new novels every month and be billed just $4.30 per book in the U.S. or $4.99 per book in Canada. That's a saving of at least 14% off the cover price! It's quite a bargain! Shipping and handling is just 50¢ per book in the U.S. and 75¢ per book in Canada.* I understand that accepting the 2 free books and gifts places me under no obligation to buy anything. I can always return a shipment and cancel at any time. Even if I never buy another book, the two free books and gifts are mine to keep forever.   106/306 HDN FVRK

Name _____ (PLEASE PRINT) _____

Address _____ Apt. #

City _____ State/Prov. _____ Zip/Postal Code

Signature (if under 18, a parent or guardian must sign)

Mail to the **Harlequin® Reader Service:**
IN U.S.A.: P.O. Box 1867, Buffalo, NY 14240-1867
IN CANADA: P.O. Box 609, Fort Erie, Ontario L2A 5X3

**Are you a current subscriber to Harlequin Presents books
and want to receive the larger-print edition?
Call 1-800-873-8635 or visit www.ReaderService.com.**

* Terms and prices subject to change without notice. Prices do not include applicable taxes. Sales tax applicable in N.Y. Canadian residents will be charged applicable taxes. Offer not valid in Quebec. This offer is limited to one order per household. Not valid for current subscribers to Harlequin Presents books. All orders subject to credit approval. Credit or debit balances in a customer's account(s) may be offset by any other outstanding balance owed by or to the customer. Please allow 4 to 6 weeks for delivery. Offer available while quantities last.

Your Privacy—The Harlequin® Reader Service is committed to protecting your privacy. Our Privacy Policy is available online at www.ReaderService.com or upon request from the Harlequin Reader Service.

We make a portion of our mailing list available to reputable third parties that offer products we believe may interest you. If you prefer that we not exchange your name with third parties, or if you wish to clarify or modify your communication preferences, please visit us at www.ReaderService.com/consumerschoice or write to us at Harlequin Reader Service Preference Service, P.O. Box 9062, Buffalo, NY 14269. Include your complete name and address.

Love the Harlequin book you just read?

Your opinion matters.

Review this book on your favorite book site, review site, blog or your own social media properties and share your opinion with other readers!

Be sure to connect with us at:
Harlequin.com/Newsletters
Facebook.com/HarlequinBooks
Twitter.com/HarlequinBooks

In Buckshot Hills, Texas, a sexy doctor meets his match in the least likely woman—a beautiful cowgirl looking to reinvent herself....

Enjoy a sneak peek from USA TODAY *bestselling author Judy Duarte's new Harlequin® Special Edition® story,* TAMMY AND THE DOCTOR *,the first book in* Byrds of a Feather, *a brand-new miniseries launching in March 2013!*

***

Before she could comment or press Tex for more details, a couple of light knocks sounded at the door.

Her grandfather shifted in his bed, then grimaced. "Who is it?"

"Mike Sanchez."

Doc? Tammy's heart dropped to the pit of her stomach with a thud, then thumped and pumped its way back up where it belonged.

"Come on in," Tex said.

Thank goodness her grandfather had issued the invitation, because she couldn't have squawked out a single word.

As Doc entered the room, looking even more handsome than he had yesterday, Tammy struggled to remain cool and calm.

And it wasn't just her heartbeat going wacky. Her feminine hormones had begun to pump in a way they'd never pumped before.

"Good morning," Doc said, his gaze landing first on Tex, then on Tammy.

As he approached the bed, he continued to look at Tammy,

his head cocked slightly.

"What's the matter?" she asked.

"I'm sorry. It's just that your eyes are an interesting shade of blue. I'm sure you hear that all the time."

"Not really." And not from anyone who'd ever mattered. In truth, they were a fairly common color—like the sky or bluebonnets or whatever. "I've always thought of them as run-of-the-mill blue."

"There's nothing ordinary about it. In fact, it's a pretty shade."

The compliment set her heart on end. But before she could think of just the perfect response, he said, "If you don't mind stepping out of the room, I'd like to examine your grandfather."

Of course she minded leaving. She wanted to stay in the same room with Doc for the rest of her natural-born days. But she understood her grandfather's need for privacy.

"Of course." Apparently it was going to take more than simply batting her eyes to woo him, but there was no way Tammy would be able to pull off a makeover by herself. Maybe she could ask her beautiful cousins for help?

She had no idea what to say the next time she ran into them. But somehow, by hook or by crook, she'd have to think of something.

Because she was going to risk untold humiliation and embarrassment by begging them to turn a cowgirl into a lady!

***

Look for TAMMY AND THE DOCTOR from
Harlequin® Special Edition® available March 2013

It all starts with a kiss

Check out the brand-new series

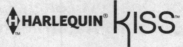

Fun, flirty and sensual romances.
ON SALE JANUARY 22!

Visit www.tryHarlequinKISS.com
and fall in love with
Harlequin® KISS™ today!